CLAIMING HIS WIFE

BOOK 4 IN THE DOMESTIC DISCIPLINE SERIES

GOLDEN ANGEL

Thank you so much for picking up my book!

Would you like to receive a free story from me as well? Join the Angel Legion and sign up for my newsletter! You'll immediately receive a free story from the Stronghold series in a welcome message, and as part of the Angel Legion you'll also receive one newsletter a month with teasers, sneak peeks, and news about upcoming releases, as well as what I'm reading now!

ACKNOWLEDGMENTS

There are many people I need to thank for helping me with this book:

Katherine, my longest beta reader, who always keeps me on track and motivated.

Sir Nick, for providing the badly needed male perspective.

Marie and Chelle, my two new beta readers, who gave such great insights about both the characters and the plot.

Marie S., for taking the time out of her busy schedule to help me with the editing... she caught a ton of the mistakes that I and others didn't and I can't thank her enough for her attention to detail and thoroughness. It's almost impossible for any book to be perfect, but I know this is the closest any of my books have ever come thanks to her!

Lee Savino, my author-sensei.

My husband. Who is awesome.

And, as always, a big thank you to all of you for buying and reading my work... if you love it, please leave a review!

CHAPTER 1

*A*n hour into their carriage ride, Grace's body was still reverberating with shock. Shock, betrayal and the smallest kernel of fear. All emotions which, at this point in her life, she'd thought herself to be far beyond. She'd truly believed she'd already lost her faith in people, that nothing they could do would surprise her, and she couldn't be hurt again. It had taken her estranged husband less than an hour to show her differently.

It was fitting, perhaps, since he was the one who had taught her the meaning of betrayal in the first place. Not that he'd meant to. But she could still hear the words, ringing in her ears, like poison in her heart.

One woman is as good as another for a wife... and, thanks to you, Grace's dowry made her especially useful as mine.

If one woman was truly as good as another, then why wasn't her husband letting *her* go and contracting a marriage with a better one? A less embarrassing one? She looked outside the window, relieved she couldn't see his straight-backed form on his horse. It would have been too tempting to throw something at his bloody stubborn head. *One woman is as good as another...* it was a chant swimming round her head, one that had tormented her for months when she'd first left Alex.

Well he'd certainly proved it, time and again, with one woman after another. A few months after she'd left him, she had just started feeling worthwhile again, enjoying the flirtations and words of men who thought she was beautiful, who thought she was desirable. Men who appreciated her for more than a business deal with her father. Then Alex had started his affairs, crushing what little had been left of her heart as he replaced her in his bed and divesting her of her last forlorn hope that perhaps she'd somehow misunderstood. Grace had faced down more than one of his lovers, who taunted her and flaunted his relations with them in her face. The women of the *ton* were catty and cruel, especially in the face of Grace's youth and beauty. They'd been gleeful when the young, stunning bride, a Diamond of the First Water, had been replaced in her husband's bed by them.

That's when Grace had finally succumbed to her first rake. At least there she'd chosen wisely. The young Marquess of Hartington had been nursing his own broken heart when he'd seduced her. There had been no expectation of a future for either of them, no painful emotions, just a joining between sympathetic souls and a great deal of pleasure. It was empty pleasure, nothing like the joyful passion she'd found in Alex's arms, but it had healed something inside of her. A belief in herself, the confidence of knowing she was desirable... and the broken edges of her heart hadn't felt quite so sharp after that.

It was the first lesson she'd learned from her lovers; there was still pleasure to be found in the world. That lesson led to many others, and eventually she'd begun to hope perhaps she had a chance for love in her life after all. Just not with her husband. Grace wanted him to divorce her, and then she could make her way to America or the Continent to start anew. Some of the gossip would follow her, but maybe not all. Paris would probably be particularly welcoming of a young, scandalous beauty. Their nobility wasn't nearly as stuffy as London's, from what she heard, in Paris scandal made a woman more desirable.

"Bastard," she muttered under her breath as her husband, seated handsomely upon his horse, dropped back into view, riding just a bit ahead of her carriage. Her hand twitched and if there had been a small enough object within reach, she definitely would have thrown it.

Immediately, Rose, her maid, looked up from the shirt she was stitching. Grace glared, filling her eyes with the hate and fury and frustration consuming her, and Rose dropped her gaze back down. At one time, Grace had considered Rose almost a friend, despite the difference in their stations. She had used Alex's money to pay the girl an outrageous wage, given her all sorts of privileges, and had even confided in her often. Now she knew Rose was just another spy in her household.

Just like Peters.

Blinking away tears, Grace looked back out the window. That betrayal might hurt the worst. She'd always considered the butler to be her anchor, her haven. He guarded her home and kept the gossip-mongers and dangerous roués away. But this morning he'd not only let Alex in, he'd instructed the household to pack her bags, and he'd been instrumental in getting her out the door and into Alex's carriage. He'd been apologizing the entire time as she'd wept and raged, but his true loyalty had been revealed; Peters belonged to the man with the stony face who'd watched the proceedings and then stepped forward to give her a single stinging slap on her rump. She'd felt the blow even through the layers of her skirts and she'd been aghast, as he ordered her to stop heaping abuse on Peters.

One woman is as good as another.

Why had he come back for her? Why did he want reconciliation instead of divorce? It couldn't be for the deal between him and her father anymore. Grace was quite sure their business together would continue no matter what; it had proved most profitable for both of them. Even if Alex divorced her, her father wouldn't back out of it; he'd basically disowned Grace when she'd left Alex's residence.

The day she'd left her husband, she'd made the mistake of trying to return to her father's house, and been rewarded with a split lip for her troubles. There had never been any love there, but she'd still somehow thought her father might at least shelter her for a night while she decided what to do, where to go. Instead she'd spent the night in a hotel, eventually paid for by Alex, nursing both her broken heart and her wounded lip. The only thing that surprised her was her father hadn't eventually come after her, demanding she return to Alex and stop sullying her family's honor by her behavior.

Perhaps he'd felt completely distancing himself from her was enough, since she and Alex were still technically married.

At least Alex continued to provide for her. She didn't know why, but she didn't particularly care either. Some form of guilt, perhaps, or maybe just to keep up appearances. It had kept her from having to contemplate less savory options for survival. Finances seemed to be the only thing he understood, the only thing that truly mattered to him. Since Grace was no longer of any use to him, she truly didn't understand why he didn't trade her out for a more willing wife.

AROUND MIDDAY, Alex called a halt for a meal. After riding all morning in the hot sun, hoping to give his wife some time to cool down after her rage this morning, he was feeling in dire need of sustenance. Perhaps it would also help give him the fortitude to get in the carriage and ride with Grace for the afternoon. He needed to do it at some point. Bath was several days away and he didn't intend to spend the entirety of the journey on his horse. While he was certainly hardy enough to, he hoped he and Grace could at least begin to repair their relationship before reaching Bath and their friends. That required being in the same space. Besides, it was never good to let a woman stew with her own thoughts for too long. Especially if those thoughts were already bound to be belligerent.

As she swanned out of the carriage, lips pursed, refusing to look at him, he sighed internally. She certainly hadn't softened since this morning. Although her eyes were still a bit red-rimmed from weeping, she looked as beautiful and unapproachable as a marble statue. Not at all like the laughing young woman he'd married. It made his chest ache as he wondered if he'd truly been the reason behind the death of her laughter.

Sometimes he wondered if it hadn't been him at all, if perhaps there had been some other reason for her disaffection. The day she'd left him, she'd called them both fools. The rest of her words had been broken, disjointed, thrown at him between tears and raging insults, and he still didn't know what he, or they, had done which was so foolish. Back then, he hadn't cared; he'd been too affronted by her insults and too hurt by her desertion of him without any warning.

As Grace swept into the inn, her maid, Rose, trailed behind her. The young woman caught his eye and grimaced before following Grace through the door. Alex knew the two had had a very strong relationship, the kind of trust necessary between a lady and a maid. He supposed he was to blame for ruining that too.

Going into the inn, he arranged for a meal and a private dining room for them. Partly so he could at least try and speak with Grace, partly because he didn't want anyone to witness the outburst he was sure must be boiling. During their short marriage, Grace had never been one to bottle up her emotions. From what he'd observed since she'd left him that was no longer true, but this morning had been an exception to that. Perhaps this afternoon would be too.

Hell, he almost wished she would rage at him again, instead of doing this damnable impression of an ice princess.

"I ordered us some food and wine," he said as he walked into the room where Grace was already settling herself down at the table. He looked at Rose and tilted his head toward the door, dismissing her. For just a moment he thought he saw a flash of anger in Grace's eyes as his presumptuousness, but then it was gone and she was back to staring at him blankly. After her fury this morning, he was all set for another scene, but instead she'd withdrawn inside herself again. Placing his hat down on the table, he sat across from her, studying her face. Grace looked over his shoulder, staring resolutely at the wall.

The idea of spanking her, as his friends had suggested, was becoming more and more appealing. Heating her bottom might break through some of her ice. Unfortunately, he didn't really think he could stomach spanking her just to make her talk to him. He didn't want to discipline her unless she'd actually done something to earn it.

The door behind him opened, admitting the innkeeper, who fluttered around them with their midday meal. Alex pasted a smile on his face, something he rarely expended the energy to do, and assured the man that the repast of meats and cheeses, with a small plate of fruit, was quite enough for both him and the lady. Anxious to please, the innkeeper poured their wine with a flourish and then hurried away, obviously picking up on Alex's desire to be left in peace.

Having a third party there certainly helped to ease the tension for a few minutes; the second the innkeeper left the room, the air seemed to thicken and Alex could feel his stomach churning with anxiety. Kidnapping his wife in order to force reconciliation sounded quite easy in theory, but in actuality, the reconciliation part was going to be anything but.

Grace was already filling her plate, her focus completely on the food in front of them rather than looking at him. With an inward sigh, Alex supposed it was enough she wasn't throwing the food at his head.

They ate in complete silence.

In fact, Grace didn't make a single noise, speak a single word, until he started to follow her into the carriage. Already seated upon the bench, she whipped her head back around from where she'd already been looking out the window, her large blue eyes even wider than usual.

"What are you doing?" she asked sharply, her voice laced with shock. Alex had thought it was pretty obvious was he was doing, but he answered her anyway.

"I thought I might join you in the carriage for the afternoon," he said, keeping his tone as amiable as possible, but also firm. He turned his head, giving Rose a jerking nod at the other carriage which was carrying several of the other servants. The maid turned, leaving him to climb in with Grace.

Firmly planting himself on the bench across from her, his legs stretched out, taking up as much space as possible. The carriage door shut and Grace hissed, like a cat whose fur had just been ruffled the wrong way. In fact, she looked very much like that cat. Alex ignored her.

There was a long silence between them, and then the carriage rocked as it began moving. He looked at Grace as she looked out the window, studying the tense muscle in her jaw, the long line of her throat, the way her breasts heaved as she sucked in air through her nose, and the tiny fists balled on her lap. It had been a long time since he'd been able to look at his wife this way, to examine her so minutely. There were small changes in her body, although she'd only become more beautiful with age, but the largest changes weren't immediately visible.

At one time they would have sat side by side in this carriage, talking and laughing, and she would have pressed herself against him while he wrapped his arm around her shoulders. One time he'd even made love to her in a carriage. After a ball, on their honeymoon, he'd pulled up her skirts and taken her right then and there, because he couldn't wait till they'd returned to the hotel, his passion for her had been so great.

"Stop looking at me like that."

Alex raised his eyebrow. As far as he could tell, Grace's attention hadn't strayed from the window. But then again, he hadn't been looking at her expression just now. His eyes rose back to her face, noting the pink tinge to her cheeks.

"What do you mean?" he asked, although he knew very well what she meant. He'd been looking at her the way a man looks at a woman, at his wife. The way a man looks at a woman who has been in his bed and found pleasure there.

"It's making my skin crawl." She shuddered, to emphasize her point.

Although the little barb pricked, the way she'd meant it to, he couldn't help but wonder if her attack was more of a defense. There was certainly something about the tilt of her chin, the way she was holding herself, that made him feel as though she was trying to protect herself from something. From him. Hope kindled in his chest. She wasn't as indifferent as she pretended to be. Perhaps she didn't hate him as much as she seemed to.

"I would think you'd become used to men looking at you like this," he murmured. Grace's eyes snapped to his face, flashing blue fire, before she tore them away again. Her pretty rosebud of a mouth was wound up tight and pinched. As he watched it slowly smoothed and relaxed, as if she was pulling down a mask over her face. "Many men enjoy looking at a beautiful woman."

"Many men enjoy doing quite a bit more than looking."

A reference to her lovers. He wasn't surprised. Jealousy had become a part of his everyday life after she'd left him, but he'd always considered it just punishment. After all, he'd been the one to drive her to that point.

"You would know, I suppose."

To his surprise, Grace flinched. Her eyes slid over to him again, wary and defensive.

"I didn't take a lover till you took a mistress," she said, obviously expecting him to argue.

"I know."

Her mouth opened and shut, surprise flitting across her face. Apparently he'd rendered her speechless. Something he hadn't thought possible. The carriage rocked as she looked back out the window, her brow creased in thought at his revelation. Her face was closed, impassive again, and he couldn't read what she was thinking. It nagged at him, even as he recognized the irony, considering many among the *ton* called him "Stone Face" for the same reason.

Alex knew many of his desires were improbable. He wanted his younger wife back, the trusting young woman whose expression had always been open, whose moments of bitterness were constantly turned to lightness at the drop of the hat. There had always been a bit of a dark core to Grace, behind her laughing face. Alex assumed her father was somewhat responsible for that; the man hadn't cared overmuch for his daughter, before or after her marriage. If it hadn't been for Alex's intervention, the Duke would have had her ostracized once she separated from Alex.

But the man had respected Alex's wishes when it came to dealing with his wife.

However badly he'd gone about doing it. Now was the time to fix their relationship though. He'd seen the marriages his friends had procured for themselves; remarkably similar to the marriage he'd once thought to have. The main difference, it seemed, was they spanked their wives when the women became unreasonable or acted inappropriately. If Alex had given Grace time to calm down the very first time she'd first ranted at him, if he'd swallowed his foolish pride and actually followed her and spanked her until she talked to him about whatever the problem was, maybe they could have avoided the misery they'd made of their marriage.

It was by no means entirely her fault, but nor was it his. Still, he assumed the burden of responsibility. After all, he was older, should have been wiser, and was the head of the household. It was past time to start making up for their mistakes and establish a new world order. He'd originally come to London this year hoping to speak with her, hoping to end the stalemate, and then he'd seen his friends' marriages and he'd begun to realize what he needed to do. Now it was time to put their advice and suggestions into action.

"Grace..." His voice trailed off and then firmed as she ignored him. "Grace, look at me." He could see the reluctance in her as she turned her head to face him once again. At least she'd obeyed, even if the eyes meeting his were entirely devoid of sparkle. They were practically doll's eyes, dead and empty. "I'm not going to hold your lovers against you. I want a fresh start for both of us. Our marriage needs to move forward, not dwell in the past."

The suggestion sparked an immediate response, but not at all the one he was expecting. Honestly, he'd thought she'd be relieved he was being so reasonable, that she would at least grudgingly agree to such a tactic. Instead, her eyes came to life with fiery anger, her lip curling in a gorgeous, derisive sneer. She was suddenly so much more alive, as if his words had lit a flame inside of her.

"Your mistresses don't concern me," she spat the words out, showing them for the lie they were. "But I have no interest in starting anew with you. Why won't you just leave me alone?"

Alex felt his expression harden, knew it was turning into the dark, rock-like features for which he was known. It was the easiest way for him to hide his emotions. "Because you're my wife."

"Well, I don't want to be anymore! Honestly, how dense do you have to be? A rock has more capacity for both emotions and intelligence than you do!"

That was it. While he was willing to make some allowances for her anger, since she was obviously still holding a grudge, outright disrespect he would not tolerate. If starting fresh wasn't acceptable to her, then he would have to impose himself on her life until she came to realize he wasn't going away and he also wasn't going to tolerate rude behavior on her part. While he couldn't control how she felt about him, he could at least control how she treated him.

He'd seen how his friends curbed their wives' behavior, and how effective it was. He'd allowed Grace to run amok for far too long, showing no outright interest in how she behaved. Perhaps she thought he didn't care, the way a spoiled child would run rampant, trying to find boundaries. Well, Alex was going to set some. Starting now.

Quick as a snake, he grabbed Grace's hand and used the momentum of the carriage to pull her across the dividing space and over his lap. Her shriek of shock and outrage didn't detract from the rush of pleasure he got from touching her. Especially once she was pressed against him, her bottom high in the air.

THUMP!

The layers of her skirt were definitely in the way. Alex immediately understood why Hugh had insisted on a bare bottom spanking. It was obvious that, while she was frozen with shock, the blow had barely touched her through all those layers of skirt.

"Alex, what the hell?!"

Insults and now cursing, which was not at all befitting of a lady. Grace wriggled on his lap, trying to squirm away, and igniting a response she probably wouldn't have expected. Then again, just being near her aroused him, actually having her softness pressed against his lap and cock would have tried a saint.

"I told you Grace, we're starting our marriage over. While I understand you may still be angry about some things, and I accept that, I will no longer tolerate certain behavior from you. Insults and cursing are both included in behaviors which are unacceptable." Ignoring her squeal and the way her nails were digging into his leg, through his pants, he flipped her skirts up.

She was wearing pantaloons beneath, but that was fine. The fabric was thin. He'd allow her some small protection, since this was the first time, and he knew he was already pushing her quite a bit.

SMACK!

The sound of his hand impacting her flesh through one layer of fabric was much more satisfying than through her skirts. Grace cried out, struggling wildly now. Holding her firmly, his arm resting on her back and his hand gripping the far side of her waist, Alex started to spank her, doing his best to keep the blows evenly spaced across her bottom.

"There will be no more insults."

SMACK!

"There will be no more cursing."

SMACK!

"You will be civil if nothing else."

SMACK!

"We will work out our issues in private."

SMACK!"

"In public we will present a united front."

SMACK!

"And there will definitely be no more men," he said fiercely, allowing his emotions to bleed through.

SMACK! SMACK! SMACK! SMACK!

Grace was howling, crying, kicking. He could feel the heat emanating off of her bottom through the thin fabric of her pantaloons, and just barely see a pink glow. This wasn't a particularly hard spanking, but it was certainly more than she'd ever experienced. He knew her father had never employed any means of discipline; Grace had said he tended to ignore his daughters unless he wanted something from them.

"There will be no more women for me, either."

"Alex, stop, please! Owwww, Alex stop!"

SMACK! SMACK! SMACK!

"Do you agree?"

"Stop, pleeeeeeeeease, it hurts, Alex, stop!"

"I need you to agree to my terms, Grace."

SMACK! SMACK! SMACK!

"I agree! I agree!"

Immediately, Alex stopped spanking her. He could feel the sobs wracking her frame, and he suddenly realized he'd never seen her cry in such a manner. The need to soothe her was almost overwhelming. Lifting her up, he sat her on his lap, letting her squirm and wriggle as much as needed to be comfortable sitting on his thighs when her bottom was probably burning. Digging a handkerchief out of his pocket, he wiped at her tears, cradling her with his other arm as he murmured about how pleased he was that she'd agreed.

Ignoring his aching erection wasn't pleasant, but it was worth it just to have her in his arms again.

CONFUSION SWAMPED Grace as her tears overwhelmed her. The spanking had hurt, it surely had, but it shouldn't be making her feel like this. The skin of her bottom burned, sparks flaring as she tried to find a comfortable way to sit on Alex's hard thighs.

She shouldn't be enjoying having his arms around her, she really shouldn't, but it felt so good to be held and comforted while she cried. It was not something she had much experience with. Crying had never done any good when she was growing up, mostly it got her banished back to the nursery where her father wouldn't have to look at her tears, and so she'd soon learned not to. The last time she'd really cried had been the night she'd left Alex, and even those tears had dried fairly quickly, because she'd been well aware how useless they were.

So why was she crying now like her heart was broken? The tears weren't slowing, if anything they were increasing as he held her against him.

Her emotions were jumbled, jangling inside of her, like too many church bells rioting inside her head. While she knew she should be furious with Alex, and she still was, she couldn't help but crave being held and comforted. Even though he was the one who had caused her distress, both in the past and today. The very idea that he thought he could spank her into compliance should have enraged her.

It would, she was sure it would, as soon as she managed to stop crying.

Some small part of her, some tiny remnant of her heart he hadn't managed to crush yet, was pulsing with hope. That's what angered her the most. He'd sounded like he cared while he was spanking her. Not the edict that they would present a respectable face to the public, which was what she'd expected of him, but when he said there would be no more men. It was the way he'd said it. Like it tormented him to know she'd had other lovers, like it had hurt him as much as his first affairs had torn at her. Stupid, really, to think it might be true. She knew how he really felt about women, how he felt about her.

One woman is as good as another.

But then why track her down like this? Why spank her? Why not just negotiate for whatever it was he wanted from her? Even if he didn't want the scandal of divorce—which she didn't understand, since she'd made herself a much greater scandal than a divorce would be—she would have expected him to come at her with a very different agreement. One which would allow him to keep his mistresses, and her to continue on with her affairs, as long as she bore his heir and became discreet. In other words, as long as they acted like the rest of the unhappily married couples in the *ton*.

Grace could have said no to that. It would have been easy. She didn't want any part of marriage to a man who had no emotions for her. She wanted her freedom. But this? The rawness in his voice when he'd said there would be no more women for him had made it sound like a promise. A vow. She wanted to believe him, which made her furious at herself.

Her tears were finally starting to slow and she tried to push away from him, but his arms tightened.

"Stay... just stay still, Grace. Let me hold you for a while." The hoarseness in his voice made him sound almost desperate. Unless, of course, she was imagining things which weren't there, the way she had when they'd first married. But his arms weren't loosening.

She was so tired of fighting. Not just today. It felt like she'd been struggling against impossible odds for years. The welcome numbness of exhaustion enveloped her, and she slumped against him, letting him hold her because it was easier than continuing to fight.

ALEX KNEW the moment Grace finally woke up, because she practically vaulted out of his arms. The wild look she gave him was replaced with an angry, pained one as soon as her bottom came into contact with the carriage bench. It was all he could do not to chuckle, but he didn't want to provoke his little wildcat of a wife any further.

Tilting her chin up, she gingerly settled back into her seat, smoothing down her hair and clothing as if pretending he didn't exist.

The past hour had been the best hour he'd had in years. Grace had reluctantly settled into his arms and then she'd fallen asleep on his shoulder, her sweet scent surrounding him, her curves resting against him. It had also been an exercise in self-control, because his body had responded to having a woman nestled up against him, especially because it was finally the right woman. Despite the aching torment of his cock, he'd fully enjoyed every last second of it.

Even now, he could barely tear his eyes away from the crease on her cheek, left from where it had pressed against his jacket.

He'd spanked her and she'd let him hold her. And she'd agreed to his terms for the future of the marriage. Obviously his friends were right. He should have taken her in hand years ago.

CHAPTER 2

$\mathcal{U}$nruly emotions clamored inside of Grace's stomach, and she was grateful Alex seemed content to finish the rest of the afternoon's ride in silence. It felt like she was burning, inside and out. Humiliation swept through her—truly, how stupid was she to pretend he cared for her?—along with anger at herself, embarrassment at how easily he'd handled her, and the small, sick hope that maybe he somehow did care. She could still feel his eyes, occasionally sweeping over her, but she resisted the temptation to look at him.

Something had changed within him, obviously, and she didn't yet know how to react. Nothing was going the way she thought it would, and it put her entirely off balance.

Her bottom still smarted a bit, although the pain had swiftly dwindled. Grace's father had never disciplined her in such a manner. It would have taken effort on his part. Whenever she'd misbehaved, he'd solved it by the simple expedient of banning her from seeing her mother or sisters. Then he didn't have to deal with her at all. Loneliness was a swift teacher for a little girl. Her father's coldness had spurred her desire for a marriage with something more; a man who was capable of loving her would certainly be capable of loving her children. After all, she'd seen Eleanor and Hugh's parents' relationship, she knew what a marriage could be.

Alex's determination to reconcile made her wonder if that faint spark of hope might have some justification. Immediately she squashed the thought. He'd already shattered her heart once, there was no need to give him the opportunity to grind it into dust.

Still, when they pulled up to an inn that evening, she allowed him to help her out of the carriage when he offered his hand. Although she avoided meeting his gaze.

After so many years of taking care of herself, it felt almost nice to allow him to take the lead. The few times she'd traveled with a lover, she'd always insisted on having her own room and managing her own affairs. They'd always let her. Now she was settled into a private room off to the side of the main dining room, being served her supper while Alex made arrangements with the innkeeper. She was able to relax, to sit in privacy, and not have to worry about the carriage or the bill or the room or anything at all.

Her thoughts wandered as she picked at her food. In less than a day, her life felt as though it had changed irrevocably—again. This morning she'd been Conyngham's lover, now it seemed as though Alex was determined to have her back in her place as his wife. While she didn't understand his motivations, perhaps they didn't truly matter. What she needed to decide upon was her next course of action. Her scandalous behavior hadn't driven him away, although he'd remained separate from her for years because of it. Obviously it hadn't been enough.

So what would be?

Would anything be enough?

Although he'd procured her agreement to the rules for reconciliation in the carriage, Grace didn't consider herself bound by those. Agreement under extreme duress wasn't agreement at all. She shifted uneasily in her chair. What would his reaction be if she were to break their agreement? Would he decide she wasn't worth the continued effort? Or would he spank her again?

A hot flush went through her at the thought and she frowned at the entirely inappropriate reaction.

Of course she didn't want him to spank her again. The entire idea was ludicrous. It had been humiliating and painful, even if being cuddled by him afterwards had been nice. In its own way, being comforted had been rather humiliating too. She shouldn't enjoy receiving any kind of comfort from the man.

Alex came back into the room, undoing the elaborate knot of his cravat and leaving it hanging around his neck. The collar of his shirt gaped open, and Grace averted her eyes, all too aware of the attraction immediately flaring in her. Her favorite time of day during their brief period of happiness had always been the evenings, when Alex would take off his jacket and cravat, the pieces of clothing he found most stifling, and just relax with her. Those were the softer times, when they would sit and talk, or read together, or play games, or when he'd start stripping off her own clothing and make love to her in whatever room they happened to be in.

She hardened her heart as Alex stripped off his jacket as well, before coming to sit down across from her. A tense silence reigned as he filled his plate, and her stomach began to roil nervously. It vexed her even more when Alex didn't seem at all affected; he began to eat, ignoring her, while she pushed her food around her plate and snuck peeks at him from beneath hooded eyes. Not once did he look at her though.

"Is my room ready?" she asked, her voice low and tense, closed-off so as not to betray her hope.

"Yes, but don't leave yet. I want to talk to you about where we're going."

Grace snorted. "Why bother? It's not like it makes a difference."

"I'm sure Eleanor will be happy to disagree with you," he said, ignoring her waspish tone. His eyes flicked up to her face, gauging her reaction to her friend's name. Even though his expression was hard, for just a moment she was almost able to believe he actually cared, just a little bit, about what she thought. "We'll be joining her and Edwin in Bath for Wesley's wedding."

Irene had told her about the engagement, and Grace couldn't help the little thrill that went through her at hearing she would be able to attend. She'd always loved social events anyway, and this would be a major one. The man was notorious for his affairs, his dangerous good looks, and his dark edges. He hadn't even had a full Season in the *ton*, but the matrons were full of gossip about his domineering manner and his scandalous perversions. Not that it made any difference; women had fallen all over themselves to trip into his bed.

Now he was getting married? That had been the stunned question on London's lips.

"Well, it will be the wedding of the Season," she murmured, her lips twisting in humor that she would be there to witness it. Those same gossiping matrons would be shocked and disapproving at her inclusion in such a major event. Especially if it was at her husband's side. The tiny smile faded immediately.

From the glint in Alex's eyes, he'd caught her small moment of weakness, but thankfully he didn't say anything about it.

"It will be large enough, although not everyone will be able to leave the capital to attend. However, Hugh and Irene will be there and I expect you to behave yourself."

Grace bristled at his patronizing tone.

"I have no issue with Irene," she snapped, feeling a rush of vindictive pleasure at the surprise on his face, knowing he could hear the sincerity in her voice. The confusion on his face was almost soothing to her temper. She smiled thinly. "She came to apologize to me before she and Hugh left London. We're quite friendly now." That was stretching the truth a bit, but it was worth it to see the dumbfounded look on her husband's face.

"Irene came to apologize to you," he repeated, as if having trouble even comprehending the words she'd used. As if he was trying to figure out what sweet, favored Irene would have to apologize to Grace about.

Irene had always been a sore subject between them, and after Grace had overhead Alex talking to her father, she'd outright hated the other woman. *One woman is as good as another*—except for Irene.

The young redhead had been so obvious in her adoration for Alex, and Alex had been devoted to her. He'd brushed off Grace's discomfort with Irene's behavior even when he'd been pretending to dote on her when they'd first been married. Then, when she'd listened to that blasted conversation, she'd realized all women were interchangeable to Alex, except for Irene. She was a constant, a woman who stood out above all the rest, and Grace's bitterness had nearly overwhelmed her every time she'd been faced with the woman.

The apology had helped, and Grace knew it wasn't Irene's fault that Alex was the way he was, but she didn't know if things would ever truly be friendly between them.

Sudden comprehension seemed to dawn on him, and it was Grace's turn to blink in confusion at his expression.

"I see," he said, nodding. "Good, then."

Tapping her finger against the table, Grace looked away from him, wondering exactly what it was he saw.

"I'm sorry as well."

Her heart stilled. Those words could not have just come out of his mouth. Alex was never sorry. He was always supremely confident in everything he did, sure of the rightness of it. Besides which...

"For what?" she asked, a bit faintly, still tapping away on the table. A little faster now as nervous energy tingled to life inside of her.

"I should have listened to you about Irene. I shouldn't have dismissed her behavior." Alex hesitated and then shook his head slightly. She could only stare in fascination as the facade of his stone face cracked, just the tiniest bit, and regret shown through. "Hugh and I spoke with her, and it's not something you'll have to worry about again."

ONE SLENDER FINGER, moving up and down, was the only sign of Grace's discomposure. Alex found himself fascinated with the small chink in her armor, wondering what it was she was thinking. Silence had never been Grace's natural state when they'd first married; she'd always been talking about something, enthusing over the latest play or book, or a story she'd heard. It made the back of Alex's neck itch to be eating a meal with her at last, and to have her shutting him out.

She stared off into the distance, her pretty pink lips pursed, as if she didn't dare open her mouth for the words that might come tumbling out. Color pinked her cheeks as her mouth twisted, as if she was seeing the humor in the situation. Years after she'd been upset about Irene, he'd finally admitted she was right and taken care of it. Alex saw the irony. Once Irene had thrown herself at him and forced his eyes open, he'd wondered if his friendship with the younger woman was part of why Grace had thought they'd been "foolish" when they'd married. Had she thought his feelings for Irene were more than brotherly, no matter that he'd told her otherwise?

Perhaps. Although he still couldn't understand why, if so. The way he'd treated both of them had been worlds apart. Irene was the little scamp he'd spent his life protecting like a little sister; Grace was his wife.

"Apology accepted," she said, finally. Yet, even then, he didn't sense any crumbling of the wall between them. Maybe Irene hadn't had anything to do with why Grace left him.

Which meant he was just as baffled as before.

They'd ridden in the carriage together all afternoon, he'd spanked her, held her on his lap while she'd slept, and now they were sharing a meal, but she was as far away as ever from him. As if during their time apart she'd erected an invisible shell keeping him from truly being able to touch her. It made him ache in a thousand different ways, from his head, to his heart, down to his cock. What he wouldn't give to just strip her down out of her dress, strip off her invisible armor, and love her back into herself.

Somehow, he didn't think she'd appreciate the sentiment. He had no desire to force himself on an unwilling woman, even if he had been rock hard all afternoon after spanking her.

Besides which, in a few minutes she was going to be furious with him for a whole new reason. His stomach full, he pushed away his plate and sighed, picking up his jacket as he stood.

"Come," he said, walking around the table and holding out his hand. "I'll show you to your room."

Grace looked at his hand like it was a viper, ready to bite and poison her, and Alex let it drop. Part of him wanted to push her to at least accept a small civility from him, but right now he was too damn tired. He just wanted to go upstairs and get this over with. The perfect end to a frustrating, and what felt like a fruitless, first day of reconciliation with his stubborn wife.

She followed him upstairs and into the room docilely enough, proof, perhaps, of her own exhaustion. But Grace was quick of mind, and it took her less than a minute to take in the contents of the room and realize exactly what he'd done. By that time he was already locking the door and tucking the key into his pocket.

"No," she said, tersely, her hands clenched into small fists at her side. "No, no, no, no, no."

"Yes."

"I won't."

"Won't what? Sleep?" He walked past her, heading for his trunk. "That's your choice, but I intend to get some rest."

The itch on the back of his neck increased, he could feel her glare slicing into his shoulder blades as he dropped his jacket onto his trunk. There was no way he was letting Grace sleep in a different room. Even if he trusted her not to try to run, considering she wasn't exactly traveling with him of her own will, one commonality his friends had was a belief their wives belonged in bed with them. Although he and Grace had had separate rooms, they'd always ended up sleeping in the same one. No more separation. Not in their marriage and not their beds.

He pulled off his cravat and tossed it onto the trunk as well, before he began to loosen the cuffs to his sleeve. Out of the corner of his eye, he saw Grace skitter to the door and test it. He hid his grin as she mumbled something under her breath, probably a curse, when she found it locked. Rolling up his shirtsleeves, he nonchalantly ambled over to the pitcher of water and large bowl laid out for their use.

Although he'd been tempted to order Grace a bath, he'd wanted to see how she'd react to their shared accommodations first. After all, she might not be interested in bathing with him in the room, and he certainly wasn't going anywhere. He'd requested a room on the upper floor, but his Grace was tenacious enough to try and make it out a window, given enough time on her own.

"I'm not getting in that bed with you."

"Which is also your choice. But you should know I have no plans to sleep on the floor tonight." Alex was gambling on Grace's love of comfort to keep her off of the floor too. He'd had the innkeeper remove the rug to make the floor even less appealing than it would have otherwise been. Splashing water on his face, Alex sighed with pleasure as he rubbed away the grime of the day.

After drying his face and arms with one of the provided towels, he looked up to see Grace still hovering by the door, a look of determination on her face.

"I'm not going to—to act as your *wife*, there," she said, pointing to the bed.

He raised his eyebrows as her chin tilted upwards in defiance. "I have no interest in forcing an unwilling woman."

Grace gaped at him, looking remarkably like a fish, and he had to hide his smile.

"I'm entirely unwilling to even be here!"

"That's different," he declared as he began unbuttoning his shirt. It didn't escape his notice when her eyes went to the bare skin revealed there before she looked away. On their honeymoon she'd told him that watching him undress was fascinating, she'd been entranced by the differences in their bodies. It heartened him to know she was still affected, even though she now had others to compare him to. Somehow that didn't wane his attraction to her, it only made him want to prove to her that he was better. Letting his shirt drop to the floor, he started walking toward her, noticing the tension gripping her—and he was fairly certain it wasn't just anger or fear which was causing her cheeks to turn pink. He put his fingers under her chin, tilted her head back to look at him. Leaning forward, he saw her pupils flare as the blush in her cheeks deepened. Male smugness wove its way around his bones; no matter what else lay between them, she was still attracted to him. "You are my wife, for better or worse, and we are going to be together. But when I make love to you again, Grace, it will be because you *beg* me to."

The moment hung between them, tension humming in the air, before she jerked away, slapping at his hand. The look she gave him made it clear she'd rather die first. Alex straightened and turned away, heading for the bed so he could remove his boots. He also needed a moment to compose himself, because his erection was throbbing, and he was already tempted to show Grace just how easily it would be for her to become willing. But it wasn't the right time yet.

"Why?"

The question cut through the air before he'd made it halfway to the bed. Alex looked over his shoulder to see her standing there, an air of desperation hanging around her that he hadn't sensed before. He'd been about to reply flippantly, but something in her eyes made him stop. The question wasn't rhetorical, it seemed to mean something to her.

"Why what?"

"Why me? I need to know Alex. Why not just divorce me and find a new wife?"

"There'd be a scandal..." he said slowly. "Where would you go? What would you do? London Society would never welcome you back into its fold, not with the way you've behaved over the years. My name has been all that's kept them from throwing you out."

"That's *my* problem, not yours," she said, scowling furiously. "I'm a bigger scandal than a divorce would be. Can you imagine what they'll say if we reconcile? I've been cuckolding you for *years.*"

Alex shrugged as he sat down on the bed and began tugging off his boots. He'd become inured to the *ton*'s opinion over those years. If they thought him a fool for taking back his wife, he didn't care, although he thought there would be just as many who approved of him taking her in hand. What he didn't understand was why Grace seemed so concerned with what they thought of him, when it was her fault they were in this situation in the first place.

He'd attempted to approach Grace, several times before. At least once a year for the past three years, actually. Every time, she'd tensed and fled, and he'd backed away, both hurt and frustrated by her response. Whenever he showed up in the same area as her, she was gone just as quickly. But he'd never shown up in London during the Season before, he'd always attempted to broach her in private. So this year he'd upped the ante in more ways than one.

"I don't want another wife, I want you," he said simply. It was the unvarnished truth as he saw it.

His wife gaped at him, apparently rendered speechless by his answer. The astonishment and shock clearly written across her face was even greater than this morning's when he'd told her he wanted to reconcile. Which he found confusing. Hadn't he always shown Grace how much he wanted her? Well, besides when he'd been foolish enough to let her go without a fight.

Cursing himself again for his idiotic pride, for allowing her to slip away from him so easily, Alex knew he would have to work to undo the damage he'd contributed to their rift. But he was determined she do the same.

To say Grace was confused was an understatement. Why was Alex so determined to have her when any woman would do for him? His behavior was completely counteracting his words to her father and she didn't know what to believe. Perhaps something had happened in the deal between her husband and her father that she didn't know about, something requiring her to be reconciled with Alex.

She didn't trust this rapid turnaround, even though some small part of her was burning with hope.

Hope hurt. Hope was what would grind her already shattered heart into dust. Hope was what had caused her to lower her defenses to Alex in the first place, to believe something more was growing between them.

So she took that little sliver of light and tucked it away, like she was closing it up into Pandora's Box, just like in the myth.

Fortunately, Alex had already gotten into the bed, after giving her a long, considering look, and his back was to her. Gritting her teeth, she followed him, practically clinging to the edge of the bed so she didn't accidentally touch him. She wasn't going give him the satisfaction of thinking she was afraid of him. She didn't want him to think she still cared, that sleeping next to him would bother her.

Tears slid silently down her face, and she told herself they were tears of anger and frustration, but she wasn't entirely sure that was true. Her emotions were utter chaos, as if all the careful walls she'd built up had tumbled down, the compartments emptied, and now she was drowning in them.

She missed Conyngham and the simplicity of their relationship. The caring of friendship without deeper emotions. Trusting him with her body had been easy, because she hadn't had to trust him with her heart.

Now she was realizing why it had been so easy to keep her heart out of her affairs: Alex had still held the battered shards.

CHAPTER 3

$\mathcal{T}$he house Eleanor and Edwin had rented out was beautifully furnished, but quite cozy, Irene was relieved to find. They'd asked her and Hugh to stay with them for the duration of their visit to Bath, since they would only be in town long enough to attend Wesley's wedding, and then Hugh wanted to move on to the estates. Edwin would be taking Eleanor to his own estates at the same time, although they were near enough for visiting, thankfully.

Irene was both looking forward to and dreading seeing her sister-in-law again. She hoped Eleanor would be able to forgive Irene for her part in Edwin's discovery of Eleanor's plans. Although Eleanor had been gracious enough in the letter she'd written to Irene, accepting her heartfelt apology, she wouldn't blame Eleanor for holding a grudge. Especially if she and Edwin were still unhappy.

But Eleanor was nothing but smiles and embraces when she greeted Hugh and Irene. Edwin, as darkly imposing as ever, kept her close by his side, but Eleanor seemed content to be there. Her face was paler and more wane than it had been in London, but Irene hoped it wasn't because she was unhappy here with Edwin.

"We've been invited by the Countess of Spencer to dinner tonight, if you feel well enough for it," Eleanor said cheerfully. "If not, we can make your excuses."

"I'd like to go and meet the future Countess," said Hugh, grinning cheerfully at his sister. The look of eager anticipation that passed between them was so filled with sibling understanding, Irene felt envious for a moment. Not that she doubted Hugh's love for her, but since she'd never had a sibling, she felt envious over the closeness Eleanor had with her brother and his friends. Her husband glanced down at her, his blue eyes sweeping over her as if checking to ensure she was well enough to go along with his plans. "As long as Irene's amenable. We can wait till tomorrow, if you'd prefer to rest, sweetheart."

"No, I'd like to go," Irene said, although she did give Eleanor a plaintive look. "Do I have time for a bath, beforehand?"

"Of course, I've already had one drawn up for you," Eleanor said, detaching herself from Edwin's side and taking Irene's arm. She gave her brother a look. "For you too, and I recommend you use it before you and Edwin disappear into the study for scotch. Come, Irene, we can have a nice *coze* while you bath."

Irene giggled as Eleanor drew her away, ignoring Hugh sputtering behind her.

LETTING Irene soak in her bath first, Eleanor directed the maids in unpacking the trunks her brother and sister-in-law had brought. She was relieved to have them in the house, as a bit of a buffer between herself and Edwin, as she still hadn't told her husband about her condition. Placing her hand over her stomach, she worried at her lower lip, knowing she wouldn't be able to hide it for much longer. Already her body was changing, not just her level of energy, but she'd noticed her stomach and breasts were becoming rounder. Her recent cravings for sweets could only explain so much of that.

Hugh had insisted he and Irene share a room, which hadn't surprised Eleanor, although she'd told him he'd have to bathe where she'd had the tub set up for him. She wanted a chance to be alone with Irene and find out what had happened in London while she was away. More importantly, she wanted to know what had happened between Irene and Hugh, since the letters they'd exchanged hadn't been especially detailed.

At first Irene seemed almost reluctant to confide in Eleanor, but once she began to tell her tale, Eleanor understood why. She gasped at hearing Hugh had punished Irene in front of someone—*Lord Brooke* of all people! Yet, she understood why as well. If she'd known why Irene had wanted to leave the capital, she would have never invited her sister-in-law to escape to Bath with her.

Of course, then Edwin wouldn't have overheard Irene talking and then come to Eleanor the way he had, and maybe they wouldn't be quite so happy now. Well, as happy as she could be when she was still worried about whether he had feelings for her. Although he behaved as a doting husband, she'd seen other marriages where the man behaved that way and the lady had no idea he had a mistress on the side. Most of the time she felt completely secure in his affections, but she still had those niggling doubts that wouldn't let her go.

If only the blasted man would tell her how he felt about her.

"Have you received any word from Lady Brooke?" Irene asked as she dressed, the maid helping to cinch her into an evening gown appropriate for dinner at the Countess'.

"No, should I have?" Eleanor asked, startled out of her reverie. She knew there was quite a bit of animosity between her sister-in-law and her best friend, so she was surprised to hear a complete lack of it in Irene's voice.

The pretty redhead worried her lower lip, sighing slightly. "Alex told Hugh and me that he wants to reconcile with her."

Eleanor burst out laughing, although there was no true humor in the situation. "That will never happen," she said, with conviction. "Grace would run to America first. In fact, I'm not sure she hasn't thought of it already."

"What happened between them?" Irene asked, settling herself down on the chair next to Eleanor's now that she was dressed. The dark green silk she'd put on brought out the emerald of her eyes and made her red hair look gloriously rich. The pale cream of her skin glowed in the firelight. "Do you know?"

"I do, but I can't betray Grace's confidence, I'm sorry."

Irene waved her hand. "No, no, of course you shouldn't. I just wish there was something I could do for them... she seems so unhappy and I know Alex has been miserable since she left him."

That made Eleanor raise her eyebrows. After all, for him to be miserable over his wife's separation from him, wouldn't he have to care about Grace? Yet, from what Grace had told her, Alex had never been particularly invested in her personally. Of course, Irene could have a different perspective.

She sighed. Marriage, as she'd learned, could be very complicated. "Perhaps when she comes to visit me this summer I'll be able to ask her."

"You don't think she'll come for the wedding?"

"No. She and Wesley know each other but they aren't close, whereas Lord Brooke is a particular friend of his." Although Eleanor rather wished Grace was coming. She would love the opportunity to observe Grace and Lord Brooke in the same locale again; there was something between the two of them that just didn't make sense.

MEETING WESLEY'S OTHER FRIEND, Viscount Petersham and his wife, was not an occasion for misbehavior, Cynthia reminded herself. Even if she wasn't feeling particularly pleased with her future husband. Two days after he'd tied her to the bedpost and done unspeakable—and incredibly pleasurable—things to her body, she still didn't know how she felt about him.

On one hand, she'd loved tracing the welts from his belt on her bottom and the subsequent soreness in her nipples from the clips he'd put on them. The pleasure he'd brought her to had been intense. On the other, he'd done unspeakable things to her bottom. Inside her bottom. The poor little hole was still tender and yet... that had been part of the pleasure. It was humiliating.

Even more so since he'd barely touched her again since then, when she was still craving him so desperately. Rubbing herself, the way she'd done before, just didn't fulfill her the way he had. She'd learned there was a very keen difference between pleasure she gave herself, and pleasure given to her. Touching herself wasn't nearly as exciting as when Wesley touched her. Besides, shouldn't he want to touch her more? Every other man she'd met had constantly been coaxing her to allow them more liberties; the man she was going to marry barely kissed her hand or cheek.

Well, except when she'd pushed him to punish her.

But she wasn't sure she was ready to do that again; the last time had left her wary of him. She remembered telling him she wanted a husband who wouldn't bore her. He would certainly be that, but now she was unsure if such excitement was a good thing. The things he'd done to her... well, they'd been unimaginable. Far beyond anything she'd thought of doing with a man. Even if it had been both exciting and pleasurable, for the first time in her life she'd been frightened by her reaction, because he'd gone far beyond the bounds she'd even thought possible. Which was why she was on her best behavior tonight, doing the pretty for Eleanor and Edwin, and the Viscount and Viscountess.

The Viscountess wasn't at all how Cynthia had pictured her, not after meeting Eleanor. Although, the Viscount was. He was as goldenly handsome as Eleanor was angelically beautiful, with piercing blue eyes and a quick, flashing smile as he looked down at his wife. The Viscountess wasn't a fashionable beauty; she had red hair and freckles, for one, but she was quite pretty even if she'd never be a Diamond of the First Water. Quite shy too, from the way she practically clung to her husband's arm as she was introduced to the Countess.

Cynthia hoped the Viscountess wouldn't be boring. She had the look of a woman who would be horrified by impropriety. Or, if she was, that her presence wouldn't make Eleanor prim and proper as well.

"May I present my betrothed, Miss Cynthia Bryant," the Earl said, pressing his fingers briefly against hers on his arm, as if telling her to behave. She stifled the impulse to stick her tongue out at him. The Earl might be wildly unpredictable in private, but he was a stuffed shirt in public and she wasn't about to purposefully court his displeasure.

She curtsied prettily, and smiled demurely. "It's very nice to meet you."

To her amusement, everyone in the room looked at her slightly askance, as if waiting for her to do something naughty. Cynthia kept the demure smile on her face, feeling her fiancé's arm tense under her fingers. From the narrow-eyed look he gave her, she was quite sure he thought her good behavior was a cover and he was trying to figure out what mischief she was up to. How galling it would be for him to discover she wasn't up to anything at all.

It was sure to frustrate him greatly.

Cynthia asked after their travels, the way a young lady should, and felt Wesley stiffen even more, if that was possible. Oh, this was going to be fun. The better she behaved, the more wound up he would get. She didn't realize the gleam in her eye was only making the Earl feel even more on edge, but she would have been quite satisfied with that knowledge as well.

"I'M DISAPPOINTED," Hugh announced, settling down in his seat, a snifter of brandy in his hand. The ladies had withdrawn to the drawing room, leaving the men at the table for their drinks. "After all the descriptions of Miss Bryant as a hellion, I expected a much more debaucherous showing."

"Perhaps Wesley has had a steadying influence on her," Edwin teased. He shot his friend a look. "Although, I have to admit, I was expecting something from her this evening as well. She certainly looked as though she was plotting mischief."

"Did she?" Hugh asked, looking somewhat confused. To him, Miss Bryant had seemed the very picture of a sweet young miss. Granted, she had quite a figure for a young miss, which he was sure had attracted Wesley, but he hadn't seen any of the spirit he'd expected.

"It's in her eyes," Wesley said, glancing at the door. Tension had gripped him all evening as he'd waited for Cynthia's behavior to degenerate. It hadn't, not once, and he didn't know whether he was relieved or disappointed by it. He certainly hoped he hadn't put her off misbehaving entirely, but going by her expression he hadn't. He just didn't know what the damned chit was up to. "She was playacting, although I don't know for whose benefit—yours, mine, or my mother's. I'm sure you'll have ample opportunity to see her antics before the wedding."

"Although she has been on better behavior the past couple of days," Edwin observed, raising his eyebrow at Wesley. "Eleanor wondered what you had done to her."

The memory of Cynthia's last punishment made Wesley grin, even as his cock hardened slightly. He'd been in a state of almost perpetual arousal following that night, which he'd only managed to deal with by keeping his distance from his bride. Given the opportunity, it was all too tempting to divest her of her virginity before the wedding night, which was absolutely not something he was going to do. Especially not in his mother's house.

Still, he wouldn't object to punishing her again. He'd taken one virginity from her the other night, indulging in his most depraved fantasy, as he'd buried himself in her tight arse after belting her creamy cheeks to a dark red. The little wanton had enjoyed herself too, for all she'd been embarrassed by the act. As much as Wesley enjoyed indulging in that particular perversion, he knew he was going to have to keep it strictly for special punishment occasions or it would lose its potent effect on her. There wasn't much his little minx was embarrassed by, and he certainly didn't want to cure her of that particular one.

"Well, well," Hugh said, raising his eyebrows. "It appears Wesley *did* anticipate his wedding night." He looked at Edwin. "You owe me twenty pounds."

"No." Wesley glared at his friends, although he wasn't truly angry. It was the kind of thing he'd bet on, and he wasn't entirely surprised they had. "She's still pure."

"Damn," said Hugh, as a triumphant Edwin held out his hand. Hugh dug into his pocket and pulled out several notes, slapping them down into Edwin's palm.

"So what did you do?" Edwin asked, curious. "Whatever it was, it definitely set her on edge."

The smile stretching across Wesley's face was pure, smug, male satisfaction. "I just used the little implements I brought back from India. There's nothing like filling a woman's bottom to make it quite clear who the Master of the House is."

Edwin guffawed as Hugh shook his head.

"I don't need that to assert myself as Master of the House," Hugh said. "Other than the oils, I haven't used your wedding gift at all."

"You don't know what you're missing," Edwin said, his eyes gleaming as Hugh pretended to try and cover his ears, a useless exploit since he refused to let go of his brandy while he did so. Before Edwin had married his sister, Hugh hadn't minded hearing about his exploits, but now he preferred not to know the details. Laughing, Edwin leaned towards Wesley, whispering loudly as Hugh pretended temporary deafness. "I haven't used the dilators yet, but I've gotten a bit of use out of your other gifts."

"At least someone is," Wesley said, grinning. Although he wasn't entirely surprised. Hugh had been the one to first introduce himself and Edwin to the idea of feminine discipline, when he'd invited them to watch Eleanor receive a birching from her father, but in many ways he was a prude. Edwin was far more adventurous, even if he hadn't reached the level Wesley had yet. While it was strange to think about Edwin and Eleanor together that way, it didn't bother him the way it did Hugh.

"I don't need such sundry instruments to discipline my wife,"

Hugh said loftily. "All Irene needs is a spanking now and then to keep her in line."

"This coming from the man who wanted a wife he didn't have to discipline at all," Wesley reminded him.

"Well... I have found it does have some benefits." Hugh smirked and gave them a significant look. "After all, disciplining a wife *is* very different from disciplining a family member."

"I should hope so," Edwin muttered, considering it was his own wife's bottom Hugh had learned on. But, he still remembered how unaffected Hugh had been when he'd brought Wesley and Edwin in to watch Eleanor's birching. Not having a sister of his own, Edwin couldn't quite imagine what it must be like to discipline someone he wasn't interested in sexually, but he knew how shocked Hugh had been by his own reaction when it was Irene under his hand instead of a family member.

All three men sipped at their brandy, contemplating their marriages. Hugh was smugly happy, having received everything he wanted and more from his marriage to Irene. His redheaded goddess was sweetness and passion, and he enjoyed slowly breaking through her demure walls. Still uncertain over Eleanor's behavior, Edwin had been much happier with his wife since their retreat to Bath; she seemed to have calmed down considerably after their first few days in town. The atmosphere here seemed much more conducive to their happiness than London had. He was in alt over her conception, and was looking forward to when she finally confirmed it and they could celebrate.

Wesley, like any soon-to-be married man was thinking about his upcoming wedding night, as well as what life would be like once his little hellion was his wife. Dark fantasies shifted around his head, all of which had sprung up since he'd belted and buggered his fiancé and she'd so obviously enjoyed it.

None of them wanted to share their current thoughts, however, so the conversation quickly turned to Wesley's company and the trade with India. Much safer topics altogether.

~

THE COUNTESS REIGNED supreme over the conversation between the ladies, which meant only socially conventional topics were discussed. Irene, like her husband, was somewhat disappointed by Cynthia's decorum. However, unlike Hugh, she was also relieved, as she didn't quite know how she would react to misbehavior. She wasn't comfortable enough in high society to know how a lady would react— although it would be helpful to see the Countess and Eleanor's reactions.

Not for the first time, Irene inwardly railed at her own mother for the lack of training she'd received. She was so used to being told exactly what to do and how to do it, that being on her own was quite frightening, especially in the presence of a woman like the Countess. Wesley's mother wore her authority like a mantle, easily and confidently. Irene could only hope one day she would do so as well.

Eleanor invited both ladies over for tea the next day, but the Countess had a prior engagement and had to decline; however, Cynthia gleefully accepted. Irene wondered if being away from the Countess' presence would mean Cynthia's true mischief would emerge. She almost hoped so. Just so she could see. Perhaps it would make her feel less guilty over her own untoward behavior a few weeks before.

~

GRACE HAD NEVER THOUGHT she'd be relieved to arrive in a sleepy place like Bath, not while the Season was still going on, but she truly didn't think she could stand another hour in the carriage with her husband. The man was driving her batty.

Both nights on the road, she'd had to sleep in the same bed as him —which, of course, meant she got very little sleep at all. Her tingling awareness of his proximity meant she could barely relax. Especially since the few times she did so and managed to fall asleep, she invariably awoke in his arms. She couldn't even blame him, because it was quite obvious from their positioning on the bed that both of them had moved toward each other.

Riding in the carriage wasn't any better. She'd truly expected him to spend at least some time on his horse. Instead, the blasted man joined her in the carriage both morning and afternoon. The confines of the conveyance seemed to shrink, as if he filled it with his very presence, far beyond his physical form. Sometimes he spoke, sometimes they rode in silence, but he was always watching her.

The worst was when she fell asleep in the carriage, exhausted from lack of sleep the night before. Every time, she awoke in his arms. The first time, she'd cursed him and immediately thrown herself across to the other side of the carriage. To his credit, he'd released her immediately, but she'd been well aware of his arousal. By the third time, she'd no longer been startled and had been weak enough to relish the feel of his arms around her. She hated herself for pretending to still be slumbering, just so she could feel the press of his warmth against her, pretend—for just a moment—that they were back in time, before she'd overheard his conversation with her father.

But she could never hold back the memories, or the bitterness, for very long. Especially because she didn't understand why he was doing what he was doing now. He hadn't spanked her since the first day, thankfully, but then again she'd been doing her best to ignore him. Once she'd realized fighting him was futile, that, for some reason, he'd decided he preferred reconciliation over divorce, she'd done her best to shut him out. It didn't seem to matter to him when she never answered; he filled the silence by speaking to her.

Things about his estate, about his company. About his life. Sometimes she caught herself beginning to smile when he made a rare quip or witticism. She could only hope he didn't notice. She didn't want him to think she was softening toward him, although she was. Even if he had apologized about the way he'd handled the original situation between her and Irene, there were so many other issues between them that they didn't discuss at all.

So she was relieved when the carriage rolled to a stop in Bath and Alex helped her out. The torment of traveling with him was over.

There would be no more falling asleep and waking up in his arms, no more being forced into a tiny space with him, and no more temptation to ask him what the hell he thought he was doing.

"Grace?"

Eleanor's familiar voice, filled with shock, was all Grace needed to push her over the edge. She looked up, into the face of her best friend, who was gorgeously attired in a blue dress and bonnet, obviously out shopping, and burst into tears. Immediately, slim arms surrounded her shoulders, even as strong fingers pressed against her back. The rush of emotions was overwhelming, and she clung to Eleanor, burying her face in the other woman's shoulder as she sobbed.

"Come here, Gracie," Alex said, his voice low and almost tender. She obediently let go of Eleanor, too overcome to even try and fight him, and let him sweep her up into his arms. Part of her knew she should be protesting his high-handedness, but another part felt comforted being held by him, letting him take over and get her off of the street before she utterly humiliated herself. Besides, her legs felt weak, and he was obviously feeling strong. "If you wouldn't mind coming in with us, Lady Hyde, I think Grace could use your company while I see to opening up the house for us."

"Of course," Eleanor said, her voice filled with worry and confusion. "I was just out shopping... I didn't realize you were here... I... just a moment." Grace heard Eleanor giving her maid directions to return to her own house and inform Lord Hyde of where she was. Relief her friend wasn't abandoning her made Grace go even limper in Alex's arms, she even felt grateful to the brute for asking Eleanor to come in with them.

How could he be so considerate and simultaneously so uncaring? Yet, she'd had proof in the past that he was. He'd fooled her for their entire honeymoon into thinking there could be more to their marriage than just convenience. Right now, she found strange comfort in the illusion.

A few minutes later, Grace and Eleanor were deposited into the main drawing room, and Grace's tears had subsided to small sniffles. Alex asked a maid to bring them tea before retreating from the room, leaving the ladies blissfully alone. For the first time in days, Grace felt like she could breathe. Unfortunately, some tiny part of her also felt a bit forlorn at the loss of his presence, but it was only a very small, very foolish part of her.

"Grace..." Eleanor's voice trailed off and she shook her head, tugging off the blue bonnet and placing it on the couch beside her as she searched for words. Or, more likely, searched for what question she wanted to begin with. "What are you doing here? With *him?*"

"I wasn't given a choice," Grace said, sniffling again. She knew she must look a fright, but neither Alex nor Eleanor had commented on it. Eleanor just reached into her reticule and retrieved a handkerchief, silently passing it over to Grace to wipe her tear-stained face with. "Peters betrayed me... he was working for Alex all along. *All* of my servants were." Tears started to flow again as she told Eleanor everything.

About riding in the carriage with Alex, his insistence on sleeping in the same room, his behavior toward her every time she fell asleep, and his determination to reconcile. Her confusion. Eleanor was the only person in the entire world who knew everything; all of Grace's humiliation, her bitterness, and her loss when she'd discovered Alex saw her as nothing more than a bargaining chip. Although Grace had been determined to keep the hurtful words to herself, this past Season she hadn't been able to hold her tumultuous emotions inside any longer when she and Alex had been in the city at the same time for the first time in years. She'd needed her friend, and Eleanor had been there for her.

So Eleanor completely understood Grace's confusion over Alex's current behavior. Indeed, Eleanor had been quite confused when she'd first met Lord Brooke, because he hadn't seemed at all the monster Grace had always made him out to be. Even after she'd found out why Grace had estranged herself from him, Eleanor hadn't seen that kind of uncaring husband in his behavior. When she'd been quite rude to him, out of loyalty to her friend, he'd asked Edwin not to punish her too harshly, because he admired her loyalty.

From what Grace was telling her now, Lord Brooke's behavior

was certainly not that of a man who had no finer feelings for his wife. Even now, he'd asked Eleanor to come in on Grace's behalf, rather than trying to isolate and intimidate her.

At any time during their marriage, he could have claimed his marital rights and Grace would have had no cause to resist. Anyone who had sheltered her would have had to give her up, under the law, if Lord Brooke had insisted. Instead, he'd let her go her own way for years. Eleanor had never seen another man do anything like it, which was why it was such a scandal among the *ton*. She was as surprised as Grace had been, to hear he wanted a reconciliation.

Of course, she was even more surprised to see Grace in Bath. Apparently, Lord Brooke's patience with the estrangement had ended.

"Perhaps once you left, he realized what he had lost," Eleanor murmured, trying to be encouraging. After all, Lord Brooke couldn't be completely uncaring if he was going through all this trouble to reconcile with Grace, rather than divorcing her. And Eleanor had some experience in recognizing affection from men who were unwilling to speak their emotions out loud. She still wasn't sure if her own husband loved her, but she knew he had great affection for her, and she was sure she saw the same signs in Lord Brooke.

"Which is how he found himself so quickly in so many other women's beds," Grace said acidly, although she didn't pull away from Eleanor's shoulder. Dabbing at her eyes with the handkerchief, she was slowly regaining control over herself. "A rather slow realization, if one happened at all."

"Men can be quite slow about such things," Eleanor said, smiling slightly, although she certainly wasn't cheery about it. She'd struggled with her own worries about Edwin's fidelity, and still did, although he'd mostly convinced her that he would remain faithful. But he still hadn't told her whether or not his emotions for her went beyond that of a childhood companion whom he desired in his bed. Hers certainly, and she worried a lack of return would make her bitter and miserable.

Quite a bit like Grace, in fact, even if Edwin did remain faithful.

"I don't know what I'm doing anymore," Grace said softly. "I thought I did... but nothing's turning out the way I planned it."

A sentiment Eleanor could whole-heartedly sympathize with. But she also thought she was much happier than if her plans had come to realization—at least, she would be once Edwin declared his feelings.

"Do you think he would let you come to tea this afternoon?" she asked, worried at the way Grace was continuing to tremble, almost shivering, despite the warmth of the day. "Irene will be there, and Cynthia, Wesley's betrothed. Surely he can't object to afternoon tea."

"That sounds like a fine idea, Lady Hyde."

Both women jerked in shock, Grace sitting bolt upright, as Lord Brooke answered the question from the door. Eleanor pursed her lips. He moved as quietly as a cat! It was more than a little disconcerting, especially since neither she nor Grace knew how long he'd been listening. She didn't think it could have been overly long, but she still ran through their conversation in her head, hoping they hadn't said anything too indiscreet.

"Come Gracie, I'll show you around the house, and then this afternoon you can go have tea with your friends."

Next to Eleanor, Grace stiffened at Alex's tone, which to Eleanor's ear hovered somewhere between soothing and patronizing. It certainly wasn't what she would have expected to hear from Lord Brooke's mouth, not the man who was reputed to be London's harshest member of the *ton*. Grace squeezed Eleanor's hand once and then stood, turning her back on her husband to face her friend again. Her blue eyes were red-rimmed from crying, but she had control over herself again.

"I'll see you this afternoon," she said softly, as Eleanor stood. They squeezed each other's hands, Eleanor in sympathetic support, Grace in a kind of needy desperation.

"Good day, Lord Brooke," Eleanor said as she passed him, giving him a sharp, warning look. While in London, she'd become fairly comfortable with the man, and while she trusted him not to harm Grace physically, she wasn't sure if he fully understood what he was doing to her friend emotionally.

"Lady Hyde," he murmured, with a slight bow.

Behind him, the butler waited to show Eleanor to the door. She glanced over her shoulder one last time, to see Lord Brooke and Grace, walking down the hallway in the opposite direction. Grace's hand was on his arm, although she seemed to be trying to keep as much distance from her husband as possible within the parameters given to her, but Lord Brooke's fingers were covering hers, as if trying to pull her closer.

Eleanor's lips twitched. Something was happening between the long-estranged Lord and Lady, although whether the change was for better or worse remained to be seen.

As ALEX LED Grace around the house, he wished he had heard more of her conversation with Eleanor. From the little he'd heard, he was sure it would have been revealing. He'd heard Grace bitterly speaking of his affairs, which had made him wince, especially because he realized she was particularly incensed at how quickly he'd replaced her in his bed. At the time, it had seemed like a good idea, guaranteed to spark her jealousy and return her to him, as well as punish her for leaving. Now it was one of his largest regrets, even more so after hearing the long-held hurt in her voice.

But he couldn't change the past now. Neither of them had been faithful. He hadn't taken a mistress until after she'd taken a lover, but she didn't know that. Sap skull that he'd been, he hadn't thought about how his reaction to her flirtations had been tempered by his knowledge she hadn't actually gone through with them. Grace had had no such assurance.

Now she was walking by his side, stiff as a board and cold as ice. Even her fingers were chilled, despite the warmth of the air, although they were slowly warming under his hand. They walked through the small library, the morning room, the music room, and finally upstairs to the bedroom. The only one he'd had made up for them.

On the trip, Grace hadn't slept very well by his side, but he was determined she'd learn. They'd spent too much time separated over the years, he wasn't about to allow her to escape him at night by retreating to a different bed. Besides, having her at his side had given him the best sleep he'd had in years; especially when she cuddled up to him and he was able to wrap himself around her.

Touching her again had quickly become addictive, and he hadn't been able to help himself when she'd fallen asleep in the carriage. He'd taken her upon his lap, able to pretend—at least for a short while —that she was completely his again.

"You must be joking," she said, snapping at him as she yanked her fingers away. Alex raised his eyebrows at her as she looked at him in complete exasperation. "You must know by now I am absolutely not going to *beg* for anything from you. Why can't I have my own room?"

"Because I like you in my bed, even if we do nothing but sleep," Alex said. He'd decided to try and keep things simple and honest between himself and Grace. Especially because he'd noticed that, for all her posturing, she was not unaffected when he did so. Before she turned away, he saw her brow furrow in confused consternation, as if she was trying to decipher some hidden meaning in his words. She did so quite often, he noticed. Hopefully soon she'd realize he meant exactly what he said. "Besides, you don't seem to object when you cuddle up beside me in the night."

"I can't help what I do when I'm asleep," she snapped.

"Of course you can't," he murmured, watching her pace around the room, checking to see where her things were.

The contemptuous look she gave him said she certainly wouldn't touch him by choice at all, much less press her body against his in the night. Which shouldn't feel like a stab to his heart, but it did. He knew he had to be patient. While she might claim she couldn't help herself, last night she'd said his name as she slept, while he held her. Even her guarded demeanor gave him hope—because if she truly cared nothing for him, then what was she guarding against? In the meantime, he had to hold firm against her barbs and attempts to push him away.

43

CHAPTER 4

"*Y*ou *like* being spanked?"

Irene's hopes to see more of Cynthia's reputed misdeeds over tea were coming to fruition with a vengeance. The brazen hussy didn't seem to have any idea of what was appropriate conversation for tea.

Not that Eleanor was helping to curb her at all. She seemed completely unaffected by Cynthia's overly familiar queries and her determined snubbing of social niceties. The young woman was dressed prettily, looking every inch the proper young lady, but after fifteen minutes of general chatting about the weather, Cynthia had turned to Irene and asked if her husband spanked her too. Which had made Lady Grace sit up, coming out of her silent reverie, and blinking her wide blue eyes with astonishment.

Up until that moment, Irene had been just a bit worried about the other woman. She'd shown up for tea unexpectedly, but had barely said a word after everyone had exchanged greetings and she'd been introduced to Cynthia. Irene had wanted to ask how Alex had convinced her to accompany him to Bath, but a surreptitious head shake from Eleanor had her holding her tongue. It became quickly obvious Grace wasn't happy about her relocation out of London, as she had been basically been lost in her own thoughts until Cynthia's completely indiscreet and inappropriate question.

When Irene had looked to Eleanor for help, her sister-in-law had already shrugged and given her a significant look, as if to say 'well, you wanted to see the real hoyden.' Irene had answered, rather stiffly, by just nodding her head, which had led to Cynthia's second question —did Irene find it enjoyable? Irene had immediately said of course not, causing Cynthia to theorize perhaps Hugh didn't do it correctly. That had motivated Irene's shocked query.

"Well, not always," Cynthia said boldly. For her part, she was rather enjoying the aghast looks on the other women's faces. Well, on Irene and Grace's, anyway. Eleanor was already inured to Cynthia's more brazen starts, she just calmly sipped her tea, although two spots of color high in her cheeks indicated she wasn't entirely unaffected by the indecent line of conversation. "The Earl's hand is very hard... but there is something quite exciting about it, isn't there?"

Irene sputtered, and Cynthia had to stifle a giggle. With such flaming red hair, she'd assumed Irene would be more volatile and less prim, but that wasn't the case at all. If anything, she was the most uptight of all the ladies in the room. Even Lady Grace looked more curious than condemning.

"What about birchings? The Earl threatened me with being birched the other day... what's it like?" she asked.

Eleanor coughed and Irene looked as though she might faint. Grace just shook her head immediately and then looked at the other two, as it became quite clear both of them had endured such a thing. The delicate blush on Eleanor's cheeks had heightened to a bright pink, and Irene's hands were beginning to tremble so badly she had to put her teacup down.

"How can you even think something like that might be enjoyable?" Irene asked, practically glaring at Cynthia.

For the first time in days, Grace felt like truly smiling. While she and Irene were on much better terms now, she couldn't help but enjoy the other woman's discomfiture. It was quite nice not to be the most scandalous lady in the room. Cynthia might be young, but

Grace already liked her quite a bit. Given a bit of polish, Cynthia would have been every bit as popular in London as Grace had been herself; having met her, Grace wasn't at all surprised the Earl of Spencer had snapped her up for himself. They were two Originals, and a free spirit like Cynthia would suit the wild Earl down to the ground.

"I don't recommend it," Eleanor replied, less vehemently, giving Irene an amused look. "Sometimes Edwin... well, he makes spanking almost nice. I don't think that's possible with a birching."

"Nice?" chorused Irene and Grace together, in matching tones of bewilderment. Eleanor's flush brightened even further, but her hand was steady on her tea cup. There was no danger of spilling even a drop onto the delicate blue and white damask of her skirt.

"When it's not a punishment," Eleanor said stoutly. Like Cynthia, she was finding her own enjoyment in being able to shock her friends. After all, she was well aware Irene would be disciplined by Hugh for misbehavior, and Cynthia had already confided in Eleanor about her own experiences. Grace hadn't seemed at all condemning over Cynthia's revelations, which had bolstered Eleanor's confidence in sharing her own secrets. "Sometimes we just do it for fun."

Now even Cynthia looked thunderstruck, not to mention more than a little intrigued. "You mean, you don't have to get in trouble to earn a spanking?"

"You *try* to be spanked?" Irene asked the younger woman, before Eleanor could answer. She looked as though she was getting a headache, trying to assimilate all these new ideas.

Cynthia rolled her expressive brown eyes; the smile on her face was pure mischief as she continued to twit Irene. "Of course... I like it, remember?" Then her expression changed, as she wrinkled her nose. "I didn't like being belted so much..." Although, she had found great pleasure afterwards. But she wasn't going to bring up the particulars of the encounter. It took quite a bit to embarrass her, but she wasn't ready to ask the other women if they'd ever been punished *inside* their bottoms.

That was too new of an experience for even her to be brazen about.

"Belted?" Irene whispered, looking horrified. "He belted you?"

Nodding, Cynthia smiled sweetly. "When I snuck into his bedroom and tried to seduce him."

Grace burst out laughing, quickly setting her teacup down on the table so it didn't spill. The laughter looked much more natural on her face than the forlorn expression she'd been wearing for most of the morning, so Cynthia was glad. Her own eyes sparkled merrily. She might not be an acknowledged beauty like Eleanor or Grace, but both of them seemed to like her. Irene was too polite to be rude, even if she was scandalized, but she didn't seem to dislike Cynthia, for all her disapproval.

They were a diverse group, not just in looks, but also in temperament. Despite Grace's maudlin demeanor when she'd first been introduced, Cynthia recognized the spark and fire of a fellow troublemaker in her. The same spark she'd felt from Eleanor. Irene would be the one to keep them toeing the line, she was sure. Shocking her was quite a bit of fun, and it was becoming increasingly obvious Cynthia wasn't the only one who felt so. The Countess would probably approve whole-heartedly of Irene as a calming influence on Cynthia. For herself, Cynthia wondered if the prim redhead, with her aura of innocence, might be corruptible.

"But you aren't married yet!" Irene said, sounding exasperated, as if she had no idea what Cynthia had been thinking.

"But we will be soon," she countered. "He'd already touched me anyway, after spanking me in the carriage. What difference could it make?"

"Now I know where Alex is getting his ideas from." The unexpected statement from Grace had all three women looking at her curiously. She hadn't spoken loudly, but her words had dropped into silence while Irene had been absorbing Cynthia's logic and Eleanor had been watching Irene with amusement. Seeing them all staring at her, Grace felt a blush rising in her own cheeks.

Listening to the other women talk about their own experiences had been quite a relief. She'd managed not to think about her first spanking for the past few days, although she'd also avoided earning another one. Being put over Alex's knee again, so intimately exposed to him, and so horribly vulnerable afterwards, was not something she would repeat by choice.

Especially right now. She knew very well that Hugh was in love with his wife, and Edwin was as well—no matter what Nell thought. It followed that the third member of their triumvirate would also marry for something other than convenience. All of the men spanked their wives, not maliciously, but because they cared enough to correct their behavior. In Eleanor's case, it sounded like sometimes it happened for other reasons as well. When she'd first set out to estrange herself from Alex, she'd felt sure she would drive him away; it would be a much easier way to handle a wife once she was no longer convenient anymore.

Instead, he had tracked her down, announced his intention to reconcile, and when she'd insulted and cursed at him, he hadn't shut her out or hit her... he'd spanked her.

Grace felt more brutally confused than ever to think her broken marriage had something common with the loving ones of her friends.

"Alex spanked you?" Irene asked looking horrified. She shook her head, her voice dropping to a mere murmur as her green eyes unfocused, as if she was looking at something only she could see. "I didn't really think he would... not even after..."

"After what?" Grace asked, both curious as to what Irene was referring and eager to turn the conversation away from herself.

Blinking, Irene looked almost surprised she'd spoken out loud. For all the blushing the ladies had been doing over tea, none of them rivaled the bright pink color Irene's face turned now. It clashed horribly with her hair. Her eyes darted around to the other two ladies, but both of them were just as curious as Grace was.

"Hugh showed Alex how to spank me," Irene whispered, her face turning nearly scarlet as a tomato. Grace's jaw dropped, Eleanor groaned and Cynthia looked enthralled. "Several weeks ago."

"He would," Eleanor muttered. She looked at Grace apologetically.

"After our father taught him, I can only imagine Hugh would take up the mantle of an instructor."

"In his defense, I had accused him of beating me, in front of Alex," Irene admitted. She sighed and looked a bit guiltily at Eleanor. "That was before I really knew the difference between a spanking and a beating. I thought he was a monster, but as he was instructing Alex, I realized how careful he was being with me. He was only proving to Alex that I wasn't being abused."

"Apparently Alex soaked it up," Grace said. Strangely, it hadn't even occurred to her to think he'd actually *beaten* her. Of course, she'd actually been hit by her own father before, and not on her bottom. Her father had never cuddled her afterwards either. It was fascinating to know all the different reactions the women had to being disciplined by their husbands.

Eleanor was the only one who had grown up being spanked, obviously. She had been resistant at first, to having such discipline continue in her marriage, but she'd also found it was very different being spanked by her husband. There were aspects she certainly enjoyed. Sheltered Irene had been horrified and frightened by her first experience, and it had taken her some time to realize Hugh had actually not brutalized her when he'd disciplined her. Now she knew, and her and Hugh's relationship was better than ever. She'd never actively court punishment, however, like Cynthia was. Cynthia's enjoyment went far beyond anything Eleanor expressed. And then there was Grace herself, who was confused by her reactions and wondering what it all meant to Alex.

Should she be worried he'd watched Irene being spanked? She considered the brief stab of jealousy she felt for just a moment before dismissing it. There was no way Hugh would be willing to share any significant part of his wife. Grace had known him for too long to think Alex had seen anything worth her being jealous over. Cringing, she remembered she didn't *want* to be jealous over anything to do with him anymore, she shouldn't care what he had done or seen with anyone. Not when she still wasn't sure of his motives.

After behaving the way he wanted and following his lead for the past few days, which had been the easiest route when she'd been trapped in a carriage with him, she was feeling much more rebellious. So he wanted to reconcile? Perhaps he thought she would just fall in line, as she had so far, but now they were no longer traveling and she had some allies here. If they were going to reconcile, they were going to do so on her terms.

She refused to have a marriage based on nothing more than his business agreement with her father and his need for a legitimate heir. If he wanted to reconcile only to show London he had control over his wife, then he was going to be sorely disappointed. Perhaps he thought disciplining her would keep her in line and that's when he decided to reconcile, but a spanking or even a birching wasn't going to keep her from behaving exactly as she wanted if he wasn't willing to give her what she needed from their marriage as well.

As if her thoughts had conjured the devil, the door to Eleanor's drawing room opened, and he was standing there, next to Lord Hyde. Even beside Hyde's dramatic dark looks, her eyes were still immediately drawn to Alex. His gaze skipped over the ladies in the room, landing only briefly on Irene, but without the usual broad smile he reserved for her. Something in Grace's chest unclenched and she realized how tense seeing the two of them looking at each other still made her. But for once, Alex was behaving the way she'd always wanted him to; his attention didn't immediately go to Irene, instead it passed over her after only a moment to land and fix upon his wife. Now she truly did believe Alex's apology, and Irene's. She'd appreciated both, but deep down, some part of her had still doubted.

"Ladies," Lord Hyde said, with a charming smile encompassing the entire room. A practiced rake's smile, but the glow in his eyes was for Eleanor alone. The look he gave her was the way Grace had always wished Alex would look at her. "I just stopped in to inform you that you're all invited for dinner, along with your husbands—and future husband," he amended slightly as he glanced at Cynthia. She beamed happily at him and he smiled back before returning his gaze to Eleanor. "I've already told Cook and Mrs. Hester to prepare dinner for eight."

"Thank you," Eleanor murmured, smoothing her hands over her skirt in an almost nervous gesture. She nodded her head at Alex. "Lord Brooke. Have you met Miss Bryant?" Gracefully she gestured at Cynthia, who was staring at Alex with fascination. Most likely because of the information Grace had just revealed about his spanking tendencies. If Irene had been gazing at him in such a manner, Grace would have bristled, but from Cynthia it didn't feel threatening at all.

"Lord Brooke," she said, very prettily, standing and dropping into a brief curtsy, proving she could behave when she wanted to.

Alex studied her in that somber, serious way of his, before giving her a slight bow in return, from the doorway. "Miss Bryant, a pleasure." His eyes returned to Grace before he backed slightly out of the room, giving Edwin space to reach for the door again.

"We'll be in the library till dinner," Edwin said to his wife, giving her a last, soft smile before closing the door behind him.

With the door safely shut between herself and her husband, Grace began to breathe again.

"Wonderful!" trilled Cynthia as she returned to her seat. "A whole meal without having to talk about the wedding!" She rolled her eyes. "The Countess is relentless."

GATHERED IN THE BILLIARDS ROOM, Wesley quickly claimed Alex as a partner, while Hugh and Edwin paired up. Neither of them had played with Alex back in London, so they didn't realize what a smashing player he was. Wesley and Alex trounced them for the first game, as Wesley had always been a keen billiards player as well, and Hugh and Edwin had demanded a change of partners for the second game. Both of them were reasonably good players, but Wesley and Alex excelled at the trickiest shots and angles.

Conversation, which had been mostly about the game itself, began to turn round to the ladies down the hall. Alex had enjoyed seeing Grace with the other women, smiling and laughing as if she was one of them in more ways than just friendship. The others were all happy wives and he wanted her to be one too. Perhaps their influence was just what she needed.

"I'm glad you and Grace could make it in for the wedding," said Wesley, coming to stand beside him while Edwin took a shot. His slightly raised brows also indicated his surprise Alex had gotten Grace to accompany him at all. "I was surprised you came together."

"It took some convincing on my part," he said. Hugh tilted his head, watching them from across the table and obviously listening in. Only Edwin seemed to be focusing on the billiards table, finding the perfect angle for his shot. "But she seems to be coming round." He hesitated for only a moment before continuing. Part of him didn't want to share too much of his marital life with Grace, but another part recognized these men all had much more experience in administering discipline to their wives and so far that was where he felt he'd made the most progress in regards to Grace. "I ah… disciplined her on the trip."

The balls on the billiards table clicked, one of them sinking into the far pocket as Edwin straightened, raising his dark brows at Alex. "Not to force her compliance I hope?"

Although the question was mild, there was an undercurrent of danger there if Alex answered incorrectly. None of these men would take it kindly if Alex was spanking Grace for anything other than deserved punishments. From someone else he might have taken offense, but he knew Edwin and the others only had Grace's best interests at heart and he couldn't be upset about that.

"For cursing at me and insulting me," he answered. Out of the corner of his eye, he saw Hugh nod his approval. "I won't tolerate outright rudeness or insults, even if she's still angry at me. Which she is, but I would never punish her for her feelings, only for the way she expresses them if she becomes disrespectful or rude." He felt the need to explain that. Even though Edwin, Hugh, and Wesley were all his friends, they hadn't known him as long as they'd known each other, and he wanted them to completely understand where he was coming from.

"That's good," said Hugh, giving him a sympathetic smile. "She's probably going to be holding a grudge against you for a while. You could wear your hand out and still not make a dent in her emotions."

"Plus, all you'd be teaching her is to keep quiet about what she's feeling, and it's hard enough to tell what a woman wants even when she's talking to you." Edwin said as he walked around the table, looking for his next shot.

"She's certainly not doing much of that," he muttered, giving a small sigh. If only he should be so lucky as to have Grace actually telling him what was going on in that beautiful head of hers.

"Give it time," Wesley said, with his usual rakish grin. "She'll come around. Women like to see us making an effort." If anyone would know what a woman wanted, it was certainly Wesley. Alex had been considered a rake as well, but he'd never seen women flock to anyone the way they had to Wesley. He was just different enough from the rest of the men in the *ton*, with his long, sun-bleached hair and tanned skin, for them to be fascinated by him.

"And be consistent," Hugh said. Something about his voice made it sound like he repeating a rule he'd learned by rote. Which, of course, he had when his father had been giving him lessons. "Don't ever let her get away with something, no matter how much she begs or pleads. Don't get distracted or allow her to seduce you. If you say she's going to be punished for something, then she *needs* to be disciplined every time she makes an infraction. Otherwise it's just confusing for everyone involved."

"Noted," Alex murmured.

A tension he hadn't even noticed was there seemed to be lifting from his shoulders as the men all showed both approval and encouragement of his actions. Since his father had never administered corporeal punishment to Alex, it wasn't something he was familiar with and he was reassured by having others to converse on the subject with. Men who knew his and Grace's history and who were supportive of the reconciliation. Before meeting Wesley, he hadn't encouraged any relationships with anyone, because most of the men of the *ton* were either vehemently disapproving of Grace or wanted to seduce her. He'd found he had little patience with men who spoke disparagingly of his wife, and none at all with the others.

～

ALEX HAD to admire Lady Hyde's acumen when it came to seating arrangements. She'd put him in between herself and Cynthia, buffering him from Irene and giving Grace the space she needed to relax. Cynthia was next to Hugh, which allowed Wesley to sit across from her and keep a weather eye on her antics. Although, so far, she'd been quite pleasant, if a trifle overly familiar with all of the gentlemen. It was obvious she didn't mean anything by it, it was just in her nature to be both friendly and flirtatious. Alex was fairly certain she didn't even realize the full extent of her attractions—she seemed to save all of her calculated flirtations for her husband.

Although that didn't stop Wesley from giving Hugh a dark look when Cynthia giggled at yet another of his many quips. Fortunately Irene didn't seem to be upset or jealous over Hugh and Cynthia's conversation.

Tonight, Alex had realized just how much he'd watched over Irene in the past, obviously to the detriment of his own marriage. His automatic response was always to check on her, ensure she was enjoying herself and she wasn't feeling left out or overwhelmed. Now his attention was more on Grace, but he still felt the old, familiar tug on his senses, demanding he protect the young woman he considered his little sister.

Even with Hugh there, it was hard to mentally hand off responsibility.

But he did his best, listening to the conversation between Eleanor, Grace, and Wesley, very occasionally adding his own input. At the head of the table, Irene and Edwin were talking about Hugh's estates and life in the country. He was telling her about his parents, whom the *ton* knew as eccentrics, seeing as they didn't even come into the capital for the Season if they could help it. As the dinner went on, it

54

became easier to ignore Irene; helped, of course, by his greater interest in his own wife.

"Where will go you after the wedding is over?" Grace was asking Wesley. Her eyes flitted over to Alex, and then immediately away again when she saw he was looking at her. The question garnered Cynthia's attention, turning her away from Hugh, as she looked at Wesley, her head cocked slightly to the side. Apparently, whatever plans he had, he hadn't seen fit to inform his future wife about.

"We hadn't discussed it yet," Wesley said, a small smile alighting his face as he looked over at his soon-to-be wife. "Probably somewhere on the Continent."

"Paris," Cynthia said definitively, her eyes coming alight with excitement at the thought of seeing new places.

Wesley raised an eyebrow at her. Paris was certainly a popular choice, but he wasn't entirely enamored of the idea of Cynthia surrounded by Frenchmen. Men were always going to be intrigued by her ample charms, but the French would certainly be the most outspoken about it.

"Perhaps," he allotted. "Italy is also beautiful this time of year."

Cynthia opened her mouth as if to argue, and then seemed to think better of it as Wesley gave her another warning look from across the table. Alex wondered if he could use such a look to the same effect with Grace. Probably not, since she was doing her best to avoid his gaze anyway. During the dinner he'd made it a point to study the other men and how they interacted with their wives. All three of them made great use of certain, firm, looks when they felt like their wives were bordering on being rude or beginning a discussion they didn't approve of. More interestingly was how they easily managed to catch their wives' eyes.

A small shift in position, a discreet cough, and that was all it took. Alex was determined to try it with Grace eventually, although from watching her he knew she was peeking at him on a regular basis anyway. He didn't even try to hide his own focus on her, he wanted her to see how she took up his attention entirely.

"Eleanor and I quite enjoyed Paris," Edwin said, grinning down the length of the table at his wife. The blushing, happy look she gave him only reminded Alex of the way he and Grace used to have such easy intimacy and significant looks. Hell, he used to smile; now, whenever he did so, it felt like a strain on his facial muscles, they were so out of practice.

Still, they were at this dinner as a couple, and despite the moments of tension, overall the evening was going well. Grace hadn't been rude or insulting, she'd even responded to him once during the conversation, and sometimes it was almost possible to forget they were the only unhappy couple at the table. This was what he'd been missing all these years.

The intimate gathering was something he'd been missing as well. This was the kind of small party which marked very deep friendships, where there was no pomp or circumstance, no social masks or pretense. Not since his school days had he had friendships this close, and it was all the more enjoyable because they were Grace's friends as well. If anything could help heal the breach between him and his wife, it was the people around this table.

THEY RODE BACK to their house at the end of the evening in silence. In some ways, Grace wished this evening had never happened. When Alex was being pleasant and charming, when they were surrounded by friends and enjoying themselves, it was almost hard to remember things hadn't always been this way between them. Tonight had been so close to being everything Grace had hoped for, wished for, in a marriage. Except it was years too late.

It made her irritable, despite the nice night she'd had.

"Come on, Gracie," Alex said, holding out his hand to help her out of the carriage.

"Can't you just call me Grace?" she asked waspishly, only holding on to his fingers as long as she had to. As soon as her feet were firmly planted on solid ground, she snatched her hand away, and felt slightly mollified by the flash of irritation in his eyes.

"If you wish," he said, his voice carefully amiable.

Which just made her want to poke at him more. After tonight, she truly believed he wanted to start over and pretend as if nothing in the past had happened. While that meant he would forgive and forget her lovers, she was finding it quite a bit harder to forgive and forget his transgressions. Perhaps because she had been ordered to, rather than being allowed to make the decision on her own. Instead, she was just supposed to go along with what he wanted.

Even if he was acting like a caring husband in public, in front of their friends, she was sure there must be some kind of nefarious reason underneath. She didn't put any credence in Eleanor's theory that he had missed her. Why would he? He'd proven very early in their marriage any woman truly was as good as another to him, just as he'd told her father. It was more likely he just wanted to eradicate the scandal of their marriage by resolving it and showing Society just what a big, strong man he was.

After all, he'd not demanded his marital rights. He could have. But he wasn't interested. As long as she behaved in public and didn't take any lovers... but then how would he get his heir on her?

Maybe he thought she was so lustful and amorous a woman that if he could keep her from taking any lovers, she would eventually turn to him out of pure need. Grace snorted as she made her way up the stairs, doing her best to ignore the looming presence of her husband as he followed her. While she had taken lovers, she hadn't had nearly as many as he. Besides, she'd learned to take care of her own needs. He could insist she sleep beside him and guard her bed all he wanted, she would be perfectly fine remaining abstinent.

But would he be?

She supposed he might be able to find another mistress, even if he was guarding his wife's bed every evening. It would just take some juggling of his time. Then again, he'd always been very busy, both with his estates and with his business. Perhaps he wouldn't have time.

It bothered her that she liked the idea of Alex being unable to indulge with a woman other than herself. Of course, she took pleasure in the thought of him being tormented by a man's need to spend his seed regularly, but she also knew it was more than that. Some part of her heart was soothed knowing he would no longer be sharing his body with other women. Even after all these years and all those other women. Although, at least she'd had her own pleasures looked after as well. And if the bloody bastard did find another mistress, after insisting on this reconciliation, Grace would hop into the bed of the first man to cross her path. But she'd go much farther than she had before. She'd tell the world about it, she'd claim Alex was an incompetent lover which was why she'd left him the first time. Some probably wouldn't believe her, and some women would know differently, but she could always claim he paid them to say so. She would make sure he knew what it felt like to be utterly humiliated. The thought should have made her feel triumphant with possible vengeance, but instead she felt heartsick at the idea of him being with another woman, *again*. Sometimes she wished she could cut her heart out of her chest. Useless organ that it was.

As usual, Grace's maid Rose was waiting for her inside the bedroom. While Grace had still not forgiven the young woman for what felt like a great betrayal, she was no longer so angry. Rose had apologized on the trip, and she'd seemed quite sincere in her guilt over having spied on Grace for Alex. Her mother had been sick and when he'd offered so much extra money, as well as better lodging and the services of his personal physician for her mother, Rose hadn't been able to refuse. It didn't mean Grace would ever trust her maid again, but she no longer felt tempted to throw the woman out of the room either.

Apparently Alex didn't agree.

"Thank you Rose, but your mistress won't need you this evening," Alex said as he came in the room behind Grace, already undoing the elaborate knot on his cravat.

Immediately Grace turned around, her eyes flashing. "I absolutely need Rose, who else is going to undo my corset?"

As soon as she asked the question, she wished she'd held the words back. The look Alex gave her was utterly rakish, as if his usual granite expression was just a stone facade and it had just dropped to make way for the Alex she'd started to fall in love with, years ago. It took her breath away. But that was just a physical reaction, she reminded herself, and it didn't have to mean anything.

"That would be me," he murmured, his voice filled with seductive intent as he tossed the cravat onto the floor in front of his wardrobe. He barely glanced at Rose as she stood, frozen in place, eyes darting between the two of them as she tried to decide who she should listen to. "Out, Rose."

The maid fled. Something else which angered Grace, even though she couldn't blame the servant for her actions. But now she was all alone with her husband. After the first night on the trip here she'd managed to have Rose undress her so she could be in bed before Alex even returned to the room in the evenings. He'd always gone down to the taproom for a glass of port before retiring, and she'd used that time to change into her nightgown and she'd be feigning sleep by the time he'd come back upstairs. Then she'd wait until he was up and gone in the mornings before she'd rise and dress for the day. Always with Rose's help.

"I hope you don't think the mere act of undressing me is going to make me eager for any kind of amorous acts between us," Grace said tartly, turning her back on him to hide the tremor in her hands as she began undoing the buttons on her dress. They were small and hard to slip through the loops, which gave her plenty to do. Just because she was about to be naked in front of Alex for the first time in years, that didn't mean she had to act like a ninny about it. If he could be unaffected by it, then so could she.

"I live in hope, as they say," he countered, his voice much closer than it had been before. She stiffened.

"I will never be interested in acting as your wife again."

"You didn't mind when we were first married," he said silkily. "You loved acting as my wife then."

"I wasn't acting, you bloody idiot," she snapped back, hating the way her body had responded to his seductive tone. It felt like something deep in her core had pulsed in response to the memories of their lovemaking. "And that was before I knew you were a lying bastard."

She shrieked as she was suddenly spun around to face him, one hard hand on her bicep, her dress gaping down the front to show the curves of her breasts as they heaved inside her corset. The expression on his face had hardened again, although his eyes did skim over her exposed bosom, before returning to her face.

"What did I tell you about cursing and insulting me?" There was suppressed fury in his voice, carefully controlled.

"Let me go!" Grace tried to pull away—she honestly hadn't thought he'd hear her—and shrieked again as she was pulled forward. Alex's hand was firm but not rough as he took the few steps towards the bed and sat down. It took him less than a moment to pull her dress down and let it drop to the floor, before tipping her over his lap.

A tremor went through her as she tried to push herself back up, but his hand splayed across the center of her back, pressing her down to the bed. She felt cool air waft over the skin of her bottom as he yanked down her drawers as well, leaving her cheeks completely bare.

"I'm sorry, okay, I'm *sorry*," she said, trying to wriggle away.

This was far worse than in the carriage when her skirts had been over her head, giving her a feeling of anonymity and protection, even as Alex had spanked her exposed arse. Without her dress on, with her drawers already fallen around her ankles, she felt horribly exposed. She sincerely doubted this was going to be anything like the pleasurable spankings Eleanor had hinted around.

The first hard slap to her bottom only confirmed that and Grace gasped, barely able to draw in a breath before Alex's hand came down again, just as firmly on her other cheek. The swats came hard and fast, so he landed four blows on her creamy buttocks before she even had time to shriek. They were sharp and stinging, and the damned man was landing them on the same two spots over and over again. Damn Hugh! He hadn't had to show Alex how to do this!

Grace wriggled under his other hand, crying out as he continued to pepper her bottom, focusing his discipline on the center of each of her cheeks. The two spots felt like they were on fire, smarting and stinging as he smacked his palm against them over and over again. It burned, and she was starting to wish he would spank her anywhere else... any other part of her bottom, just to spread out the punishment. His relentless focus on those two specific spots was undoing her far faster than the spanking in the carriage had.

"Please, Alex, I'm *sorry*, I won't do it again, I promise," she begged between cries and sobs. Her legs kicked uselessly and she tried to reach back to stop him—since this time her skirts weren't in her way —but he just paused to catch her hands and press them down into the small of her back before resuming the stinging blows.

"No, you won't," he replied, his voice hard as he did his best to hide his arousal from his squirming, crying wife. Not that he took pleasure in her pain, but there was something gorgeous about the two bright red splotches on her creamy, quivering bottom. "I won't tolerate insults, Grace. There are other ways to show you're displeased with me which are much more productive."

Something about the way she cried out then made him sure she wanted to yell another insult at him, but she didn't. She just squirmed and begged, trying to placate him with apologies, what Hugh had described as a "spanking chant:" a series of meaningless pleas and promises that fell from a woman's mouth to try and stymy her punishment. Alex had gotten a much more in depth lecture from all of the men that afternoon in the library, as they'd compared notes on the kinds of discipline they'd meted out and what was most effective.

He supposed he should be thankful Grace wasn't like Cynthia. Unlike Wesley, he didn't feel confident enough to wield a strap or a cane. Edwin's creative use of a spoon sounded much more his style.

Deciding Grace had probably had enough, he gave the bright red spots on her ass two more sharp slaps each, holding her in place as she bucked in response, and then he settled his hand down over one of her heated cheeks. Sensing her punishment was finally over, Grace slumped across his lap, sniffling, although she'd finally stopped squirming. Which was surprising, he'd thought the moment he'd finished that he'd have to hold on to her to keep her from running.

Remembering another suggestion the other men had made, he let his hand begin to slip down to the plump lips between his wife's legs.

"Alex! *No, stop!*" Grace squealed, bucking again. Which only made her cunny press against his fingers, and he knew immediately why she'd wanted him to stop.

The others had been right. She was wet. Her pussy had creamed as he'd spanked her. Despite her protests and pleas, some part of her had liked everything he'd just done to her—hell, *loved* it, from the feel of her.

"Well, well, well, what do we have here?" he murmured, dipping his finger into her soft folds and swirling his finger again. It was torture for his cock, to know her heated quim was so close, yet quite sure he wouldn't be burying himself in heaven tonight. Grace moaned in humiliation, hanging her head as much as she could in her current position as she tried to close her legs and force his hand out. She wanted to keep fighting, but at the same time, she didn't want to incite him back into spanking her. Worse, she didn't want him to stop what he was doing. It felt so good, so right, to be touched by him.

He let his finger slide further, finding the swollen pleasure pearl and rubbing against the sensitive bud while she gasped and writhed.

"Alex, *please.*" The husky, throaty plea made his cock throb even harder, and he knew he was already seconds away from cumming. Months of abstinence combined with Grace over his lap, slick and ready for him, her bottom red from a spanking, had done that to him.

"Please what? Are you ready to beg for me Grace? If you want me in your bed, all you have to do is ask."

She shuddered, and he swore he could hear her teeth grinding together, right before she made a sound like a little growl. Even though she was aroused and had been right on the point of begging, his reminder had her pride rearing back up with a vengeance. Drawing a small circle around her clit with his forefinger, he slid his thumb into her wet hole as he tormented her a little bit more, feeling the tightness of her inner muscles clamping down on him. She gasped, but she still didn't say yes, she still held herself back.

Then he sighed, letting his disappointment fill his voice. "I suppose not. Very well, Gracie."

With great reluctance, Alex pulled his hand away from the soft heaven between his wife's legs and released her wrists. It took a moment, and then Grace pushed up and away, both of her hands in front of her *mons* as if to cover herself from him, since her drawers were pooled around her ankles. The red heat in her cheeks wasn't only from embarrassment, he would wager his title on it.

As she stared at him, breathing heavily and looking like a chaotic mix of confusion, anger, embarrassment, and passionate arousal, Grace's mouth opened and closed several times. Very deliberately, Alex brought his thumb to his mouth, making sure she could see her juices coating the digit, and then he sucked it between his lips. The sweet, musky taste of her exploded on his tongue and he felt the ache of it all the way into his kidneys as his cock and balls tightened even further.

"You still taste delicious, Gracie," he said, after pulling his thumb back out of his mouth. He wasn't at all averse to showing her how much he desired her. Especially because right now he was sure she desired him too. Her pretty pink lips made a small 'o' of shock as she blinked, completely stunned. Alex grinned at her, feeling so much like his old self that even his aching cock didn't bother him. "Turn around, sweetheart, and I'll undo your corset so you can go to sleep."

Surprisingly, she didn't argue with him, she just turned and he was treated to the sight of the hem of her chemise hovering over her spanked bottom. The sheer material did nothing to hide the bright red splotches from his gaze. It was quite erotic.

Very quickly, Alex undid his wife's corset. Knowing he wasn't going to find relief with her tonight, he wanted to touch her as little as possible right now. He had no desire to torture himself any further.

The unlacing of her corset should have made it easier for Grace to breathe, but she still felt utterly breathless. Her bottom was throbbing on its fiery surface, but that was nothing compared to the hot, pulsing need between her legs. Part of her wanted to throw herself at Alex and just sate the need. If she thought she could give her body to him without endangering the walls around her heart, she would... but she wasn't sure of her defenses at the moment.

Alex's gentle hands as he unlaced her, the way he'd aroused her after punishing her, had her completely off-kilter. When he turned her to face him again, she found she couldn't look up at him. The hard shell she'd cultivated over the years, that she'd clung to the past few days she'd spent in his presence, felt like it was crumbling around her.

"You took your punishment very well, but no more insults, Gracie. I won't tolerate it," Alex murmured, pressing his lips against her forehead. His hands were gentle on her shoulders, sliding over the thin fabric of her chemise. "Next time I'll use a hairbrush."

She shivered, wondering how he could sound so threatening and so tender at the same time. The spot on her forehead where he'd kissed her felt feverish. Part of her wished he would hold her again, comfortingly, the way he had after he'd spanked her in the carriage.

Instead, he released her and walked over to her dresser, pulling out one of her nightgowns. Grace let him dress her like a doll. Everything felt surreal, as if she was dreaming rather than being awake. Except that her bottom hurt too much for this to be a dream.

"Grace..." Alex's voice was deep, seductive. "Tell me you want me." She looked up into his glowing eyes, and for one horrifying moment she felt herself weaken. The shock of it made her jerk away and she shook her head, clutching her arms, thankful for the covering of her nightgown.

Whipping around, she fled to the other side of the bed and practically threw herself under the covers. She didn't trust her voice right now. Why being spanked lowered her defenses so much, she didn't know. She would have thought it would make her even more determined against him, but for some reason it made her feel almost cared about. Of course, his behavior after punishing her might have something to do with that too. While she didn't like the spanking, and she was shocked at her arousal even after hearing Cynthia's brazen report, she did like the comfort and praise he gave her afterwards. Somehow she felt closer to him.

Which was just idiocy on her part.

Closing her eyes, she tried to even her breathing, hoping to force herself into sleep before Alex finished with his nightly ablutions and joined her in the bed.

Glancing over at the lump of sheets covering his wife, Alex stifled a sigh. She was on her side, he could tell, probably protecting her bottom from any further stimulation. Part of him had hoped she'd relent and let them at least join together physically. A woman who was well satisfied in bed was halfway to being well-satisfied with her life. He wanted to connect with her again, and the best way he knew how was physically. Even when he'd been younger and less cynical, he'd always had trouble expressing himself in words.

His cock was still throbbing painfully, and as he stripped down he could see it was a dark, angry red color. He'd seen plenty of women naked before his marriage, and in the years after it, but none of them ever caused the same kind of reaction Grace did. That pale, creamy skin made him want to search out all of her sensitive pink parts with his tongue. Hours could be spent, worshiping her from head to toe, discovering what spots made her whimper and what spots made her moan. Helping her change her clothes had been torture, but well worth it, just to see her bared to him again. Glancing over his shoulder to make sure Grace was still facing away from him, he picked up one of his handkerchiefs. Gritting his teeth, he faced away from her, leaning one hand against the vanity as he wrapped the handkerchief around the turgid rod and began to pump his hand.

Immediately, the taste of her in his mouth seemed much more vibrant, the memory of her quivering buttocks danced before his eyes, and the sound of her moan as he'd teased her pussy filled his ears. It only took a few hard strokes of his hand before he was spilling into the handkerchief, the relief of culmination making his knees feel weak. Fortunately, he'd managed to keep from making even the smallest sound, only the faster pace of his breathing indicated he'd been doing something illicit.

Glancing over his shoulder again, he made sure Grace hadn't moved, and was both relieved and disappointed to confirm the fact.

Discarding the handkerchief, Alex made his way back to the bed, completely nude. He'd allow Grace to keep her nightgown as long as she wanted to, but he was no longer going to be uncomfortable in bed. Tonight, she'd wanted him. He knew she had, even though she'd turned him away. The fact that she'd hesitated before doing so gave him hope.

As he crawled into the bed, all too aware of the proximity of his wife, he wondered what she had meant by calling him a lying bastard. Grimacing, he acknowledged this was not the time to ask. If he'd wanted to know, he should have said something before her spanking. Because, as far as he could remember, he'd never lied to her about anything, ever.

CHAPTER 5

*C*ynthia was bored. Which, in and of itself, was not unusual, but she did take exception to being bored when she was at a dance. Looking wistfully over at the floor, filled with whirling couples, she wished she were one of them. Instead, she was trapped within the Countess' circle, all of whom wanted to know every detail about the upcoming wedding.

There were even more of them than usual to flutter over her, as people had been pouring into Bath once they'd received their wedding invitations. Most of them had made it a stop on their way back to their estates, following the Season. Eleanor had told her the wedding certainly wouldn't empty the capital, but it would tempt quite a few of the *ton* to depart earlier than they normally would. Unfortunately, that just meant she had to be at the Countess' side for what seemed like endless rounds of interminable introductions and bland, socially acceptable interactions.

She glanced over at her fiancé, who already knew everyone and didn't seem to be held to the same strictures. No, he was able to speak with his friends, visit the refreshments table, and even dance if he wanted. Although if he did dance with one more flirtatious beauty, fresh from London, Cynthia was not going to be responsible for her actions. After all his threats about her talking to other men, she would have thought he'd be more circumspect with his own attentions.

Granted, his friends were also dancing with women other than their wives, but Eleanor and Irene were also on the dance floor, and the moment the music ended Edwin and Hugh were back at their sides, reclaiming their women. Only Grace wasn't dancing, and that was because Alex was looming over her and glaring at any man who dared come within two feet of her. Going by the increasingly irate expression on Grace's face, only the fact they were in public was keeping her from exploding.

Really, she should just accept one of Lord Brooke's many invitations to dance. It was obvious he wasn't going to let his wife dance with another man until she danced with him first. Cynthia had even seen the scowling lord shake his head at Hugh when he'd begun to approach.

If only she could do the same with her own fiancé.

Cynthia scowled at him across the room, where he was talking with some blonde beauty who was practically clinging to his—oh... that was Eleanor on his arm. Well, Eleanor was alright. But still. Shouldn't the Earl have asked his fiancée to dance at least once? Perhaps he was too scared to approach the gaggle of women around his mother, but that didn't mean Cynthia should have to pay the price for his cowardice.

"Excuse me, my lady," she murmured to the Countess, "I must visit the retiring room."

"Of course, my dear, hurry back," the Countess said, smiling benignly. She was fully decked out in all her best clothing, a glittering array of gold and ruby red, guaranteed to attract attention. Obviously, she was in alt over finally having her eldest son about to be married. Bemused, Cynthia hurried away, sliding between the ladies and nodding inanely as she passed.

In her own dress of dark rose pink, edged with cream, Cynthia knew she looked quite attractive tonight. The color matched her nipples perfectly, which made her feel wonderfully naughty, even though no one else was aware of it. Well, the Earl might be, but he certainly wouldn't say anything even if he realized.

As she made her way across the room, the frustrating man materialized at her elbow.

"Where do you think you're going?"

Cynthia scowled up at him, not at all intimidated by his low, threatening voice. "Anywhere but back there," she said, jerking her head back towards where his mother was standing holding court. The Earl's lips twitched as he almost smiled. Ha. She knew he had a sense of humor in there, even if he did tend to present his stuffiest side to her.

Well, stuffy when he wasn't baring her backside, turning it bright red and then putting his... well. Now her own cheeks were starting to match her dress as she looked up at him. It wasn't like her to be easily embarrassed, but she couldn't think about him doing *that* without blushing.

"You, of all people, shouldn't be left unchaperoned for even a minute," he said, taking her hand and putting it on his arm. Since Cynthia didn't actually need to use the retiring room, she didn't protest.

"Then you can chaperone me," she said, smiling up at him with such saccharine sweetness she knew he'd be suspicious. She'd noticed he was always the most wary of her when she was behaving correctly. It set him on edge. "After all, you seem unable to go more than a minute without a female on your arm, it might as well be me."

The Earl's eyebrows raised and a little gleam entered his eyes. He really was devastatingly attractive. "Jealous?"

"Hardly," she said, airily, blatantly lying through her teeth. It had surprised her, actually, how possessive she felt of him. The good news was, she knew he was just as bad and she intended to use that. "There are quite a few gentlemen who would be eager to make up for your neglecting me."

They changed direction with a suddenness that almost made her stumble, but the Earl caught her with his arm around her waist, his grip tight, as he maneuvered them toward the doors to the outside.

Silent, imposing, and completely in control, he ushered her out into the night. The darkness was broken up by the lights throughout the gardens, a few shadowy figures moving in the distance along the less well-lit pathways. Couples, who were searching out intimacy.

Leading her onto one of those darker pathways, Wesley was filled with satisfaction he no longer had to worry about her reputation. Betrothed couples were always given a certain amount of leeway, and with the wedding day looming so close, they'd be given even more. No one would look askance, as long as he married the chit, and Wesley had no intention of changing his mind about that.

Wesley knew once they were married, the rakes would be hovering... waiting. His soon-to-be wife was exactly the kind of treat they'd like to indulge in, with her sensuous curves and eager passion; if he ever made the mistake of letting her become a bored matron, they would pounce. However, Wesley had no intention of ever allowing that to happen. For once, he was fairly certain Cynthia was one of the few women in the world who would be able to satisfy his baser urges and his need to indulge in them on a very regular basis.

Right now he was suffering, waiting for their wedding night, but he knew it was going to be worth it. Keeping her in line was a full time job; he certainly hadn't wanted to risk leaving the house to find a willing woman, only to return and find she'd run rampant in his absence. Although, if he were being entirely truthful with himself, he would admit the attractions of other women had paled after meeting Cynthia anyway. He wanted her, very badly, and trying to find a substitute didn't hold any real appeal. Wesley was experienced enough with women to know a substitute never appeased him.

Waiting for his wedding night would be worth it.

In the meantime, he'd enjoy stolen moments, like he was about to right now. Judging the current pathway they were on to be dark enough no one would be able to immediately discern their identities, Wesley pulled her off the gravel and pushed her up against a tree. Cynthia squeaked, but before she could speak or protest, his mouth was on hers in a possessive, passionate kiss. A conqueror's kiss, meant to dominate, to claim.

His senses thrilled as she softened against him, opening her lips to invite him in, her hands pressed against his chest but not pushing him away. Trapping her, his hands planted firmly on either side of her body, the bark of the tree digging into his hands, Wesley kissed her with all the expert knowledge of a degenerate rake. Cynthia melted against him; he could practically feel her submission to him as he pressed his body against hers, his cock digging into the softness of her stomach.

Nipping at her full lower lip, he raised his head slightly, glaring down at her in the dim light.

"No other men, baggage," he said, his voice darkly serious.

Cynthia glared back up at him, not at all cowed. "No other women, my Lord," she retorted tartly.

"Agreed," he said immediately, lowering his head again. "Shall we seal our deal with a kiss?"

The man knew how to seduce with his mouth... his tongue... Cynthia moaned as he pressed her back against the tree, allowing it to hold her up while he made free with his hands. The low neckline of her ball gown made it easy for him to pull her breasts free, resting them on top of the fabric, so he could pinch and roll the tender buds between his fingers. Whimpering against his lips, Cynthia arched, the slick folds between her legs aching with envy as he plucked her rosy, throbbing tips. She could feel his hardness rubbing against her and her insides clenched.

Would he ruin her now? Finally?

She wasn't sure how she felt about being ruined in the gardens behind the Assembly Rooms, but right now her body didn't care. It craved his touch, the rising pleasure in her core, and the fire he created in her belly.

When he pulled away from the kiss and put his mouth to her breast, she moaned loudly and he immediately put his hand over her lips, muffling the noise. Eyes wide, she stared at their surroundings, remembering they were outside where anyone could walk by and see them. Although they might not see her face, it was unmistakable what they were doing. Excitement and terror filled her equally.

71

She'd never allowed a gentleman to take so many liberties with her, because she hadn't wanted to chance being caught and shaming her family or the Countess. If she'd ever thought she could get away with it, she might have, but before the Earl she'd always had to be worried about her reputation. Now, if anyone were to come upon them, Wesley would be the one blamed, not her. No one would blame her for following her betrothed's lead... she wouldn't be ruined... and it gave her a sense of freedom like she'd never had before.

Cynthia almost wanted someone to walk by, to see Wesley bent over her breasts, to see her skirts as they slowly slid up her legs... her alabaster skin was glowing in the moonlight. It would be shocking. Scandalous. And horribly exciting.

Fingers slid underneath her skirts, only the Earl's body would keep a passerby from seeing her completely at this point. She moaned against his hand, panting as his fingers slid through her folds, becoming soaked in her cream. The Earl moaned too, and bit down on her nipple. It was pleasure and pain all rolled into one, and she was reminded abruptly of the little clips he'd put on her nipples when he'd last punished her.

As if in remembrance, her bottom throbbed. Cynthia writhed against him, rubbing her pussy against his hand as her passion grew exponentially with each stroke of his fingers. She couldn't contain herself, and if he hadn't kept his hand firmly planted over her mouth, her sensual cries would have been heard all over the gardens. Then Wesley's mouth replaced his hand, his desperate kiss drinking in her cries as cool night air wafted across her wet nipple and his fingers shoved inside of her.

Every muscle in her lower body seemed to clench, all at once, and she felt her clit rubbing hard against the heel of his hand as he rocked against her, applying rhythmic pressure against her tender parts. Cynthia was on fire, the pleasure building between her legs somehow much more intense than when she touched herself there. It was almost more exciting when it was the Earl touching her, more pleasurable... his fingers pushed back and forth inside of her, making her clench around him as her juices dripped over his hand.

She cried out, her passion muffled by his lips as he pressed her hard against the tree. Writhing, she could hear the rip of fabric as her dress tore against the bark, and she didn't care. It only excited her more. Ecstasy pulsed through her core as his fingers stroked her insides, her hands clutching at him as her muscles went weak with the overwhelming pleasure sizzling along her body. Her ears filled with a roaring sound as she rode his hand, in the middle of a garden, the excitement of their surroundings enhancing her rapture.

When he withdrew his hand, letting her skirts fall back into place, she moaned as he lifted his mouth from hers. Every inch of her skin felt like it was fizzing, like the top of the glass of champagne, effervescence escaping the only way it could. Her knees were weak, too weak to hold her, and she found herself sliding down the Earl's front until she was on her knees in front of him.

Shocked that he'd let her fall, she looked up at him in the darkness, just as the Earl's hand slid into her hair and tilted her head even further back. Her face was shadowed, but he could still see her swollen, parted lips, as she panted, and the creamy swells of her breasts hanging free of her gown in the night air. Wesley was too far gone to care about propriety or being caught; he desperately needed relief after having Cynthia writhing and moaning against him in such a wanton manner.

It was the work of a moment to undo the front of his breeches, something he could easily do with one hand, and then he was pressing the head of his cock against her mouth.

"Open," he hissed at her, his balls throbbing with need as the softness of her lips pressed against his sensitive tip. "And don't use your teeth."

Wet heat surrounded him as he thrust forward, one hand still tangled in her hair, using it to guide her head, and he braced the other against the tree behind her so he could bend over and watch as she took his cock into her mouth. The shocked look on her face made him feel rampantly possessive; it was obvious she hadn't done this before and he relished the knowledge he was the first—and only—

man to have her body. Even if she'd flirted and played with danger, she hadn't indulged.

She was his. All his. To corrupt and play with, to mold and teach, and to conquer and claim. He was on fire for her, and he didn't think it would ever be quenched; every touch only seemed to feed it, like the bellows of a blacksmith. Even when it was banked, the embers glowed, waiting to be reignited to full strength.

Feeling the vibrations of her moans traveling up the length of his cock, he had to stifle his own groan as he began to thrust back and forth in her mouth. Her small hands pressed against his thighs; she didn't try to push him away, she was bracing herself against him as he pushed deeper.

"Relax..." he murmured as he felt her gag, the small muscles in the back of her throat massaging the head of his dick. He dug his fingers into the base of her skull, massaging her scalp to help her follow his order. "Breathe through your nose, you're doing very well."

At any other time, Cynthia might have been insulted by his praise. Especially when it came to men—and the Earl in particular—she didn't want to do very well, she wanted to be wonderful. Perfect. Unforgettable. But right now she was too busy trying to breathe without choking.

When Mr. Carter had suggested she use her mouth on him, this hadn't been quite what she pictured. This was much more raw, much more primal. She felt incredibly small and submissive, for the first time in her life, on her knees before the Earl. The desire to please him was overwhelming, and not something she would have expected. The taste of male flesh was salty, musky, and had awakened a kind of craving inside of her. Her tongue explored the underside of his cock, relishing the forbidden flavors, as tears smarted in the back of her eyes from trying not to gag.

It was obvious the Earl was enjoying using her mouth this way, and it was much less embarrassing and painful than when he'd used her bottom. Even though she was becoming somewhat lightheaded, Cynthia was enjoying it too. The decadence of having her breasts exposed, the revelation of the Earl's cock between her lips, the hunger she felt from him even though his face was shadowed... and all of it tempered with the knowledge someone could walk by at any moment. That if they were seen, there would be no socially acceptable excuse for what they were doing... it wouldn't ruin her reputation, but it would certainly cause a scandal.

Cynthia had spent her life chasing the forbidden, but she'd always drawn certain lines. Now she didn't have to; the Earl was drawing them for her and he was putting them much farther out than she might have—if she'd even had the knowledge. She lived for excitement, adventure, and the pleasures that came from disobedience. The Earl had brought entirely new avenues for all of those things into her life.

"Suck, harder," he groaned, his thrusts into her mouth becoming harder, going deeper. The fingers pressing into the back of her head actually did help keep her relaxed, although she almost panicked when she first felt him actually enter her throat.

It was dizzying, exciting, terrifying... she felt so small and vulnerable on her knees before him, feeling his masculine strength and knowing she could choke on him... but she didn't bite down. She tried to do what he said, relaxing her throat and suckling on the thick rod pumping between her lips. Immediately she was rewarded with a hoarse, low cry, and she felt him actually swell larger.

The soft skin on the underside of his cock pulsed against her tongue and she tried to jerk back as something hot slid down the back of her throat.

"Swallow."

Not that he left her much of a choice, his hand pressing firmly on the back of her head, holding her in place as he emptied himself. She could feel the pulsing of each jet of liquid pressing down on her tongue, before her throat tightened, convulsively swallowing the subsequent spurt. The Earl's tight grip on the back of her head began to loosen, his breathing becoming ragged, and he softened inside of her mouth, slowly shrinking in size. Unsure of what to do, she continued to suckle, gently sucking, fascinated by the way it felt as he dwindled. The hand holding her head began to caress her. Her pins had already mostly fallen out of her hair, leaving the long strands tumbled down to her shoulders, and he ran his fingers through it, humming low in appreciation.

Looking down at the young woman who was still laving his cock with attention, Wesley had never felt so damned lucky in his life. Who knew his ward would turn out to be such a treasure? He was glad he hadn't followed his original plan of foisting her off on some other sap. Cynthia was all his and he didn't have to share her with anyone.

Gently, he moved to pull himself away from her all too tempting mouth, aware they'd probably exceeded the amount of time they could reasonably spend in the gardens without being caught. They were only lucky no one had walked by while they'd been occupied.

"Did I do it right?"

Cynthia's sultry voice, tempered by uncertainty, nearly made Wesley laugh aloud. Little minx. Helping her to her feet, he looked down into her bright eyes, which were peering at him as if searching for clues.

"Yes, baggage, that was delightful," he murmured, enjoying the look of pride and pleasure lighting up her face. Unable to help himself, he leaned down and took her mouth in another kiss, taking the opportunity to caress her breasts one last time as he tucked them back inside of her gown. From the way she murmured and squirmed against him, he was sure, if he'd wanted to, he'd be able to stoke the flames of her passion again already.

Unfortunately, that wasn't going to be possible.

Pulling reluctantly away from her, he realized returning to the Assembly Rooms wasn't going to be possible either. He thought Cynthia looked delightful with her swollen lips, tumbled hair and rumpled gown (which now also had green stains at her knees), but no one else should see her like this.

"Come on, sweetheart," he said, wrapping his jacket around her to hide the worst of the damage, and wincing when he saw the tiny tears all over the back of her gown. Damn. He was probably going to have to explain this to his mother later, when she asked why he and Cynthia left early, and if she heard about the state of Cynthia's gown, she'd never believe whatever he came up with. Maybe he could bribe the maids to burn the thing and never mention it to his mother.

Sadly, that was doubtful.

Well, it's not like he wasn't going to marry the chit.

A small smile curving his face, Wesley led Cynthia out of the gardens and around the building on the outside, keeping to the shadows. Humming softly to herself, she leaned into him, her fingers holding the edges of the jacket closed at her chest, trusting him to lead her to the carriage. A strange sense of clairvoyance whispered up Wesley's spine, as he suddenly realized this would be his life. The life he was meant to lead, with this brazen, sensual woman at his side. He could see them, walking just like this, in old age. Perhaps even after some fun ravishing each other in the garden.

At least, he was certainly determined to be a randy old goat, and somehow he was quite certain Cynthia wouldn't object in the least bit.

Grinning now, he held her even more firmly to his side. He couldn't wait to be married.

"Does anyone know where Wesley and Cynthia have gone?" Eleanor asked, looking around. She was utterly stunning in an ice blue gown which set off her eyes and her golden hair.

Grace fluttered her fan in front of her face to hide her smile. "I believe I saw them step outside a few minutes ago," she murmured quietly. "Probably to explore the gardens."

Beside both of them, Edwin snorted and Eleanor looked up at him and giggled. "Oh dear."

"We could go explore the gardens," he said, giving his wife a lustful look, his eyes trailing over her cleavage. Grace couldn't help it, she tensed immediately. She didn't want to ruin Eleanor and Edwin's night, but at the moment, the presence of her friend was all that was keeping her sane.

Because, unfortunately, she wasn't having a nice coze in the corner with Nell and her husband. No, there was a fourth standing with them. Silent. Watchful. Standing far too close to her shoulder. And Grace desperately did not want to be left alone with him. She knew Eleanor sensed that immediately, and she felt both guilt and relief when Nell shook her head at Edwin and tapped his chest reprovingly with her fan.

"Absolutely not, you reprobate," Eleanor said chidingly.

"But sweetheart, that's what you like about me," Edwin said, his eyes darkening even further as he grabbed Eleanor's hand and held it to his chest. The look Eleanor gave back to him said she'd love to go exploring the gardens with him, but she still shook her head. Grace watched them rather wistfully, although she was sure her envy was hidden behind a suitably blank expression.

"We could go explore the gardens." Alex's deep voice rumbled in her hair, sending shivers dancing up and down Grace's spine. By the time she looked over her shoulder at him to pierce him with an icy glare, she had her reactions back under control.

She didn't say a word. She didn't need to. The bastard just smiled at her, his eyes glowing as they traveled down from her face and straight into her cleavage.

Grace had dressed to impress tonight. She'd played up her creamy skin and dark hair with a rich, ruby dress, trimmed with navy blue lace, to go with the sapphire and rubies around her neck and in her hair. The sapphires were too dark to match her eyes, but she knew she looked stunning, nonetheless. Alex hadn't been the only one looking her over appreciatively this evening.

Not that any of the men who had come forward had lingered. Without saying a word, Alex's looming presence had somehow gotten across the message that Grace was off limits. She wasn't entirely sure how he did it, but every single man who approached walked away within a few minutes after exchanging no more than a few pleasantries.

Turning away from him, she tapped her foot impatiently, only to realize she was tapping in time to the music. Again.

"Dance with me, Grace."

She sighed. All night Alex had been asking and she'd been refusing. This time, it sounded more like an order than a request. Maybe if she danced with him, he'd leave her alone.

"Fine." It wasn't the most gracious answer, as she held out her hand, but Alex bowed over her fingers anyway, entirely courteous, before leading her out onto the floor.

Of course it was a waltz. He held her far too tightly, his hand splayed over her back as he began to rotate, inserting them between the other couples, masterfully maneuvering her around the floor. Alex had always been a wonderful dancer. It felt like her skin was becoming tight, having him touch her and hold her this closely.

Other than after he'd spanked her, or when she accidentally moved toward him in her sleep, Alex had barely touched her at all. Now she was letting him. Had agreed to it. Had she been mad?

She kept her face tilted away from him, unsure if she'd be able to hide the confusion and distress she felt over her pleasure at his nearness.

"You look ravishing tonight," he said, his voice low so others passing by them wouldn't be able to hear them over the music. "Then again, you always look stunning, but I do like this dress in particular. Did you wear it because you remembered how much I like you in red?"

Pursing her lips, she shook her head, but in her heart she suddenly wondered. Had she dressed to taunt him or to please him?

"You think rather highly of yourself, don't you?" she asked tartly.

"Why shouldn't I, when I have the most beautiful woman in the room in my arms?"

Her heart skipped a beat, and she wished he didn't sound so sincere. It was hard to maintain her anger when Alex was being charming. Complimentary. Acting as though he cared. It brought up the most awful feelings of wistful hope inside of her, made her think about Eleanor's theory that perhaps he truly did value Grace for herself and he just hadn't known it till she was gone. But then Grace had to remind herself it had apparently taken him years to figure it out, and he was probably motivated by something other than emotion.

After all, he'd proven himself to be just like her father, valuing business and money over emotions and caring.

But it was hard to remember that in moments like this, when he was holding her so closely and looking at her like she was the only woman in the world. Heat high in her cheeks, she kept her face turned away, not knowing how to respond to him.

Alex took her silence as a positive sign. If she were stone, holding firm against him, then he would be water, slowly wearing down her resistance. He was certain he was wearing her down. Just like tonight, when he'd waited patiently by her side, hoping eventually she'd relent and dance with him. Now she was. That had been his first major victory of the evening.

Smaller victories included making her shiver and blush, which she was doing right now. She couldn't completely contain her physical responses to him, and he was more than willing to play on those.

The more time he spent with her, the easier it was to remember his former, more charming, happier self. Even if she was angry with him all the time, at least she was there. And she was softening. The fact that he held her in her arms and made her blush was proof. She didn't protest about sleeping in the same bed anymore either.

When the dance was done, Alex took her back to the side of the ballroom. Edwin and Eleanor had vacated the space, but Hugh and Irene had taken their place.

"Edwin took Nell home, she wasn't feeling too well," Hugh said. He didn't appear concerned, however, so Alex knew it wasn't anything dire. Smiling down at Grace, Hugh patted Irene's hand and then released her to hold his hand out to Grace. "Lady Brooke, would you like to dance?"

"Yes, please," she said, with every evidence of relief, shooting Alex a triumphant look before turning away to take Hugh's hand.

Alex hid his smile. Even that was a victory, because she'd cared enough to make a point to him. It didn't matter what the point was. He turned to Irene. "Well, pet, would you like to dance?"

"Absolutely," Irene said, smiling up at him enthusiastically. They hadn't quite managed to return to their old camaraderie yet, Alex still felt a bit strange about touching her after that scene in the garden, but they were on their way. Fortunately, the current song was a quadrille, which didn't require the same kind of intimacy a waltz did.

While he was dancing with Irene, he couldn't help but watch Grace. She was aptly named, her every movement was long and elegant, like a siren's call to his senses.

Unfortunately, Hugh's dance with her seemed to be some kind of signal to the other men in attendance. No sooner had the dance ended and they'd returned to the sidelines, than a young lord stepped up to ask Grace to dance. Of course, at events such as this, that was completely normal. Alex's behavior tonight, keeping the men from even asking her for a dance, had been decidedly unusual amongst the *ton*. In London, it would have been more than frowned upon, he probably would have found himself overrun by outraged matrons.

After all, most of the time, husbands didn't hover over their wives at balls, so if the women wanted to dance, it wasn't going to be with their spouse.

Although, Alex had only meant to keep Grace off the dance floor until she acquiesced to dance with him, it was still hard to see her take the floor, laughing and smiling with another man. With an internal sigh, he turned and asked one of the young matrons at the edge of the floor to join him. If Grace was going to dance, he was going to dance.

He'd learned his lesson about hurting his own cause though. The moment the dance ended, he returned the flirtatious matron to her place and took his own beside Grace. The musicians were resting for the moment, and the young buck she'd been dancing with had taken it upon himself to retain her hand as they chatted. Alex had absolutely no compunction about pushing his way between them and taking Grace's hand back for his own.

"Lord Brooke," the younger man said, immediately letting Grace go. He might be a rake-in-training, but he knew when he was outclassed.

Alex eyed him without malice. "My apologies, I don't believe we've been introduced."

"Marbury," he said, with a grin.

"Ah, the name I've heard," Alex said, raising his eyebrow. Marbury was a bit more than a rake-in-training, but he was also known for not poaching protected preserves. As long as Alex made it clear he wasn't going to stand for any dalliances with his wife, he would have nothing to fear from Marbury. "Your grays are superb."

Other than his exploits in the bedroom, Marbury was also known for being a notable whip. Alex had seen his team, a matching set of feisty grays, on the street, although he'd never gotten a good look at the man driving them.

"Matchless," Marbury said with an almost boyish grin. "But they should be considering the cost."

Beside them, Grace made an indelicate snorting sound. "Men and their horses."

"Ladies and their ribbons," Alex said teasingly back to her, his heart lightening. It was an old retort, teasing words exchanged more than once back when he'd started courting her. Grace had asked him to go shopping with her and he'd made some kind of pompous remark about ladies always needing new ribbons; she'd tossed her head and haughtily informed him she was going to New Market to choose a new horse, but if he wanted ribbons she would send him out with her mother so he would at least be educated in choosing the best.

That was the day Alex had decided he was going to marry her.

A gentleman Grace had met earlier that evening, Mr. Lowell, interrupted just then, asking Grace to dance. Somewhat in a daze, she accepted, looking over her shoulder at Alex as Mr. Lowell led her away. Alex's eyes were trained on her, watching her walk away.

She hadn't expected him to remember their old repartee. It had fallen from her lips before she'd thought about it, sparked by the conversation, and she'd thought it a mistake even before she'd finished saying the words. But then Alex had responded. He'd remembered.

That had surprised her even more than his appearance by her side at the end of the dance. She'd thoroughly expected him to remain with the blonde beauty he'd ended up dancing with. After all, he'd been hanging on Grace all night and he'd finally gotten what he'd wanted. When she'd first seen him take to the floor, her heart had dropped somewhere around the vicinity of her feet. She thought by accepting Marbury's invitation, that her action had spurred Alex to seek out another companion.

Even though she'd tried to tell herself she was glad he'd gotten the message, it had still hurt.

Then he'd reappeared at her side, the blonde nowhere in sight, as aggressively possessive as he had been earlier in the evening. Even though she tried to remain aloof, how could such attention *not* turn her head, just a little? Then, to know he'd remembered such a simple little thing from before... a tiny joke between them she'd been sure he'd forgotten. Such little interactions had meant something to her, but what could they have meant to him?

Yet he'd remembered.

For the rest of the night, Grace was utterly taken aback. Alex danced with woman after woman, just as she did with the men who came to ask her, but he always returned to her side after each set. Without the lady in question on his arm. And he never danced with a single one twice.

Except for Grace. He claimed every single waltz with her, apparently content to dance with her held close, even though they didn't exchange a word between them. She truly didn't know what to say.

CHAPTER 6

"*B*ut what do I do?" Grace whispered into Eleanor's ear.

They were doing their best not to catch the Countess' eye while she went into raptures, showing them the ballroom as it was being decorated for the wedding. The event was two days away and Cynthia looked like she was reaching the end of her patience, but Grace was too wrapped up in her own issues to help with that. Besides, the Countess had her arm firmly wrapped around Cynthia's. It would be like trying to detach a leech. A well-meaning, motherly, and completely wedding-crazed leech.

"You could always try giving him another chance, he might surprise you," Eleanor whispered back, glancing over to make sure they weren't being watched. They were, but only by Cynthia, who was gazing at them beseechingly as the Countess directed one of the footmen to raise the valances another foot. They both looked back at her with sympathy and shook their heads.

She stuck out her tongue at them and Eleanor giggled. Even Grace smiled, although she was currently feeling far too rattled to truly feel any humor. Eleanor kept pushing her to give her marriage another chance, to take Alex at face value—again. The worst part was, Grace could feel herself weakening and wanting to do exactly that.

But if Eleanor was wrong, and Alex was only using her again, Grace didn't know if her heart could take it.

Irene looked over at them curiously. She'd been following the Countess through the ballroom much closer than Grace or Eleanor had. Probably conditioned to follow closely by her harpy mother, poor thing. Lately Grace had been tempted to talk to Irene, wondering if she might have any insights into Alex's behavior. After all, she had known him the longest. But, even though there was some obvious cooling of untoward affection between them, she was sure Irene's loyalty remained to Alex. She didn't know if she could trust Irene to keep her confidence.

The doors on the far side of the room opened, and the Earl peered in, looking around. His mother saw him immediately and started half-dragging Cynthia across the room, stopping mid-tirade as she barreled towards her son, her voice rising as she neared him.

"Wesley! There you are! What do you have to say for yourself, sirrah? I cannot believe your behavior last night!"

"Oh dear," Eleanor murmured under her breath, holding her hand over her mouth to muffle her giggle as Wesley's friends abandoned ship and left him to the tender mercies of the Countess.

Apparently, Wesley had taken Cynthia out to the gardens at the dance last night and had rendered her into such a state of disarray that they'd had to make a hasty trip home. The Countess was infuriated, although she hadn't shown it before, as she put the blame solely on her son's broad shoulders. Cynthia appeared fascinated by the diatribe, while everyone else displayed varying degrees of amusement. Grace coughed to cover her own laughter, and she couldn't help catching Alex's gaze. For one delightful, pure moment, they looked at each other, laughter filling their eyes. He was heart-stoppingly beautiful when he smiled.

Then the moment was over, and Grace pulled her gaze away. She couldn't drop her guard too much. Not yet.

If only she could find a way to test him, to discover what his motivations were. Perhaps she should search the study of their current residence, see if he had any of his business papers. They might hold a clue. Or his correspondence. Something to tell her why he might need a wife by his side, or her as his wife in particular.

In the meantime... perhaps there were other ways of ascertaining just how serious he was. Her scandalous reputation didn't appear to currently bother him, but what if she was seen as being even more so? After all, he was intent on reining her in, and everyone now knew it, and if she refused to let him, perhaps he'd find her too embarrassing to hold on to. Especially if his reasons had to do with business. She had thought she'd already broken the line of what a man would be willing to tolerate before divorce, but perhaps she hadn't gone quite far enough.

And, if by some miracle, he held on to her no matter what she did... then perhaps she would have her answer.

His wife was drunk.

At a dinner party.

Unfortunately, one which included more than just their close friends. The Countess had invited quite a few guests into her home, to celebrate Wesley and Cynthia's upcoming nuptials. Fortunately, Grace was far enough down the table from their hostess that the Countess hadn't noticed and so wasn't distressed, especially since she was more focused on ensuring her son and his fiancée behaved, but quite a few people at Grace's end of the table were already shooting her glances and whispering behind their hands.

Her voice was a little too loud, her laughter a little too brazen, and she was being remarkably indiscreet about, well, everything. Most of the high-flyers were seated with the Countess, but he could see several of them eyeing Grace from down the length of the table. She was creating more talk, and he was too far away to be able to do anything about it. Interrupting dinner would only draw more attention to her behavior and fuel speculation. He gritted his teeth, trying to decide what to do. Grace's manners had always been impeccable, especially after they'd become estranged, because she realized what a fine line she walked on in Society. If she had done anything more extraordinary than indulge in her private life, the high sticklers would have had all the excuse they needed to drive her from Society completely. Now that Alex was back in her life, trying to reconcile, did she think she no longer needed to follow the other social conventions? Or was this for his benefit alone?

"I'm sorry, Lady Brooke, I didn't catch that," a pretty, dark-haired lady said, politely, as Grace muttered something under her breath. Mrs. Locklear, if Alex remembered her introduction correctly, a widow who had been escorted there by her friend Lord Hereford. Although Alex was quite sure they were probably more than friends.

"Well, Mrs. Locklear," Grace said, her rising tones contemptuously superior, "if you had been listening instead of mentally undressing everyone else's husbands, you wouldn't need to ask."

Both Mrs. Locklear and Lord Hereford went beet red, for very different reasons. Alex coughed, nearly choking on the piece of chicken he practically swallowed whole. The actual remark didn't surprise him, Grace had always said outrageous things, but she had always said them *sotto voce* to a trusted companion. Not announced it so everyone could hear. Well, not everyone, but enough people to bring conversation around their part of the table to a grinding halt.

On one hand, all the women around them looked more than a little gratified to have Mrs. Locklear called out. On the other hand, it still reflected badly upon Grace and upon himself that she had spoken so rudely to anyone, no matter how well it was deserved. Propriety demanded the social faults of others not be publicly remarked upon, although of course many would gossip about it privately. Fortunately, Mrs. Locklear didn't respond in kind; instead she seemed to shrink in on herself, barely looking at any of the men, as Grace turned to answer a question Edwin asked her. He shot Alex a look of apology which was unnecessary; Alex didn't think Edwin would have any real control over Grace, even though he was sitting next to her, but he was grateful to his friend for distracting her.

Damn the social conventions dictating a man and wife should sit apart. Alex could have kept more control over Grace's drinking if he'd been sitting closer. Granted, he hadn't noticed her drinking to excess, but he had been immersed in conversation with his dinner companions until her behavior had distracted him.

WHEN THE WOMEN left the table to the men, dispersing to the drawing room, Eleanor swiftly caught up to Grace. She'd been watching her friend carefully all evening and she could tell Grace was up to something. Something that was probably going to earn her nothing but a hot bottom at the end of the evening, if the expression on Lord Brooke's face was any indicator.

Eleanor was fairly certain his desire to reconcile with Grace was sincere. Ever since the couple had arrived in Bath, he'd already appeared more open and approachable. She'd even seen him smile several times. Usually when Grace couldn't see him do so. Both of them appeared to be playing their hands very close to their chests, but there was definitely something between them.

"What are you doing?" Eleanor whispered into Grace's ear, snagging her friend's elbow and pulling her close.

After all, she didn't want to draw any more attention to Grace. The high sticklers had already been looking at her askance by dessert, and even the Countess had noticed there was something going on with her, although she'd been too far down the table to know what. Thankfully.

Grace sniffed, turning her nose up into the air, stumbling over her feet a bit as she did so. "I don't know what you're talking about."

"You're not drunk, so stop acting," Eleanor whispered back. Grace looked at her in surprise, and with a bit of guilt, her cheeks turning the faintest shade of pink. "You're going to end up causing a scene."

"Yes, and then I'll be able to see how Alex reacts."

Eleanor groaned. She should have known. Sometimes she and Grace were so alike. Grace wanted to provoke a reaction from Alex to try and discern his true feelings, just as Eleanor wanted to do with Edwin. However, she knew from trial and error that forcing such a declaration was near to impossible. No matter what Edwin did in response to Eleanor's provocation, she could always find multiple motivations to assign to his actions. It never helped clarify what his feelings might be toward her.

"It's not going to work," Eleanor told her. "You're probably just going to end up not being able to sit down tomorrow."

"If he spanks me, instead of giving up on this idiotic notion to reconcile, then that will say a great deal, won't it?"

It would, but it wouldn't be enough. Something else Eleanor knew, because her own doubts still gnawed at her. She did find it reassuring Edwin would rather spank or birch her bottom then send her out of his sight, but then again, he needed an heir. So did Alex. Although, it truly would be easier for him to divorce Grace than to put forth an effort to keep her in line. No one would blame him. If Edwin wanted to divorce, or even separate, it would be a huge scandal. Not to mention it would wreck his friendship with Hugh. Whereas, most of Society would probably applaud such a step by Lord Brooke. Perhaps Grace was right and she would find it more indicative than Edwin's responses were for Eleanor.

"I hope you know what you're doing," she murmured, and then there wasn't a chance to say anything more, because the Countess came sweeping up to them as they entered the drawing room.

It was obvious the older woman had realized something was going on with Grace and was determined nothing happened to ruin the dinner. Not that Grace would ever take her antics so far, especially not when Alex wasn't around to be witness to it. Eleanor watched, amused, as the Countess seated Grace next to her, surrounded by some of the highest sticklers in Society, ones who would have probably given her the cut direct if they'd happened upon her in London... and Grace proceeded to charm them all.

Some of them quite unwillingly. The Duchess of Kent looked like she'd swallowed an egg about two seconds after she laughed at one of Grace's quips, realizing who she was laughing with. None of them would dare cut her with the Countess right there, obviously sponsoring her, and Alex having escorted her, but they clearly weren't quite sure how to treat her either. Eleanor had to swallow her own laughter as she made her way over to Cynthia and Irene, who were sitting on one of the window seats and chatting.

Irene was describing Hugh's estates and their honeymoon there. Smiling, Eleanor sat down with them, enjoying hearing about her old home from a new perspective.

"I don't know if I'll make a very good lady of the house," Cynthia said ruefully, when Irene was done. "The Countess has been doing her best to train me, but I can't imagine why anyone would listen to me. Manfred certainly doesn't."

Eleanor laughed at the disgruntled look on Cynthia's face. Apparently she'd at least attempted to give the Countess' butler an order and it hadn't gone very well. "He didn't listen to Wesley either, before he became the Earl, if that makes you feel any better," she said, her eyes sparkling. "Besides, he'll likely stay with the Countess. I can't imagine her being agreeable to letting him go."

Cynthia immediately perked up. "So we'll have a different butler?"

"Yes, I imagine he's probably at either Spencer House in London or out on the estates right now," Eleanor said, giving Cynthia a supportive smile. It couldn't be easy, knowing she was about to be mistress of a whole horde of servants she hadn't even met yet. At least Eleanor had known most of Edwin's before they were married, and Irene had met quite a few of Hugh's. Not that any of them were as stuffy as Manfred anyway, she knew Irene had been welcomed with open arms at Stonehaven and Westingdon.

"Oh good. I can deal with someone who doesn't know me, I think," Cynthia said, obviously gaining in confidence already. "Manfred knows me a little too well by now." Her wince made both Irene and Eleanor laugh.

"You could always try behaving," Irene said, although her green eyes were sparkling with amusement.

The saucy smile she got in return left no doubt of Cynthia's opinion on that. "You could always try having some fun," she teased.

"I have plenty of fun," Irene retorted, with affection. "And I can sit down the next day when I do."

All three women dissolved into giggles.

Unfortunately Eleanor wasn't able to enjoy her mirth for very long, as her belly twinged. She'd started to become nauseous at all sorts of odd hours through the day, especially in the mornings. Swallowing hard, she prayed she wasn't about to humiliate herself by vomiting in the middle of the Countess of Spencer's drawing room.

"Eleanor? Are you all right?" Irene was looking at her with concern, Cynthia turning to see what was wrong as Irene reached out her hand.

"Yes... yes," Eleanor said faintly, pressing her hand against her stomach. "I'm fine, I just need a moment." She glanced over at the gaggle of women around the Countess, hoping none of them had noticed her incapacity. To her relief, they were still involved in their conversation. If they knew she was increasing, they would be lenient about any feminine issues she had, of course, but since she hadn't told Edwin yet, she certainly didn't want that gossip making the rounds.

Although she was going to have to tell him soon. Her increasing nausea and bouts of fatigue were becoming harder and harder to hide.

As if her thoughts had summoned him, the door opened and the men began to trickle into the room. Alex and Edwin were among the first, and his dark gaze slashed around the women, searching for her. The moment he saw her, he frowned, and something inside of her shriveled. She realized, after a moment, she didn't like feeling as though he was upset with her. Unless, of course, she meant him to be.

Doing it unintentionally made her feel small and sad, her mind grasping for what she might have done wrong and how she could make it right.

Her insides warmed as he immediately strode toward her, while Alex headed straight for his own wife, and she realized Edwin was frowning in concern. Not upset. Some of her tension dissipated.

"What's wrong, Nell?" he asked, in a quiet voice, as soon as he reached her.

Part of her wanted to blurt out exactly what was wrong, but this was not the time or the place. "Nothing, really," she said, mustering up a smile as his frown deepened. "Just a *megrim*."

"She got very pale all of the sudden and clutched at her stomach," Cynthia said helpfully. Eleanor shot the woman a glare, but Cynthia wasn't looking at her at all; her gaze had immediately moved to Wesley as he came into the room.

His mouth drawn in a hard line, Edwin held out his hand. Not wanting to refuse him and make more of a fuss, Eleanor took it and allowed him to help her up. She was sure no one else realized the smile on his face was false, as he made their excuses to the Countess for an early departure. Perhaps Hugh might have noticed, but he was too busy fetching tea for Irene as the trolley came into the room while Edwin and Eleanor made their goodbyes.

But she felt entirely too nauseous and, now that she was standing, a bit dizzy to worry over it. Edwin was like a pillar of strength beside her, one she could lean on both physically and mentally, trusting him to say and do the right things so they could leave. She let him maneuver them out the doors and into the coach, where he sat her beside him and folded her into his arms.

Happily snuggling into his chest, Eleanor didn't see the continued worry creasing his brow, or the anxiety in his eyes as his finger stroked over her shoulder.

It took Alex less than two minutes, after he inserted himself into the circle of women around the Countess, to realize his wife wasn't drunk after all. She'd been bamming him. And he'd been taken in completely. Which meant her behavior over dinner had been deliberate. No wonder she'd been able to skate the line so well, making a minor scene without causing an actual scandal.

He grated his teeth as he sat and listened to her chatting with some of the most influential movers and shakers within the *ton*. None of whom knew quite what to make of her at this moment. They'd all become used to thinking of her as a walking scandal, but now her husband was back by her side and dancing attendance on her. On top of that, the Countess was one of the most influential women when it came to Society. She was considered a force to be reckoned with, and she was showing her obvious support of Grace.

Which he appreciated, since she was doing so at his request. She'd raised her finely arched eyebrows when he'd made the request, but had agreed readily enough.

When the teacart came in, his wife began testing his patience again.

He'd gotten up to fetch her a cup, joining the other gentlemen as they handed out the cups to the ladies, and by the time he'd turned around, she had separated herself from the Countess' circle and was flirtatiously batting her eyes at Lord Northrup as she accepted a cup of tea from him. Stony-faced, Alex took the cup he'd procured to the Countess instead, bowing over her hand, before grimly stalking to his wife.

The amusement in the Countess' eyes as she'd accepted the tea from him had not improved his mood.

"Northrup," he said, rather shortly, as he settled next to Grace. He could practically feel the tension in her begin to tighten, the moment he placed himself beside her.

Reaching out, he placed his hand on the small of her back, a possessive movement which didn't go unnoticed by Northrup. The other man's dark eyes showed confusion that quickly cleared, as he realized no matter how the lady might have been acting toward him, the lord was not going to be amenable.

"Brooke," he responded mildly. "Your lovely wife and I were just discussing the new Sheridan play."

"Ah yes," Alex said, putting a smile on his face as he shifted closer to Grace, his body language implying an intimacy between them that didn't actually exist. He could feel her tension ratcheting up even higher, although she didn't move away. It was like she was waiting for something... maybe just to see what he was going to do. "My Grace does love Sheridan's works. I prefer Shakespeare, myself."

Northrup chuckled, smoothing down his black mustache in a kind of nervous gesture, although he seemed to be relaxing now. "Who doesn't? The Bard is always popular."

"I think something new is preferable to something old," Grace said, her voice filled with gaiety, and yet her tone had an edge as well. "We've all read and seen the Bard's plays a hundred times over. I like to see new characters and plots on the stage, it's so much more engaging." As she spoke, Alex slid his fingers along her back so the tips could subtly grip her waist, a calm satisfaction filling him as he felt her stiffen despite her outward composure.

He knew she was trying to prod him, but strangely he felt more placid every passing minute.

"Yet there is always much to be appreciated about the old," he countered, looking down at her. Her bright blue eyes lifted to his, guarded but searching. Emotion seemed to churn underneath the smooth social mask, the blankness of which was wearing thin. "Not just the comfort of the familiar, but a depth of emotion that can only be built over time. New is not always better."

They were both speaking of more than just theater now, and something flickered across her face before she turned away from him, her lips curving into a smile as she tilted her head at Lord Northrup. Like so many men, he smiled automatically in response. When Grace was in a mood to be charming, she was like bright sunshine, nearly impossible to ignore and even more impossible to be unaffected by.

He was still going to spank her ass when they got home, charm or not. While her antics, surprisingly, weren't riling his temper at the moment, he certainly wasn't going to let her get away without any consequences.

"As you can see, Lord Brooke and I can never agree on anything," Grace said, with an airy little laugh, even as Alex tightened his fingers warningly, pressing them into her side. She kept her gaze on Lord Northrup, and something about her demeanor made her words an open invitation. "We appreciate very different diversions."

"Which is a good example of why opposites attract," Alex said, his temper starting to stir again. Pretending to glance at the clock on the far wall, he pulled Grace into him, his anger soothed as she was pressed against his side and he could feel her own ire leap up again. For some reason, setting her off balance helped him to keep an even keel. "Excuse us, Northrup, we really should be going." He gave Grace a look full of so much sexual heat she froze, staring up at him like a mouse who had just noticed it was being stalked by a cat. "I'm sure you understand."

"Oh ah... hmm, yes," Northrup coughed, covering his stutter as he looked back and forth between them. "Good evening, then."

The man actually blushed as he turned away. Ninny. Alex nearly snorted. If Grace truly wanted to test his possessiveness, she needed much more stalwart quarry than someone like Northrup.

Keeping a hold of his wayward wife, Alex hurried them through their goodbyes. The Countess wished them a good night with a knowing little glint in her eye that made Grace look distinctly uncomfortable. Obviously the woman thought they'd reconciled fully, and Alex was eager to go home and claim his marital rights.

If he thought Grace would be willing, he absolutely would be, but at the moment the only thing he was going to be doing this evening was turning his wife's bottom a bright red. Of course, he'd already found that was enjoyable in its own way.

GRACE STOOD in the middle of their bedroom, watching warily as Alex locked the door behind him. He'd been silent the entire carriage ride home, the glimpses of his face in the moonlight had shown a contemplative expression. Honestly, she would have been more reassured to see anger. There had been times during the evening when she'd been sure his temper had been stirring; his control over himself made her feel anxious for some reason.

Maybe because she wasn't sure how he was going to react now.

If she'd ever behaved in such a way with her father present, he probably would have dragged her from the dinner and confined her to her room for days. Probably with as little food as possible. If she resisted, she would earn a cuff or two from his fist. Then he'd ignore her again, even after she was released, unless she did something else to gain his ire.

It occurred to her that she was more comfortable with such visible anger and predictable repercussions than she was with Alex's silent contemplation.

Was he fed up with her now? Was he going to leave her? But if he was, then why lock her in the room with him? Did that mean Eleanor had been right and he was going to spank her? A warm flush seemed to shudder through her, from her core up to her cheeks and back down again, at the thought. It might be perverse, but she would rather be spanked than sent away and rejected again.

Spanking her took effort on Alex's part. Effort he didn't actually need to expend when it would be much easier to give up on her and divorce her. Spanking meant he wanted to correct her behavior, *because* he wanted to keep her. At least, she hoped that's what it meant. She knew where her hope had gotten her before, but at least this was hope tempered with a kind of proof.

It made more sense for him to divorce her than to reconcile with her. Especially when he still hadn't claimed his marital rights. If all he wanted was an heir from her, then wouldn't he have done that already? She was his wife; legally it wouldn't be seen as forcing her. In fact, legally, she was the one currently in the wrong by denying him.

Alex turned around, his eyes looking darker than usual in the candlelight, fixing her in place with his gaze. She felt the tremor through her body, half excitement, half fear. When he looked at her like that, she couldn't help her body's response, the way her nipples tightened and her womanhood became hot and wet with need. She swore she could already feel an anticipatory tingle in her bottom, and her hands reflexively went behind her back, covering her cheeks.

"Turn around, Gracie, I'm going to help you take your dress off."

She didn't protest the use of his nickname for her anymore. It made her ache bitterly, for the memories, but at the same time it warmed her. Besides, he always went back to calling her that, even if he stopped for a bit.

Taking her hands off of her bottom, she turned around and wrung them in front of her, waiting for his touch.

Fingers drifted over the back of her neck and down her exposed spine. The gown she was wearing wasn't scandalous, but it was fashionably low, and she shivered as he traced a line down the center of her back until he reached the neckline. She could feel his hot breath on the back of her neck as her gown started to sag, drooping a little more with each button undone.

Grace told herself she wasn't enjoying this.

However, she did enjoy his low, tortured groan as he relieved her of her corset, leaving her only in a thin, translucent chemise. She had to admit, she was having trouble standing firm in her resistance to him right now. Especially because he obviously had no intention of sending her away. No, he still wanted to reconcile. She still felt like there must be an ulterior motive, but it must be a damn good one. Tomorrow she'd search his study and see what she could find.

Alex walked around her and sat down on the bed. He'd taken his jacket, waistcoat and cravat off already and was undoing the laces on his sleeves to roll them up. Seeing him bare his forearms, the same way he'd done the last time he'd spanked her, sent a jolt of butterflies through her stomach.

She still didn't understand his motivations, but she did know his firm resolve to correct her behavior aroused her. Comforted her in some way. Why go to all the effort of taming a recalcitrant wife? Why hold her afterwards? Unless there were emotions pressing in.

Hope had slayed her heart the last time, and she was afraid to hope again, but it burned in her chest anyway. Nearly choking her with the unresolved desires and dreams she thought she'd given up. Because, deep down, she'd never wanted Alex to divorce her, she'd never wanted to travel to the Continent or America to start over with some other man; no, she'd wanted him. Him, the way she'd dreamed they would be.

To wonder if such a thing might be within her grasp again... it made her heart sing at the same time it terrified her.

∾

BEAUTIFUL DIDN'T BEGIN to describe his wife. She was staring at him with the strangest expression on her face, one he couldn't possible interpret. Something had changed within her. Even though she was still his little firebrand, now she wasn't acting like her usual spirited self.

He'd expected a fight to undress her. Instead, she'd meekly acquiesced. Now she seemed to be waiting for his next move. But not exactly warily... almost expectantly. Hopefully. Her arms hung at her sides, not at all trying to cover herself. The pert pink nipples of her breasts were rosy against the fabric of her chemise, the shadow of her womanhood easily visible. Tension shimmered in the air between them, her soft lips open as her breath quickened.

Had she wanted to be spanked?

"Come here, Gracie," he said, keeping his voice stern and his face blank as he patted his lap. She shook her head, her hands clenching into little fists at her sides. "Yes. Now, Grace. Or I'll get your hairbrush. Considering how you've behaved tonight, you shouldn't tempt me to be harsher."

As he watched, her cheeks flushed and then paled, and she took one step closer. He waited patiently, keeping his eyes trained on her face, not saying anything more. There was a struggle going on within her; as long as she made her way to him eventually, he didn't want to make it harder for her.

Each step brought her closer, coming faster as she neared him, her head ducking down as if she was too ashamed or embarrassed to look at him. Alex had her over his lap the moment she reached his side, rubbing his hand over the soft flesh of her ass as he crooned to her.

"Good girl," he said, placing one hand on the small of her back to hold her in place as his other hand squeezed the fleshy globes of her bottom. His cock was snugly caged between her body and his, eagerly rubbing against the front of his pants. The thinness of her drawers would provide no protection, but then that wasn't really the point, was it? He drew them down, feeling her squirm as he did so. "I won't be as hard on you, sweetheart, since you came to me of your own accord. But you do deserve a spanking."

Giving the pale flesh of her ass, one last caress, Alex raised his hand and let it fall with a snap.

SMACK!

The little noise Grace uttered couldn't rightly be called a whimper or a moan, but it was something in between.

SMACK! SMACK! SMACK!

Spanking her, the advice he'd received from all the men whirled around his head. Hitting her over and over again in one spot would hurt the most eventually. The crease of her bottom and the undersides where the curves met her thighs would be the most sensitive areas to spank. Her thighs would sting her in an entirely different manner. Direct hits to her quim should be gentler than those administered to her bottom.

"You will not feign drunkenness to try and justify your abominable behavior."

SMACK! SMACK!

"You will absolutely not actually *become* drunk and lewd in public."

SMACK! SMACK!

Grace was starting to cry, her soft mewls and whimpers making his cock even harder as her rosy bottom darkened. Her legs had begun to move restlessly; not kicking yet, but soon they would be.

"You will not flirt with other men."

SMACK! SMACK! SMACK! SMACK!

She howled, bucking slightly, as he landed the blows on her sit-spot in a small flurry, as if to emphasize that particular command. Over and over he repeated himself, and every time he returned to his rule about other men, his hand came down on her most sensitive spots.

Despite his anger and frustration with her, he felt completely in control of himself. It was a cold kind of anger, one he'd learned to live with. However, he didn't intend to have to live with it for very much longer.

He had to admit, roasting Grace's bottom for her offenses held much greater appeal than he would have ever thought. Feeling her soft body squirming on his lap, her breathy cries filling his ears, her promises to "be good"—well, he wished he'd done this years ago instead of behaving like an utter fool. Especially because she seemed to enjoy it.

Every so often, in between raining spanks down on her tender flesh, he would pause and rub his hand over it instead. From the way she wriggled and whimpered, he knew it wasn't entirely soothing. The heat of her skin told him she was very sensitive as he dug his fingers into her pliable flesh. A few times his fingers had brushed over the swollen lips of her pussy, which were pouty and wet with arousal.

Still, he didn't think she was getting any kind of pleasure from the punishment itself. Humiliation broke her voice when his fingers probed, and that was when she tried hardest to squirm away. Because she was embarrassed by the wetness coating her nether lips.

It took Alex's breath away to feel her hot, wet slickness at his fingertips. Knowing it wasn't an aberration; this was not the first time she'd responded like this. He groaned as he slid two fingers into her wet heat, feeling her pussy tighten around them. Using his other hand to squeeze a reddened cheek, he held her tightly on his lap, enjoying the way she squirmed against him while he stroked her insides.

"Alex... oh no...." She gasped and writhed as his fingers found the most sensitive spot inside her body. Since she wasn't actually telling him no, just saying it as if she could ward off the pleasure with her words, he kept going. Pressing. Stroking. Squeezing her buttocks and sending tingling pain to mix with her pleasure.

His cock was rock hard and throbbing, eager to replace his fingers... but he wasn't going to. Not unless she asked. It was almost a trust exercise for them, and he would keep to his word.

Grace cried out, her body shuddering as she climaxed. Her insides clenched around his fingers, especially when he squeezed her bottom. Hips bucking, she rode out her pleasure.

"You don't need other men," Alex murmured, thrusting his fingers in deep. "I'll take care of whatever needs you have, Grace. I want to."

She moaned in response.

Pulling his fingers from the clasp of her body, he had her on her back on the bed within seconds. Although her expression was slightly dazed, her eyes flashed with fear and mistrust as she saw him looming over her.

"I'm not going to take you unless you ask, Gracie," he said, even as he undid the front of his breeches and pulled out his cock.

Although he could understand why she would think so. Her drawers had been left on the floor and he was kneeling between her spread, bare legs. The lips of her pussy glistened in the candlelight, pink and plump and utterly tempting. Her chemise was pushed up, above her gorgeous breasts, her nipples slowly softening from their ripe little buds.

Her lips formed a shocked little 'o' as he grasped his cock in hand and reared up on his knees, looking down at her body, all flushed and feminine. The look of shock on her face as he fisted himself only encouraged him. They'd never done anything like this before. Apparently she'd never seen a man rub himself before, because her wide eyes were glued to the sight.

That shock only heightened as thick, white fluid spurted and arched in the air, painting her naked breasts and stomach with his essence as he groaned his release. The last spurts fell on the dark curls of her mound and the parted lips of her pussy as she drew in a shuddering breath.

Sighing in repletion, Alex released himself and reached down to tug off her chemise. To his surprise, Grace didn't argue with him as he pulled it over her head and then used it to wipe his seed from her body. She just watched him with hooded, confused eyes, nibbling her lower lip the entire time.

His cock was already starting to stir again, but he ignored it. Settling beside her on the bed, he wrapped one heavy arm around her body and dragged her into him. She whimpered a bit as her hot bottom pressed against his groin, his semi-hard cock settling into the crack between her cheeks, but she didn't try to pull away or fight him.

It was the first time she had let him cuddle her like this, as the light of the candles went out one by one.

Tenderness and triumph ran through him as he stroked her belly and whispered in her ear how beautiful she was. How well she'd taken her punishment. What a good girl she was.

His chest clenched as he felt her relax and then slump into slumber, her body pressed against his and her head resting on his arm.

It might not seem like a very large step, but he knew it was. He was winning her over, slowly but surely. Surprisingly, spanking seemed to have something to do with it.

Edwin, Hugh, and Wesley were definitely onto something.

CHAPTER 7

he all-too-familiar stirrings of nausea woke her, stronger than ever before. Eleanor groaned, her hand going immediately to her belly. Normally she could hold off in the mornings, at least until Edwin had risen and left the room. Since she often slept a little later than him anyway, he'd never known she was hiding her sick from him.

But now she felt as though she was going to vomit immediately, and he was still in bed with her, his arm around her head and shoulders, which she had been using for a pillow.

Just stay calm... swallow... breathe... oh God...

She lurched off the bed, stumbling, unable to answer as she heard Edwin call her name, his voice disoriented and confused as she abruptly left the bed. Fortunately, the water basin wasn't too far away and had been left empty. Poppy had learned it was usually for the best to bring a fresh basin every morning, after her mistress had already used the empty one.

Bending over, gripping the sides of the basin, Eleanor heaved, and tears sprang to her eyes. Not just from the bitter taste or the stinging in her throat, but because she'd never wanted Edwin to see her like this. So many men lost interest in their wives as soon as they were with child, considering their duty done, but even if Edwin wasn't like that, this was disgusting. Unfeminine. Messy. Smelly. How would he ever be able to look at her the same?

So it shocked her when she heard him sharply calling out the door for Poppy's immediate assistance, and then felt him approach from behind her. The hairs on the back of her neck and arms lifted, making her horribly aware of his presence.

Her robe was placed over her shoulders, and Edwin helped her straighten, pulling her away from the basin as he coughed a little in reaction. Eleanor bit her lip to keep from moaning her humiliation aloud as he wrapped her up in the robe, helping her slide her arms into the sleeves. She couldn't look up at him to see his expression, she was too scared to.

"Oh my lady," said Poppy, rushing in with an expression of concern on her face. "I'm sorry I wasn't prepared, this is so much earlier than usual."

Out of the corner of her eye, Eleanor saw Edwin's mouth open, close, and frown. She winced.

"Earlier?" he asked, his tone sharp. "This happens often?"

Poppy halted mid-stride, nearly sloshing some water on the floor. Her soft brown eyes darted between the master and the mistress as she realized the lady of the house hadn't been quite as forthcoming about her condition as Poppy had thought. Not that the servants knew everything which went on between the Lord and Lady, but none of them had realized he was completely unaware of why his wife never joined him first thing in the morning to break her fast.

"Ah..." she said, obviously searching for words. Eleanor just let out a little groan, which distracted him completely as she swayed slightly. Pulling her into his arms, Edwin let her press her face against his chest while he rubbed her back. She made a small sound of content-ment; her nausea wasn't gone, but it had lost a lot of its immediacy.

Sensing the master was now distracted, Poppy quickly changed out the basins, taking the soiled one from the room. Holding on to Edwin's robe, Eleanor closed her eyes, wishing she could stay just like this forever. Because she knew questions were coming that she didn't want to answer—wasn't sure how to answer.

She was right.

"Nell, why didn't you tell me you were having problems in the mornings?" Edwin's voice was soft, not stern, and filled with concern, but the question still made her feel stubbornly tetchy. Mostly because she was being forced into telling him about her condition, and it definitely wasn't on her terms.

"Why do you care?" she muttered, just barely loud enough for him to hear. She almost winced at how waspish she sounded.

"Nell." This time he said her name a little more sharply, a warning for her to behave and to answer. Instead, she just tried to burrow even more closely into his chest and he sighed, somewhat exasperated. His hands caressed her gently, from shoulders to waist, and she melted against him as his voice lowered to a murmur. "You're going to be the death of me, woman. If I'd known how bad the mornings were for you, I would have been here to take care of you."

Suddenly Eleanor felt as though they were standing on a precipice together, one they'd been moving toward for a long time. One that could make or break her heart.

Tilting her head back, her expression completely serious, she looked up at her husband. "Why?"

THE SEARCHING, almost desperate look in Eleanor's big blue eyes made Edwin hesitate. There had been quite a few times, since their wedding, that he'd felt Eleanor wanted something from him. He just didn't know what and she never seemed inclined to tell him, or even proffer a hint. This was another such moment.

Cupping her face in his hand, he couldn't help but worry his answer would—again—be found lacking. Her soft skin almost looked translucent, she was so pale after her morning sickness. Ever since he'd realized her condition, he'd also seen her becoming more delicate. Never frail, but she seemed more vulnerable, less robust. It made him feel even more protective of her than usual, and he'd done his best to ensure she didn't over exert herself, even as she'd insisted on carrying on almost as normal.

He'd been waiting for days for her to reveal her condition. Part of him had even started to wonder if she hadn't realized why she was so fatigued, but if she didn't know by now she was carrying his child, then he would eat his hat. It was for the wife to announce when she was carrying, but who knew what went on in the feminine mind. He had no idea why Eleanor hadn't told him yet, but as long as she did nothing to endanger herself or the child then he was content to wait.

Still, he didn't want to cause her any distress either. So he parried the question back to her.

"Why wouldn't I want to take care of my wife?" he asked, rubbing his thumb across her cheek as she leaned into the caress. Her eyes sparked, with temper, and he could barely hold back his grin. Even sick and feeling weak, his Eleanor never completely lost her spirit.

"But why would you want to take care of *me*?"

Edwin had quite a reputation with the ladies. He knew what they liked, what they wanted, but when it came to moments like this with his wife, he found himself floundering. The look in her eyes told him quite clearly there was a right answer and a wrong answer, and unless he wanted to see more than just a flash of her temper, he'd better figure out what was what and quickly.

"Because... that's what I do. I'm your husband. I care about you... I want to take care of you..." The waiting expression on her face frustrated him further, as he knew he still wasn't getting it quite right. "Bloody hell... Nell, what do you want from me? I love you, I want to take care of you... what is so wrong with taking care of you?"

Sudden tension in her body had her nearly vibrating as she suddenly refocused on him with an intense look that took his breath away. "You love me?"

Gods above, he would never understand women. "Yes, of course, what—Nell, why are you crying? Stop... dammit, what did I say?"

Eyes awash in wetness, huge tears were welling up and beginning to trickle down her cheeks, too quickly for Edwin to halt them. He had no idea what he'd said wrong, inducing an unaccustomed panic. Usually when she was this upset with him, he at least knew why.

"You really love me?" Her voice was watery, wavering, as she pressed her face against his chest again, frustratingly hiding her expression from him. But the wistful happiness in her voice was something he understood.

"Yes, of course I do, Nell..." he said soothingly, wondering if her condition had affected her head as well. He rubbed her back in small circles, doing his best to placate the little woman.

Suddenly she smacked his chest with her palm, making him yelp in surprise as she pulled away. Dammit, her mood had volleyed again and now she looked incensed. "What do you mean 'of course?' How was I to know you love me when you've never said it before?"

Edwin rubbed his chest, trying to think back. "Haven't I?"

"No, you dolt! I would remember it if you had!"

He gave her a stern look. "No insults, sweetheart. I wouldn't spank you right now, because you're not feeling well, but believe me, I will be keeping a tally over the next seven months and once you're recovered from birthing, you will be getting your due."

To his surprise, his wife froze again, eyeing him warily. Her hand went automatically to her stomach, covering it, and Edwin felt his usual masculine surge of smugness at knowing she was carrying his child.

"You know?"

"Know what?" This might be one of the most confusing conversations he'd ever had with his wife. He'd heard women could become quite volatile during pregnancy—and considering Eleanor could be volatile most of the time, perhaps he shouldn't be surprised he was having a bit of trouble keeping up with her now.

She nibbled her lower lip, looking worried all of the sudden. "That I'm with child."

"Yes, of course, sweetheart," he said gently, wondering at the nervous tension hovering around her. "I've known for a while... I can count you know."

A blush suffused her cheeks, making her look less sickly, which was a relief. "Oh... and... you don't mind?"

It felt like a megrim was growing in the front of his head and he resisted the urge to rub at it. After all, he didn't want to set his wife off. Taking a deep breath, he reached out and pulled her into his arms. She didn't resist, thankfully. Holding her nice and tight, enjoying the way she felt pressed up against him, he lowered his head to murmur in her ear. Obviously, her morning illness *had* affected her mind, and it was his duty to put his wife at ease.

"Nell, I'm thrilled you're carrying our child. I will love him or her, as much as I love you. I'm going to take care of you, when you're ill and when you're well. I will discipline you when you need it. And I will do this for the rest of our lives. Everything about you, including your penchant for occasionally being an unmanageable hoyden, makes me happy. Alright?"

Nodding her head, Eleanor rubbed her face against him. His robe clung damply to his skin.

Dammit, she was crying again.

SOAKING IN HER BATH, Eleanor didn't think she'd ever been so happy. Edwin had taken care of her all morning, until he'd received some correspondence from London that he'd had to answer immediately, and he'd handed her over to Poppy for a bit.

The poor man had seemed a bit at a loss this morning, especially when she'd cried. Which amused her, because he certainly didn't mind her tears when he was turning her bottom a hot, bright red. But when he wasn't doing that, they seemed to panic him a bit.

She still wanted to kick him, just a little, because of his confusion and complete lack of understanding as to why hearing him say "I love you" was so important. When she'd tried to explain, he'd said, "If ever a day should go by when I don't say I love you, may never a moment pass without you knowing I do. Do you hear me sweetheart?" She'd nearly swooned.

Although he'd then admitted to having read it somewhere in the past, but he'd insisted the sentiment was his. A small smile slid across her face as she remembered the panicked expression on his face when he thought she might cry again. Silly man. But his words had warmed her and he'd seemed willing enough when she told him she would like to hear it more often. Even if he didn't understand it.

"You look quite a bit better."

Playfully, she scowled as she opened her eyes, focusing on the darkly handsome man who was closing the door to their bedroom behind him. She couldn't summon up any true ire at the moment. Her mood was far too happy and relaxed.

"Are you saying I looked unattractive earlier?"

Edwin just grinned at her, his dark eyes dancing. "When? Before, during, or after you were emptying your stomach into the basin?"

"Wretch," she said, laughing as she flicked water in his direction. Her heartbeat seemed to pick up as his eyes traveled down to the water she was laying in, lingering on her rounded breasts and pert nipples. Eleanor was feeling *much* better than she had been this morning. Smiling wickedly, she reached for the washcloth hanging on the side of the tub. She had already used it to clean herself, of course, but that wasn't the point.

Her husband's gaze sharpened as she dragged the cloth up her arm, and to her shoulder, watching as the droplets of water ran down her skin. The water was perfectly clear, nothing to obscure his gaze as she moved the cloth down and rubbed the nubby material over her breasts. Her nipples, which had already been hardening, tightened into tiny buds instantly with the stimulation.

"Mmmm," she purred, rubbing them a little harder than was necessary, arching her back to thrust them up. Droplets slid down the exposed curves of her breasts as they rose up out of the water.

"Temptress," her husband rasped. She smiled, hearing the slithering of clothing that indicated he was already undressing.

With a soft little sigh, ignoring his accusation, she ran the washcloth down her stomach and between her legs. The little pleasure bud there stood to attention as she rubbed the cloth in a slow, circular motion over it, making her moan with true pleasure. Warmth pressed against her shoulders and she opened her eyes to look into her husband's.

Dropping the cloth, she tilted her head upwards for a kiss.

"Oh no," he murmured, sliding his hand into the water and picking up the cloth to press it back against her sensitive folds. "Keep going."

Eleanor scowled at him. "I only did it to get you over here."

The rakish grin Edwin gave her made her heart flutter. It looked like he had the very devil in his eyes. "I know... but I want to watch you."

A blush crept up her cheeks. It was one thing to behave like a wanton in order to tease him, quite another to have him so close to her, watching her as she touched herself in a completely unladylike way. Yet, the intense hunger in his dark eyes made her want to please him.

Almost hesitantly, she took the cloth back from him, the water swirling as she circled it over her pleasure nub. Edwin shifted, moving behind her, his mouth lowering to her neck to kiss and suck at the sensitive skin. His hands lowered into the warm water, cupping her breasts and squeezing them. It felt strange and erotic on her slick skin, especially as his fingers pinched her nipples and slid off of them.

Sensations collided, enhancing her pleasure, and she found herself pressing the cloth harder as she rubbed up and down. Edwin's hands plucked and rubbed her nipples, unable to get a firm grip thanks to the water. Arching her back, she found herself moaning as he sucked at the tender skin connecting her neck to her shoulder. Knowing he was watching the movements of her hand under the water, the way the blue cloth contrasted to her golden curls as they swirled in the currents.

The needy itch was growing, blossoming, and she realized she was going to climax from touching herself.

Just as she reached the cusp, Edwin suddenly released her breast, grabbing her arm and pulling it away. She cried out at the interruption, her body straining for the orgasm that was just out of reach.

Leaning over her, Edwin's mouth caught hers, stifling her distress with his kiss. It only made her burn more.

When he pulled away, she glared at him.

"Time to get out of the tub, sweetheart," he said, giving her a knowing look. She gritted her teeth.

"Damn you," she cursed, as he helped her to stand on shaky legs. Then she cried out, shuddering as he pinched her nipple. The tender bud was even more sensitive than usual, and the flash of pain had her clinging to him.

"Don't be naughty, Nell," he teased, although there was a firm note in his voice that indicated he meant what he said. Just because she was with child didn't mean she would be able to run amok, saying and doing whatever she wanted without facing any consequences. Eleanor was sure Edwin would prove creative if he felt the need to punish her. She bit her tongue against cursing him again as he helped her step out of the tub.

Her body felt exquisitely sensitive as he toweled her off, rubbing it briskly over her limbs and spending more time on her breasts and between her legs. Eleanor had her hands pressed on his shoulders to help her keep her balance. She rocked her hips as his fingers slid through her slit, trying to keep the contact.

"Edwin, pleeeease," she said, moaning in distress when he pulled away, leaving her aching.

"Patience, sweetheart," he murmured, dropping the towel down next to the tub. He unpinned her hair, letting it tumble down her back like a cascade of sunlight. Sweeping her up in his arms, he carried her to the bed as she wound her arms around his neck and peppered kisses across his shoulder. Her teeth scraped against his collarbone, making him shudder slightly, and he tightened his arms around her to ensure he didn't accidentally let her drop even an inch.

Handling her like she was made of fine china, he laid her down on the bed, crawling eagerly on top of her and sliding his hands up her arms until he reached her wrists, which he pinned down beside her head. The soft little whimpering noises she made in the back of her throat went straight to his cock, which was already rock hard from watching her touch herself. She rocked underneath him, rubbing herself against him, seeking to be impaled on his rod.

Eleanor's passion never failed to inflame him, making him struggle for self-control as his wife tried to quicken their pace. All his experience as a rake helped, but only so much. He desired Eleanor like he had no other woman in his life. His to cherish, to protect, to love. It still made him chuckle to think how insistent she'd been on hearing the words. Not that he'd ever meant to withhold them from her, he just hadn't realized he'd never said them.

After all, their love match was the talk of the *ton*. Every society matron was constantly commenting on how he doted on her, the way his eyes always followed her. The men were well aware of his affliction, especially the dangerous rakes and seducers. They might eye Eleanor from afar, but they were well aware her husband would be less than accommodating, and none of them had a desire to meet him at dawn merely for flirting with her. Or speaking with her. Or even looking at her. Edwin didn't care that he'd gained a reputation as a possessive and overly affectionate husband. Although he was amused his wife was apparently the only person who hadn't heard the news.

Wrapping his long fingers around both of her slender wrists, he used his free hand to pick up one of the ropes he'd permanently attached to their headboard. It was a soft, silky length of material that he could wind about his wife's wrists without worrying it would harm her delicate skin. And having the rope readily available meant his valet had no more cause to complain about ruined cravats.

"Edwin, no, please," Eleanor begged as he wrapped her wrists tightly, securing them over her head, knowing having her hands tied meant he was going to take his time. Tease her. Play with her. Torment her, while she was bound and helpless and unable to even urge him along.

This was what she got for trying to tease him when she was in her bath.

"Perfect," he murmured, sliding his body back so he could admire the pretty picture she made, with her golden hair spilling across the pillow, her arms stretched upwards, and her breasts thrust up with their pretty pink tips, like a sweet offering for his mouth and hands. He cupped her breasts, watching her face as he pinched her nipples tightly.

Eleanor writhed, the stinging sensation of pain mingled with pleasure shooting through her and making her already sensitive body wind even tighter around the tension in her belly. Her husband was looming over her like a dark god, his eyes boring into her, watching every nuance of her expression as he pinched and rolled the tender buds, tugging on them and making her pant as she twisted and squirmed beneath him. Rubbing her thighs together did nothing to ease the growing need between them, and she groaned, arching her back and begging him for more.

Scooting back, Edwin straddled her thighs, one hand still on her breast, the other gliding down her stomach toward her mound.

"Edwin, please, touch me," she begged, trying to lift her hips, but unable to with his weight on her lower body.

"I am touching you, sweetheart."

She moaned. "More... please... touch my... my pussy."

Those were the magic words. Edwin loved to hear her breathlessly begging him, using terms that would never pass her lips in any other situation. On the other hand, she knew that too, and she was becoming more comfortable using them. Hoping it would push him into doing what she wanted.

So he slid one finger down her slit, feeling the scalding heat of her folds, gliding through the slick cream.

"Like this?" he asked, swirling his finger in a small circle.

Eleanor groaned, squirming beneath him even more as she tried to trap his hand, to rock against him. "No, Edwin, please, more."

"So bossy," he said, shaking his head. "But you're not in charge, are you, Eleanor?"

"No," she said, her blue eyes pleading with him to give her what she wanted. Needed. She was willing to say anything to get it.

Leaning down, he kissed her belly, amazed it held the spark of life beneath its slightly rounded surface. His finger probed and she gasped, shuddering as he pumped his finger slowly in and out of her grasping channel. When he withdrew again, her voice broke on a sob.

Quick as a wink, Edwin had her flipped over, settling her on her knees with her upper body stretched out before her. She looked over her shoulder at him, her expression a mixture of sexual frustration, need and outrage.

"You said you weren't going to spank me while I'm pregnant!"

"I said I wouldn't punish you," Edwin said, holding one hand on her lower back to keep her in place, his other hand raising and coming down on her rump with a sharp smack. His wife let out a low moan, her hips pressing up against his hand on her lower back, as if trying to lift her bottom to ask for more. "I don't want you distressed... but this isn't distressing you, is it Nell?"

His voice was a low, seductive croon, and as he spanked the other side of Eleanor's bottom, she moaned again. It was true, she wasn't the slightest bit distressed. If anything, she was more turned on than ever. Edwin's darker fantasies were beyond anything she could fabricate for herself, but whenever they indulged in them, it aroused her to wild heights. She trusted him not to harm her, and truthfully she couldn't see the harm in being spanked like this, as he wasn't anywhere near her belly, but she'd had to protest anyway. Even though she liked it, sometimes, when he spanked her, she always felt as though she should voice the proper, feminine outrage.

She really shouldn't enjoy it when he ignored her protests completely.

The flurry of stinging slaps to her backside had her burning up, inside and out. She moaned as Edwin's hand punished, then caressed, and then stroked her soaked slit, before rising up and peppering her bottom with sharp smacks again. Tugging at the restraints, she begged him for more every time he thrust his fingers inside of her, the pleasure rising up until she felt like she might orgasm from the feel of his hand coming down on her burning, aching flesh.

Edwin spanked her until her bottom was a hot, flushed pink and her arousal was dripping down her thighs. His cockhead was dark red, angry looking and demanding to be buried inside of her. Something he wasn't going to deny himself any longer.

Flipping his wife on to her back, Edwin grasped her thighs and pulled them apart. The swollen lips of her pussy blossomed like a flower, coated with creamy dew, her clitoris so plump and eager that it was engorged larger than he'd ever seen before. Hooking her legs over his arms, he reached up to cup her breasts as he lined up his cock with her wet heat.

"Yes, oh please, Edwin, please, yeeeesss!" Eleanor screamed as he thrust forward, her body bowing and clamping down around him as he pinched down on her nipples and used them to hold her in place as he filled her.

Her pussy spasmed around him, her legs bending and trying to draw him in further as she sobbed out in ecstasy. Making a low, growling noise in the back of his throat, Edwin leaned forward and began to pound into her, hard, fast and mercilessly, knowing she was aroused enough she could take it. In fact, Eleanor had started to orgasm almost the moment he'd entered her, stretching her open with the delicious friction of his cock sliding inside of her.

With her wrists tied to the bed, and her lower body in Edwin's complete control, there was nothing she could do but shriek and convulse around him as he ravished her. Her pussy tingled and fizzed as her first climax began to subside, unable to fully dissipate while Edwin was still moving inside of her, his body rubbing against her sensitive swollen lips and the fat bud of her clit.

He was rock hard, a length of steel invading her body, and rubbing over an exquisitely pleasurable spot with every thrust. Eleanor writhed, knowing he was watching her every shudder, every twist of her body, and she enjoyed it. Knowing his entire focus was on her was a blissfully satisfying experience, even if the rush of pleasure was becoming almost painful in its intensity.

A second orgasm overtook her as he ground his body against hers, trapping her clit between them and using his pelvis to send waves of ecstasy surging through her. Eleanor cried out, her pussy tightening around the thick rod inside of her, trying to milk it of its seed.

Instead, Edwin continued to thrust, hard and deep, making her scream as her body bowed and tried to move beneath him. She tried to press her legs together, but his arms held them too tightly. There were no defenses for her vulnerable pussy as his merciless assault on her most tender spots continued.

She sobbed with relief and release as he groaned and surged, his cock swelling inside of her, throbbing against her inner walls as spurt after spurt of hot seed filled her. Drops of moisture clung to her long lashes as they fluttered, her eyes rolling upwards as the last spasms of pleasure were wrung from her body.

Edwin's forearms kept him from putting his full weight on Eleanor as he released her legs and leaned over her, finding her lips with his. He was careful not to put any pressure against her stomach, although she didn't seem any worse for wear from their vigorous lovemaking. Kissing him back, she made those happy, dreamy sounds that indicated he'd tamed her—for now at least.

Pulling his lips away, he looked down into those sapphire blue eyes which had captured him from the very beginning, even if he hadn't known at the time quite what that had meant.

"I love you, Eleanor," he said, shifting his weight to one arm so he could cup and caress her cheek, loving the softness of her skin, the submissiveness he felt in her every languid movement. "You're the perfect woman for me, never doubt it."

The happiness shining out of her eyes was unshaded, and he knew he'd finally found the right words, the ones she'd been waiting to hear.

CHAPTER 8

*D*amn his mother and her blasted notions of 'fun' traditions. Scowling into his cup, Wesley contemplated disobeying a direct order from his mother, so he could at least spend the evening in the company of his bride. Whose bloody awful idea was it to keep the bride and groom apart for the night before the wedding?

He could hear the gaggle of females, even from half a floor away. Another one of his mother's ideas; having Cynthia's friends over to help entertain her the evening before. Or, possibly, just to keep her occupied while his mother attended to all the last minute decisions and tasks necessary to any major event. She was absolutely in her element with this wedding nonsense.

Truthfully, he didn't begrudge his mother her fun—he just wished it didn't come at the expense of his own.

If Cynthia had been alone... well, he wouldn't have anticipated the wedding night of course, but they'd already done a few things and he wouldn't be averse to indulging in more of those. After all, there was a certain illicit thrill to engaging in sensual activities with his bride before she was actually his wife.

Growling under his breath, Wesley decided to quit the house and head to Edwin's for the sake of his own sanity. It was only a short carriage ride from here to the house Edwin was renting. An even shorter distance to Alex's, although he was fairly certain Alex had joined Hugh at Edwin's. Nell was here, with Cynthia, Grace, and Irene, so the husbands had all gathered at Edwin's. Originally Wesley had intended to stay in his own house, hoping for a chance to see Cynthia at some point—not that he would ever admit the sentiment to anyone—and sneak her off somewhere for a bit of fun.

If they'd been in London, he would have indulged in the expected stag night, although he privately admitted to himself that he would have still preferred to try and debauch his bride a little further rather than sit in some smoky den with women who didn't actually interest him and a host of other drunken men. Although, considering his closest friends were now all happily married, it was distinctly possibly there wouldn't have been any loose women at his stag night anyway. Which would have been fine with him. The only loose woman he was interested in was Cynthia, and the damned wench had better only be loose with him.

He'd been hoping to get a little stag night celebration with her, but it seemed like she was doing just bloody fine without him.

Another peal of feminine laughter rang down the hallway.

Tossing back the remains of his drink, Wesley swallowed, ignoring the burn in his throat, and slammed the glass down on the table next to him. Enough was enough. Bounding up and into the hall, he stalked toward the front of the house, resigned to the fate of becoming just like his friends, patiently waiting for their wives to come home. Although at least they could look forward to warm bodies in their beds tonight, unlike him.

Well, perhaps Alex might be sympathetic. The man had been as quiet as ever when it came to discussing what was going on between him and his wife. Maybe Wesley wasn't alone when it came to an empty bed.

～

DESPITE THE CONCERNS nagging at her all day, Grace was thoroughly enjoying herself. She'd hoped to be able to sneak into Alex's study and go through his things, to find some clue as to his desire for a reconciliation, but he'd been in the blasted room all day. In fact, he'd still been in it when she'd left the house to come to Cynthia's.

The atmosphere with the other three women was so relaxed she could almost forget the tension dogging her every waking hour. Although the Countess had greeted them upon their arrival, she'd quickly excused herself to go attend to other matters, leaving the younger women to their own devices. Dressed in their less formal gowns, they'd sipped sherry (probably a bit more than was wise, and Eleanor had had weak tea because her stomach was feeling unsettled), eaten chocolate, and given Cynthia all sorts of interesting marriage advice. Discussion and celebration of Eleanor's pregnancy, once she confided the news to them, had led to a discussion of intimate bedroom proceedings.

Grace was actually learning quite a bit.

Especially when Cynthia had told them about using her mouth on the Earl.

"Your *mouth?*" she said, shocked. Not just from the stunning visual, but from the very idea of it.

"Yes," Cynthia said, looking at her curiously. "You mean, you've never?"

Shaking her head, Grace fought back a blush as she tried not to contemplate the idea. When she glanced at Eleanor in an appeal for help, she was surprised to see her friend's cheeks turn pink as well.

"Really?" Irene's astonishment was just too much for them to handle, as she asked the question in a kind of superior surprise. All three of them turned to look at the redhead, whom they'd all considered a bit of a prude, shocked at her nonchalance. She looked back at them, as primly as she always did. "What? Is it an unusual thing to do?"

"Good grief, what kind of wedding night talk did you have with *your* mother?" Eleanor asked, sounding absolutely scandalized.

Considering the icy coldness of the Baroness, Irene's mother, Grace couldn't imagine the woman sharing that kind of information either.

"She didn't really tell me much of anything," Irene said, shrugging her shoulders. "I just do whatever Hugh wants me to. He likes it when I use my mouth. It's quite a lot of fun, actually."

"Oh no, no," Eleanor said, shaking her head as she put her hands over her ears. "I'm not listening... I think my ears are bleeding!" All of them fell over giggling at her antics and the horrified expression on her face. Grace pressed her hand to her stomach, trying to control her mirth as tears sparked in her eyes she was laughing so hard. She'd never seen Eleanor so perturbed.

When they finally regained control over themselves, she couldn't contain her curiosity. "But really... what do you do?"

"Oh no, don't ask them about it," Eleanor said, giving Cynthia a stern look. "I can't tell you the amount of trouble I got into when I tried it with Edwin. He was sure I had learned it from some other man."

It was like a thundercloud suddenly shutting out the sun. Grace's chest went tight inside, as if her rib cage had wrapped around her heart and squeezed. While Edwin's suspicions of Eleanor were definitely without merit, if Grace and Alex were to reconcile and she was to try something so new with him... would he be upset? The others were exchanging glances, and Eleanor looked incredibly regretful of what she'd said.

"I'm sorry, Grace," she murmured, reaching out and grabbing Grace's hand, a forlorn expression on her face. "I wasn't thinking... I just spoke..."

Giving her friend a wan smile, Grace patted Eleanor's hand. "I'm alright. I know you didn't mean anything by it, and you're right." She gave a brittle little laugh. "With all my lovers, you'd think I would have been the one with the most experience."

That was certainly true. Although, she'd never been particularly adventurous in the bedroom. Once Alex had left, she'd been careful to keep things pleasurable, but light. She knew from her time with him that it was very possible to get creative, and some of her lovers had tried, but Grace hadn't encouraged any kind of experimentation. That was the quickest way to get kicked out of her bed, in fact. Keep things enjoyable and rote, that had been her motto when it came to her lovers.

"Who was the best lover?" Cynthia asked. The question made Irene shriek with horror. Eleanor whacked the curious brunette with her fan, and Grace burst into laughter. Trust the unmanageable hoyden to be the one to break the tension. She wished she could keep Cynthia with her all the time. Eleanor might be her best friend, but she didn't have Cynthia's irreverence, which had proven remarkably effective at jostling Grace out of her misery whenever it came crashing down.

"You can't ask her that!" Irene was so appalled she was actually trembling, her voice a high-pitched squeak. It made Grace want to cover her ears, the way Eleanor had done a few minutes ago.

"But I want to know!" Cynthia protested. "She's the only one who can tell me if I'm going to get bored with one man or not, isn't she?"

"Well I can tell you I'm not bored," Irene snapped.

"You don't have a point of comparison."

"I don't need one!"

"Children, children, calm down," Grace interjected, since Eleanor was laughing too hard to. She gave them both a slightly strained smile. Although Cynthia's question had made her laugh and loosened the tension in the room, answering it kept her spirits dampened. "Alex was always the best."

Silence descended and she avidly wished her life wasn't so complicated. Just like her to bring down the happiness of everyone else right before a wedding.

"Why?"

Irene groaned. Eleanor laughed. Cynthia looked at both of them in exasperation. "What? What did I do now? The why is important, don't you think?"

"It's the most important thing," Grace said. Perhaps her own relationship with Alex had fallen apart, but since they were all handing out marriage advice to Cynthia, she was going to give the young woman the best words of wisdom she had. Maybe Cynthia would be able to make a better go of it. Certainly, Wesley was head over heels in love with the young chit, and she was fairly certain Cynthia loved him back. It wouldn't do for her to accidentally ruin their relationship because of her natural curiosity, and Grace hoped her words would help Cynthia to realize that. "It was always the best with Alex because, for me, it wasn't just about the physical. I loved him and it made everything we did together transcend regular pleasure. With my lovers... it was enjoyable. I found my pleasure. But it wasn't the same. There's nothing more incredible than making love with someone you love."

This time the silence in the room was different. Reverent. Irene and Eleanor were glowing, but also looking at her with a kind of sympathetic sadness. She refused to think of it as pity. Cynthia looked thoughtful.

"So, why are you fighting becoming reconciled with him?"

Maybe it was Cynthia's guilelessness. Maybe it was the sherry. Maybe it was because she was finally starting to seriously consider Alex might be genuine in his desire to reconcile.

The whole story came spilling from her lips. They all listened, Eleanor with the sympathy of a friend who had already heard everything, holding Grace's hand and giving it the occasional supportive squeeze. Across from them, Irene listened with pursed lips, as though she was keeping in some of her thoughts, allowing Grace to fully have her say. Which made Grace wonder what insights Irene might have into Alex's behavior. It still hurt her, a bit, how close Alex and Irene had been, how much more Irene had known him, but it was a distant kind of hurt. Irene no longer flaunted their relationship the way she had back then, and she'd apologized for her previous actions.

Cynthia was listening very carefully, chewing on her lower lip. She brightened when Grace got to the part about wanting to search through Alex's papers, to see if she could find a hint or even some evidence about any business transactions that might be spurring his decision. Of course, Eleanor groaned in disgust at Grace's plan, since she hadn't heard it before.

"That's a terrible idea," Eleanor said, shaking her head. "What if nothing's there? Then will you believe him?"

"It would help," Grace argued. "I know it's not definitive, but if there's nothing condemning there, then at least I know."

"I think it's *brilliant*," Cynthia gushed, leaning forward in her seat, her hazel eyes sparkling with mischief. "In fact, I think we should do it tonight."

"We?"

"Tonight?"

Irene's squeak came right on top of Grace's question. The prim and proper redhead looked horrified at the idea she was about to become a part of this.

"Of course!" Cynthia said enthusiastically. She pointed at Irene and Eleanor. "You told us your husbands decided to spend the evening together, yes? Do you really think Alex isn't there? They'll probably be up all night drinking, thinking us safely tucked away *here*. Besides, she certainly won't get a chance tomorrow. And don't you want to know what his correspondence says?"

Reckless Eleanor looked like she wanted to say yes, but Irene was already shaking her head. "What if we're caught? How are we going to avoid being seen by the servants? Don't you think Manfred will notice if we all go missing from this room? Besides, I can tell you right now I'm fairly certain Alex loves you," she said, looking beseechingly at Grace. Her words made Grace's heart jump in her chest, even though she couldn't quite bring herself to believe them. "When you were married, he was the happiest I've ever seen him... and after you left, it was like all his emotions just closed up and went away."

"That could have been because I humiliated him by leaving him," Grace countered, keeping her heart cold against the hope always trying to batter its way in. "My father is completely closed against me as well."

"Alex isn't like that..." Irene said, but then she shook her head, a rueful expression crossing her face. "But then, sometimes I wonder if I know Alex as well as I think. I would have never expected him to spank his wife, and I certainly wouldn't have thought he'd ever say one woman is as good as another for his wife. I know he would do anything for his business, he loves his work, but..." Irene sighed. "I'm not helping am I?"

"Nope," Cynthia said, turning her attention back to Grace. "Which is why we should absolutely search his study tonight."

Even though part of her was clamoring to say yes, Grace hesitated. "But... Irene made some good points. What about Manfred?"

The Countess' butler checked in on them every so often, ostensibly to see if they needed anything, but probably also to reassure himself Cynthia wasn't running amok without the Countess to watch over her. Grace was under the impression he didn't trust the other women to be able to control her. He probably didn't realize how true that was.

"What if I stay here?" Irene said, rather eagerly. She glanced at the clock on the mantle. "Manfred hasn't checked on us in a while, he'll probably be by soon. If you leave after he checks on us, there should be plenty of time for you to return, and if you aren't back before he comes again, I can say you've gone to the retiring room."

All of them looked at Irene with varying degrees of admiration. Despite the fact that she obviously didn't want to be party to the search of Alex's study, her deviousness and willingness to contribute in a very key way was impressive. Grace would probably have given up, rather than come up with something so sneaky.

Eleanor sighed, pulling her hand away from Grace and laying both of her palms over the very slight swell of her stomach. It was only visible because she was sitting down and she wasn't wearing a gown requiring a corset. "I should probably stay here as well," she said, regretfully, her hand briefly caressing her stomach. "It would still look suspicious if Irene was just sitting here alone. Besides, someone should keep her company." The two women smiled at each other, Irene looking rather relieved she wouldn't completely be on her own.

"Well I'm going with Grace," Cynthia announced, her eyes sparkling with anticipation. Even in the face of her enthusiasm, Grace could still feel herself hesitating. There would still be the other servants to contend with. And what if Alex came home early? But

Cynthia was also right about this being a golden opportunity. "Please," the younger woman begged. "It sounds like so much fun—think of it as a wedding present to me."

The happy eagerness with which she made her suggestion had Grace laughing again. Truly, she had laughed more in the company of her friends here in Bath than she had in years, and mostly due to Cynthia. The young woman was, quite simply, outrageous. When Wesley did take her to London, she would either be a hit or even more of a scandal than Grace had been. Although, since he was already considered a bit of an eccentric, due to his flaunting of fashion and his bronzed skin, as well as his outspoken interest in trade, Cynthia would probably be dubbed an Original, rather than a scandal.

"Very well," said Grace, her heart beginning to hammer inside of her chest. "We'll do it."

COMFORTABLY ENSCONCED IN A PLUSH CHAIR, Hugh swirled his brandy and raised his glass.

"To Wesley and his bride—may she ever keep him on his toes."

"Which will keep her bottom very red," Wesley parried, raising his own glass amid the laughter. Hugh could only shake his head.

Although he did admit it aroused him to discipline his wife, he certainly didn't consider it a necessity to life, like Wesley did. Edwin too, although Hugh did his best not to think about that. He was more than content with Irene's sweetness, her passion, her eagerness in his bed. The occasional spanking surely added a bit of spice, but he was happiest when she didn't require it. As he'd thought, he preferred a wife who wasn't constantly getting into trouble, like his sister had. A wife like Cynthia would probably put him in his grave decades early; Wesley seemed to thrive on it.

"Do you think she does it on purpose?" Alex asked, tapping one long finger against his glass.

To Hugh's surprise, the usually stone-faced lord seemed almost relaxed tonight. It was the first time Hugh had really seen him enjoying himself. Since arriving in Bath, Alex had sought out advice from all three of the other men about disciplining his wife, but he hadn't talked about the results at all. He kept everything very close to his chest, unlike Wesley, who had a tendency to share a bit too much.

"Does what on purpose?" Edwin asked.

"Gets into trouble," Alex said. His hazel eyes were slightly out of focus, as if he was looking at something far away, or deep within. "I think Gracie has started deliberately trying to provoke me."

"I wouldn't put it past either of them," Wesley said. A small, sadistic smile played on his lips. "However, I would hope Cynthia's punishments are enough to keep her from misbehaving in a way I would truly be upset over."

"Or it'll just teach her not to get caught," Hugh said. "I'm sure Eleanor didn't receive half the punishments she likely deserved." He'd even covered for her a few times, as a good big brother should. Usually when the offense was minor, or he himself was somehow involved in her antics. That had only been when they were children though, as he'd gotten older and taken on more responsibility— including disciplining her—he'd stopped participating in her wild schemes and she'd started hiding them from him.

All of the men mulled over this likely scenario. Wesley looked like he anticipated the challenge and Hugh silently wished him luck. He was sure his friend would need all he could get.

Before another topic of discussion could be raised, a knock sounded at the door, making all of them look up, and then at Edwin, in surprise. He shook his head, looking just as caught off guard as the rest of them. Although they knew quite a few people in Bath, as the *ton* had come trickling in for the wedding on the morrow, they hadn't been expecting anyone to join them. Edwin's butler opened the door, an expression of concern on his face and he gave an apologetic bow to all of them as he handed his employer a note.

Edwin's countenance darkened as he read over it quickly, his jaw clenching. "Speaking of getting caught..." He thrust the note at Hugh as he nodded to the butler. "Thank you, Banks. Get our coats, please, it appears we're going out."

The other two crowded 'round Hugh as Edwin spoke, wanting to know what had perturbed him.

The short note was written in a heavy, severe hand.

My Lord Hyde,

I regret I must request you inform the Earl of Spencer he is needed at the house at once. His ward and one of our guests have gone missing. Your wife and Viscountess Petersham are currently still in the drawing room here.

With regrets for the intrusion,

William Manfred

The curses came fast and furious as all of the gentlemen swiftly downed the last of their drinks and set them aside. So much for thinking his own wife had become a paragon of virtues. He didn't doubt for one moment Irene knew where Grace and Cynthia had got to, if they'd disappeared.

And he was prepared to do whatever was necessary to convince her to part with the information.

THE MOMENT the men came storming through the door, Irene knew they were caught. Not that it stopped either her or Eleanor from putting on their most innocent expressions. The gimlet look in her husband's eye as he strode toward her said he wasn't buying her act for a second. Nervous butterflies flocked to her stomach.

Defying Hugh wasn't something she was cut out for, but she would do her best. She completely avoided looking at Alex, not wanting to give anything away. Besides which, she was feeling more than displeased with her old friend at the moment. Although she hadn't liked Grace at the beginning of their marriage, that still didn't mean he should have said the things he did to Grace's father. Now, having become friendlier with the other woman, she no longer blamed Grace for her behavior at all.

Irene knew full well she herself was lucky Hugh cared so deeply for her that he had fallen in love with her. But he'd also started out their marriage with the appropriate sentiments. She was appalled at Alex's attitude toward marriage. Why should Grace treat their relationship as something worthwhile when he didn't?

She didn't realize it, but her chin tilted up at a stubborn angle as she looked back at the men, feigning calm. Only her hands, clenched in her lap, gave away her nerves. That and the tiny tremors shivering through her body. Beside her, Eleanor, much more practiced at being in trouble, raised a questioning eyebrow at her approaching husband.

While Wesley and Alex hung back, it was clear they were even more agitated than Hugh or Edwin, who looked like avenging furies as they loomed over their wives.

"My Lords," Eleanor said smoothly, and Irene mentally blessed her. Her own throat was so tight with nerves she could barely breathe, much less talk. "To what do we owe the pleasure?"

Edwin crossed his arms over his chest, the stern look on his face making Irene quail. She didn't know how Eleanor managed to remain so collected, looking up at him as if she didn't have a care in the world. Peeking at her own husband, Irene felt her tremors increase at his severe countenance. Every inch of her wanted to squirm under his authoritarian gaze.

"Where are Cynthia and Grace?" Edwin asked, his mild tone completely at odds with the stern look on his face. Deceptively mild, that was what it was, Irene thought. She didn't trust it any more than the men trusted her and Eleanor's wide-eyed innocence.

"Why the retiring room, of course," Eleanor said with a little laugh, her eyes meeting each man in turn, with a look that said they were all being silly. More than ever, Irene admired her sister-in-law. The lie wouldn't hold up for more than a few minutes, but Eleanor looked completely serene, even facing off against the four large and very intimidating men in the room.

Even knowing her and Irene's bottoms were going to pay for it.

Irene bit on her lower lip. She hated the look of disappointment on Hugh's face as she didn't speak up and avoided meeting his eyes, even when she peeked at him through her lashes. Eventually either she or Eleanor would break, and she was honest enough to know it would probably be her, but she would delay the men for as long as possible. Give Grace and Cynthia the time to search, so at least their punishments wouldn't be in vain.

"I think we both know that's not true." The growing menace in Edwin's voice made Irene shiver again. She actually shrank into herself as Hugh spoke up.

"Perhaps Irene and I should move to a different room to talk," he said. "Wesley, do you have a room we could use?"

Staring at her hands in her lap, Irene's bottom clenched. She instinctively knew why Hugh wanted privacy. It was what she had expected. Eleanor was protected by her condition, but going by the look on Edwin's face, he was already thinking about lighting into her bottom once it was safe to. Not that it quailed Eleanor in the slightest, unlike Irene.

She knew she was their weak spot. Unused to standing up to her mother. Unused to being spanked. Unused to doing anything other than what was expected of her.

"My study," Wesley said, his voice hard, not at all like the laughing, flirtatious rake she was used to seeing him as. Quite suddenly, she realized this was the side of him Cynthia probably saw most often. Stern, imposing, and, as Cynthia would say, a "stuffed-shirt." Although, right now he certainly had reason to be. "The chair is in there."

Irene stifled a little moan as Hugh reached out and took her arm, lifting her to her feet.

"Wait," said Eleanor, reaching out to grab Irene's hand. The men all stilled, looking at the rebellious blonde as she tugged Irene back down beside her. Hugh allowed it, although he kept his hand on Irene's arm. His thumb caressed her skin, even as his fingers remained firmly gripping her. It was both reassuring and anxiety inducing. Irene knew she was going to be spanked tonight, but she was relieved it had been put off for at least a few minutes. Eleanor's cool sapphire gaze slid around the room again, not lingering on any single man. "They went for a walk."

"Where?" Wesley demanded through gritted teeth. He stepped forward from his place by the door, Alex only a pace behind him. Irene tried to lean back, away from them, even though they were nowhere near her, but Hugh's hand held her in place. "It's far too late in the evening for them to be out walking alone."

"Nell, where did they go?" Edwin asked, his voice foreboding as he loomed over his wife in a most intimidating manner. The little smirk she gave him said she wasn't nearly as daunted as Irene was. Leaning over, he whispered in Eleanor's ear, softly enough that none of the other men could hear what he was saying, but Irene could just make out the threat. "I may not be able to spank you right now, but for every minute you wait to tell me, I will add on a day you will not be allowed to climax."

Irene's cheeks paled along with Eleanor's.

She could only assume the two of them had at least as lusty a relationship as she and Hugh; she couldn't imagine being with him every night and not being able to climax. That was awful! Irene almost thought she'd prefer to be spanked. At least she was still allowed to find her pleasure after that particular discipline.

But Eleanor's primrose lips still firmed in rebellion. Her head tilted up as she gave her husband a saucy smile, the tension stretching between them as their wills collided. Irene bit down on her own lip, looking back and forth between them. Eleanor's expression was almost taunting, while Edwin was looking at her with a mix of frustration and the same hunger Irene often saw in her own husband's eyes. Everyone in this room knew Eleanor would never play this game if Cynthia and Grace were up to something truly dangerous, but now the stakes had been laid down, she would follow it through to the bitter end.

"That's one," Edwin said, after glancing at the clock.

Eleanor's chin tilted up even further, her smile becoming taut, and Irene saw the other men exchanging glances, as if wondering what Edwin had threatened her with. As she looked up, Hugh caught her gaze, and Irene immediately dropped her eyes back to her lap again, squirming a bit as she felt his scrutiny boring into her.

"They're perfectly safe," Eleanor said, sound like a prim and proper matron at tea. Irene was in awe of her composure. "They didn't go far." Neither Alex nor Wesley looked very reassured by her words, if anything, they looked more anxious now.

"Two."

The fingers on Irene's arm tightened, and she knew Hugh was considering removing her from the room to find out where the women were. The stalling tactics were doing nothing to help her or Eleanor. She couldn't stand the thought Eleanor was going to be punished for trying to shield her; even if they had both been trying to give Grace the time she needed, it was different when Irene was sitting right there, knowing what Eleanor was going to have to live with (or, really, without) during the next few days.

"Three."

"Grace went to her and Alex's house, and Cynthia went with her," Irene blurted out.

The look Eleanor gave her contained almost as much exasperation as it did gratitude. Somehow, Irene didn't think Eleanor's pride would have allowed her to give in at this point, so in some ways, Irene was protecting her now. Although she had given up Grace and Cynthia, but that was always a foregone conclusion. Either way, the men would get their hands on them, and it didn't make sense for her and Eleanor to suffer more than they had to, just to give the other women time to get back.

Hopefully by now they'd had enough time to go through Alex's correspondence.

"Let's go." Alex spun on his heel and stalked out of the room, Wesley right behind him.

"I believe we'll be leaving as well," Edwin said, holding out his hand for Eleanor to take. She didn't look like she wanted to, but she did anyway, with a small sigh, as if in acknowledgement she'd gotten herself into enough trouble for tonight.

"Us as well," Hugh said, pulling Irene up. His voice sounded grimly determined and her insides quivered. It had been a while since Hugh had felt she needed discipline, but she hadn't forgotten how much a spanking hurt. Even though she'd eventually spoken up, she knew it would only gain her the slightest of reprieves, considering her prevarication. "Irene and I apparently need to have a very long... talk."

She gulped, meekly moving with her husband as he led her purposefully toward the door.

Oh she was in so much trouble.

CHAPTER 9

*G*rimly leading his suddenly submissive wife to their bedroom, Hugh could only wonder what she had been thinking. He'd been glad she'd made friends with the others, especially Grace since there had been such friction there; now he was wondering if his approval had come too swiftly. Apparently none of them were a good influence on her.

Although at least she and Eleanor had stayed behind from whatever trouble Cynthia and Grace were getting into.

"Why did Grace and Cynthia go out?" he asked, leading Irene to the bed.

She looked quite soft and feminine, like a sweet paragon of virtues in her pale green dress. The look she gave him, however, was anything but. "For private reasons."

Hugh raised his eyebrow. It was obvious Irene knew she was going to be punished, and yet she was still defying him? On the other hand, if she had been sworn to secrecy by her confederates, then he could understand her stubbornness a bit.

"Anything that will affect us?" he asked, mildly. As much as he wanted his wife to share everything with him, he also knew he had to accept there would be occasions when she was the confidant of other people's secrets. It would be unreasonable of him to expect her to disgorge another's confidence, as he certainly didn't tell her everything he, Wesley, Edwin, and Alex talked about.

To her credit, she thought it over for a brief moment before shaking her head. "No... It will only affect Grace and Alex."

His curiosity roused, but he wasn't going to punish Irene for being a true friend. Unless he planned on utterly controlling every aspect of her life, including her relationships, he couldn't. And he wasn't that kind of man.

With her hands twisting together in front of her, Irene glanced at him and then down at the ground, and then back at him, obviously nervous. As she should be. Even if he wasn't going to press for why Grace and Cynthia had left the house, as they weren't his responsibility, he was still going to discipline his wife for her part in their machinations. Not too harshly, because she had stayed where she had told him she would be.

So had Eleanor, but he doubted it was for the same reasons as Irene. His wife preferred to be good, which was part of why he loved her. It was his duty to ensure she had reason to remain that way and not be tempted or corrupted by her friends and his sister.

"Very well." He had to suppress a smile as Irene relaxed slightly with a long sigh of relief. She so badly wanted to please him, to not disappoint him. No man could be unaffected by such sweet devotion. "But we still have to deal with your own transgressions. I understand you wished to protect your friends, but you did them no favors by prevaricating. Have you heard from them since they left Wesley's house? How do you know they arrived safely at their location? How do you know they remain safe?"

The questions made Irene feel suddenly sick. She'd known from the beginning Cynthia's idea was questionable, although her objections had mostly focused on how easily they could all be caught. It hadn't even occurred to her to worry about Grace and Cynthia's safety; after all, the house Alex had rented wasn't too far from the Countess'. Yet, it was nighttime and they had left unescorted by any male protection, and even if they did reach Alex's house unmolested, they wouldn't be able to send a servant with a message for Eleanor and Irene. Even if the entire mission had been successful, and the men hadn't found out they'd gone missing, that would have meant a second trip back through the streets in the darkness. Obviously, Eleanor had been convinced they were in no danger, but what if—

Her hand swung up to cover her mouth as her mind whirled with terrible visions, and suddenly Hugh was standing before her, pulling her into the safe, warm circle of his arms and murmuring soothingly. "Relax sweetheart, I'm sure they're fine. They didn't have very far to go between the houses. Alex and Wesley will find them, and woe betide anyone who sought to molest them. I just wanted to point out the dangers, not distress you so."

He actually sounded rather contrite, and she frowned, realizing he had exaggerated the danger just a bit. Although he'd still made some good points.

"I'm not sure I'll be able to sleep tonight, if we don't find out what happened to them," she muttered, smacking his chest lightly. Her heart still felt like it was in her throat as her mind raced with all the things that could go wrong, when two ladies stepped out into the night on their own. Of course, they weren't in London, and Bath was much safer.

"I'm sure I can help you to sleep, wife," Hugh said, and for just a moment she saw the anticipatory glint of passion in his blues eyes. Just as quickly, it faded, to be replaced by a stern look. Worries about Grace and Cynthia moved to the back of her mind, as worry for her own person rose up to take precedence. "After we finish your spanking."

Hearing that she was receiving a spanking, instead of a harsher punishment, should have been a relief, but it was hard to feel relieved when she knew how much a spanking from Hugh could hurt. A lesser punishment was still bloody painful, as Eleanor would say. Of course she would choose a spanking over a birching or a belting, but Irene would rather not have any punishment at all. But she knew she deserved it.

She didn't regret her actions, or trying to give Grace and Cynthia more time, but she'd known when she made the choice that she would face the consequences later.

Releasing her from his arms, Hugh walked over to the bed and sat down, patting his lap. "Come here, Irene."

Sometimes she wished he would just drag her. It would be so much easier than having to willingly walk to her own punishment. There was a sharp fluttering in her stomach increased the closer she came to him. Stifling a little moan, she lay herself over his lap, her legs hanging down on one side, her upper body across the bed.

The feel of her skirts sliding up her legs, and then Hugh's warm hand on her thigh and bottom, made her shiver. His finger traced little patterns on the creamy flesh of her buttocks, as if inspecting the area he was about to redden.

"Do you understand why you're being punished, Irene?"

"Yes," she said, her voice tight. She could already feel the tears rising in the back of her eyes, even though he hadn't even started yet. The anticipation was wringing her nerves. At this moment, she wished he would just get on with it, but she knew once he started, she would wish he'd kept stalling. "Because I didn't tell you where Grace and Cynthia had gone."

"I commend loyalty to your friends, but your loyalty must, first and foremost, be to me," he said, still stroking her bottom. His palm felt hot against her skin and she squirmed a bit again. This part felt good, which was only going to make the actual spanking feel even worse by comparison. "I will not tolerate lying to me, not directly and not by omission."

"I'm sorry, Hugh," she said, miserably. She really was too. If she had to do it all over again... well, she wasn't sure what she would do, but she did feel guilty she had made it seem like she valued her friends over her husband. Not to mention guilty for putting Cynthia and Grace at risk. This was her penance, and she would take it, because she knew she deserved it. "I don't like lying to you."

"I know, sweetheart," he said, his voice softening a bit. "You're normally a very good girl, but that's why I have to put my foot down when you do step out of line." His voice had hardened again by the end of his sentence, and his hand lifted from her bottom and came down with a sharp slap.

Irene jerked, mostly in surprise, and then clutched at the covers as his hand began to come down in earnest, smacking her bottom over and over again.

SLAP! SLAP! SLAP!

The fire built up quickly as his hand peppered her bottom, covering every inch of creamy skin in a bright pink. At first it was easy for Hugh to tell where to land his palm: anywhere her skin was still white. Once the first blush rose in her cheeks, he had to be a little more focused to make sure he didn't hit the same spots over and over again. He wanted each layer of the spanking to be even, although it did wear his hand out more.

His wife began to pant and then moan as she squirmed on his lap, her soft belly rubbing against the hard ridge of his cock. As her buttocks began to turn a darker pink, her soft cries became more distressed, the sound going straight to his groin as her skin began to feel hot beneath his hand. Holding her firmly in place, he ignored her squirming as she began to plead with him.

"Hugh, I'm sorry, I am, I'm sorry, I won't do it again, I promise!"

Knowing better than to listen to the words, which were properly contrite but also really just part of trying to get out of her punishment, Hugh kept smacking his hand down on the jiggling flesh of her bottom. Each blow had a ripple effect through the rest of her pink skin tantalized him, making his balls tighten as he yearned to plow into his wife. Even better, as her legs began to kick, he caught flashes of her pussy with its frame of soft red curls, glistening slightly.

As usual, Irene had become aroused while she was being punished.

She didn't enjoy the discipline, just as he would prefer he not have to discipline her, but both of them had physical reactions to it that they couldn't deny. It was pure torture for Hugh to have to hold back, waiting to take his pleasure, because his wife had to be soundly spanked before either of them could enjoy themselves. Although, Irene's pleasure was almost a punishment in and of itself, because he knew she was embarrassed by her reaction to being spanked. Especially since the first time he had done it, she had considered it abuse.

"Hugh, pleaaaaaaase, I've learned my lesson! Please, please, please!"

Her buttocks had turned a nice rosy red now, hot to the touch and probably quite painful. In some ways, his wife was lucky she was the one to speak up and tell them where Grace and Cynthia were. If she hadn't, Hugh probably would have gotten her hairbrush at this point and laid its hard surface down atop her already burning cheeks.

But he had decided she had done the right thing in the end. He gave her one last resounding smack right in the center of her arse, and then began rubbing the abused flesh. She choked and made little sobbing noises, relaxing in relief as she realized her punishment was over.

"I'm stopping now because you were good in the end," he told her sternly. "That's your reward, otherwise this would have been much worse."

Irene nodded her head to show her understanding, because her throat was too choked up from tears. This hadn't been a particularly hard spanking, truthfully, even though she had wailed and carried on in an embarrassing manner. Of course it had hurt, it was supposed to, but she knew it could have been so much worse. Unfortunately she'd discovered her bottom could take quite a bit more punishment than she would have ever thought possible. It always hurt so much more than it looked like it would.

Lifting her up from his lap, Hugh stood her up and pulled off her dress and chemise. Irene moaned a bit as his hands and fingers caressed her breasts, pinching her already erect nipples. It felt like her face flamed as bright as her bottom when his fingers slipped between her legs, coming away covered in her cream. The smirking, rakish grin on her husband's face at the proof of her body's incomprehensible reaction only made her blush harder.

When he tossed her onto the bed, on her back, she squealed and immediately tried to roll over as her bottom flared with pain at the contact.

"Oh no, wife," Hugh said firmly, reaching out and rolling her back as he finished shucking off his own clothing. His cock was rigidly hard, standing out in front of him. "I want you on your back with your legs spread."

The aggressive, almost crude words made Irene shiver. She was enamored of Hugh as a gentleman, but when he became demanding and coarse in bed, she almost liked that even more. The fiery pain in her bottom made her moan as it came back in contact with the bed, her weight pressing down on it. Planting her feet on the bed, she kept her thighs spread wide, blushing at the open and vulnerable picture she must make, but doing it anyway to keep as much space between the bed and her bottom as possible.

Hugh chuckled as he climbed between her legs, the head of his cock rubbing against her slick pussy lips as he hovered over her. "You can give me that appalled look all you want, sweetheart, I can see how aroused you are. Your pretty pussy is nearly as pink as your arse."

Even as he caught her lips in a deep, passionate kiss, Irene whined in embarrassment that he'd pointed out her shameful reaction. She whined again, the sound muffled by his lips, as his body weight came down on her, pressing her into the bed. There was no way her legs could hold up both of them, and the pleasure of his body against hers mingled with the flaring sparks in her poor bottom. Writhing against him, trying to escape the fiery burn, her nipples and body rubbed against his hard muscles and wiry hair, further stimulating her senses. She could feel his cock bobbing between her thighs, the tip coated in her juices.

With his own groan, Hugh thrust his hips forward, impaling her on his shaft. She gasped, opening her mouth even further, and he took full advantage, his tongue sliding in deep just like his cock. Irene clutched at his shoulders, her nails digging in, as she was driven into the mattress by his hard thrust, her bottom bouncing painfully against the bed.

Almost immediately, Hugh started moving, hard and fast, slapping her pussy with his body and making her bottom bounce and rub against the mattress. Irene cried out at the painfully pleasurable sensations, her body confused as to what it was feeling as his cock massaged her insides and her sore buttocks were further abused. One of Hugh's hands slid down to grip a red cheek, fingers digging in and making her mewl as she squirmed beneath him, her pussy clenching in lustful passion as he rode her hard.

Their lovemaking was always passionate, but Hugh was rougher with her, harder on her, after a spanking, as if punishing her woke some kind of animalistic urge inside of him. Irene was caught in the waves of his desire, almost as though she was being dragged into his ardor along with him. All she could do was cling to him as they came together, hanging on to him for the duration and hoping not to get left behind.

Her body was clamoring for more even as she shrieked with pain and pleasure. The same part of her that loved the discipline reveled in being ravished and dominated by her husband, her own urges making her hotter and wetter as he pounded between her thighs. She gave herself over to the sensation, letting him take complete control of her body, accepting both the ecstasy and the exquisite burn.

Hugh could feel her softening beneath him, her pussy clutching at him as he lost himself in her sweet heaven. The slight pain from her nails digging into his shoulders gave way to a masculine pride at how she clutched at him, writhed for him, cried out for him. The wet slickness of her body coated his cock, making it easy for him to pump in and out of her. The soft, breathy noises she made whenever her bottom was pressed against the bed—half enjoyment and half distress—sent shudders of pleasure down his spine.

"Cum for me, sweetheart," he growled in her ear, his raspy, heated voice making her insides clench and dance. "I want to feel your pussy milking me while I fill you with my seed."

His dirty, salacious words, combined with all the incredible sensations, finally sent Irene careening over the edge of pleasure. She opened her mouth to answer him and ended up screaming his name instead as she clawed at his chest. The pleasure surged, lifting her high, and then dropping her into a free fall of ecstasy. It was stars and light and surging warmth all around her and inside of her. Hot liquid splashed her insides and she clenched, her pussy squeezing and milking Hugh's cock of his seed, just like he'd wanted her to.

The connection between them felt so incredibly deep, so completely encompassing, both of them were breathless as Hugh's body partially collapsed on top of hers. Still joined intimately, they breathed deeply, inhaling each other's scents, nuzzling and holding each other as closely as they could. Irene's eyelids fluttered as she felt contentment and exhaustion sliding through her.

As the pleasure high began to wear off, she was more and more aware of the throbbing pain in her bottom. She whimpered, shifting beneath their combined weights, and Hugh immediately knew what was wrong. Holding her tightly, so she moved with him, he rolled on to his back and she lay atop him.

His softened cock slid reluctantly from the warm haven of her body as he reached down to gently caress her ass. The soft cheeks were still emanating heat, and he was sure they retained their bright pink color even if he couldn't currently see it. Irene made a soft little noise as he stroked the sore flesh, wriggling to find a more comfortable position, since he seemed determined to keep her sprawled across his body.

"Go to sleep, sweetheart," he murmured, one hand still cupping her bottom as the other drifted up to brush the hair off of her neck.

"But what about Cynthia and Grace?" Irene asked softly, her voice sultry with sleepiness. "I need to know what happened to them."

"We'll see them tomorrow at the wedding," he said, letting a hint of authority trickle into his voice. He didn't doubt Wesley and Alex had the situation well in hand, otherwise he would have heard from them by now if they'd needed assistance.

A small smile went across his face as he stroked his sleepy wife, his own contentment making him smug. All of their women would be sitting very uncomfortably at the wedding tomorrow.

~

GETTING BACK into the house Alex had rented proved much easier than leaving the Countess' home unnoticed. On the way out, Grace and Cynthia had hid several times from maids and servants. They'd slipped out a side door Cynthia said she had used on occasion to sneak out, both of them giggling with relief when they weren't stopped. Neither of them had seen the eyes following them out the door, watching with disapproval. For the first block, as they hurried down the street, Grace kept looking over her shoulder, the hairs on the back of her neck standing up as if in warning, but no one called after them.

The darkened streets had made her heart beat faster—or maybe it was just because she was finally going to achieve her goal. Most of the house was quiet and dark, and she was relieved, because that meant Alex had certainly gone out with the other men. His study was at the front of the house, and she was sure he would have been in there still working if he were home. The darkness of the window in particular was reassuring.

They'd slipped in through the front door, moving silently so as not to alert the butler, and easily made their way up into Alex's room. Grace hadn't hesitated to light the candles and gas lamps available, brightening up the room enough so they could look.

Surprisingly, despite the fact that most of the documents on Alex's desk were completely standard business correspondence, Cynthia didn't look bored at all as they leafed through them. She occasionally held one out to Grace, wanting to know if a particular transaction or deal might have something to do with Grace or her father, but nothing had. The documents on Alex's desk were entirely benign.

"Time to go through the drawers," Cynthia said gleefully, when they finished the third small stack, not even bothering to whisper.

For some reason, Grace's stomach did a little flip when Cynthia opened the first drawer. It seemed more invasive to go through the drawers than it did to go through the things on top of his desk. Something disturbingly like guilt wiggled in her belly. But it was far too late to turn back now; curiosity, and a strange kind of desperation, drove her onward.

"You take that side, I'll take this side," Grace said, shooing Cynthia to the left. The younger woman eagerly pulled open the first drawer.

"Boring... boring... boring..." Cynthia was muttering under her breath as Grace did her best to ignore the soft chant. Her own drawer wasn't proving to be very interesting either. Mostly it was long-term contracts between Alex and others with whom he did business. She did find the one between Alex and her father, but it hadn't been updated since it had been signed.

Which meant the deal between her father and Alex hadn't changed at all, despite her and Alex's estrangement. Not that her father had ever been the type to allow sentiment or family to get in the way of refilling his coffers. The man had decadent tastes, and didn't mind dabbling in business to support himself, especially if he could do it under the guise of a socially acceptable transaction like a marriage.

Scowling, Grace shoved the papers back into the drawer and moved on to the middle one.

"Grace," Cynthia whispered excitedly, making Grace's head jerk up. But Cynthia wasn't holding papers, she was holding out a portrait in miniature, which had been carefully wrapped in paper in the middle drawer of the left side of the desk. "Look! This is you, isn't it?"

It was. A younger her. Grace hadn't realized how much the face in her mirror had changed over the past years. In some ways, she was exactly the same; oval face, creamy skin, bright blue eyes with their extravagant lashes, deep black hair. Looking at this image of her past self, she could see the innocence of youth, the lack of lines around her eyes, and the artist had even managed to capture some of the hope Grace had always felt when she was younger.

When had Alex had this done? It wasn't a portrait Grace had ever seen before, and yet it was irrefutably one of her younger self. This wasn't something he'd commissioned recently. So when? And how long had he been carrying it around with him.

Something painful pressed inside of her chest, as if her heart was growing and pushing against her rib cage and lungs, making it hard for her to breathe. *What does this mean?*

The question echoed inside of her head, so loudly she didn't even realize Cynthia was talking to her until the other woman shook her.

"Grace? Grace, are you well? You've gone white as a sheet!"

Blinking, her eyes refocusing, Grace looked up at Cynthia's panicked gaze, although the panic immediately lessened as the younger woman realized Grace was back with her.

"I'm fine," Grace said, although it was a lie. She didn't feel fine. She felt... unsettled. The hope which seemed to never quite die away was blossoming painfully inside of her again, as if the portrait was a spark that had hit some very eager tinder. She hardened herself against the hope, gathering the hurt she'd used to build her walls and reminding herself of why he wasn't to be trusted.

But there were cracks in her defenses. That bright, shining hope leaked through, tempting her. Why did her husband have to be so bloody confusing?!

Looking slightly worried, Cynthia took the portrait back and carefully wrapped it back up in the paper, the exact way it had been before. Grace couldn't help the little smile when she realized how very good her friend was at making it appear as if the drawer she'd just rifled through was untouched. No one, looking at the portrait's carefully wrapped package, would realize they'd opened it. Cynthia was quite practiced at snooping, it appeared.

It was in the final drawer on her side Grace found her prize. Packets of letters, all from business, and one from her father. This was what she had been looking for. Saving her father's for last, she skimmed through the other packets, quickly confirming that none of them had anything to do with Alex's marital status. The hope pulsing outside of the fortress around her heart felt as though it was pressing inwards as one by one, each packet was set aside without any evidence to condemn Alex. Without revealing some ulterior motive or purpose for their reconciliation.

But she didn't allow herself to crumble. After all, she still had the packet of letters from her father to go through. Who knew what her father and her husband had discussed during the years she and Alex had been estranged. She certainly hadn't spoken with her father in all that time.

As she peeked back at the bottom of the stack, to the earliest letters, and work her way to the front, it quickly became clear why.

Alex had kept every single letter from her father, from the approving ones when they had first been married, to the ones which became almost threatening in tone when she left Alex. Her father had demanded Alex get her "under control," or he would do it himself. The very next letter following that one had been filled with frustrated fury and confusion which indicated Alex had not only refused to give in to her father's demands, but had actually ordered her father to stay away from her.

Each letter was successively angrier, although it was obvious from the rest of their correspondence that the business deal they had made was making them both quite a bit of money. From the tone of her father's letters, it appeared he became resigned to the fact that Alex wasn't going to curb her behavior or allow her father to either. He called Alex a fool and worse, but bowed to his dictates. Apparently, her father had needed Alex far more than Alex had needed her father.

Chewing her lower lip, Grace's mind raced as she flipped through each piece of correspondence, wishing she could read Alex's letters to her father. What had he said that had convinced her father to leave her alone? Why had he been protecting her?

Her father even said if Alex divorced her, he would continue business with Alex as usual. That didn't surprise Grace at all, what did surprise Grace was that Alex hadn't taken her father up on the offer. It had been made almost two years ago. During all this time, she had assumed her father had at least something to do with Alex continuing to pay the bills she sent to him. She'd thought something in the agreement he'd made with her father required him to, that her father must have put something in the marriage contract about Alex keeping her in the proper style. After all, her father cared more about appearances and money than anything else.

She'd been wrong. Her father hadn't even cared that much about her.

Why?

The question pounded at her head. Why had Alex protected her from her father's wrath? Why had Alex paid for her dresses and food and houses when she'd been estranged from him and taking lovers? Why had Alex decided he wanted to reconcile when it would have been so much easier for him to divorce her and take another wife? Even easier than she had supposed, as her father obviously wouldn't have put up any kind of fight, not even for the sake of appearances.

Apparently she had become enough of an embarrassment that her father was ready to pretend she wasn't his daughter, but not enough for Alex to abandon her as his wife.

Why? Why? WHY?

Beside her, oblivious to her turmoil, Cynthia's head snapped up and she let out a soft little shriek. "Someone's home... Blast! Quick! Put everything back!"

Fear coursed through Grace, horror overtaking her, and she shoved the packets of letters back into Alex's desk drawer. If—when —he opened the drawer, it would be obvious someone had gone through it, but that couldn't be helped now. The fast, heavy tread of masculine steps was getting closer, ominous and otherwise silent. More than one pair of boots, too.

Next to her, Cynthia was jumping to her feet, frantically brushing out her skirts to hide the evidence she'd been sitting beside the desk. Grace followed suit. She took two steps for the door and then stopped. The heavy tread was already coming down the hall and there was only one way out of this room. It wouldn't matter if she stepped out; if Alex was home, he already knew where they were. The light in the room would have been visible from the street.

"Blast and damnation, what the devil is he doing home so early?" Cynthia muttered, just before the door swung open and slammed into the wall. Grace winced at the crashing noise, and then took a step back as she looked up to meet her husband's furious eyes. Right behind him was the Earl of Spencer, looking every inch his title and nothing at all like the playful and flirtatious Wesley she'd always known. Cynthia groaned. "Dammit."

"What have I told you about cursing?" Wesley growled, moving so quickly Grace was taken aback. Even Alex looked a bit surprised as Wesley snatched up his ward and fiancée, tossing her over his shoulder as she let out a shriek, and then striding back out the door without saying another word.

Cynthia's demands to be put down echoed through the hall, growing fainter until they heard the sound of the front door opening and then closing decisively.

Both she and Alex stood there, listening, almost as if they both wanted to ascertain they were alone. Her mouth was dry, her heart feeling as though it might burst from her chest it was beating so hard. She could barely look at the man, at her husband, whom she didn't understand at all.

"What are you doing in here?" The question was clipped, sharp. Dangerous. It sent a shiver down her spine.

She looked down at the desk in front of her, her fingers tracing the edge of it in a nervous movement.

"This is where we are staying, is it not?" she asked, trying to think through the fog suddenly clouding her mind. Part of her wanted to ask him all the questions that had arisen when she'd read through her father's letters, and when Cynthia had found the portrait, but another part of her didn't want to say anything until she'd had more time to think it through. That part of her was also curious what he would do now. She'd been caught invading his privacy, snooping through his things, and she was being deliberately obtuse. Not to mention, she wasn't supposed to be in this house right now. Would his temper overcome him? Would this be too much trouble, even if it wasn't going to cause a scandal since no one knew about it?

"Yet it is not where you are supposed to be and there is no reason for you to be in this room."

Still not looking at him, Grace shrugged, her hand wiping damply over her skirt. She felt as though she was teetering on a knife's edge, waiting for his next move. Wondering what the unpredictable man would do, and what it would mean when set alongside his other actions.

Standing behind his desk, Grace looked almost like a naughty little debutante. She avoided his eyes, traced patterns on the wood top of his desk, fiddled with her skirts, and did everything she could not to actually challenge him. Which was unusual for her. Someone was definitely feeling guilty.

"Did you find what you were looking for?" he asked, his voice rough with his anger and frustration. He didn't know what Grace was looking for. Letters from a mistress perhaps? She would be sorely disappointed on that score. Although he'd received a few letters from women since he'd given his last mistress her *congé*, he'd tossed them all in the fire without even opening them.

The way Grace jumped at his question, looking even guiltier, he knew she hadn't found whatever she'd been looking for. Probably some kind of evidence to further condemn him in her mind. Knowing she hadn't found it allowed him to relax slightly, some of his tension leaking away. They'd made a lot of progress since coming to Bath and he was loathe to find he'd lost ground.

"I wasn't looking for anything," she said sharply, still avoiding meeting his gaze.

"Bend over the desk."

Now she looked at him, her blue eyes wide with shock at his rough order, cheeks flushing and then paling. Alex stood there, his anger leaching away as calm overtook him. Patiently, he stared back at her, crossing his arms over his chest. The door was behind him, there was nowhere for her to go.

But he'd still expected her to argue. To his surprise, she stepped forward and very slowly began bending over the desk. Confusion was clear on her face, as if she herself didn't quite understand why she was obeying him. Seeing her submit so quickly had his cock standing upright, the rush of lust hitting him so fast he nearly groaned aloud. Perhaps it was her guilty conscience, Alex wasn't sure, but he wasn't going to argue with the results either.

"Stretch out and grip the other side of the desk."

She was short enough that she had to squirm forward, her fists uncurling so her fingers could wrap around the far edge. Walking around behind her, Alex could see her toes were barely touching the floor. Perfect. The vulnerability of her position was incredibly arousing.

When he flipped up her skirts, she made a soft little whimpering sound that wasn't quite a protest. Surreptitiously, he rubbed the front of his pants, making his cock swell even further as he looked down at the creamy expanse of skin revealed. The mounded hills of her buttocks were thrust upwards by her position, the pouting lips of her pussy, fringed with dark curls that made the cream and pink of her skin stand out, peeked from between her thighs. They weren't wet, not yet.

Settling one hand down on the small of her back to both hold up her skirts and keep her from squirming too much, Alex raised his hand.

SMACK! SMACK! SMACK! SMACK!

"Ow!" Grace protested, although he noticed she still hung on to the desk, even as she tried to wriggle out from underneath his hand. His cock approved.

"I know when you're lying to me, Grace," he said sternly. "I won't tolerate it."

SMACK! SMACK! SMACK! SMACK!

He kept the slaps to her ass steady but fast, placing them randomly across her buttocks so she wasn't able to guess where each blow would land. The flesh of her bottom danced and jiggled, from both the spanking and her squirming as her legs kicked a little bit. This was probably the hardest spanking he'd given her yet, but it was well deserved.

The little minx had not only snuck out of Spencer's house, but she'd done it in order to go through Alex's private space, and then had the audacity to try and lie about it. A firmer punishment than he'd given her before was definitely called for.

"Ow! Alex, please, it *hurts.*"

SMACK! SMACK!

"It's supposed to, sweetheart," he said, somewhat grimly. "It's going to hurt a lot more by the time I'm done. Did you even think about what you were doing?"

SMACK! SMACK!

"Would you like it if I disappeared from where I told you I was going to be?"

SMACK! SMACK!

"Have I gone through any of your private things?"

SMACK! SMACK!

"What if you'd been accosted in the streets?"

SMACK! SMACK!

"You and Cynthia could have been attacked and hurt, coming over here unaccompanied at night!"

SMACK! SMACK! SMACK! SMACK!

The idea she and Cynthia might have been attacked on this little excursion left him breathless with anxiety. Although he loved Grace's spirit, he wouldn't tolerate her putting herself in danger. He was just starting to win her back; it would kill him to actually lose her. Anger surged through him again at the lack of care she showed for her own person.

"Ow! Dammit, Alex, we were perfectly fine!"

SMACK! SMACK! SMACK!

Grace howled as Alex's hand came down between her legs rather than on her ass, smacking against her pussy lips with a humiliating wet sound.

"But you might not have been!"

The panicked rage in his voice took her aback, even in her own self-involved little world of pain and embarrassment. The way he said it, sounded like any injury to her would have hurt him. He sounded like Edwin or Hugh or Wesley... like he really, truly *cared*. And wasn't he showing it right now? Behaving just like them, punishing her because she'd put herself in danger? Well, and also the other things he'd said, but there was no doubting from the force of his blows what he was most upset about.

SMACK! SMACK! SMACK! SMACK!

His hand came down on her pale thighs, making her gasp and kick at the new sensations. It stung so much more than when he was spanking her ass. The fiery sparks were licking at her all over, her bottom, between her legs, the backs of her thighs... it felt like her whole backside was being roasted. She cried out, louder, not caring anymore if the staff might be able to hear her.

"Please, Alex, I wasn't! I won't do it again, I promise!"

"No, you bloody well won't."

His hand moved back up to her bottom, which was already bright pink and sensitive, and Grace howled. Tears were beginning to slide down her cheeks and on to his desk, but even though she kicked and squirmed beneath his hand, she found she couldn't let go of the far edge of the desk. Her fingers curled around it as if she was hanging on for dear life. Why couldn't she let go? Was it because she felt like she deserved this punishment?

Because she really did. She was feeling more than a little guilty about going through Alex's things, especially since she hadn't found anything against him. There was no righteous anger to give her cause, no vindication. All she'd found was a portrait of herself and letters from her father showing Alex's protection of her. Not to mention, she would have been furious if she'd found Alex going through her things. Or if he'd lied about where he was. Or if he'd put himself in some kind of dangerous situation. Because she cared too.

The tears spilled faster, not because he was hurting her— although it did hurt quite a bit—but they came out in a cathartic rush as she accepted her punishment. She cried because of her father's lack of care, because Alex carried a portrait of her and—it seemed—had for years, because he'd protected her from both her father and Society, and because he still cared enough to punish her. To spank her instead of pushing her out on the streets, alone and unprotected. To discipline her, the way her well-loved friends were disciplined.

"Grace?" Alex's voice was almost hesitant, his hand gentle as he smoothed it over her burning, throbbing bottom. "Sweetheart, are you alright?"

Part of her wanted to say something bratty, to point out he'd just roasted her bottom, so how could he expect her to be alright? But all she did was nod her head, still crying.

"I was going to give you a taste of the belt, but I think you've had enough," he murmured, still sounding worried. Then his hand slipped down between her legs. "Ahhh." Not so worried now; the exhalation of sound was smug and almost triumphant, to her shame.

Grace couldn't explain her body's reaction or why she was still clinging to the desk as his fingers slid through the slick wetness of her womanhood. She just whimpered, her hips bucking upwards to encourage the contact. The pleasure helped to ease the throbbing ache of her bottom, even though she was fairly certain the same ache was what had caused the arousal. She moaned and shuddered as his finger drew the wetness down around her little pleasure nub, rubbing against it.

Other men had touched her like this, but she'd always felt some-what disengaged, as if she'd had to concentrate in order to focus on the pleasure. With Alex, she'd never had any difficulty. Her own emotions kept her riveted to whatever he was doing to her body, completely engaged in the feel of his fingers as they massaged her clit and slid between the folds of her nether lips, spreading her cream around the entire area.

The edges of pain, from the spanking, seemed to balance out the ecstasy of his touch, pulling her even further into what he was doing. She moaned again as he swirled his fingers, throbbing and burning inside and out.

"Dammit," he cursed, his voice hoarse, and then suddenly she felt him kneel behind her, both of his hands on her bottom cheeks, spreading them open so cool air and his hot breath wafted across her pussy lips. Grace whimpered. "I'm just going to taste you, sweetheart, if you want to stop me, all you have to do is stand up."

Stop him! The voice in her head shrieked, but her body just clamped down tighter around the desk, silently begging him to continue.

The first swipe of his tongue went straight through the center of her pussy, and Grace cried out. His fingers dug into her sore bottom, sending more sensations rioting through her as he began to suck and nibble on her pussy lips, licking her all over except the one place where she wanted it most. Hanging on to the desk, Grace moaned. Because of her position, she couldn't really move her body, all she could do was lie there and take whatever Alex would give her.

But it wasn't enough.

She felt like screaming in frustration as her pleasure built, but not fast enough, not high enough. The vast emptiness inside of her only seemed to grow as Alex took his time, savoring her taste. From his own moans, she could tell he was enjoying feasting between her thighs, and that aroused her even more.

"More, more, Alex please, I need *more*," she begged, her insides contracting as his tongue slid around her swollen clit. If she could have lifted her hips, she would have, but with her toes barely brushing the floor there was no chance of that.

"Tell me what you want, Gracie," he said, and then his tongue slid between her folds and inside of her, thrusting but not filling, and she moaned. "Remember what I told you in the carriage on our way here? If you want me, you're going to beg me, so there's no mistaking what you're asking for."

How was it possible his arrogant words only fanned her inner flames even higher? Maybe it was the controlled passion she heard in his voice, the hungry plea she do what he demanded and beg him. His tongue thrust inside of her again, making her body try to clench around him to draw him in further.

"Alex, please, I need you inside me," she begged, letting her pride go, letting her walls down. Any night before this and she wouldn't have been able to, but he'd already been planting creepers along those walls, cracking them open, slowly but surely weakening them. Tonight she'd found new cause for hope, in the portrait, in the letters. In his determination to protect her, to discipline her... to keep her. Doing the same things he saw his friends doing with their wives. She wanted that. She'd always wanted that. The leap of trust wasn't so big, she told the small voice at the back of her head, she was only trusting him with her body. Not her heart, not yet... but tonight, she wanted this. Needed it even. They could come together like this. An unspoken reward for what she hadn't found in his desk, and for the unexpected surprises she'd discovered instead.

"More specific, Grace," Alex said, his tongue sliding around her clit as a finger pressed inside of her, pumping and stroking, but far too slender for her greedy passion. "Tell me to fuck you. Beg me."

The tip of his finger rubbed over a sweet spot inside of her and every inch of her quivered with need. She was lost in a maelstrom of emotions and passion, no longer thinking, no longer caring about the bigger picture. Alex's authority, his demands, they swept through her and carried her along with them.

"Fuck me, oh Alex please, fuck me, fuck me, fuck me," she chanted.

It took Alex less than thirty seconds to undo the front of his pants and line his cock up with his wife's swollen, soaked pussy. She was practically dripping cream, and had been from the moment he'd started spanking her. The heat of her body nuzzled against the crown of his dick, her slick wetness like a kiss on the tip. Then he thrust forward and both of them cried out.

Tight, hot... heaven. Sliding into Grace wasn't like any other woman. His emotions engulfed him for the first time in years, making him feel a sense of rightness, of completeness missing from his life for so long. The silken grip of her body nearly unmanned him, and he held himself tightly against her, buried inside, fighting against the urge to empty himself immediately into her hot channel. The small muscles inside of her body massaged the length of his cock as the heat from her rosy bottom warmed his groin.

"Please, Alex, please... more... it feels so good..."

Those breathy, demanding words were new. A sudden flash of possessive jealousy had him wondering who had encouraged that. His own fault, he knew, for letting things go the way they had. The only positive note was it helped him get his own impulses under control.

Wrapping his fingers around her hips, he pulled his own back, reluctantly ceding the warmth of her cunt, before shoving back in again, deep and hard. Grace groaned and tightened. He liked this position, where she couldn't move, trapped between him and the desk, totally at his mercy. The rosy hue of her bottom as it jiggled with each thrust was just as enticing and exciting as when he had her on her back so he could watch her breasts.

He started thrusting hard and deep, so her pleading words were blurred into moans and whimpers, those same needy noises in her throat he remembered. Holding her hips tightly, he slammed into her, working his cock in and out of her pussy in feverish action, fighting the urge to spill... wanting this moment to last forever.

Grace screamed his name when she came, her body shuddering around his, her pussy clinging to his cock so tightly he almost feared he'd hurt her as he kept moving. The sobbing note in her voice told him how intense her orgasm was. He kept riding her, reveling in the way she trembled and gasped beneath him as the waves of pleasure continued, forced out of her by his thrusting cock.

"Too much... Alex, oh it's too much... I can't... oh please... not again... I can't..." Her broken words trailed off as she let out another gasping scream, and he realized she was climaxing again. Even harder and more intense than before.

He couldn't hold back any longer. Bracing himself against her, he pummeled her pussy with a series of brutal thrusts that had her writhing and screaming his name again, before he held himself tightly inside of her. He groaned as her pussy milked his cock, sucking at it with her inner muscles, as he swelled and exploded inside of her. It felt like years of pent-up desire, flowing out of him and into her body, filling her and fulfilling him at the same time.

Feeling weak in the knees as his balls emptied, he leaned over Grace, feeling her hot bottom flush against his stomach, her smaller body limp beneath his. If it wasn't for her contented sighs, he would have worried he'd hurt her, she was so still. Although, he could still feel her pussy occasionally spasm around his softening cock.

Kissing the back of her shoulder and neck, a contentment he'd never known warmed him. Even back when they'd been on their honeymoon, he hadn't felt quite like this. Although, back then, he'd known she was important to him, that he had developed some very deep feelings for her, now that he'd been apart from her for so long, he had an even deeper appreciation for what she meant to him. There would be no letting her go this time.

"Sweetheart," he whispered, brushing back her hair to kiss her cheek.

Her eyes were closed and she was smiling. "Mmm?"

Not awake then. Alex sighed ruefully. He'd been hoping to talk more about why Grace had been in his study, find out what she'd been looking for—and why she'd begged him to fuck her when he'd been sure she would keep resisting. He hadn't questioned the sudden turn around while his cock was practically bursting in his pants, now he wanted to know what had instigated it. But talking to Grace when she was like this was useless, unless she'd changed drastically in the years since their marriage, and he doubted she'd altered quite that much.

Right now she was in a pleasure induced hazy state of satisfied exhaustion. If he got more than meaningless noises out of her, he'd be shocked.

Making himself decent again, Alex gathered his wife tenderly up into his arms, resting her head against his shoulder. She sighed and snuggled in, making those happy little noises he loved so well, her eyes still closed. Tomorrow he doubted she'd even remember these moments. But he would. This was how their marriage should be, always.

Taking her to their room, he stripped her limp body naked, letting her curl up under the covers while he attended to his own bedtime needs. The only time she roused even slightly was when he used a warm, damp cloth to clear away the evidence of their activities. She curled on her side, grimacing sleepily a bit whenever her bottom touched the mattress.

Blowing out the candles, Alex crawled in behind her, tucking her into the curve of his body and holding her possessively with his arm and leg. Tonight had been unexpected, and he didn't even try to hazard a guess what tomorrow would bring. Perhaps she would try to pull away again, perhaps she wouldn't.

All he knew was he would never let her go again.

CHAPTER 10

"Put me down, you... you..." Cynthia clenched her jaw against the multitude of insults which sprang to the front of her mind. Inwardly, she cursed that she was already changing her behavior for the bloody man who had her slung over his shoulder like a sack of potatoes, but she knew she was in enough trouble as it was. She didn't need to add insulting him to her punishable crimes.

The Earl utterly ignored her, and the passersby, as he strode through the streets. More than one man let out a drunken hoot and cheered him as he went past.

"Git 'er, laddy!"

"Tup 'er good!"

Cynthia let out a strangled sound of outrage. "Put me down! They think I'm a trollop!"

"Better they think you a whore than realize who you actually are," the Earl said grimly, not loosening his iron hold on her for a second. She wanted to kick him, but she was too afraid of falling. If he hadn't put her over his shoulder like some kind of demented barbarian, no one would have even noticed them going through the streets.

Granted, some part of her was excited by his high-handed ways, but she was also embarrassed. Cynthia didn't like to be embarrassed

—it wasn't an emotion she was very familiar with, as she normally didn't find herself in situations out of her control. At least, not until she'd met the Earl. As a punishment, it was probably far more effective than the more physical discipline the Earl had used on her. Well, other than the things he'd done to her bottom hole, but that was also due more to embarrassment than anything else. That area should have been sacrosanct and private.

Hanging her head, she tried to cover her face so at least no one would guess the 'trollop' the Earl was with tonight was the same woman he'd be marrying on the morrow. It was one of those strange situations where, if she had plotted for this to happen, she wouldn't have been embarrassed at all. But since she hadn't, she felt humiliated by her position. Cynthia had truly meant to be to the Brooke's house and then gone before Wesley returned home.

She didn't like to think what his presence meant for Eleanor and Irene. Although she'd learned Irene was more adventurous than Cynthia had ever guessed, it was obvious the redhead didn't enjoy spankings the way Cynthia did. Eleanor did, but only some of the time—and in her current condition, Cynthia doubted she'd enjoy it at all. As for Grace... well, considering the portrait Cynthia had found tonight and the look on Grace's face as she'd read through the letters she'd found, perhaps whatever punishment Lord Brooke doled out would be worth it to her. Cynthia certainly hoped so, since she was going to be punished for it as well.

Curiosity was certainly one of her besetting sins. She'd just *had* to go along on the adventure with Grace. Sneak out of the house. Search through a lord's private affairs. Normally not the kind of thing she would regret, but she was a bit worried about what the Earl might come up with as a punishment. Spankings were all well and good, whether with his hand or a belt, because even though they hurt like the devil during the process, the pleasure that followed was immense. On the other hand, the last time he'd punished her, her bottom hole had paid the price, and Cynthia had found the pleasure from *that* to be rather shameful. It had made her feel utterly out of control and vulnerable in a way nothing else ever had.

She squeaked as Wesley started up the steps to the house, bouncing her on his shoulder as he did so. Clutching at the back of his coat, her position felt extremely precarious.

"Manfred," Wesley said, in acknowledgement as the door opened, just a tinge of gratitude coloring his voice. The older gentleman looked shocked at the sight of Cynthia upended over Wesley's shoulder, her rump high in the air, one of his arms wrapped around her knees and the other firmly gripping her thigh.

The butler swallowed and blinked several times. "My Lord," he said finally, coming to himself and quickly closing the door behind Wesley. Obviously hoping no one had seen.

Personally, Wesley didn't care. Most people would probably assume what the drunken men in the street had—that the woman over his shoulder was a ladybird. Even if they recognized him, they'd think he was celebrating his last night as a bachelor. Hardly something to be remarked upon, although it wouldn't be considered good taste to have brought the woman to his mother's house, it wasn't something anyone would mention either.

Besides which, there was something extremely satisfying about carting his annoying baggage through the streets as her protests rained down on his ears. After all the aggravation she'd caused him this evening, it only seemed fair. When he'd first opened the letter from Manfred and realized Cynthia had gone missing, he'd thought his heart was going to stop. His chest had ached, thinking she'd gone back on her word and had gone out in search of another man before their wedding. It seemed like the kind of thing his overly adventurous and rebellious hoyden might do, although some part of him had held out that there must be some other explanation, because she wasn't the type to go back on a deal.

Hearing she'd gone off with Grace hadn't helped. Although he, personally, liked Grace quite a bit, Cynthia didn't need any encouragement from the *ton*'s favorite scandal. He would have been less agitated if Eleanor or Irene had been with them.

Discovering them in Alex's office, going through his things, had been a relief for Wesley. He was sure Alex didn't feel the same way, but at the moment Alex's feelings weren't his concern. His concern was ensuring Cynthia understood this kind of behavior wasn't going to be tolerated.

He wouldn't have her running around at night, on her own, doing who the hell knows what. If she wanted adventure, he could provide her with that. Hell, if she wanted to go snoop through somebody's things, he'd be willing to go with her. It could be fun. He'd put his foot down about his own friends of course, but still. The point was, she needed to recognize she now had a partner in life and he should be included in her little escapades. Wesley needed to watch over her, to know she was safe. He needed to be there to extricate her from any situation when she got in over her head. It wasn't just possessiveness he felt—she'd rattled every protective bone in his body.

"We're in the house, you can put me down now," she said, her voice reasonable, placating, as if she was talking to a dunce or an intelligent animal. Wesley gritted his teeth and kept walking. "My room is that way."

He ignored her words, and her exasperated sighs, as he took her to his study. That's where everything he needed was. He'd stopped for a moment on his way out of the house, earlier, to give one of the maids orders to set up his study just the way he needed it to punish his wayward bride. It would also separate him enough from the rest of the house that their slumber wouldn't be disturbed. Especially his mother's. Doubtless, if she knew what he was up to, she wouldn't even let him discipline Cynthia.

"Your mother didn't want you to see me tonight!" Cynthia said, as if she could sense he was thinking about the Countess. "She said it's bad luck!"

"Bad luck for you," he replied, letting go of her thigh and smacking her bottom over her skirts. It wouldn't hurt her with all that padding, but it was still satisfying. She squealed in outrage, not pain, making him smirk.

He wiped the smile from his face as he set her down next to the chair. The items he'd requested from the maid were laid out on his desk, precisely as he asked. Cynthia was too busy glaring up at him, her fists propped on her hips, to even notice.

"I can't believe you just carried me through the streets!"

"I can't believe you left *here* and walked through the streets unaccompanied," Wesley growled back, watching her eyes go wide with defiance and guilt. "Putting yourself and Grace in danger. Not to mention, getting Irene and Eleanor into trouble as well. Don't think I can't guess whose idea this was." The guilt in her expression ratcheted up, as well as concern for her friends. Disobedient wench. The only person she should be concerned for right now was herself. "Plus, going through Alex's private room. Turn around and bend over the chair with your skirts up around your waist."

Her pert pink lips gaped open as she stared up at him in surprise. "Don't you want to know why I did it?"

Wesley snorted. "I could care less, sweetheart, I just know you did it and your arse is going to pay for it."

"Don't speak to me like that, I'm a lady," Cynthia snapped at him, even as she turned around and started to lift her skirt. "Your mother always told your brothers not to curse in front of ladies."

That got another snort, especially since the last part of her sentence was somewhat muffled as she bent over the chair, offering up her bottom for his inspection in a completely unladylike manner. He didn't apologize, but he didn't counter her argument either. If his mother ever did overhear the language he used in Cynthia's presence, she'd probably wallop him herself.

"Ladies don't go wandering off in the night without an escort," he said sharply, his hand coming down hard on her backside. Tonight he wasn't going to bother giving her a warm-up to the spanking. This spanking was going to be a warm-up to the birching she'd be getting. The muffled cry which greeted the blow indicated his force had been unexpected. Good, he hoped this got her attention.

Cynthia shrieked again as his hand came crashing down. She hadn't realized how much she relied on having her bottom sufficiently warmed up before he really started swinging his hand. Normally her buttocks were already bright pink by the time he used this much force, receiving it cold was a shock to her system that was both painful and arousing. Already she could feel her hard nipples rubbing against the chair's cushion through the fabric of her dress, and her pussy beginning to tighten and cream as his hand came down again and again.

Just being in this position was exciting for her, because she knew what was coming. Even if right now it did hurt like the dickens.

"Ow, ow, ow, ow," she chanted into the seat of the chair, her feet beginning to move and dance. Almost immediately the spanking stopped.

"Hold still, Cynthia, and keep your legs well spread or I'll tie them apart."

The very idea made her shudder as a gush of wetness leaked from her pussy. She'd been quite excited when he'd tied her hands to his bed the night she'd tried to sneak into it, the idea of having her legs tied apart so all of her privates would be vulnerable and on display... she wouldn't be able to keep him from touching her anywhere.

The Earl chuckled. "Like that, do you?

Before she even realized he had the necessary equipment nearby, Cynthia found herself with her ankles spread much wider than she'd initially had them, leather thongs wrapped around them to secure them to the legs of the chair. The position made her press herself down into the chair, offering up her butt even higher to keep her balance. She whimpered as his hands ran up her thighs, pulling the flesh apart to reveal the wet pink lips between them. When his thumb ran over her exposed anus, she made a small sound of protest, squirming as if she could actually get away when she was tied up and helpless like this.

"You're a dream come true, sweetheart."

The admiration in his voice did nothing to lessen the power of his next slap against her exposed flesh.

SMACK! SMACK! SMACK! SMACK!

Cynthia shrieked and squirmed, wagging her bottom up and down in the air because it was the only movement she could make. Her fingers clutched at the cushion beneath her, using it to muffle her cries as the Earl's broad platter of a hand abused her backside.

The spanking stopped, his hands gripping her flesh and squeezing hard enough to make her gasp as his fingers dug into her heated buttocks. Hot pleasure coursed through her, making her clench and try to push back against him as he confused her senses. Then his fingers released and she automatically braced herself for what was coming next.

SMACK! SMACK! SMACK! SMACK!

She moaned and wagged her bottom, knowing he would be watching the way it danced for him. Aroused by it even as the pain of each swat jerked through her. Still, now that her bottom was well warmed, the initial shock of the beating had lessened. Even though tears sparked in her eyes at the painful sting, Cynthia knew she could take it.

Watching his bride's bottom jiggling and squirming as he turned it a bright pink was pure pleasure for Wesley. Cynthia's tiny pink anus was completely exposed to him, because he'd tied her legs down so far apart, and he could see the glossy slickness of her pussy lips, open and vulnerable like a blooming rose. Spanking Cynthia wasn't a true punishment, not for the level of misbehavior she'd engaged in this evening, but it was a good warm-up for the main event.

Since she couldn't see him, he didn't bother to hide his grin as he gave her a final two swats right on her sit-spots and stepped away. The whimpering noise she made was halfway between pained and needy eagerness as she heard him move away from her. The bright pink skin of her bottom contrasted heavily against the cream of her back and thighs.

His hand hovered over the items on his desk. He'd never intended to use all of them tonight, but he'd wanted to leave his options open. For a moment he considered the nipple clips, but he decided against them. No need to help her by giving her any kind of distraction from punishing her rump. And he could always use them tomorrow. Picking up the ginger root, he couldn't help but wonder if his mother's staff knew why he would want it. The root was carved perfectly, which made him think someone in the household was familiar with this style of discipline.

Thick as two of his fingers at its widest point, the root was blunt-ended with a tip as thin as just one of his fingers. There was a deep groove just under its thickest point, which would help hold it in place. Small cuts had been made in the bulb to allow the juices to flow. He was so looking forward to how Cynthia would react to this.

With his other hand, he slid his finger along her wet slit. The horny little wench moaned and tilted her hips as much as she was able to.

"Please... Wesley... fuck me..."

The sound of her pleading voice, saying his name, was almost enough to make him drop the ginger plug and give in. Except he'd come this far without ruining his bride before their wedding night, and he would hate to have wasted all his effort. Besides, she'd more than earned a much harsher punishment than she'd received. All she'd gotten so far tonight was the warm-up.

"Is that really what you think you deserve, baggage?" he asked, somewhat amused. Moving his wet finger up her slit, he rimmed her tight little arsehole with it, watching as she immediately tensed.

But because her legs were so far apart, her buttocks couldn't clench shut, they just jiggled as she tried to. The effort of holding herself completely closed against his finger as it began to press against her little rosebud wasn't something she could maintain for any length of time. After barely a minute, Wesley's finger started to push in.

"No..." she moaned, her voice thick with lust and confusion.

Even more amused, he watched as she covered her face with her hands, hiding her blush from him. The tight grip of her ass pulled at his finger. He was just going to stretch her the smallest bit before inserting the ginger, lubing her with her own juices, because anything else would take away from the sting of the irritant. Pumping his finger back and forth, he enjoyed the tight heat of her asshole scalding his digit, especially when accompanied by her protesting whimpers.

"Please, my lord, do it the right way," she begged, as his finger pushed deeper. "Oh please... stop..."

"But you enjoy it so much, sweetheart," he murmured, watching as her arse completely engulfed his finger. "Why would I stop?"

She moaned again, as if protesting his declaration, but was unable to voice the lie to tell him that she didn't. The shudder going through her was as much shame as it was pleasure.

When he withdrew his finger, she slumped in relief, her body relaxing, which made it very easy for him to press the ginger against her tiny hole and shove it in with one thrust. Cynthia shrieked, her body arching, in surprise as she was invaded. Not by his finger, she could tell that. Her anus closed around whatever it was, holding it inside of her. The slight burn from being stretched wasn't too terrible, it had just startled her.

The Earl's hand caressed her bottom, as if judging the amount of heat emanating from her skin. It had been a fairly hard spanking, but he hadn't gone on long enough for it to be considered the worst one he'd administered to her. Cynthia panted, feeling the heat growing inside of her as he smoothed his hand over her sensitive skin. The tingling burn from her anus stretching hadn't started to dwindle yet.

In fact, it was growing.

"What's happening?" she asked, gasping as her bottom clenched, increasing the burn. It was an itchy, stinging burn that was beginning to get hotter and hotter inside of her. Whimpering, she shuddered, trying to reach back to grab whatever it was and pull it out, but the Earl easily caught her hands before they'd even reached the red cheeks of her bottom.

"Ginger," he said amiably as he switched sides of the chair so he could tie her hands in front of her, lashing her wrists together.

His brown eyes were hungry as he gazed into hers. The way he soaked in her expression, she knew he was enjoying every flash of discomfort he saw on her face. The thing in her bottom was making her squirm and wriggle as she tried to get away from the burn, but it just hurt worse as her bottom tightened around it.

"Just relax, baggage," he murmured, stroking his fingers over her cheek and bringing her attention back to him. "It will hurt worse when you tighten your ass around it. I want your sweet little bottom to be nice and relaxed when I birch you, this will help."

Help? This was meant to help? Cynthia opened her mouth to protest, but he leaned forward and caught her lips with his. The kiss was aggressive, his tongue sweeping into her mouth and muffling her words. One hand slid through her hair, tilting her head back at an almost uncomfortable angle so he could have complete access to her lips. The other slid under her front as she felt his finger sliding into the neckline of her dress, reaching down to squeeze her breasts.

Her pussy was creaming, even with the embarrassment of having ginger stuck up her bottom and burning her up inside. Perhaps she even liked it. Not that she had a choice either way. Being tied up like this meant there was nothing she could do, and that did help a bit with her humiliation, even though she still didn't like him touching that area, much less shoving things into it.

But she submitted to his kiss, relaxing the way he wanted her to, and the tingling burn did lessen as her ass unclenched from around the ginger plug. He'd told the truth.

When he released her, she felt almost dizzy from the myriad of sensations. Not to mention lack of air due to his thorough kissing.

So the first slash of the birch across her pink arse came as a shock. It was like a thousand tiny bees stinging into her flesh, and her bottom tightened around the ginger and she shrieked twice as loud as the burning spread both inside and out. When it came down again, she heard the swish through the air before it landed across her bottom, stinging and slashing at her skin.

She arched and jerked so hard the chair actually moved for a moment, panicking her as she thought she would fall over with the heavy thing on top of her. The Earl had quickly settled the heavy piece of furniture back down, and his hand tapped against her bottom.

"Hold still, sweetheart, you have eight more to go."

Cynthia moaned. Eight?! She cursed herself for even wondering what a birching would be like; Eleanor and Irene had been right, it was awful! "Please, I've learned my lesson, please Wesley, no more!"

If Wesley had actually thought she was telling the truth, he would have been more tempted to stop. But a birching wasn't going to truly harm Cynthia, and he didn't miss the way her pussy was still glistening with her juices. In fact, he thought they might have actually grown. Her pussy lips were quite plump, her bottom dancing as it clenched around the fiery ginger and then immediately released again.

THWAP!

The short, sharp scream she emitted was as furious as it was pained. Her bottom clenched and danced, the sharp red welts across the pink skin standing out as they swelled.

THWAP!

Another scream and more tugging at her restraints... and then she finally submitted. It had only taken four strokes for her to let go and sink into herself. Even though she screamed again when the birch came down, it was different. Her bottom didn't clench as much around the ginger. There was an acceptance to her tone, as well as sincerity when she cried out again that she was sorry.

THWAP!

THWAP!

Wesley gave her a moment between each stroke, not just to gather herself, but also to extend the anticipation. Naughty girls needed time to reflect on why they were being punished and think about how they were going to behave in the future.

THWAP!

The stroke caught her across her plump pussy lips, eliciting a shriek even higher and more piercing than the ones that came before. The red welt across them made her folds swell even more, but Wesley didn't miss how her juices had started to coat her upper thighs. The more he punished her, the more his bride creamed. Cupping his cock, he gave her an extra moment before laying down the tenth stroke, as he squeezed his erection tightly to relieve some of the ache in his balls.

THWAP!

Her sobs were of relief as she slumped down in the chair, her bottom streaked with the evidence of her birching. The enticing rump was high up in the air, propped up by the arm of the chair, while her face burrowed into the seat. With her legs spread apart and restrained, her cunt gaped at him, as if begging him to slide in as he admired his handiwork.

But that would have to wait till tomorrow.

Wesley removed the ginger from her anus, coating his fingers in a soothing balm which he then slid into her ass. It amused him to watch as she squirmed and whimpered, more unsettled by the feeling of his fingers in her arsehole than she had been by the birching.

Because it felt good. Cynthia didn't want it to feel good. She didn't welcome the coolness that came from the balm as his fingers plumbed her depths, making the roasted skin of her cheeks feel even hotter by comparison. It had hurt, far more than a spanking had, and yet she had the same aching hot need that made her want to rub her pussy. Or have the Earl rub her pussy. Damn him for choosing the wrong hole! Damn him even more for making it enjoyable.

"What do bad girls get, Cynthia?" he asked, his voice a low purr as his fingers thrust back and forth in her ass, twisting and making her whimper as the abused hole spasmed. "Where do naughty girls get fucked?"

"Noooo... please..." She covered her face with her hands, the bindings on her wrists rubbing against her chin. The Earl was going to put his cock in her arse again and, even though it was wrong, she knew when he did, she was going to cum. Why couldn't he do it the right way? The way other men wanted to?

His fingers delved deep and spread, stretching her and making her pant as her pussy clenched emptily. Part of her knew her reaction was why he insisted on making this an aspect of her punishment. But she couldn't help the feelings of embarrassment and shame washing over her as he played with her most private area, knowing he was going to shove his large cock into it, and make her climax even though she didn't want to. The whole thing would be much less humiliating if she didn't enjoy it, to be honest.

"Did you want my cock in your ass again, before our wedding?" he asked, almost taunting. "Is that why you went out tonight? Did you want to get caught doing something naughty?"

No... That couldn't possibly be why she'd done it. She just liked the adventure. The thrill of doing something she wasn't supposed to. Cynthia shook her head, as if denying both him and the thoughts inside of her head. While she liked being spanked, this was not how she'd imagined spending the night before her wedding! It wasn't! She'd thought she and Grace would be able to make it back to the house with no one the wiser, that she'd be spending the night in triumph, not with a scorching hot backside waiting to be violated by her soon-to-be husband.

"I think you did, sweetheart."

"No." Cynthia shook her head again, shaking as his fingers twisted and receded, just as something stroked over her clit as if to emphasize how swollen and aroused the little bud was.

The Earl chuckled, a dark, cruel sound which had her shuddering in anticipation. The fingers stroking her clit pinched at the little bud and she cried out, panting as pleasure surged and she nearly came.

"It doesn't really matter, since it's going to happen anyway... but one day, you're going to admit how much you like having my cock in your ass."

She moaned in denial again as his fingers retreated and something much larger and thicker pressed against the rosebud. It had been stretched enough by the ginger and his fingers to allow a fairly easy entry at first. The burn wasn't nearly as bad as when he'd put that awful spicy plug into her, even though her tight hole was being forced open much wider.

The Earl's hands wrapped around her hips, her buttocks were spread wide enough by the position of her legs that he had no need to press them apart with his hands to gain entry. The little pink hole grew paler, turning almost white as it stretched open for his cock. Groaning with pleasure, he stared down at those streaky red and pink mounds framing her pretty, forbidden hole. He could feel Cynthia's trembling, the spasms of her tight channel as he pressed forward, and the way her hips subtly lifted to welcome him in.

He doubted she even realized she was doing it, because her mind told her this act was wrong and shameful, even though her body enjoyed it. There was so little propriety in the brazen minx, he relished the taste of it. Tonight her ass, under protests, tomorrow her cunt, with her encouragement.

It didn't escape his notice how much his Cynthia wanted to lose her virginity. The anticipation, his self-control, only emphasized who was in control of their relationship.

Sinking deeper, he groaned some more, wanting her to hear his pleasure as he invaded her backside. The little tremors of her anus massaged his cock, her tiny whimpers as she squirmed making him even harder. It was the beautiful and erotic sound of a woman submitting her body, taking the discomfort in order to please him, acknowledging his right to both punish and pleasure her.

When his groin came flush against her bottom, he rocked against her, making her squeal as his body rubbed against the tender welts the birch had left behind. The mixture of pleasure and pain left her gasping and clenching. Sliding his hands up from her hips, he yanked on the top of her dress so he could reach her bare breasts. The fabric of her dress was now bunched around her middle, enhancing the feeling of vulnerability as she was clothed but not covered.

Possessive need swamped him as he began to thrust into her ass, squeezing her breasts tightly. The wet slap of his balls against her pussy made both of them moan. She was saying something softly, so softly he couldn't hear it, and he leaned closer, causing his body to press more tightly against her roasted bottom and the heat seemed to coat his stomach.

"Oh please... oh please... oh please..."

Masculine triumph surged. She was caught, somewhere between begging him to stop and crying out for more, totally ensnared by the sensations coursing through her. He'd pushed her beyond her thinking reactions and into a state where things like embarrassment and shame meant nothing. All that mattered was the pleasure and the pain, and her body was confusing them.

Wesley practically roared his triumph as he began fucking her hard, using her breasts for leverage, and wallowing in her shrieks of pained pleasure as he fucked her ass. Pinching her nipples, he could feel her tight hole contract around him, increasing the friction burn for both of them as he plundered her depths.

When she screamed again, he knew she was climaxing, her pussy spasming and creaming itself even though it was empty. The grip on his cock tightened nearly to the point of pain as she bucked and clenched. Pinching her nipples hard, he thrust in completely, grinding himself against her rump and awakening the stinging welts the birch had left behind.

Cynthia was lost in a maelstrom of pain and pleasure, she couldn't tell where one ended and the other began... darkness, scattered with blazing sparks, covered her vision. Heat spurted, filling her, her ass clenching around steel and protesting the thick, hard length piercing it, even as it spurred her ecstasy to greater heights. It was heaven and hell, warring in her body, and she'd never felt anything so intense.

GENTLY COVERING HIS BRIDE UP, Wesley stroked her damp hair back from her temples. He couldn't have asked for a better stag night, despite the panic he'd felt earlier when he'd gone looking for Cynthia. Frustrating baggage. There'd been a moment of lesser panic as well, when he'd unsheathed from her ass and she hadn't moved. For a moment he thought he'd been too rough, but when he pulled her up to look at him, the dreamy smile on her lips had quieted all his qualms.

His bride had barely been lucid, she'd been limp in his arms, and unable to walk, but she'd been smiling.

It had been monumentally satisfying to carry her to her room, a soft, submissive bundle of chastised beauty. Of course, it would be even more satisfying after tonight, when he'd be able to carry her to *his* room. He was sure there would be many occasions for that. With the exception of the night she'd tried to sneak into his bed, he'd decided the bedroom would be for pleasure, the study for punishment.

Not that he would ignore his darker and more perverted tendencies in the privacy of their bedroom, but he wouldn't punish her for naughtiness there either.

Leaning down, he kissed her soft lips and she murmured in her sleep, her dreamy smile making him feel almost tender, despite how frustratingly out of bounds she'd been earlier.

"Sleep well, darling. Tomorrow you're mine."

CHAPTER 11

*T*he wedding ceremony was beautiful. The groom was a handsome devil incarnate. The bride was stunning, a mix of innocence and sultry promise. The vows surprisingly sincere, causing many a woman in the audience to frown and many a man to sigh with regret, as another hardened rake had evidently fallen victim to love—and to such a buxom beauty! The men were especially displeased they hadn't even had a chance to approach such a sweet armful before the Earl of Spencer had snatched her up. Those who had been lucky enough to meet her before, cursed the Earl for both his good fortune and the possessiveness they'd already had the dubious privilege of experiencing when they'd flirted with her after he'd met her. Several of the young ladies, mostly in their second or third seasons, sighed in envy at the romanticism of it all, hoping they would be as fortunate to find such handsome, doting husbands.

Throughout all of it, Eleanor was miserable.

Well, perhaps miserable wasn't the right word. Murderous might be more apt.

Seated between the Countess and her own parents in the front pew, she glared at her husband throughout the entire ceremony. He was splendid looking, so tall and dark, and with a rakish smirk decorating his lips. She could hear the sighs of the women behind her as they admired the looks of the men who were standing up for Wesley. If only those women knew that one of the men was the very devil incarnate.

After taking her home last night, Edwin had punished her with pleasure. More specifically, withheld pleasure. He'd kissed and caressed and stroked her until she was wild with need, and then he'd pumped his seed all over her breasts and belly, without allowing her to climax. Holding her tightly in his arms, he'd kept her from touching herself and relieving the ache which had taken hold.

The worst part was, she could tell he wasn't even truly upset with her. In fact, he'd seemed rather proud she hadn't gone wandering off with Cynthia and Grace. Defying him had been fun, but the punishment she'd received had not been the one she'd expected.

Of course she'd known she wouldn't get away with withholding information from him, but she'd thought she'd at least receive ecstasy at the end of it, as she so often did. Although, even if she'd known what his devious mind would come up with, she still wouldn't have told him where Grace and Cynthia had gone. Part of her was relieved Irene had caved, so she hadn't had to. Knowing Grace and Cynthia hadn't been up to anything harmful had given her the chance to pit her will against Edwin's again.

She would hate for him to think she was becoming too meek. It wasn't in her nature, so any time she could find some small way to test his will (and his patience), she happily took it up. Last night had proven to be such a moment. Eleanor had exulted in her rebellion, in proving to herself and him that being in love, being disciplined by her husband, hadn't changed who she was at her core.

But then the bastard had gone and turned it all around on her.

Even now, glaring at him, she couldn't help but want him. The entire ceremony she could barely concentrate on the words, or on the way Cynthia kept shifting uncomfortably, or Grace as she peeked at Alex from across the dais. Eleanor was too busy thinking about all the naughty, decadent, perverse things she wanted to do with her husband.

A spanking would have been better than this.

Actually, if she was being honest, she'd been looking forward to a bit of discipline. It wasn't until she hadn't gotten it that she realized how much her body craved her husband's firm hand and the hot sting of a spanking. There was truly something wrong with her.

CYNTHIA MIGHT HAVE IMAGINED IT, but she would swear Wesley's eyes gleamed even brighter as she promised to love, honor, and obey him. Vowing to obey him felt right, even as she knew she would break the vow many times throughout their life. She wanted to obey, she really did, but it was just so very difficult. But she would obey as best she could, and she'd probably do better at it when she had a sore bottom than when she didn't. Still, she did love him. She had no idea what "honoring" him meant, but she'd just vowed to do that too.

The fierce way he spoke his own vows made her heart dance inside of her chest. He was looking at her with a possessiveness she'd seen Edwin looking at Eleanor with, and Hugh looking at Irene, and even Alex looking at Grace. It was a heady experience, being at the center of all that attention—not just the congregation's, but his as well.

Putting the ring on Cynthia's finger was the highlight of the ceremony for Wesley. Finally, *finally*, she was marked as his. The gleaming gold band wasn't a shield against other men, he knew that, but it still made him feel incredibly, smugly triumphant to see it on her hand. A physical indication she was his and no one else's, for the rest of their life.

If another man even thought of touching her, Wesley now had all the reason he needed to blow the bugger's head off.

"I NOW PRONOUNCE YOU, man and wife. You may kiss the bride."

The pastor was grinning as he said the words, but his expression quickly turned to shock as Wesley behaved in his usual irreverent manner. Edwin, Hugh, and Alex all chortled with amusement as Wesley reached out and grabbed his bride by her hips, drawing her into him and bending her back for a completely improper and passionate kiss. Even more improperly, Cynthia flung her arms around his neck and was obviously kissing him back with enthusiasm. The sounds behind Eleanor, from the *ton* at large, ranged from gasps of shock or disapproval to cheers from a few of the men— quickly quieted as they were whacked with fans from the ladies seated nearest them.

Eleanor covered her mouth, pretending to cough to cover her own laughter. Beside her, the Countess shook her head, but Eleanor could see the sparkle in her eyes and the amused twitch of her lips as she watched her son finish the kiss and bring Cynthia upright again.

The shameless little hussy was pink-cheeked with excitement, not with embarrassment, as Wesley wrapped her hand around his arm and they began to walk back down the aisle. Eleanor couldn't help but grin at her. She was going to set the *ton* on its ears and Eleanor was looking forward to it. Already Cynthia had created a bit of a scandal by having Grace as one of her bridesmaids. If only Eleanor's morning nausea was less severe, she would have been standing up there as well.

As the wedding party followed the bride and groom down the aisle, the entire audience was treated to watching Lord Brooke extending his arm in an exaggerated offer to his wife. But that wasn't the biggest surprise—the whole room seemed to take an indrawn breath when she actually accepted it. Rumors had been going around since their arrival together in Bath, especially after the dance the other night, but this seemed even more indicative of their general state of affairs.

Eleanor rolled her eyes. Such small scenes would be dissected to tiny bits by the gossips, and then it was likely their entire demeanor toward Grace would change. Everyone would assume the couple was reconciling to create an heir, and now that Grace was doing her duty, the scandal would die down again as long as she didn't take another lover until after said heir was produced. She saw more than one woman looking at the couple with blatant consternation on their faces.

Probably the ones who had hoped Lord Brooke would divorce his wife and remarry. Or women who had hoped to become his lover. Many of them were the same women who flirted with Edwin, only to be brutally rebuffed. It took considerable effort for Eleanor not to smirk at any of them as she passed, arm in arm with the Countess.

THE RECEIVING line at the wedding brunch was boring Cynthia to tears, right up until she saw two of her favorite people in the world. She fairly launched herself at them, tears of joy sparkling in her eyes.

"Matthew! Vincent! What are you doing here?!"

Behind her, Wesley had to still his sudden and violent desire to punch his own brothers in the face. Fortunately for both of them, they responded to his new bride's enthusiastic greeting with laughter and brotherly hugs, giving no indication they regarded Cynthia as anything other than a little sister. Which made Wesley wonder about the state of their eyesight. Matthew might be a bit young to appreciate Cynthia's charms, which were evident even in the innocent and modest white dress she was wearing, but Vincent was old enough to know what a treasure she was.

Vincent laughed and kissed her forehead. "My gawd, Cyn, I almost didn't recognize you... you look like a real lady now." A statement which she immediately contradicted by sticking her tongue out at him, which made him laugh again. He had the same hazel eyes and brown hair as all the Spencer men, but his hair was fashionably styled as was his clothing. Matthew, of course, was wearing his uniform, and was eyeing some of the other young ladies who were fluttering and fanning themselves over the dashing young officer. "What happened to all the mud?"

To Wesley's surprise, Cynthia blushed, but then turned up her nose at him in an admirable imitation of the Countess. "A gentleman doesn't remind a lady of her past indiscretions."

"Too right, my dear," the Countess—now the Dowager-Countess since Cynthia had just become the Countess—said, coming up behind Cynthia and giving her sons a pleased smiled. "I'm so glad you two made it in time, although you should have come and sat with me."

"Hullo mother," Matthew said dutifully, leaning down to buss her cheek. "We arrived a bit too late for that, so we just sat in the back and watched." He grinned at Wesley. "Congratulations brother, or should I say good luck? Because you're going to need it with this little devil." He opened his arms and Cynthia immediately squealed and jumped into them, squeezing him about the waist.

Wesley plastered a smile on his own face, even though right now he felt a bit like growling. He and Cynthia were going to have to have a talk about the proper way to interact with other men. Even his brothers. His smile became a bit more relaxed as he remembered their "talk" last night. From the way his bride had been fidgeting all morning, he knew she was still feeling the marks from her birching. His marks, on her skin, reminding her of whose she was. That salved some of the possessive aggression boiling up inside of him.

Strangely, being wedded to her didn't make him feel more secure. If anything, he felt more possessively guarded than ever. As a wife, she was even riper for seduction by the rakes of the *ton*. Not that he thought she would fall to their blandishments, she'd kept them off before he'd ever met her, but that didn't mean he liked them looking or thinking. It almost made him feel sorry for all the husbands he'd cuckolded over the years. Except they'd been stupid enough to neglect their wives, leaving them unprotected and needy.

Not a mistake Wesley would make.

Pulling his wife back to him and tucking her in neatly at his side, he grinned at his brothers. With Cynthia properly secured, it was easier to enjoy seeing them. "I didn't know you were going to be here, but I'm glad you are."

His younger brothers both clapped his shoulder, expressing their congratulations on his wedding. "Not something I thought I'd ever be able to say to you," teased Matthew. "But I'm glad Mother was right."

"What do you mean?" Wesley asked, frowning as he turned his head slightly. The Dowager was surrounded by her friends, all gleefully congratulating her on getting her rakish son settled.

"As soon as Cyn came to live with us, Mother said she'd be perfect for you, once she was trained up a bit," Vincent said. The sparkling of his mischievous hazel eyes were filled with laughter; it was obvious he knew his elder brother had had no idea.

"She did?" Wesley and Cynthia chorused the words, in the same surprised tones, which made him feel slightly better. Slightly less trapped as well. For a moment his temper rose, but it quickly slid into amusement as he looked down at his wife, who was glaring from across the room at her new mother-in-law. "Well, she was right, much as I hate to say it."

Cynthia muttered something under her breath, and he gave her a warning squeeze. Even though he couldn't hear the words, he was fairly sure she'd just cursed.

Looking up at him, her expression was puzzled. "Aren't you mad?"

"At my mother's machinations?" He sighed and shook his head, his smile slightly crooked with resignation. "You'll get used to them. Besides, how can I be mad at her when she brought me you?"

Both of his brothers made gagging noises as Cynthia's cheeks blushed a sweet pink. She looked so charmingly innocent at that moment, despite Wesley's firsthand knowledge that she certainly wasn't. It took quite a bit of willpower not to drag her off to divest her of the last of her innocence this very moment.

STANDING with Hugh and his parents, Alex kept one eye on Grace, who was talking with Eleanor and Irene. Edwin hovered behind the chair he'd seated Eleanor in, which had already sparked quite a bit of speculation among the guests that she might be in an interesting condition. Many of them had tried to surreptitiously coax one of the Hydes' friends into confirming, so far without success. It helped that Eleanor's parents weren't hovering as well, most of the gossips were sure Lord and Lady Harrington would be watching over her as well if she were *enceinte*.

Alex only had eyes for Grace.

Last night she slept in his arms without protest, warm and soft, and he'd fallen asleep filled with hope. This morning she'd pulled away immediately, a wary expression back on her face. Studying him. Judging him. If only he knew for what.

Unfortunately, they hadn't had any time to talk as they'd had to prepare for the wedding. Cynthia had asked Irene, Eleanor, and Grace to stand on her side, so Grace had disappeared to join the women as soon as she'd dressed. At least Alex had had the pleasure of looking at her barely pink bottom before she'd gotten dressed. The spanking she'd received the night before hadn't left much visible evidence behind, but he could tell she was still sore from the way she'd winced when she'd sat down for her maid to do her hair.

They needed to talk.

It was a thought he'd had before, especially when she'd said things that confused him, but he'd always allowed himself to be distracted by other means of communication. Alex always felt actions spoke more than words. It was why he'd waited until after Grace had taken her first lover to take a mistress to his bed. Now that had translated into spanking her when she was naughty and holding her for comfort afterwards. Actions were easier than words.

But it was looking as though words were going to become necessary, because every time he spoke, he felt as though Grace was weighing what he said. And when she spoke, half the time he wasn't sure what she was talking about. There seemed to be some third part of the conversation he wasn't aware of. It would be so much easier if she would just trust in him, in his return, his worship of her body, his discipline... after all, he was taking the time to correct her behavior and continue to try and reconcile, rather than giving up on their relationship. Shouldn't that speak volumes?

Well, perhaps he was just being impatient, because it did seem like things had changed between them—for the better. But he didn't think they could go much further without him knowing what was going through her pretty little head, and she seemed to feel the same. Because every time he told her, she didn't act as though she trusted what he said.

"Why don't you just go over to her?"

Alex came back to himself with a start, guiltily turning to look at Hugh. Lord and Lady Harrington had already moved away, leaving the two men alone. "Sorry, I didn't mean to ignore you."

"No apology necessary," Hugh said, shooting him an amused look. "I just don't understand why you're standing here with me, when it's obvious you want to be over there with her."

"I just thought I'd give her some space," he muttered, looking back at her. She was laughing at something Eleanor had said, looking gorgeously happy and making his chest ache. "She never smiles like that when I'm nearby."

Hugh studied her for a moment, his own expression softening when his gaze lit upon his own wife. "Give it time. You've already made a great deal of progress from when you first arrived in Bath."

"Yes, but she's keeping something from me... and I'm sure whatever it is makes up part of the reason why she's so determined to remain estranged." His jaw clenched. "Or become divorced."

"Have you asked her?"

He felt just the slight hint of a blush tinging his cheeks. "I've meant to... but there hasn't been much time to really sit and talk and when there has..."

"You've gotten distracted," Hugh finished for him, grinning at Alex's discomfiture. Alex cleared his throat, searching for his usual indifference and finding it was harder to slide the blank expression over his face than it used to be. Fortunately, Hugh understood. "I know how that can be. But you should make the time now the wedding's over. If I'd made the time to truly talk to Irene, perhaps things wouldn't have ah... gone quite the way they had this Season."

Remembering the horrifyingly awkward scene in the garden, Alex shifted uncomfortably. Just thinking about that night made his skin crawl. He still didn't understand what had come over Irene, although she'd explained what had gone on in her head; her actions had been shocking. Most of the time he could forget about it when they talked now, but he still held back from the way their friendship used to be. Not just out of respect for Hugh and Grace, but also because it made him anxious.

"It'd be easier if, when I did tell her something, she actually believed me," he muttered.

"Well then maybe it's you that needs to listen, instead of talking," Hugh said, shrugging. They both looked across the room at Grace. "She's stubborn and when she gets an idea in her head, it can be the devil to knock it out again. When she and Eleanor were younger, our Cook at the time told them that if you eat a pie just out of the oven, before it's had the a chance to cool, it's poison. Eleanor didn't believe her, but Grace still won't eat a fresh made pie."

Now that was something Alex definitely hadn't known about his wife. The very silliness of it made his lips twitch, wanting to smile. "She's never said anything about it to me."

"She wouldn't, it's just one of her habits now," Hugh said, grinning. "I daresay she doesn't even realize she still does it... it's just an idea that got stuck in her head."

So what idea did she have stuck in her head about Alex and their marriage?

He was just about to excuse himself from Hugh when a seductive waft of feminine perfume made him turn his head. Beside him was Lady Astor, a beautiful young widow who had just recently come out of mourning her much older husband. She looked like delicate springtime, all soft creams, pinks, and golds. Even her doe-like brown eyes were soft looking as she smiled up at him, completely sincerely and with open invitation.

"Lord Brooke, Viscount Petersham," she said, with the tiniest curtsy allowing her to dip just enough to lean forward and show off rather splendid cleavage.

"Lady Astor," they chorused together. Alex's bow hid his wince.

"You look splendid this morning," Hugh said, somehow managing to strike just the right note of admiration in his voice, without making it sound as though he was interested in her personage.

"Thank you, Viscount," she said, obviously pleased by the compliment. She glanced at Alex, her lashes lowering as if inviting him to compliment her as well. When he didn't immediately speak up, it didn't seem to faze her at all. "The wedding was beautiful, I'm so glad I was able to come to Bath for it. Quite the event of the Season. Those who stayed in London will be sorry they missed it."

They exchanged meaningless social niceties for another few minutes, Alex shifting away every time Lady Astor tried to reach out and touch him. He didn't want her damn hand on his arm. It didn't take very long for her to smile and excuse herself, having finally gotten the hint.

Unfortunately, that seemed to be the cue for the other women to take their own run at him. Alex held himself stiffly aloof, although he had to be polite, and let Hugh do most of the talking. Unlike himself, Hugh had a wife who felt secure in their relationship, one who wouldn't mistake the necessary social graciousness for something more than it was. His own situation was more precarious.

When he next glanced across the room, and saw Grace was watching him with an expression of surprise and wariness on her face, he was even gladder he'd decided to be so aloof to the flirtatious ladies.

It was like a game of cat and mouse.

Grace watched Alex, but only when he wasn't watching her, making sure their gazes never crossed. Part of her mind was busy with the conversation going on around her, while the other was completely occupied by observing Alex. She was still trying to decide whether or not to trust him.

Last night had been... wonderful. Terrible. Her body ached to repeat it. Her heart ached to believe in it.

"Are you going to be alright on his estates?" Eleanor asked her softly, leaning in so the other women around them couldn't hear what she was saying. They were involved in their own conversation anyway, so none of them were trying to listen. While the *ton* hadn't lost interest in the continuing saga of Lord and Lady Brooke, this morning they were far more interested in the Earl and his new Countess. "I'm not sure if I'll be able to talk Edwin into leaving the Manse once we get there... considering..." She gestured discreetly at her belly.

"I think I'll be fine... I don't know." Grace let out a huff of air. She'd told Eleanor everything she'd found—and hadn't found—in Alex's study last night. Although she hadn't told Eleanor about what had come after Alex had disciplined her. "I just... I want to believe maybe this is real, that maybe he does feel something for me... but I've been wrong before, why would I be right this time? I don't think I can go through it again, Nell... it just about killed me the first time. Why would I set myself up to fall a second time?"

Eleanor grasped her hand, her serious blue eyes filled with earnest sincerity. "Maybe you should confront him. You've been doing everything you can to find out his motives, *except* actually asking him. If he knew why you left him, why you don't trust him now, maybe it would help."

"Or maybe he'll see me for the little fool I was," Grace said bitterly, wincing. She didn't want to talk about that with him because she was too afraid he would ridicule her.

So she was afraid to question him because he might turn out to be a man she couldn't love, and at the same time, she was afraid to love him anyway because she hadn't confronted him. Maybe she really was a little fool.

"Talk to him," Eleanor whispered, squeezing her hand. "I wish I had talked to Edwin sooner. I kept hinting around what I wanted from him, because I wanted him to say what he felt in his own words, but he didn't realize what I needed to hear. I thought the declaration only mattered if it came, unasked for, from him... but if I had asked, he would have told me. He would have reassured me until I believed it, the way he did as soon as he realized what I wanted. I was too stuck in wanting something specific from him, instead of appreciating what he was doing to show me how he felt."

Nodding, Grace admitted to herself, in some ways, she'd been unreasonable ever since Alex had shown up in her life again. Not that he'd been entirely reasonable. Hence, the kidnapping her to Bath. She hadn't been ready to listen before.

Watching as yet another woman stepped away from Alex and Hugh, a look of disappointment on her beautiful face, Grace knew she was ready to start listening now. Alex was making an effort to show he could be the same kind of caring husband his friends were to their wives; eschewing the company of other women, staving off the flirts, and demonstrating he was serious about this reconciliation. More serious than Grace had originally thought, certainly.

"I'll talk to him. But not tonight."

Eleanor made an exasperated noise. "Why not tonight?"

"Because we're leaving Bath tomorrow and I will be stuck in the carriage with him for *hours*, if the trip here was any indication. I'd like as pleasant a ride as possible, so I might as well wait until we're at the estate to say anything. At least that way I'll have a whole house, not to mention the acreage, to get away from him if I need to."

The reasoning made sense, but she couldn't help but giggle when Eleanor did. Just having a course of action, knowing the end of her current Purgatory was coming in one way or another—although she didn't know whether she'd fall into Hell or rise into Heaven—made her feel better. Even if she did fall, at least then she'd *know*. The constant doubt and anxiety was turning her mad.

"You can come stay with us if you need to," Eleanor said, the giggles subsiding as she turned more serious. "You'll be right next to Hugh and you know he'll do whatever he can to help you, if you need it."

He would too, even though he was now Alex's friend, Grace knew that. Hugh was, by far, the most serious of the trio which had grown up together, he would consider it his duty to protect his sister's best friend. After all, he had often enough when she was younger. It was a position she had never put him or his family in when she and Alex had separated, because she hadn't wanted to take advantage of their feelings toward her in a way that could cause them some strife among the rest of their peers. They'd never kept her from Eleanor, and that had been enough.

If she had to take shelter with Hugh...

Hopefully it wouldn't come to that. Because if she did, and Alex was determined to keep her in their marriage, the law would be on his side. Hugh could actually be arrested if he tried to keep Alex from her. If a husband wanted his wife under his roof, there was very little anyone could do. She truly would flee, rather than forcing her friends to make terrible choices.

But even thinking about such things couldn't stop the almost painful burgeoning of hope in her chest, spurred by both Alex's recent behavior and Eleanor's encouragement. Her life had been a kind of Hell for years now; perhaps it was finally time for redemption.

As much as Edwin wanted to hear exactly what his wife and Grace were whispering back and forth, he could tell from the way they were huddled together that leaning down to overhear would only result in the end of the conversation. From the way they both kept peeking over at Alex, he was sure it had something to do with Grace and Alex's marriage. Just as he was certain last night's escapades were about that as well.

He couldn't figure out exactly what they thought they'd accomplished last night. Sometimes women just did inexplicable things.

Although, it had led to some very satisfying moments for himself. There was something exquisitely erotic about teasing Eleanor into a needy frenzy and then denying her pleasure. The look of aghast disbelief on her face as she realized the control he had over her body and her climaxes had been hotly arousing for him. He'd held her close all night to ensure she wouldn't cheat and pleasure herself.

Today he amused himself with little touches to the nape of her neck, her shoulder, her lower back... small caresses meant to tantalize without satisfying. The angry, sexually charged dirty looks he received in return only made him grin. He wanted to get his Nell to a frustrated boiling point, and then tomorrow he'd wake her with his mouth between her legs. This was a punishment he was going to have to remember even after he didn't have to worry about disciplinary spankings again.

He didn't doubt he'd need plenty of creativity through his life when it came to disciplining Eleanor. Their marriage would be a constant testing of wills, but he was sure he would always win. It wouldn't be restful, as Hugh would put it, but it was what Edwin loved about her.

This time, when he caressed the back of her neck and she glared up at him, her gaze almost immediately softened. Perhaps because of the way he was looking at her. He could practically feel his love for her flowing out of him, as if it was water spilling out of a too-full glass. It still baffled him that she hadn't known how he cared for her.

"There you are!" Lady Harrington pushed through a knot of people, beaming at her daughter, son-in-law, and daughter's friend equally. Since returning to Bath, it was obvious her health had improved greatly. Trailing along behind her with an indulgent look on his face, Hugh and Eleanor's father just smiled at them, without the excitement Lady Harrington was showing. "I've been looking all over for you."

To their surprise, she reached out to Grace, leaning down to give her an affectionate kiss on each cheek. Murmurs from the people around them, showed Lady Harrington's preference had not gone unnoticed. Edwin coughed to cover his laughter. He smelled a motherly plot afoot. The Countess had also been marked in her attentions to Grace this past week, keeping her from the censure of the high sticklers who had been invited to the wedding. He wasn't sure if Alex had asked her to help or if she had just decided to do it on his own, but Grace's mother and Lady Harrington were best friends, so it wasn't too surprising she would be putting her own foot forward to further Grace's re-entrance into the higher echelons of Society.

For herself, Grace looked surprised, pleased, and—strangely—a bit worried. Edwin saw her glance at Alex before turning her attention back to Lady Harrington, a happy smile on her face, although the tension hadn't quite left her shoulders. She was another one who obviously didn't know how much her husband cared for her, but that wasn't his problem. That was something Alex would need to work out on his own; Edwin had his own stubborn wife to deal with.

He stroked his fingers down the back of Eleanor's neck, watching her shiver.

Reaching back, she grabbed his hand and tugged, pulling him downward. To any onlooker, it would seem she just wanted a wifely word in his ear, but her tone was viperish as she hissed at him.

"If you don't stop touching me, Edwin... I swear... I'm going to explode! A spanking would be better than this!"

The feverishly bright look in her eyes made him immediately contrite. The entire point of this exercise, other than to punish her, had been to provide discipline in a way which wouldn't cause her undue distress. A disciplinary spanking would have her bucking and crying, stressing her both emotionally and physically; he hadn't meant to drive her quite to that point now. It seemed he would have to be more careful than he realized with this kind of creative sanctioning of her behavior.

At least while she was pregnant.

"I'm sorry, sweetheart, calm down," he said, his voice full of apology. He'd only meant to tease her, not to torture her. While it was gratifying to know the effect he had on her, he also needed to maintain his control.

When he straightened and put his hand back on her neck, it was no longer the seductive, light touch he'd been tormenting her with.

Instead, he used his fingers to massage and soothe her, affection running through him as he felt her relax under his ministrations.

Soothed, Eleanor allowed herself to be drawn into the conversation with Grace and her mother.

"Well, you two seem to be happy as two peas in a pod," Lord Harrington said jovially, sidling up to Edwin. He looked down indulgently at his daughter, who (fortunately) hadn't heard a word he'd said. "I knew she'd come around once she had a chance to settle."

"She's perfect," Edwin said, conveniently ignoring the various escapades Eleanor had put him through. After all, they were his concerns to deal with now, not her father's. Besides, those same escapades were what made her perfect for him. As long as she wasn't putting herself in the way of harm, he quite enjoyed her high-spirited antics. Playful spankings were arousing in their own way, but he knew his favorite ones were those Eleanor had earned. He would miss seeing her tear-stained, contrite face following a well-deserved punishment, and her hot, red bottom, until her pregnancy was over... but he would also be tallying all of her misdeeds and build his anticipation for the day of reckoning once their child was born.

"Just like her mother." The loving look Lord Harrington bestowed upon his wife left little doubt to his own feelings. "Have you spoken to your parents yet?"

"I wrote them, of course," Edwin said. He shared a knowing look with the older man. "They encouraged us to visit the Manse as soon as possible. We'll be leaving tomorrow to make our way there. They're thrilled, of course, especially mother."

Lord Harrington nodded, knowing his friends' vagaries very well. None of them had truly expected Edwin's parents to leave their estate, not even to meet his new bride. If they'd had enough advance notice of the wedding, they would have come, but once the deed was done—and to a young woman they knew quite well—they'd be content to wait for him to come home.

"Penelope and I will be in Bath for another week before we leave for Stonehaven. After that, we've been invited to come stay at the Manse."

"I'm sure Eleanor will be particularly glad of her Mother's company by then," Edwin murmured, careful to keep his voice low. They hadn't announced her condition yet, and they wouldn't until they were ready to leave Bath, but he knew she was going to tell her mother sometime today or tomorrow. Dropping a discreet hint to her father wouldn't ruin that. "I hope you plan to stay for a while."

The sharp-eyed Earl looked down at his daughter and then back up at Edwin and grinned, making him look years younger. "I'm sure a visit can be arranged. Penelope will probably insist."

"So will Eleanor." Truthfully, Edwin would be grateful to have Lord Harrington there as well. While his own father was a good man, he could also be rather absent-minded and unreliable. Lord Harrington was like a bulwark of paternal strength to lean on, whereas the Earl of Clarendon was just as likely to be buried in the library with his research as he was to be attending to his parental duties. It wasn't that he meant to be distracted, but Edwin was still glad Lord Harrington would be there to help as well.

Sometimes he wondered if the reason they kept putting off announcing Eleanor's condition was because he found the reality utterly terrifying. He'd told his closest friends, of course, in the first rush of excitement, but with every day that went by he found himself less excited and more overwhelmed by the impending life growing in his wife's belly. To the best of his ability he would keep Eleanor safe and healthy, but the dangers of childbirth were unavoidable. Only so many factors were within his control.

Then once his son or daughter was born... would he be a good father? Would he be able to keep his sons from running wild? Instill in his heir the right amount of responsibility? Teach his other sons they mattered, even though they weren't the heir? He certainly didn't want them to feel the way Wesley's younger brothers had felt under their father's iron fist. Then again, he didn't want to be like Wesley's father at all. What if it was a daughter? What would he do with a daughter?

A hand on his arm jerked him out of the spiral of thoughts that seemed to engulf him whenever he started to think about his future progeny. Lord Harrington's clear blue eyes were filled with fellow feeling and understanding. He clapped Edwin on the shoulder.

"You'll be just fine, son. Just fine."

Simple words really, and yet they brought Edwin a large measure of relief. After all, Lord Harrington was the man he looked up to the most when it came to fatherhood. If he believed in Edwin, then maybe Edwin could as well.

CHAPTER 12

*E*nough was enough. The inane social niceties were driving Wesley absolutely up the wall. Normally he eschewed conversing when he was out in Society, unless it was with a particular man or woman he actually wished to speak with. Being trapped in a room filled with gawkers who wanted to congratulate, gossip about, or seduce him and his new wife made his skin crawl.

The disappointed women were the worst. Their underhanded, catty comments seemed to slide right off of Cynthia, but they were infuriating Wesley. Worse, there wasn't much he could do about them, other than remain glued to his bride's side and do his best to deflect. If they were men, he could call them out. Then again, if they were men, they'd be direct instead of backbiting.

"It's too bad the Countess didn't bring you to London," a beautiful young matron was saying to Cynthia. Wesley couldn't remember her name. She was beautiful, but obviously spiteful. The man she'd come in with, whom he assumed was her husband, was talking with a different buxom beauty across the room. "A little bit of town bronze is always helpful when it comes to marriage. So many poor young women from the country become married without truly under-standing Society... it leads to so much disappointment on their part when their husbands don't behave as they expected once back in Society."

The flirtatious glance she gave him made it clear what she meant. The invitation in her eyes did not appeal to him at all. It just made him furious she was implying to Cynthia—on her wedding day—that Wesley would not remain faithful and she shouldn't expect him to. Even if he and Cynthia hadn't made their deal, he would have been furious. Cynthia was worthy of more than a husband who chased other women. Wesley was that worthier husband and he didn't like this woman implying he wouldn't be. Especially because he certainly didn't need his bride getting any bright ideas about the sincerity of his promise to her—the little minx would certainly retaliate and then Wesley would have to kill someone.

"Oh, the Countess was too afraid to bring me to London," Cynthia said brightly, stealing the woman's attention back to herself before Wesley could completely lose his temper and tell her exactly what he thought about her brazen blandishments. "I'm sure I would have created quite the scandal... I have the most awful manners. Especially when it comes to things I consider mine. Why, I tried to stab her son Matthew with a fork when he poached one of my potatoes at dinner." She giggled and batted her eyes, making Wesley practically choke. "Imagine if I'd done that at a dinner party to a Duke!"

His unapologetic hussy of a wife pressed against him, beaming at the other woman, but Wesley could see the hard look in her eyes, despite the silliness of her demeanor. The message had gotten across, making the young matron look a bit leery. After all, this country girl had not only understood exactly what she'd been saying but had indicated a penchant for violence.

"Yes... that would have been quite unfortunate," she said, rallying, although she still eyed Cynthia warily. "Excuse me... I ah, see my friend needs me."

Wesley forced his face to a stern countenance, hiding his mirth, as the woman hurried away. He bent his head slightly, his arm wrapped around Cynthia's hips, giving the impression he was saying sweet nothings in her ear. The image wouldn't hurt, and perhaps it would help keep more of the harpies away.

"That wasn't well done, baggage, what if she gossips? My mother will be horrified."

"I'd rather horrify your mother than have to deal with any more women like Lady Vetch," Cynthia said tartly, turning up her cute little nose. Wesley had the most insane urge to kiss it. Marriage was getting to his head. "If she tries to poach you, I will use something much sharper than a fork."

"It doesn't matter if she wants to poach me," he replied, trying not to think about how adorable her possessive jealousy was. "What matters is I have no interest in anyone but you. She can want whatever she likes, it makes no difference to me."

"Well it does to me." Cynthia scowled at him. "I'm a Countess now. They'll respect me."

"Or you'll stab them with a fork?"

"Exactly."

The worst part was, he wasn't quite sure whether or not she was serious, and he was definitely sure he didn't care. In fact, part of him was highly amused by the idea of a fork-wielding Cynthia, chasing away amorous would-be paramours.

Staring up at her new husband, Cynthia had to admit, she hadn't been expecting the twinkling amusement in his eyes. While he was wildly exciting when it came to amorous pursuits, and she was incredibly attracted to his dominating authority over her, she'd honestly thought she'd set herself up for a wedding day spanking. Not that she wanted one, but she wouldn't have regretted it for a moment. Lady Vetch had been the most recent in a long line of women hinting to her that she shouldn't be upset if her new husband chose one of them as his lover. If the woman gossiped and it kept any more hussies from appearing on the scene, all the better.

Cynthia hadn't even been deflowered yet, she was certainly not sharing her husband. She would keep him busy enough in the bedroom. There were so many things she wanted to learn. He wasn't going to have time to attend to any other lady's desires.

Not that he'd seemed interested in any of the importuning women, but still. If Cynthia had to put up with his stuffed-shirt ways and wicked punishments, she was certainly going to reap the benefits of being married to him as well. She hadn't wanted another spanking over top the welts decorating her bottom, but it had been worth the risk. Especially since he seemed more amused than anything else, which was a relief for her poor bum.

She was probably the only bride in history to have absolutely no desire to sit down, no matter how much her feet hurt or how tired she felt. Every single part of her bottom was sore, and the welts left from the birch stung when she pressed on them. She knew because she'd poked at each and every one of them this morning while she'd been admiring them in the mirror. At long last, she'd had some physical evidence of what she'd gone through. The sight had fascinated her to say the least, although she was less enamored of how it felt when any pressure at all was placed on her tender cheeks.

"I think it's time we left, baggage."

"Oh but..." Not that she wanted to put off the good stuff, but she'd missed out on the last round of éclairs to go through the room, and the footman she'd snagged had promised to bring her some. Plus, she'd barely gotten to speak to Matthew and Vincent.

Unfortunately, the Earl was not impressed by her protest. His stuffed-shirt persona was firmly back in place, not a hint of amusement to be seen. He swept her up into his arms, one arm behind her back and the other under her legs as she gasped with shock. Titters and whispers swept through the room as he headed straight for the door, and Cynthia sighed. Apparently she wasn't going to get her éclairs after all.

Of course, she was going to finally find out what all the fuss of being a married woman was about. That perked her up. She gave a cheery wave over Wesley's shoulder, spotting Edwin and Eleanor, who were both laughing, and the ever-scandalized expression of Irene as Wesley swept past.

"Wesley, put Cynthia down this minute!"

"Sorry Mother," he said, blandly, as he reached the door, turning to look over the crowd. Most of them looked utterly overjoyed at this new display of the Earl of Spencer's unusual behavior. "Thank you all for coming, my bride and I are going to step out now for a private discussion, but stay as long as you like and enjoy yourselves."

"Here, here!" Several of the men shouted, raising their glasses of champagne and drowning out the Dowager-Countess' protests as Wesley pushed through the door.

"You're going to be in trouble later," Cynthia said, rather admiringly. She would have never dared ignore Wesley's mother in such a fashion. It was quite impressive.

Her new husband made an exasperated noise and eyed her. "You're more afraid of my mother than you are of me, aren't you?"

"Wouldn't you be?"

The repartee made him laugh. Cynthia watched, fascinated. With one arm around his neck to help her stay in position, this was the closest she'd ever been able to observe him. She could see the pulse in his neck, the way his throat worked as he laughed, the small dark hairs curling around the shell of his ear because they were too short to be tied back... With her free hand, she reached up to stroke his hair.

Immediately he stopped, in the middle of the hall. The sounds from the ballroom had mostly faded away and there wasn't a servant to be seen, giving them momentary privacy. The heat in his eyes when he looked at her made her heart beat faster.

"What are you doing, sweetheart?"

Her mouth went dry at the growling rasp in his voice. Beneath her dress, her nipples tightened into little points, rubbing against the fabric as his hands tightened on her.

"Touching you?" she asked, doing it again, and this time letting her finger slide down the side of his throat.

A muscle in his jaw clenched and then suddenly she found herself pushed up against the wall, her legs dropped down and no longer in his arms. But her feet didn't touch the ground either; his leg was wedged between hers, and he was tall enough she could just barely feel her toes brushing the floor. All of her weight rested on her core, and even the sharp pinches flaring in her bottom as it was pressed against the wall didn't stop the flash of pleasure that streaked through her like lightening.

His lips devoured hers, his hard cock digging into her stomach, and Cynthia clutched at him, reeling from the suddenness of his passion. The gloves had come off, and she suddenly realized how much control he'd always retained in his dealings with her. Control he obviously no longer felt such a keen need to hold onto now they were married. She'd been poking a tiger in his cage, only to find he'd slipped through the bars and now kitty wanted to play.

Cynthia whimpered as he rocked against her, making her clit pulse as her weight moved over it. The hardness of his thigh was almost painful against her soft folds, even through the cushioning fabric of her wedding dress. His tongue was dancing in her mouth, sliding against hers as if dueling for possession of the space, until she could barely breathe. It felt like all of her intimate parts, from her breasts down to her pussy, were swollen with arousal.

When his hands cupped her buttocks, making her rock even more firmly against his thigh, the welts fizzed with pain and made her writhe in intense, torturous pleasure.

It wasn't until she heard ripping fabric, as the train of her skirt came loose, and the Earl pulled away that she was able to come back to herself. Her lips felt swollen from his rough kisses, her breasts heavy, and she stared up at him, dazed as she gasped for air.

"I am not deflowering you against a wall in a hallway," he said, clipping off the end of each word in his frustrated angst, glaring at her as if it were her fault.

Maybe it was. But how could she have known such a small touch could incite such a disproportionate reaction? Definitely something to remember later, if by some miracle her brain was still working.

Wesley hauled her up into his arms again, this time holding her in such a way that her own arms were trapped against her sides. Gritting his teeth against the temptation to throw caution to the winds and just take her here and now, he strode down the hallway as quickly as he could. Fortunately, for both their sakes, his bride remained absolutely silent as he kicked open the door to his room.

Their room.

A wave of masculine smugness washed over him, helping to temper his anxiousness to sink into her body. She was all his now. In his arms, in his room, and about to be in his bed where she belonged. Never again would she sleep anywhere but beside him. There would be no more nights waking up alone, aching for her. She'd be right there, beside him, soft and warm and reachable.

He tossed her onto the bed.

Blinking, her cheeks rosy and pretty pink lips slightly parted, she stared up at him in a kind of sensual daze. Wesley yanked off his jacket, enjoying the way her eyes widened as he started to strip. She sat up, watching with eagerness as piece after piece of clothing fell to the ground. The way she was looking at him had his balls aching, her eyes focused on his cock as it stood out from his body as if reaching for her.

As he stood there, enjoying watching her look at him, her eyes slowly went up his body to his face. Her little pink tongue flicked out, moistening her lower lip, reminding him of how sweet her mouth was. But that's not where his cock was going today.

"We're... going to..." Surprisingly, she flushed. It was charmingly erotic, to see his brazen little bride turning pink. She could crawl into his bed in the middle of the night, looking to be ruined before her wedding, but now they were married she turned slightly shy.

"I'm going to make you mine. My wife."

He moved forward, kneeling on the bed and leaning over her as she began to slide slowly down onto her back, staring up at him.

"The right way?"

"What's the right way, sweetheart?"

She scowled up at him as he loomed over her, his mouth hovering just above hers. "In my *pussy*."

Dirty girl. Wesley didn't answer, he just lowered his lips to hers, kissing her again. Tasting her. Conquering her. The fabric of her dress scratched at his body, annoying him as he lay out his full length on her. She gasped into his mouth, her legs automatically spreading for him, cradling him against the unwelcoming fabric.

Blasted dress.

With a sound of annoyance, Wesley pulled away and grasped the neckline in both hands.

Cynthia shrieked as he rent the dress in two, revealing her corset and chemise beneath. "I liked that dress!"

"I'll buy you a new one," he muttered, tossing the ruined fabric on the floor, quickly sending the rest of her clothing after it. It was like unwrapping a present on Christmas morning, and he'd never been the patient type. He'd always liked to rip the wrapping paper from the boxes, and Cynthia was far better than any holiday gift he'd ever received. Chances were this wouldn't be the last dress of hers he shredded. Of course, once she was naked, he fully intended on taking his time and savoring his bride.

Lush curves beckoned to him, her spread legs revealing glistening lips peeking out from her thatch of brown curls. The wide-eyed excitement on her face made her unlike any virginal bride he'd ever heard of, but it also made her perfect for him.

He bent over to take on pert nipple in his mouth, making her gasp and writhe as his hands pressed down on her thighs, keeping them open. His thumbs traced little circles on the soft, inner skin, slowly moving closer and closer to her untouched pussy. Well, he'd done a bit of touching, but that was different.

Moaning, Cynthia clutched at his head, sliding her fingers through his hair, because there wasn't much else she could do. She was on her back, spread and helpless, and utterly aroused. The slight pain of her bottom pressing against the bed was nothing compared to the fires her new husband was stoking inside of her. If anything, that bit of sting was like a sharp bite which made everything else more pleasurable by comparison. When she tried to move her legs, wanting to clasp them around him, she felt a surge of wetness gush through her pussy as he held her in place.

The domineering, conquering lord had complete dominion over her body, and it left her absolutely breathless. Any lingering ire over his treatment of her dress had completely washed away. She had more important things to focus on.

"Please... more..." she begged, as his switched nipples, leaving one wet and cool in the open air as he engulfed the other in his hot mouth. The steady sucking sensation and the flicking of his tongue against the sensitive bud had her arching as her pussy clenched. Her legs were forced farther apart as his hands slid higher on her thighs; she wanted to scream with frustration as they brushed against her pussy lips and then stopped. "Oh! Wesley..."

He groaned around her nipple as she said his name, and she shuddered at the vibrations through her breast. It felt like her body was on fire, and she knew he had the means to quench it. The wetness seeping from her cunt did nothing to douse the heat, her needy wriggling only frustrating her further as she sought some kind of pressure for her clit and found nothing.

"Patience, sweetheart," he said, lifting his mouth from her nipple, the look of amusement on his face rousing her temper again.

She scowled at him. "*Now*, my lord."

"It's going to hurt, this first time."

Cynthia just rolled her eyes. As if being spanked didn't hurt. Or birched. Or when he put his cock in the wrong place. If all of that could hurt and feel good at the same time, she was sure she could survive whatever he was talking about.

Especially since she wanted it.

He shifted upwards, his eyes boring into hers, and she felt something hot and hard pressing against her pussy. Her breath caught in her throat as the most immense pressure suddenly assaulted her core, and then something tore. It didn't just hurt; it stung, pinched and burned all at the same time. Cynthia cried out, hitting at Wesley's chest with her small fists.

Catching her hands, he pinned them down on either side of her. She tried to close her legs, but his big body blocked the way.

"Ow!" she said, her voice full of outrage and shock, not to mention just a bit of disappointment. "Take it out!"

"Shhh," he said, soothingly. Patronizing, really. "It will feel better in a moment. I won't move right away so you have time to get used to it."

She squirmed, trying to get away. If it was going to feel like that, then she definitely didn't want him moving at all! "I changed my mind, put it in the other hole."

Having him in her bottom might be shameful, and somewhat painful, but it had never felt like that. It didn't occur to her to consider how he'd always been much more careful about preparing her bottom, and he might have taken the same care with her virginity if she hadn't been so impatient. But he'd been impatient as well, and he hadn't expected her to be quite so well protected. Her maidenhead was broken now, but it had been rather thick, so he could only imagine it must have hurt when he'd forced himself through. He'd wanted her to truly feel him taking her for the first time, but if he'd realized how painful the initial breach would be, he would have prepared her more with his fingers. That's what he got for giving into her pleas; he'd return to his original plan of taking his time with her.

Her offer of her bottom hole both amused and concerned him, because he knew she didn't like it very much at all. There was no way his wife was going to leave his bed anything but blissfully satisfied.

Pushing both of her arms up above her head, he grasped her wrists in one hand so he could free up the other hand. "It won't ever hurt again, sweetheart. That was your virginity being breached. With it gone everything will feel much better."

The suspicious look she gave him would have been insulting if it wasn't so amusing. It changed immediately as he caressed down her body, pinching her nipple on the way, until he could flatten his palm across her hip and reach between them to rub her clitoris with his thumb. The expression on her face shifted to cautious wonderment as she clenched around him and then gasped. As soon as her muscles relaxed, Wesley took the opportunity to rock himself forward, thrusting a few more inches into her body.

"Oh!" Her back arched, thrusting her breasts up at him, as her head fell back and she offered up her vulnerable throat to him. Leaning down, Wesley nipped at the soft skin, continuing to rub slow circles over her clit, giving her as much additional sensation as possible to help with the slow invasion of her deflowered pussy. The tight channel fluttered around him as he pushed in, testing his self-control with its hot grip, making him want to sink into her over and over again, hard and fast, until he filled her with his seed.

One day he'd be able to do that, but not today when she was too new to the activity. He wasn't exactly small, or even moderately sized, and she was going to be sore enough after this.

"That feels... oh goodness..." Cynthia writhed as he worked himself deeper, her arms only tugging slightly at his hold on her wrists. In some ways, it was easier for her to accept him into her body now that she wasn't able to move or try and push him away. Besides, the way he was rubbing her clit had her clenching in pleasure, even though the stinging burn of inner muscles stretching hadn't quite subsided.

"Good girl," he whispered, before leaning over and capturing her lips. He shifted again, laying his full length over her as his hand traveled back up her body.

That was when Cynthia realized he must be fully inside of her.

He hadn't lied, the movements he'd made didn't hurt in the same way at all. Not from when he'd first entered her and not the same as when he'd gone in the bad hole. Now it just felt like she was stretched and so very full, but it felt much better and much less shameful than when he filled her other hole. The stretch didn't burn quite as much, it didn't feel as though she should be pushing him out... in fact, having him inside of her like this, with his weight on top of her, felt so wonderfully right that she thought she could stay just like this forever.

Then he started to move.

Even though his thumb was no longer caressing her clit, the little bud was swollen and sensitive, and when he fully sheathed himself inside of her again, his body pressed up against it in the most amazing way. Cynthia cried out, lifting her hips, trying to get more contact as the ecstasy buzzed through her body. His kiss was demanding as he slowly thrust in and out of her pussy, his tongue spearing her at the same time his cock did, muffling her cries and moans.

She could feel every inch of him, rubbing inside of her, hard and hot and so very fulfilling. It was far, far better than when he'd put his fingers in her.

Slowly his movements began to come faster, harder, and his lips pulled away from hers as they both panted for breath. His expression was almost a grimace as he pumped his hips, making the most incredible groaning noises that seemed to pierce her right down to her core. Cynthia couldn't believe how wild, how primitive he looked. Naked and above her, joined with her, it was shockingly intimate and improper.

"Put your arms around my neck," he ordered as he released her wrists.

She obeyed with alacrity, wanting to hold onto him. To touch him. Her fingers slid into his hair as he changed his position slightly, both of his hands sliding under her body to grip her buttocks. The welts stung as his fingers dug into her fleshy bottom, forcing her to tilt her hips upwards, but that was nothing compared to the surge of ecstasy as his cock rubbed over the most wonderful spot inside of her. The pleasure soared higher as, at the end of his stroke, his body pressed against her clit and the two jolts of sensation connected.

Without realizing it, Cynthia clawed at his shoulders, coming apart beneath him as he ground himself against her sensitive pussy. The clenching tremors of her muscles nearly undid him, but Wesley grit his teeth and held on to his own release. He had his pride after all.

"Oh... oh Wesley... I can't... it's too much... I've never... Oh!"

The shock and awe on her face were wiped out by rapture as she screamed with passion, obviously overcome by an immense climax, the likes of which she'd never experienced. It was exactly what he'd been aiming for, waiting for, as he'd positioned her so both her inner and outer sweet spots had been stimulated by his thrusting. Now he could let himself go.

Cynthia screamed again, writhing and dragging her nails down his back as she shook with the intensity of her orgasm, which was only increasing as he began to seek his own pleasure. The pounding thrusts between her thighs had her pussy spasming. They came much harder and faster than before, as Wesley wallowed in the tight sheath of her body, fucking her as hard as he could.

He wanted every inch of her to feel him, to submit to him.

"Mine," he growled, feeling the tingling in the base of his spine that signaled his own oncoming orgasm. She was his, all his, and no other man's. Ever.

"Yes!" she screamed, as he got even harder, thicker inside of her.

Tears were leaking down her face, which he was sure she was unaware of, her body straining against his. Her pussy convulsed and squeezed, and he groaned her name into her hair as he thrust home one final time and began to empty himself inside of her. They rocked together, his groin grinding against her clit and swollen lips as jet after jet of thick cream completed her deflowering.

He continued to rock, his movements becoming more gentle as she jerked beneath him, whimpering from the onslaught of over-whelming sensations. Slowly they came back to earth together as he kissed the salty tears from her cheeks, stroking her hair and soothing her... calming her... The tempestuous currents that had carried her away slowed and eddied, allowing her to relax her grip on his shoulders.

From the sting, he'd have marks there tomorrow. Possibly for several days to come. The thought made him grin.

"Oh!" she whispered, shuddering again as his softened cock finally fell from its warm haven. "That felt so strange."

Snorting, Wesley carefully rolled off of her, getting up to retrieve a cloth and wet it in the basin. When he turned back around, his bride was right where he'd left her, soft brown curls resting on the pillow, her arms at her sides, and her legs still spread. The sight of pink cream smearing her inner thighs made him feel both guilty that he'd hurt her when he'd taken her maidenhead and yet intensely, posses-sively, triumphant in a barbaric way.

She watched with half-lidded eyes, not the least bit bothered by any kind of modesty, as he carefully cleaned the mess they had made, sighing a bit with relief as the cool cloth swept over her heated pussy.

When Wesley returned to the bed, after wiping his cock clean as well, he pulled Cynthia to the other side of the large piece of furniture, away from the lingering dampness on the sheets. She snuggled into him immediately, her hand resting on his chest, making a sound of sleepy contentment.

"Well, baggage, what do you think of sex?" he asked, twining one of her curls about his finger. It wasn't the kind of question he'd ever asked a lover, but he was curious about her answer.

"It's not going to hurt at the beginning every time, is it?" she asked, her voice lilting a bit with sleepiness.

"No, sweetheart," he reassured her, feeling the smallest pang of remorse. "It was only this once."

"Mmm. Then it was worth it."

Wesley chuckled at the satisfied way she said it. His cock responded as well, but he knew she needed some rest. A nap. They had plenty of time for more bed play. Their whole lives in fact.

A year ago he wouldn't have thought it possible to be this satisfied, thinking about having just one woman in his bed for the rest of his life. But he was savagely determined she be his, all and only his. And he would be hers.

"Well, I don't think they'll be coming back," Eleanor said, highly amused by Wesley's antics. His mother looked equally resigned and pleased as her son carried Cynthia away from the room. Probably weighing the social scandal (which wouldn't be all that great, really, as newlyweds were always granted quite a bit of leeway) against the possibility of grandbabies sooner rather than later.

Speaking of...

"Are you ready to go, my dear?" Eleanor's father put his hand down on her mother's shoulder, taking the Countess' attention away from Grace. Her mother looked up and smiled.

"Yes, I think so."

Before Eleanor could speak up, Edwin was already stepping forward, keeping one hand on the back of her neck. It was no longer a teasing touch, but more possessive than anything else. As if he couldn't bear not to touch her. She rather liked it, even if she didn't want to like anything about him right now. He may have stopped teasing her, but that didn't mean her body's needs had quieted.

"May Eleanor and I accompany you? We'd like some time with you before we depart tomorrow."

The Countess brightened, beaming at her son-in-law. "Yes, that would be lovely." She turned her head to look at Grace. "Would you like to come too, dear?"

The invitation was made out of social necessity, although Eleanor didn't mind if Grace was there when she and Edwin told her parents she was with child. But Alex was suddenly standing beside his wife as well, holding out his hand to help her stand.

"Grace and I are staying in tonight," he said mildly, his voice ever so polite, but firm as well. "We have our own discussions we need to have."

Grace bit down on her lip and shot Eleanor a look as she placed her hand in Alex's and stood. Eleanor could only shrug in response. Even though she did think Alex and Grace should talk, she couldn't blame her friend for wanting to wait until tomorrow. But there was nothing Eleanor could do right now.

"Write to me, as soon as you arrive," she said to Grace, accepting Edwin's hand to help her stand. He came around from behind the chairs so he could stand next to her, his hand on the small of her back. Again, not teasing, and yet her body reacted anyway.

Damn him.

"I will," Grace promised. They kept their voices light, but Eleanor was quite sure neither of the men were fooled. Surprisingly, Alex just smiled at her.

Then again, perhaps she shouldn't be surprised when he'd praised her loyal friendship to Grace in the past. Still, she hadn't thought he would still be appreciative when it was his actions she was checking up on. That smile reassured her more than anything else could have.

Eleanor was sure Grace and Alex could have a happy marriage like the rest of them, because she was sure they were in love with each other. If only they could bring themselves to admit it.

"I wonder if Wesley and Cynthia will come visit when the others do," Edwin said, musing, on their way out. "Or if they'll be too ah... busy."

"They had better not be that busy," Eleanor said, her hand automatically going to her stomach, where her and Edwin's child rested. "I'll want friends around."

Edwin's dark eyes glowed as he looked down at her. Taking her hand in his, he raised it to his lips. "Then I'll make sure they're there, love."

Frustrated with her husband or not, Eleanor's heart filed with warmth.

CHAPTER 13

$\mathcal{J}$t was such a lovely day that Alex chose to dismiss the coachman and walk with Grace back to their house. She seemed tense for some reason. Being cooped up in a closed carriage with him, even for a short period of time, probably wouldn't help, he decided. They had made a great deal of progress in becoming more easy in each other's company, but today she'd seemed to take a step back from him again.

Indeed, she relaxed the moment he suggested strolling home.

The hot air didn't seem to bother her at all as she turned her face to the sun, basking in its glow. Alex couldn't help but smile, remembering the scandalized high sticklers back at Wesley's wedding brunch, all of them horrified that he'd carried his bride off while it was still daylight. At his and Grace's wedding, he wouldn't have dared to do such a thing. They'd waited, very properly, for night to fall before consummating. Although he wished he'd had the balls to do as Wesley had.

He wished he had the balls to do it right now. It was probably fortunate he didn't, as Grace would not thank him for carrying her off down the street. They were causing enough talk as it was, just by being in each other's presence.

"Did you have a good talk with Eleanor and her mother?" he asked. He already knew she had, she'd been smiling the entire time, but he didn't want to spend the entire walk in silence. Perhaps they couldn't discuss the important issues, but he enjoyed conversing with her, and the more they did so, the more natural it was becoming again. Their conversations had become much less stilted, especially over the past few days.

"Yes, it was lovely to see Lady Harrington," Grace said, a sincere smile flitting across her face, before wariness edged into her expression again. She peeked up at him through her lashes, watching him.

It was something he'd seen a lot from her, both when he'd first started courting her, and since he'd demanded a reconciliation. As if she was watching him, waiting to see what he would do, and hiding herself from him until she was sure he wasn't a threat. Alex was fairly certain the tactic came from when she lived in her father's household.

As if making some kind of decision, her chin lifted a bit. "She and my mother are very good friends, you know."

"Yes, I remember," he replied, smiling as he looked down at her. Out of the corner of his eye, he saw a passerby gawking at them. Possibly because they'd both been recognized together, or possibly because he'd been recognized and been seen smiling.

The smile worked on Grace. She seemed to relax and started to tell him about Lady Harrington's recent charitable activities around Bath, Eleanor and Edwin's intention to stay at the Manse for the foreseeable future, and everything else she'd talked about with them. Alex was content to let her talk, occasionally adding his own observations or thoughts, and just enjoy walking beside his wife while she actually conversed with him. They were the very picture of matrimonial harmony. He just hoped they could become more than the picture.

By dinnertime, Grace was starting to feel hunted.

At first she'd enjoyed Alex's efforts to spend time with her after the wedding. They'd walked and talked, and it had been almost like old times. He'd listened quite attentively and never seemed to become bored or annoyed with her chatter, although she'd focused on the most mundane and trivial of topics. She'd been quite careful to avoid any conversation that could lead to the more serious issues between them.

When they'd returned home, she'd expected him to go to his study, which he had, but he'd joined her in the library after barely an hour when she'd thought she wouldn't see him again till dinnertime. At first it had been uncomfortable to have him sitting so closely to her, on the same couch, even if he was concentrating on his own book. After a bit, he'd asked what she was reading, and she'd been almost relieved to tell him about the silly Gothic romance she'd been pretending to read.

Pretending, because once he'd sat down, she'd barely been able to concentrate on the book. She'd turned pages, but only because she hadn't wanted him to know how distracted he made her. With his presence crowding the couch, his body heat so close to hers, she'd become rather tense, waiting for whatever he was going to do. Wondering if he would try to seduce her again. Kiss her. Or even touch her at all.

When he'd kept to his side of the couch, the tension had spooled about her unbearably, tightening with every passing minute. She'd started to wonder if she wanted his attention. If she wanted him to try and seduce her. His query about her reading material had allowed her to put the book down and stop pretending.

Strangely, he seemed almost interested in the ridiculous plot. Grace enjoyed her Gothic romances because of their darkness, their silliness... but she certainly hadn't expected to witness her husband chuckling at her villainous description of the Mad Baron and his evil plans. She'd almost jumped out of her seat when Alex had laid his arm out on the couch back behind her, leaning forward to inspect the cover of the book. Her heart had leapt up into her throat, fluttering madly, as he invaded her space.

Heat flushed her cheeks.

It wasn't that her reaction was new—it certainly wasn't—but it seemed to have intensified since last night. When she'd let him, begged him, to make love to her. At the wedding and the brunch, they'd been far enough apart she could retain her peace of mind.

Now, alone in their house, it was all she could think about.

"I'm feeling a bit warm," she'd said, hastily getting to her feet. "I think I'll take a stroll in the garden."

Alex had studied her face as he stood, taking the book from her hands and placing it down on the couch. "I'll join you."

Once in the garden, she hadn't been able to think of anything to talk about, so she'd questioned him more about the estates. He'd talked to her of them on the carriage ride to Bath, but she hadn't been quite in the mood to listen at the time.

Listening to his enthusiasm about the estates, she was again reminded of the Alex she'd married. He didn't just tell her about his plans or what was happening, but also what he hoped to achieve in the future, what he would like her to look into... the small things which indicated he saw her as a wife and partner and not just a figurehead. Not the way her mother had been part of the pretty family picture her father had painted, the way he'd expected Grace and her sisters to become similar pictures. She wondered if, once he heard she and Alex had reconciled, she might be able to see her mother and sisters again. They'd all adhered to his edict of silence when it came to her, which she didn't blame them for. Besides, it meant she hadn't had to listen to pressure or guilt from them about her behavior; equally it meant her scandalous behavior hadn't reflected upon her sisters once they'd begun looking for husbands. It was well known she was the black sheep of her family and they'd cut her off.

Still... it would be nice to be able to attend the same events without worrying her own family members would cut her.

"I'd like you to ride out among the farms with me," Alex told her, his eagerness growing as they talked about his estates. "I want you to talk to the women about the possibility of a school in the area."

That had especially appealed to Grace. She wondered if Alex had somehow discovered the donations she made for the education of

children in London. They'd all been made discreetly and anony-
mously, because she'd known her name would actually hinder rather
than help any of the causes she'd backed, but she supposed it was still
possible. Grace wasn't a bluestocking, but she'd always found an
escape from life in books, and she wanted to make it possible for all
children in unfortunate situations. She was lucky she'd been taught to
read. Lucky she'd been born a Duke's daughter, even if sometimes
she'd chafed at the restrictions such a position came with.

That had led to a much longer conversation than she'd anticipated
about what Alex hoped to do with schools, or at least a traveling
teacher, for the children on his lands. The time flew by, until she realized she needed to dress for dinner. It was her first break from Alex
all afternoon, and she'd been a bit relieved by it.

Being constantly in his presence had unnerved her. Weakened
defenses which were already crumbling. She didn't even know why
she bothered to try and shore up the walls around her heart, except
she still couldn't bring herself to fully trust him. The last time she'd
had hope for her future with him, he'd ended up crushing her. It was
making her far more wary this time around.

Especially because, during dinner, he kept trying to slide the
conversation around to the very things she didn't want to talk about.
It became a verbal game of cat and mouse. He would begin alluding to
things like marriage or communication, their friends' marriages, their
separation, and Grace would immediately slide the conversation back
to something innocuous. It was not relaxing dinner conversation and
her tension was beginning to rise again.

Alex tolerated Grace's evasions because of the servants that were
in and out of the room, serving them dinner. Although he trusted his
people to be discreet, there was no way to completely stymy gossip.
Especially if the Lord and Lady of the house aired their issues too
loudly and too openly in front of the staff. It was human nature to
talk.

He'd hoped to at least begin to broach the subject, to ready her,
because he was determined they have an in depth conversation
following dinner, but he could tell he was causing her quite a bit of

anxiety. It couldn't be helped. The lack of communication between them was frustrating him. There were too many questions going unanswered.

Why did she call him a liar?

Why did she speak and behave as if he'd never cared for her?

What had she been looking for in his study?

Why had she left him in the first place? What was opening her to him again now?

He supposed it was possible she'd meant for him to chase after her the first time, but somehow that just didn't align with Grace's character. Other women played games, but Grace had seemed truly furious when she'd first left him. Not to mention disdainful, cutting, and frankly disgusted by him. Which was why his response had been so prideful. He'd been young and stupid. If she tried such a tactic with him now, he would not only follow behind her but, once he caught up with her, he would blister her bottom until she explained herself.

Looking at her across the dinner table, he noted she was wearing the dark red color he liked on her so much. It emphasized her dark hair, pale skin, and the red in her cheeks and lips. Even her eyes seemed a brighter blue in contrast. Not for the first time, he thought he needed to buy her a sapphire and ruby necklace and tiara set.

Almost as if she could read his mind, Grace's pretty pert lips twisted into a little smirk. "You're thinking about rubies and sapphires again, aren't you?" she teased.

He laughed, shaking his head. "How do you always know?"

At least, she always had known, years ago. She claimed it was a look on his face, but he could swear not a single part of his expression changed.

"You haven't altered as much as you might think," she said, her eyes sparkling just a moment before they began to dull, as she realized she'd tread too close to the topics of conversation she was avoiding.

But Alex had already realized his tactics were only making her uncomfortable, so he just leaned back and patted his belly. "That's not what I've been told."

Grace burst out laughing, immediately relaxing since he hadn't picked up on the lead she'd given him. It was reward enough for continuing to be patient and waiting until after dinner, when they were completely alone, to begin their conversation.

"You're just fishing for compliments, no one would dare say anything to you about your waistline!"

Giving her a look of mock outrage, he put an affronted hand over his chest. "Are you implying there's something to say?"

The rest of the meal went much better as they fell into teasing each other. He hadn't felt so lighthearted since he was a boy. Was it Grace leaving him that had turned him into Stoneface? Or was it her absence in his life throughout the years? Probably a bit of both. She brought out a side of him that was far more relaxed and playful than he felt able to show to anyone else—although his friendship with Wesley and the others had begun to bring out some of those facets as well.

They both became more tense as the meal ended and he asked her to join him in his study for an after dinner sherry. Well, sherry for her and brandy for him. For a moment he thought she would refuse and he would have to insist, or even force her, but then she nodded. The grim expression on her face didn't make him feel any better.

As they walked down the hall, the serious mien melted away and she started chatting again. He hoped she didn't really think he would be distracted by talk about tomorrow's weather and how fast the carriage might travel. Whatever she thought he wanted to talk about, it was obvious she knew it was more serious. This time, he wasn't going to be diverted.

At least, that's what he thought until they got to the study. No sooner had he closed the door behind them, than Grace threw herself on him.

∾

WHATEVER IT WAS Alex wanted to talk about, Grace was sure it impinged on the topics she *didn't*. What was wrong with the blasted man? Hadn't he thought through how awful their traveling situation could be if they argued tonight? Things were going so well between them, why did he have to try and ruin it?

When he'd escorted her out of the dining room, she'd realized there were other means of distracting him, however. Enjoyable means. After all, they'd already revived the physical portion of their marriage, why not enjoy the benefits while she could? Just in case she ended up having to flee him again. At least she'd have another night in his bed. Because she did still love him, and not a single night with another man had ever compared to being with him.

So, when he turned around from closing the door to his study, she plastered herself against him. It was an unprecedented move on her part. Before their estrangement, she'd certainly never thrown herself at him. Partly because she had never needed to, but even if she'd had the opportunity, she probably would have been too shy to take it. During their estrangement, she'd had all manner of men chasing after her. She'd been content to pick and choose among them, and to indulge when they wanted her, without actually pursuing them herself. She'd ended up with a reputation for being choosy, and so the men had flocked. Some matrons had to exert effort to find their lovers, Grace had never been one of them. If men hadn't presented themselves, she probably would have gone without.

Alex was the only man she'd ever truly wanted to throw herself at. Now, spurred by her need to put off the conversation she knew he wanted to have, it was easy. Especially because, the second she touched her lips to his, she realized she was hungry for him.

The romantic wedding this morning, the way he'd spurned the attentions and flirtations of other women, the little looks he'd given her across the room, and then his stalwart attention to her this afternoon, combined with the fact that they had already made love the night before, opened the way for her. She'd held herself back physically because her emotions wouldn't allow her to give in. She no longer had that barrier.

His body fell back against the door and she could practically feel his surprise. One arm slid around his neck, the other hand clutched at his cravat, and she refused to give up his lips when she felt him trying to pull away. His mouth opened and she thrust her tongue brazenly inside, standing on her toes and rubbing her body against his. Resistance was futile, unless he was prepared to bodily tear her away from him. For a moment, she feared he would do just that as his hands settled on her hips, prepared to push, and then she felt him give in.

Instead of pushing her away, his fingers tightened on her hips. He stopped trying to pull away and drew her in closer, taking control of the kiss with a dominating force that left her breathless. Grace moaned into his mouth as their tongues dueled, pulling at the knot in his cravat and tearing the thing away from his throat. Her calves ached from the effort of keeping her tall enough to kiss him, but she didn't care.

His arousal pressed against her stomach and she was on fire with need. Overwhelmed by urgency. If things went badly tomorrow... if he couldn't give her the answers she needed... she might very well have to flee. She might never see him again. For tonight, at least, she could push away thoughts of the future, ignore her fluttering hopes, and just pretend there was nothing more between them than their desires. Let their bodies do the talking.

Sliding her hands down, she tugged his buttons through their holes and pushed his jacket open, sliding her hands in. Alex made a growling noise, deep in his chest, which reverberated through her palms. She pushed against him as he tried to lift his head again, refusing to give up the kiss, and he grabbed her by the back of her hair, pulling her head back so she had to look at him.

"Grace—"

"Shut up," she said fiercely, arching her hips away to undo the front of his pants.

"Grace, we should talk."

Hunger was hot in Alex's eyes, but she could also see his intent to refuse her. The control he was struggling for. She shoved her hand in the front of his pants, wrapping her fingers around his erection. Pleasure washed over him, his eyes unfocusing as the hot length throbbed in her hand. For just a moment, his fingers loosened in her hair and she immediately took advantage of it to drop to her knees.

"Later. Not now."

Pulling his cock free of his clothing, it bobbed in front of her face.

"Grace!"

"Shut up! I want to try this."

"*Try this?*" Alex sounded like he was being strangled. She looked up at him, from her position on her knees. He was still leaning back against the door, his cravat gone, his jacket open, shirt rumpled, and the front of his pants hanging open. For once, she was the aggressor and it was surprisingly erotic.

"Eleanor says she does it for Edwin, I want to try."

She could almost see the thoughts flitting across his face. Shock at knowing what she and her best friend discussed. Curiosity about what else they might have talked about. The revelation that this was an act Grace had never indulged in. That was something she'd wanted to be sure of, that he knew she'd never done this before. Not just because Eleanor had warned her he might be jealous, but also in case she was bad at it.

Alex knew he should stop her, knew she was probably just diverting him as she had all day, but when her hot mouth closed over the head of his cock, all rational thought flew from his head. When they'd first been married, he'd spent quite a bit of time between Grace's thighs, with his fingers, his mouth, his cock... but they hadn't been together for long enough to begin exploring some of the more exotic aspects of love-play. At the time, Alex certainly hadn't needed anything but his wife, naked and willing, to excite him to the point of losing control.

Knowing she'd never done this with any other man, that she wanted to do it with him... who was he to deny her? Later, he would rationalize those thoughts. Remind himself that she hadn't wanted to touch him for so long, the change in her attitude needed to be encouraged. That he didn't want to deter her turnaround.

But right now, all he could do was hold on for dear life as her tongue delicately licked the underside of his cock, and the wet heat of her mouth took him deeper. He groaned, struggling to keep from tightening his grip in her hair, not wanting to take control from her when she seemed so delighted to be exploring his cock with her mouth.

She made a pleased humming sound which nearly sent him to his knees, the vibrations traveling up the length of his cock. When the head bumped against the back of her throat, she gagged a bit and backed off, but he didn't mind. After a moment, she began to move her mouth back and forth again, always taking him as deeply as she could, pushing her limits.

It was heaven and hell.

There was no mistaking her for anything but a novice. She was too fascinated by what she was doing, her eyes flicking back and forth between looking directly in front of her, and looking up at his face. When she wanted to lick him, she would pause, exploring with her tongue, especially around the head of his cock, rather than keeping up a steady tempo. He didn't hold back vocally, moaning and practically whimpering at times, letting her know exactly what he most enjoyed about what she was doing.

Even though she was on her knees in front of him, he had no doubts about who was truly in control of this interaction. But the torturous teasing was becoming too much for him, he needed more; wanted to give her the same pleasure she was bestowing upon him.

When he tightened his fingers in her hair, reluctantly pulling her mouth from his cock, she glared up at him. "I don't want to stop yet."

"We're not stopping, sweetheart," he said, with his best rakish grin. It was feeling a bit wobbly, just as he was, but from the way her face changed to interest and arousal, the effort was satisfactory. "I'm just making some adjustments."

Lying down on the floor, he pulled her atop him, startling a laugh out of her as he flipped her skirts up and positioned her knees on either side of his head, rather than his hips as she obviously expected.

They were both almost completely fully clothed, on the floor of his study, as her mouth slid back over his cock and he pulled her pussy down onto his tongue. The very depravity of the situation made it even more exciting. Grace moaned around his length, her hips bucking as his tongue slid up the wet lips of her pussy. His hands splayed across her bottom, holding her firmly in place. The pretty pink lips of her pussy were parted, her creamy cheeks of her bottom quivering as she shuddered with pleasure, and the tiny crinkled bud of her anus winking at him. It was a sight that would make any man ragingly hard, even if he hadn't been already.

Alex enjoyed the view nearly as much as he enjoyed the musky sweetness of her pussy on his tongue, the scent of her filling his nose. The wet sounds of pleasure being given and taken filled the room, muffled moans interspersed with the rustling of clothing and slick sounds of his cock sliding in and out of her mouth and his fingers thrusting in her pussy.

Pleasure was making it hard for Grace to concentrate... but at the moment, breathing seemed highly overrated anyway. The way Alex was feasting on her pussy, the perversion of what they were doing together and where they were doing it, was all making her even more excited than she'd thought possible. Precautions and worries about the future had fallen by the wayside, pushed out of her head by much more immediate needs and desires.

He stroked the inside of her pussy, finding a spot that made her clench and suck harder as she clutched at his thighs. The slickness of his cock made it easier for her to take more of him, this position on top of him allowing the head to slip into her throat without gagging her. The frantic quality of her movements, as he licked and stroked her pussy, didn't hurt either. The more he teased her, the more her pussy tingled with need, the harder she sucked him into her mouth.

The musky flavor of him was different from anything she'd ever tasted, not at all unpleasant, and she found herself craving more and more of it. The texture of his cock was part of that too, so soft and yet hard at the same time, the bumps and veiny ridges that gave way when her tongue pressed against them... she wanted more of it. All of it. As she moaned and sucked, his hips were moving, pushing his cock back and forth between her lips even if she was holding still.

When her fingers crept down to touch his balls, she felt him shudder, just before he thrust up even harder and the suction of his lips on her pussy redoubled. She nearly screamed around his cock as he fluttered his tongue of her clit, simultaneously sucking on the swollen bud. None of her lovers, not even Alex when they were first married, had encouraged any kind of exploration of their manhoods. They were more interested in getting her on her back so they could put it inside her. Some of the more adventurous would get on their own backs so she could ride them, but even then, their goal was to be buried inside of her pussy.

She had never even thought of exploring a man's body, never needed to, and so she had never realized the effect her touch could have on him. Now she was getting quite a lesson. Holding his sack a bit more tightly, she squeezed gently, and was rewarded with another lusty moan as he writhed beneath her. Grace became almost lost in the sucking and squeezing, her hips moving as she climbed closer to climax.

When it hit, she jerked her head off of his cock, afraid she might bite down as she spasmed with ecstasy. He sucked hard on her clit and she wrapped her fingers around his dick, releasing his sack, squeezing his rod so hard she could feel it pulse between her fingers as she came.

Suddenly, she was on her back and Alex was between her legs, shoving his cock into her. Her pussy was still convulsing with orgasmic rapture, and she screamed his name as the rough invasion sent her soaring even higher into ecstasy.

Feeling her climax around him, Alex didn't waste a second worrying about Grace's pleasure—she had already reached it and didn't show any sign of coming down from it. Sliding his hands under her shoulders, he held her in place as he began a steady, almost brutal thrusting, using her climax-wracked body for his own pleasure. Her cries became higher, her fingers clawing uselessly at his clothing as she writhed. The grip of her pussy was almost painful as he fucked her hard, pounding between her thighs with every bit of his forceful need.

He could feel the pressure rising, tightening, and he roared her name as he thrust home, holding her so tightly he swore he could actually feel his cock exploding against her womb. Grace mewled and shuddered beneath him, tears rolling down her face from the intensity of her ecstasy, her breath sobbing out as her fingernails raked over his jacket.

They'd never bothered to undress.

It was the most frantic coupling of his life, and yet he couldn't regret it for a moment. Even though she'd distracted him from their conversation. He'd learned a few things about his wife, not the least of which was that she was just as passionate for him as he was for her. Perhaps she'd only meant to divert him, but she'd quickly become caught up in their lovemaking as well.

And he'd been the first man to know her sweet mouth. Alex did his best not to think about her with other men. After all, he wasn't blameless. But he did feel a surge of masculine satisfaction at knowing he'd had things from her that no one else had.

Leaning down, he kissed her swollen lips, just as her eyelashes fluttered. She was all limp, satisfied female beneath him. Loved into a dazed state. Still panting for breath. The corset she was wearing probably didn't help.

Alex drank her in like she was a tonic for all his ills. She whimpered a bit, but she kissed him back, her hands moving more slowly across his shoulders. Sliding under his jacket, caressing him through his shirt.

"Mmmmm..." Grace sighed as he pulled away, feeling absolutely boneless. She didn't even care about the indecent sprawl of her body or that her skirt was up around her hips.

"Come on, sweetheart, I'll take you to bed."

She didn't protest as he lifted her in his arms. Sleepily, she nestled against his shoulder. As a distraction, her tactics had worked admirably. However, she was fairly certain they'd also had a hand in the further crumbling of her walls. All she wanted to do was burrow into Alex's arms and never come out. What was she going to do if he dashed all her hopes again?

CHAPTER 14

*F*ortunately, Alex showed no sign of wanting to talk the next morning. They were too busy closing up the house, settling the affairs with man he'd rented it from, and packing up the carriage. Grace felt rather jumpy, worrying over what the ride would be like, but she supposed she could always seduce him again. This morning she'd been in his arms, his cock pressing against her stomach, and he'd started to roll atop her when his valet had knocked and reminded him that he'd asked to be woken early.

She'd been surprised at how disappointed she'd felt. Especially considering their activities last night. How was it she craved him more than ever, when last night should have satisfied her for at least a week?

It was because it was Alex... no other man had ever come close to touching her heart, and so the physical act had never been anything more than a means to release. With Alex, it was so much more. Last night, as he'd been touching her, loving her, she'd felt sure there was more to their encounter than just her emotions. She would have been willing to swear he felt something for her too. Of course, once the rush of pleasure was over, she was no longer so sure, but there was no denying that when they were intimately joined, she felt something was there.

Perhaps that was what she was truly craving. Not the physical intimacy, but the emotions she felt when they were engaged in it. The emotions she felt from him.

Soon they were going to be trapped in a carriage together. Then she would be trapped on his estates. But she refused to be trapped in a marriage she didn't want for the rest of her life.

The only thing now was to decide whether or not she still wanted it.

"You still look tired, sweetheart, sit down," Alex said, suddenly appearing beside her, concern clear on his face. Grace had to admit, she liked that he was becoming more expressive. "We'll be ready to go soon. You can direct from over here."

He took her hand and led her to a bench in the front hall, not far from where she'd been standing. Even though she did feel a bit fatigued still, she had been perfectly fine standing... but she liked his solicitous attention. It still felt a bit strange to have someone watching over her again, sharing the burden of her day-to-day life. While she'd gotten used to it in some areas, this was the first time they'd ever packed up a house together and moved on from it.

"Oh, be careful with that!" Grace said, jumping up as one of the footmen hurried past her with a vase in his arms. One of the ones she'd gotten in Paris, when she and Alex were on their honeymoon. It was the only thing he'd bought her that she took with her everywhere she went. Seeing the look on his face, as he recognized it, she scowled. "I just like the vase. Don't... don't read anything into it that's not there."

"Of course not," he murmured, bringing the hand he was still holding up to his mouth to kiss, his dark eyes never leaving hers. But she could tell by the look in his eyes, he knew she was lying.

The vase had represented many things to her. The bitterness of being let down. A reminder not to trust too easily again. But also a memory of what had been good, the happiness they'd had for a short time before reality had intruded. Even though she'd been let down, she hadn't completely given up hope on love.

"Sit down, sweetheart," he said, his mild voice at odds with the intense look he gave her. It was both dominant and sensual, a voice to be obeyed. Grace found herself sitting back down without even thinking about it. "Now stay here, I'll take care of everything else."

Somewhat bemused, Grace decided to obey. Although she'd been the aggressor when it came to their love-making last night, she had no doubts about who was in charge of the relationship in general. Part of her still felt a bit of resentment that the staff she'd once trusted was completely his. Another part of her warmed to the idea he'd cared enough to watch over her—after all, it's not as if any of the staff had interfered in her life in a negative way until the day he'd come to retrieve her. She told herself he'd been spying on her, but even that made her feel strangely happy in an odd sort of way. Because he'd cared enough to both keep tabs on her and, at the same time, allow her to live her life the way she wanted.

Perhaps she was just fooling herself again, but it did seem the most logical explanation. Or maybe Eleanor's optimism was rubbing off on her.

From her perch in the hallway, Grace sorted out several issues, deciding which items would go in the coach with her and Alex and which would be part of the baggage train, which would travel much more slowly due to its weight. It felt rather nice to only have one thing to oversee, instead of rushing around the house and trying to make sure every single aspect of closing up the house was being handled.

By the time Alex was handing her up into the carriage, before climbing in after her, Grace was having a great deal of trouble beating back the hope pounding inside of her chest.

As much as Alex wanted to have a real discussion with his wife, he decided a carriage ride was not an appropriate venue. Even if she hadn't looked so tired. Yesterday had been exhausting, on several levels, and they'd been woken up earlier than Grace was used to rising, and she hadn't had a moment of rest yet.

Sitting himself next to her, he felt her tense slightly as he wrapped his arm around her. Pulling her into his chest, he tried to soothe some of her tension away, running his hand down her arm.

"Try and get some more sleep, sweetheart," he murmured, stroking her hair. Almost immediately she relaxed, and he realized she must have been worried he was going to try and do something else. Seduce her perhaps? Or talk to her? Which would concern her more, he wondered.

Going by how vocal they'd both been the past two nights, he didn't think seducing her would be any more appropriate than the discussion he had in mind. Loud talking would easily be heard by the coachman, much less shouting of any kind. Besides which, they had a very long ride ahead of them, he didn't particularly want any kind of encounter with his wife which would make it awkward or uncomfortable.

Leaning his head against the back of the coach, he looked out the window and watched as the streets of Bath rolled by to give way to meadows. Grace fit under his arm perfectly, her soft snores making him smile. On the ride into Bath, she'd barely been able to look at him, much less sit beside him. Now she was snuggled up right where she was supposed to be.

For now he could wallow in contentment, but he knew they would have to talk eventually. Hopefully it wouldn't ruin the way things had been going between them.

THAT NIGHT, at the inn, Alex didn't try to press Grace into deep discussion. He thought about it, but when she gave him a saucy look and asked if he could help her disrobe, he allowed himself to be distracted again. Hopefully the foundation of physical intimacy they were building would help to promote emotional intimacy.

He certainly felt as though they were becoming more joined together, as he moved inside of her, their eyes locked together, bodies moving in tandem. Every touch, every kiss, every moan, broke apart the barriers between them just a little bit more. It was tempting to think they wouldn't need to talk at all, but even with Grace cuddling beside him, her hand on his chest and her head nuzzled into his shoulder, he knew it wasn't possible.

This was an idyllic moment out of time, where they were neither here nor there, but traveling both physically and metaphorically. They were both acting as if there was nothing wrong between them and never had been, but until they addressed the past, they couldn't really move into the future. Even though she gave herself to him every night, even though their conversations had become much more natural, there were still times when she would hold herself back. Times when he would feel his own anger and mistrust rising—especially when a letter from Conyngham caught up with her.

She'd given him her return letter to mark and post. It hadn't been sealed. He'd gritted his teeth, sealed it and sent it on without reading it, hard as that had been. Even though he knew she'd left it unsealed so he could read it, he was determined to show he trusted her.

Besides, she'd read aloud the letter Conyngham had sent her, which had mostly been full of gossip from the capital, including his current rivalry with his best friend over another woman. Grace had seemed quite amused and Alex had told himself he had no cause to be jealous. She certainly didn't seem upset that Conyngham had already moved on from her, so why should he be upset the man was contacting her?

Still, that night he made her climax over and over again until she was nearly limp and begging him to stop, before he took his own pleasure. Proving to both of them that he had full mastery over her body, doing his best to wipe away the memory of any other man.

After almost a week of traveling, they finally reached his estates, and Brookeside, the main house. Everything looked exactly the same as he'd left it, the rolling hills around the house, the white walls of Brookeside's impressive front, flowering bushes decorating its edges, but it felt completely different. Because, for the first time in years, he was here with Grace. In fact, they'd only been here as a married couple for a few nights. The rest of their time they'd been on their honeymoon or in London.

Now he was returning home, with Grace on his arm, fiercely triumphant in getting her back where she was supposed to be. The look on her face, as she stepped out of the carriage, was both wistful and wary.

Peters opened the door for them, and Alex felt Grace jerk beside him. He supposed he should have warned her that her former butler was at Brookeside, but he truly hadn't thought of it. There'd been too many other things to consider. However, her stiffness told him that might have been a mistake. Just seeing Peters was bound to remind her of her staff's betrayal when Alex had come to collect her—as well as the fact he'd had to collect her at all, that they'd been apart, and all the reasons for it.

"Welcome home, my lord, my lady," Peters said smoothly, stepping back and bowing his head slightly.

"Don't pander, Peters, it doesn't become you." The waspish tone of Grace's voice grated over Alex's nerves. She'd lost her edge during their time in Bath and he wasn't happy to hear it back, even if he understood why.

Putting his hand on the small of Grace's back, he pushed her gently forward, away from the butler. Recriminations weren't going to help any of them right now. A quick glance at Peters showed the man wasn't offended by Grace's reaction, he was watching her with a mixture of regret and worry. Alex shouldn't be too surprised, after all, Peters had gotten to know Grace's whims and moods quite well over the years.

He *was* surprised to feel the slightest twinge of jealousy about that.

"Peters was just doing his job, sweetheart," he murmured, as he guided Grace toward to staircase to the upper level. "Don't blame him."

The look Grace gave him was not promising. "So you're saying I should blame you?" she asked, smiling at him in a poisonously sweet way that made his hackles rise.

"We'll discuss this later," he said, firmly. Because he could tell this discussion was going to go straight to their past and their estrangement, and he didn't want to start that in the hallway, when they'd just finished traveling. Both of them were tired, dirty, and in no kind of mindset for such an important conversation. Besides, if he let her have her way now, they'd end up fighting and he didn't want that either. "For now, I'll have a bath sent to our room so you can bathe and change."

Dark eyebrows rose as she looked up at him, her venom tempered by confusion. "What will you be doing?" She blinked. "*Our* room?"

"I need a quick word with my steward about the estates, now that I'm back. And yes, our room. I sent word ahead to prepare the rooms accordingly. By now you should be used to sharing a room with me."

Pushing open the door to said bedroom, which was actually his room, he ushered Grace in before she could protest. Her mouth worked, but snapped shut when she saw Rose was already in there, waiting for her. Alex grinned at her suspicious look, which was also tempered with relief. Perhaps a bath and then some food would soothe the savage beast.

Once they were calmer, and in a better frame of mind, they were finally going to talk about why she'd left him and how they were going to go forward from here. This time, he didn't care if she stripped naked and danced for him, he wasn't going to be distracted again.

GRACE ALMOST HATED to admit how much she needed the bath. It had been prepared while Rose helped her undress, and the hot water had soothed muscles that ached from riding in the carriage. The roads hadn't been too horrible, but there was always a bit of bouncing, and her neck ached from sleeping on Alex's shoulder the day before. The hot bath also soothed other aches, between her legs.

They'd made love every single night, and sometimes the next morning as well. Alex had been absolutely voracious, even more so than he'd been on their honeymoon. Not that she'd been protesting, although she certainly wasn't used to this much activity down there. Before her lovers had always been at her beck and call, coming over only when she desired company or comfort or pleasure. Now, she had no choice. Although, Alex always made her want it, despite the aches of her inner muscles. He always made sure she found her pleasure too, before he found his. Sometimes multiple times.

Sighing, Grace relaxed against the tub, feeling rather drowsy from the heat surrounding her. Rose puttered about the room, unpacking Grace's things. At this point, Grace had nearly forgiven the maid for actually being in Alex's employ. She supposed she should forgive Peters too, although somehow she felt his betrayal even more keenly than Rose's.

Perhaps because she'd confided in Peters about her innermost thoughts and feelings nearly as much as she had in her lady's maid, Rose, but she'd always seen him as a protector. He'd stood between her and Society, stalwart and unbending, keeping the worst of the gossip-mongers from her and removing anyone who upset her. More than one person had found themselves in the bewildering position of being dismissed from her house by a mere butler, with all the civility and manners one could expect, and yet the dismissal was just as firm and just as final as if it was from a Duke.

Yet he'd let Alex through the door.

Maybe if she and Alex truly managed to reconcile she'd feel better about forgiving Peters. Even if it was unrealistic to expect him to protect her from his true employer, she'd still trusted him. Up until the day he'd let Alex in, she would have sworn Peters was on her side. That had been half the reason she'd hired him.

She was drying off when Alex came in and immediately began stripping off his clothing.

"Alex," she said, rather sharply, as Rose squeaked in dismay, halting the shedding of his clothes. She looked at her maid. "You may go, Rose."

"Thank you, my lady," Rose said, hurrying from the room, avoiding looking at Alex even though he was still quite respectable in his shirt and pants.

"I forgot she was here," Alex said, chagrined, as he began to take off the rest of his clothing. "I'm so used to it being just us." The warm way he said it, and the almost loving look which accompanied the admission, made Grace's heart dance inside.

"You'll have to get used to more of the servants being around," Grace said mildly. Brookeside required a much larger contingent of staff than the small house they'd stayed in when they were in Bath. Especially now that Grace was in residence. It wouldn't surprise her to know that, other than his valet, Alex rarely had to contend with servants inside his bedroom. But if he wanted Grace in his rooms, he was going to have to accustom himself to Rose being there as well, as well as some other maids.

Grimacing, Alex stepped into the tub, lowering himself into the lukewarm water. "I suppose I will."

Unlike Rose, Grace had no desire to look away from his long, lean body, enjoying the view as he began to scrub away the dirt of the road. However, there were still things to do.

Sighing, she pulled on a simple day dress, one she didn't need Rose or anyone else to help her with. Since they were at Brookeside and not expecting visitors, there was no need for her to dress up at all.

"I'm going to go arrange dinner," she said, pulling her hair back in a simple tie. "I assume Mrs. Stewart is still in her position?" The housekeeper had been as efficient as a general in the army, Grace couldn't imagine Alex dismissing her.

"Yes, and she'll be happy to see you," Alex said, his lips twisting into a wry smile. The older woman was starting to get on in years and, although she was quite practiced in her role, she'd been the first in the household to start pushing Alex to either collect his wife or get a new one. Surprisingly, she hadn't seemed to have a preference, although Alex had assumed she would be disapproving of Grace. Servants could sometimes be even more prudish than the upper classes when it came to scandal.

He thought he heard Grace mutter something as she went out the door, but he couldn't quite make out what. If she was worried about her reception from the servants, she shouldn't be. Alex had prepared his staff, they all knew he'd be bringing her home and to treat her with the respect due the lady of the house. He'd gotten the impression most of them weren't resentful over her absence, just relieved it was now being rectified and their household was finally going to become like any other.

Just as soon as they had their talk.

GRACE HAD BEEN TEMPTED to stay and watch Alex bathe, but she also wasn't quite ready to give up the dreamy happiness she'd found and ruin it with the discussion she knew was coming. Once she confronted him about why he wanted to reconcile with her, things were going to change irrevocably, one way or another. She wasn't avoiding it exactly... but just putting it off, holding onto the illusion of everything being wonderful, if only for a little while.

Doing something as normal and mundane as seeking out the housekeeper only added to that illusion of a happy husband and wife.

"My lady," Mrs. Stewart said, as soon as she caught sight of Grace heading her way, immediately interrupting directions she'd been giving to a maid. Grace was surprised to see a look of pleasure on the older woman's face.

Somewhere in her sixties, the steely-haired, sharp-eyed hawk of a housekeeper wasn't the type to put up with any nonsense. Part of the reason Grace had wanted to seek her out while Alex wasn't around was in case Mrs. Stewart wasn't very respectful. She knew very well Alex wouldn't let the woman go, and so she'd hoped to have a private kind of confrontation, but from the welcoming expression on Mrs. Stewart's face, it appeared there wasn't going to be a confrontation at all. Maybe Alex hadn't been sarcastic when he'd said Mrs. Stewart would be happy to see her.

"Mrs. Stewart," Grace said, trying to sound confident, although she could hear the slight hesitation in her voice. "If you have a moment, I'd like to talk to you about the menus for this week, now that Lord Brooke and I are here."

"Very good, my lady," Mrs. Stewart said, giving a nod of approval as if Grace was a young student who had just said something clever. Looking at the maid, Mrs. Stewart waved her hand. "Go on girl, just don't let me find a speck of dust anywhere or you'll regret it."

The maid bobbed a curtsy to both of the ladies before rushing off, looking both determined and worried. Mrs. Stewart's standards were incredibly high.

"Would you like to sit in the yellow room?" Mrs. Stewart asked, although it sounded more like a firm suggestion than a true question. Grace couldn't help but smile, rather astounded Mrs. Stewart remembered her preference for that small but cheery room. She was also aware she was being herded into the "proper role" of lady of the house by the housekeeper.

But she much preferred that over being met with accusing eyes, recriminations, resentment, or disrespect.

Mrs. Stewart was prepared, not that Grace expected anything less. They spent the next hour in the yellow room, at one of the small tables, going over the purchases Mrs. Stewart had made in advance of the Brookes' arrival and devising menus for the week from it. Something she had done quite often on her own, but now she was thinking about Alex too. Remembering his preferences, his dislikes. And Mrs. Stewart dropped several helpful hints along the way when Grace's memory failed her.

The housekeeper also filled Grace in on the state of the house, the number of servants currently employed, her recommendations about what linens needed to be replaced and what rooms needed to be looked at. When Grace asked about the bedroom usually reserved for the lady of the house, Mrs. Stewart coughed delicately and said the lord had decreed it was not to be opened up for any reason. She looked slightly scandalized as she said it, which nearly made Grace giggle.

Apparently her own scandalous behavior was going to be

forgiven, but the staff was still a bit taken aback by the sleeping arrangements. After all, it just wasn't done. Of course, neither was deserting one's husband without giving him an heir. She was glad Mrs. Stewart wasn't holding a grudge, but sometimes she just didn't understand the way the staff viewed things.

"I think that's it," Mrs. Stewart said cheerfully, gathering her papers back up. "Thank you for your time, my lady. It's good to have you back where you belong."

The words were said perfectly respectfully, but at the same time carried subtext indicating Grace had better fulfill her duties as Lady Brooke or Mrs. Stewart would have something to say about it. Grace nodded her head to indicate understanding. Perhaps she should call Mrs. Stewart on her implied directive, but she was too relieved it wasn't worse. Housekeepers of Mrs. Stewart's quality were coveted by the *ton*. Certain positions within a household were much harder to fill than others, and Mrs. Stewart was an exemplary member of her kind. It was the same reason Grace had ultimately decided to keep Rose on as her lady's maid, finding and training a new lady's maid would be difficult, and other than working for Alex, Rose was a wonderful lady's maid.

"Thank you, Mrs. Stewart," she murmured, keeping her face composed. It wouldn't do to show her amusement or her relief. The housekeeper probably wouldn't consider it proper.

To Grace's surprise, Peters slipped in the door just after Mrs. Stewart slipped out. For a moment they just stared at each other. The man she'd trusted to keep her safe, whom she'd occasionally confided in, the one and only man who had stood by her through all the years she'd been apart from Alex. The only man she'd allowed herself to rely on in any way.

No wonder it had hurt so much when he'd let Alex in the door.

"Hello Peters," she said, softly, her voice heavy with resignation. The bitterness, the anger was gone, as she understood she'd been let down by yet another man in her life. But then again, had she really? Peters must have known Alex's plan. Perhaps he even thought he'd been doing the best thing for her.

"My lady," Peters said, just as softly. There was remorse on his usually inexpressive face, which made her feel a bit better. The *ton* might have referred to Alex as "stone face" because of his usual lack of expression, but her husband had nothing on a well-trained butler. "Would it be possible for me to have a moment of your time?"

Such a request was unprecedented. Some bitter, petty part of Grace wanted to deny him, to lash back at him for hurting her, but she pushed it down as unworthy. Just a month ago, she probably would have ignored the small voice inside of her head to let him speak. She hadn't cared much for anyone's pain or feelings but her own, and only her closest friends had escaped her indifference. Although, even there, she'd had a waspish tongue as well. It shamed her to think of how poorly she'd occasionally treated Eleanor, who had stood by her side anyway. She wanted to be a better person now. In fact, she felt as though she already was. Even if it turned out Alex just wanted an heir or needed her for a business deal, Grace didn't want to continue to be the bitterly unhappy person she'd turned into.

"That's fine, Peters, come on in," she said, doing her best to keep her voice even.

Standing across the table from her, hands at his sides, he looked a bit like he was facing a firing squad. It was almost enough to make her smile, but the very serious expression on his face helped her keep her own in check.

"I just wanted to apologize, my lady," he said, bowing his head slightly. "I didn't get a chance to before you left. Although I had no choice but to follow my lord's orders and keep his involvement in your staff a secret, I want you to know I never bore you any ill will and I would have never done anything to upset you if it had been in my power."

Studying the earnest expression on his face, Grace felt another little crack in her heart heal. Peters was an amazing butler, and he truly had done everything he could to keep anyone from upsetting her. She never thought he'd meant to hurt her, it was just an inevitability that the men she trusted hurt her. Although, unlike Alex and her father, Peters had done his best, within his limitations. Unfortunately, Alex just happened to be one of those limitations.

"Lord Brooke is a good man, my family has been with his for years," Peters continued, after pausing for a moment to see if she would respond. "My instructions, when he first asked me to seek a post with you, were to ensure you never came to any harm and to protect you from the gossipmongers."

"Not to keep out my lovers?" Grace asked, arching one eyebrow. It was a question which had crossed her mind more than once, when she'd allowed her thoughts to dwell on the past and Alex's sudden attitude reversal.

Peters hesitated, and she was fascinated to see a slight blush creep into his cheeks. "Lord Brooke never gave me any instruction about ah... male visitors," he said, his head tipping back slightly and she had the impression he was putting his nose in the air. "And, if you'll excuse my frankness, I thought perhaps such visitors might jolt him into admitting to the fraudulent nature of his own affairs. I didn't realize it would cause further pain on both your parts when I first made my decision to tell him that your flirtations were nothing but flirtations."

"Fraudulent nature?" Grace repeated, trying to understand what Peters was saying.

"Why, yes, I assume his lordship..." Peters' voice tapered off as if realizing perhaps his assumption about his lordship was just as incorrect this time as it had been the last. "I think perhaps I should let you speak to his lordship first."

"Oh no you don't," Grace glared up at him, pointing her finger accusingly, as she fell back into the pattern of speaking easily and frankly with Peters. They had been together long enough that she didn't often stand on ceremony with him when they were alone. "You owe me. Exactly what about Alex's affairs was fraudulent?"

After shifting his weight back and forth, looking increasingly uncomfortable, Peters blew out a long breath of air. Unlike Grace, he seemed to be clinging to the proper respect between servant and mistress, perhaps to create the emotional distance he needed to answer her.

"Although Lord Brooke didn't give me any specific orders regarding male visitors to your household, he did initially ask for reports on your guests. When he became aware none of your flirtations were... ah... serious, he decided to embark upon his own. Um, I believe with the intention of making you jealous. To my knowledge, he did not obtain a true mistress until after I had to report your first overnight guest."

Grace's jaw dropped for several reasons. The first—Alex had cared enough to keep such close tabs on her when she'd initially left him, even as he'd given her the space she'd demanded. Although the presence of his servants in her household had intimated as much, she'd still struggled with the idea that he hadn't just left her completely alone. The second was the knowledge that Alex's first mistress hadn't been anything more than a prop.

That bitch!

That *bastard!*

When Grace had first left him, heart-broken and crushed, she'd found her self-confidence again in the admiration from other men. Perhaps her husband hadn't cared about her, hadn't valued her as anything but part of a business transaction, but other men found her beautiful and appealing. So she'd flirted. Part of her had even hoped maybe Alex would come to her, maybe he'd realize she was worth something for herself. She hadn't actively thought about making him jealous, but that was part of it, she was sure... but the main part had been reassuring herself she was a beautiful and desirable woman, one who was worth more to men than just her father's money.

Then whispers had come when Alex had taken a mistress, Lady Clarissa Heathmore. A beautiful, tall, icy blonde with dark, haunting eyes. Grace's opposite in every way.

Lady Clarissa had cornered Grace in the retiring room at a ball, mocking her for being unable to keep her husband's attentions, inferring he'd abandoned Grace rather than the other way round. She'd praised Alex's prowess in bed and told Grace not to expect to return to it any time soon.

One woman is as good as another.

With his choice of Lady Clarissa as his mistress, Grace thought he'd proven those words. Because if he was content with such a harpy gracing his bed, then he must truly not care what woman gave him pleasure. She'd chosen her very first lover that night, and been lucky the rake was eager to please her and fully lived up to his reputation. The next morning Grace had had a few regrets, but they were all emotional, not physical, and all of them had easily been dismissed when she'd remembered Lady Clarissa's taunts.

They hadn't been true. Grace was fully willing to believe Peters over that lying tart.

But for Alex to choose such a woman... what the hell had he been thinking? Had he taken Clarissa into his confidence? Told her he wanted Grace jealous? Encouraged her?

"My lady? My lady, please!" The alarm in Peters' voice finally drew Grace's attention, and she realized she was standing, fists clenched at her side, fairly quivering with rage.

That blasted bastard. She was going to gut him.

CHAPTER 15

*W*hen the door to his study flew open, Alex jumped in surprise and looked up to see his wife stalking into the room like an avenging fury, Peters hovering over her shoulder looking distraught. Tension gripped him. What the hell could Peters have told her to make her look like this?

Her eyes blazed with rage, cheeks flushed, bosom heaving. If he didn't feel sick to his stomach, worrying about what had gone wrong, he might have been aroused by the picture she presented.

"You *bastard.*"

Alex opened his mouth—although he wasn't sure whether he was going to protest, ask what she was talking about, or scold her for her language, but it didn't matter because he didn't get a chance to say anything anyway.

"You utter *bastard.* Lady Clarissa Heathmore? *Lady Clarissa Heathmore?* Of all the back-stabbing, mealy-mouthed, three-penny uprights, you had to choose *her* to try and make me jealous?! Do you have any idea how awful she was to me?"

He nearly choked at Grace's description, which was all too true, but he hadn't realized she knew that bit of slang. She shouldn't have even known what a three-penny upright was, much less be able to use it in a fairly correct context. The women who procured their clientele from the streets would take a man to a back alley for three pennies and have him right up against the wall... not something a delicate flower of the *ton* should have even passing knowledge of.

Obviously Grace and Peters had been having a bit of a talk. He should have spoken with the butler beforehand and warned him that, although things looked well enough from the outside between himself and his wife, they hadn't actually discussed any details from their past yet. Peters knew far too much of what Alex had done and why. He'd never betrayed that trust either, until now. Apparently his allegiance belonged even more firmly to Grace than Alex had realized.

"Grace, let me explain—" he started to say, and then ducked, as she shrieked wordlessly at him, throwing the pen she was holding in her hand at his head.

She wasn't done though.

After one horrified look, Peters quickly closed the door to the room. Alex knew he could count on the man to keep the other servants away, so they wouldn't be privy to overhearing the scene about to commence in here. He ducked again as Grace launched a decorative vase at his head, growling when it shattered against the far wall.

"Stop that!"

"Bugger off! You... you... nodcock! Bastard! Did you and she laugh together about fooling me? Did you tell her to spread all those rumors?"

Ducking yet another flung object at his head—Alex couldn't even tell what she'd picked up off the shelf—he practically charged her. She was so overwrought she was practically hysterical, he didn't think she even realized there were tears rolling down her cheeks. It was breaking his heart.

He grabbed her, wrapping his arms around her, and she immediately started struggling against him.

"Grace, stop it! Of course I didn't! As soon as I heard what she was telling people, I refuted her!"

"Too late!" she shrieked, kicking at his ankles, struggling harder against him, trying to scratch at him. It felt like all the pain, all the anger, was raging inside of her like an inferno, driving her mad, and she was going to pop if she didn't find some way of venting it. "And the Baroness was just as bad!"

Baroness von Wender had followed Lady Clarissa Heathmore, and she'd been only slightly more discreet. She hadn't searched Grace out to taunt her, but when they'd run into each other, the thinly veiled innuendos and insults had come fast and thick.

"I cut her too!"

"Maybe you should have just stayed away from women altogether!" She tried to bite him, but the jacket he was wearing prevented her from snaring anything more than fabric in her teeth.

Realizing Grace was only becoming more hysterical, that she wasn't in any state of mind to listen, Alex gritted his teeth and decided to revert back to the only method which had worked in curbing her behavior so far. Besides, the way she was cursing and throwing things at him, she certainly had earned a spanking. Keeping his arms wrapped around her, so she couldn't hit out at him—the kicking was bad enough—he lifted her and quickly walked over to the nearest chair. She managed to bang him a couple good ones on his shins as she shrieked and hurled insults at him.

Grimly, Alex quickly flipped her over his knee, wrapping his leg around the back of hers to keep her from kicking and placing his forearm along her back as she struggled to push herself up.

"Let me up, you jackass! Don't you dare!"

She screamed in outrage as he yanked her skirts up and bared her bottom, cursing again as the first blows landed on her creamy skin. Alex didn't hold back, he spanked her hard and fast, barely letting her catch her breath as she starting yelping and shrieking for an entirely different reason. To his relief, he felt her starting to relax under his arm, her angry struggles melting away as she started truly crying.

SMACK! SMACK! SMACK!

Every time his hand landed, her flesh flattened and then bounced back, rosy and bright, her bottom jiggling with the force of each blow.

He was careful to cover the entire area, working his way over each cheek, the delicate crease beneath them, and then down her thighs. Despite the circumstances, he was becoming hard as a rock, watching Grace's bottom turn from creamy ivory to a hot, roasted red.

The fight was going out of her, until she seemed almost defeated, slumped over his thigh, crying out as he spanked her. Slowly her insults and accusations melded into pleas for him to stop, she'd had enough.

Alex kept his arm on the small of her back, keeping her in place, as he rested his other hand on her bottom. The heat of her skin sank into his palm, which was also a bit sore from spanking her. His arm had gotten tired as well. Maybe he should invest in a paddle or the like, that's what Wesley had recommended.

"Do you know why I spanked you, Grace?" he asked, keeping his voice light, reasonable. He caressed her hot bottom, soothingly.

The little sniffles accompanying her reply somehow made him even more aroused. "Because I threw things at you. And insulted you."

"You acted like a child, throwing a tantrum, didn't you?"

"Yes." It was said resentfully, but at least she admitted it.

"We need to talk, Grace. This wasn't quite how I planned on doing it, but since you've forced my hand—literally—I think this might be the best time."

Grace wanted to die. Not because her bottom hurt so much, although it did, but because she couldn't imagine a worse time for the discussion they'd both known was coming. Hanging over his lap, with a freshly beaten bottom? She started to wriggle.

"Let me up!"

SMACK! SMACK!

He landed a blow on each cheek, making her shriek, although she immediately went still afterwards. Alex returned to running his hand over her reddened rump, patting and gently caressing the tender, red flesh.

"I think I like you right here, where I can make sure you listen. Now. Apparently you've talked to Peters. I will admit, I made mistakes when you left me. I was prideful and arrogant. I should have gone after you, rather than trying to make you jealous and trying to force you to come to me. I chose the wrong woman to make that point with, and when I became angry you'd taken a lover, I chose wrongly, again. Not just in my choice of mistress, but in taking a mistress at all. Again, I should have come after you." He allowed his regret to fill his voice. "I cannot express how much I wish I had. I'm your husband. I should have never let you run wild the way you did and I take full responsibility for that. I am sorry for all the pain those women caused you. I wish I had never put them in a position to be able to do so."

His voice was so sincere, Grace found herself confused. She was also a bit peeved at his taking responsibility for letting her 'run wild,' even though it was his fault she'd taken it in her head to do so. Still, his apology about the women was entirely sincere. As was his admission that he should have come after her.

"It wouldn't have made a difference."

Alex's hand stilled. "What?"

"It wouldn't have made a difference if you'd come after me," Grace said, fighting against the part of her that wanted to give in and forgive him. The part of her which had apparently forgotten how much he'd hurt her. "You couldn't have said anything that would have made a difference."

"Why not? Why did you leave, Grace? I've never understood that. You called us foolish... told me I was a liar... and you've never explained." The frustration in his voice was accompanied by fingers digging into her flesh, sparking little flashes of pain in her stinging bottom. Grace wriggled, panting, and the tight grip of his fingers relaxed. "Why did you leave me, Gracie?" The pain in his voice set off her temper again.

"I didn't think you would care!" Bitter fury engulfed her again. Somehow it was easier to say everything when she couldn't see his face; when she was over his knee, her poor bottom throbbing from the spanking he'd given her, she could just shout out her emotions to the floor. "After all, *one woman is as good as another*, isn't she?"

"What the hell does that mean?"

"That's what you said to my father!" Grace started to struggle again, tears filling her already swollen eyes. She could barely believe she had any left to shed. "You and my father, bastards, both of you, congratulating yourselves on your damned business deal... he got me off his hands and you got a wife. It wouldn't have mattered who your wife was, you didn't care, but at least you got some extra benefit out of marrying me because of that damned arrangement!"

Something clicked inside of Alex's head. The hazy memory of a conversation from so very long ago, when Grace's father had come to talk to Alex after they'd returned from their honeymoon. Although Alex had never particularly cared for the Duke, the deal they'd arranged had been highly lucrative on both sides. Yes, Grace had come as part of the bargain, but...

SMACK!

SMACK!

SMACK!

He spanked her already pained bottom until she stopped struggling again, taking the time to get his chaotic thoughts under control, until she hung limply again.

"I hate you."

Alex's heart contracted. "You listen to me, Grace Eileen Greville, and you listen to me good. Your father is an unmitigated arse. At times, I may behave like one too, but I definitely cared who I took to wife. I wanted you. Not any of your sisters or any other woman, just you. But when you're making a deal, you don't show your hand. You should know that from all the shopping you do. The less interest you show, the better off you are. If your father had known how much I wanted you, he would have wrung me dry in the financial part of the bargain. When you heard our conversation the papers hadn't been finalized yet. I couldn't let him know how I felt about you because there were still some small details being worked out in the deal. You were the best part of the deal. No matter how much money I made from it."

Silence hung in the room, only broken by Grace's sniffles.

"Do you believe me?" Alex asked, after a few minutes, his chest tightening with worry. She didn't answer.

SMACK!

"Answer me, Grace."

"I don't know."

The sad, soft little voice was one he'd never heard from her before. Immediately, Alex had her pulled up onto his lap, cuddling her close. The heat of her bottom pressed against his erection, but he had no impulse to indulge in that right now. Holding her tightly in his arms, he snuggled her against his chest, tucking her head under his chin.

"I'll pull out, if you want me to," he said softly. While both he and the Duke had made quite a bit of money together, over the years, there were other ventures he could make just as much money from. "We're secure. I don't need the deal with your father, I can find another. Grace? Do you want that?"

"I don't know." The sad repetition made him feel almost panicked, because he truly didn't know what to do, but he took heart from the fact that she wasn't trying to get away. If anything, she was snuggling closer to him, seeking comfort from him.

"You don't have to decide anything right now," he said, suddenly realizing she must be wrung out. Not only had she been furious when she'd first come into the room, but he'd spanked her for quite a while. She was so limp in his arms... she must be exhausted. "I'm going to take you to our room."

Lifting her up, he was both relieved and a bit worried when she didn't argue.

As he'd expected, Peters was out in the hall, about a hundred feet away. Far enough he probably hadn't been able to overhear much, but he'd be able to warn others away from the hall. After a few quick directions to the butler, Alex headed for his room, Grace lying unmoving in his arms.

In their room, Alex practically babied her. Not to make up for the spanking, she knew that... but she wasn't entirely sure why. Because he felt guilty? Because he'd been telling the truth and he cared for her?

Peters brought food and drink, which Alex practically hand fed her, while holding her on his lap. To her surprise, she was both hungry and thirsty. Especially thirsty. She would have thought she wouldn't be able to eat a thing, but once she got started, she devoured nearly the entire plate. Alex undressed her and tucked her into bed, before disrobing and crawling in behind her.

She lay somewhere between sleep and wakefulness as he curled himself around her, his front pressed against her back. The thick ridge of his cock wedged between her sore buttocks, but he didn't press himself on her. Instead, he just seemed to want to stroke her. To be as close to her as possible.

"Why didn't you come and talk to me?" she asked, her voice a mere whisper in the room. Facing away from him, yet surrounded by his body, it was once again easier to make herself vulnerable. To speak about the past that had hurt her so badly.

"I don't have a good reason," Alex said, tucking her even more tightly against him as he buried his face in her hair. "Youth and stupidity are the best explanations I have. I was hurt you left me. Angry. I wanted to make you come back to me instead of going to you."

His fingers stroked between her breasts, down to her stomach, up and down and up and down. It didn't feel sexual. It felt comforting. The kind of small, intimate touches he'd used on their honeymoon, as if he just couldn't get enough of touching her.

"If I'd known..."

"I was too hurt to tell you." Although now she wished she had. Youth and stupidity indeed. Too hurt. Too proud. Too angry. Although, even if he had told her, would she have believed him?

Maybe eventually. If he'd acted the way he was now. But she wasn't sure he would have, back then. They'd both changed over the years. Matured. They were different people. Grace no longer saw the world as so black and white, she also no longer saw it as always rosy and good. Being in love didn't mean life would automatically be easy and wonderful. Watching her friends had taught her that. Edwin and Eleanor's path had been particularly rocky, even though it was obvious they loved each other.

Was her and Alex's relationship something like that?

"I don't blame you." Now Alex's voice was bitter. "If I had heard you saying something similar about me... I almost wish I'd never made the deal. I could have had you without it."

Grace snorted. "You may be underestimating my father's lust for money. It's all he cares about."

That was the difference, she suddenly realized. Her father only cared about money. If Alex was the same as her father, he might have faked his way through their courtship and wedding, maybe even their honeymoon, but once the deal was set, he would have turned his back completely. That was how she'd always interpreted Alex's behavior when they came back to London. He didn't need her anymore.

But her father would have never protected his wife in such circumstances. While he might not have divorced her, he wouldn't have paid for her housing and clothing either. He would have used his money to force her back to him. And if he did go after her, he certainly wouldn't have done it in the same method as Alex. No, her father liked to shut his wife and daughters away when they caused him trouble.

Alex didn't just let her see her friends, he took her to them. He stayed by her side. Allowed her to go out when she wanted, even without him. Showed her tenderness, caring. Spanked her to correct her behavior, rather than caging her in punishment. And after he spanked her, he comforted her. Held her. Like he was doing now.

She couldn't remember if her father had *ever* held her in such a way. She'd certainly never witnessed him doing so with her mother or sisters.

The offer to withdraw from business with her father floated through her mind. That was definitely something her father never would have done. Not for anyone.

"Will you really end the agreement with my father?" Grace asked, twisting slightly so she could look at her husband. When he answered, she needed to see his face. Her eyes felt swollen and gritty, and she was sure she looked a fright, but this was too important to hide away from. Alex's face was serious, and at least he didn't seem repulsed by her tear-stained face.

"Absolutely. I'll send a note to him first thing tomorrow morning."

"Don't."

"Don't?" he echoed, looking confused.

Grace nodded. "I believe you would, and that's enough."

Her throat tightened, even though there were other things she wanted to say... but she just couldn't yet. It didn't matter. The look on Alex's face was almost euphoric, like she'd just given him the greatest gift in the world. Swiftly, he turned her, pulling her face against his chest and cradling her there. One hand stroked up and down her back, the other reached down to cup her still burning bottom.

Strangely, even though it stung where his fingers pressed against her sore buttocks, it also made her feel safe. Loved. Closing her eyes, she nestled in. Exhausted, she found herself quickly dropping into sleep.

ALEX WASN'T sure what eventually woke him. He and Grace had slept in a tangle of limbs, both of them needing it after the emotionally fraught afternoon.

At first, he thought he'd be more frustrated that such a stupid miscommunication had kept them apart for so long. Then he'd realized it had been far more than that. Their relationship hadn't had the foundation of trust it needed. If they had been more open about their feelings for each other, she would have felt more comfortable coming to him, questioning him, rather than running with little to no explanation. That was just as much his fault as it was hers. As was his conversation with her father.

He'd never make that kind of stupid mistake again.

Grace should always feel valued. Cherished. No matter whether he thought she could hear or not, he'd never disparage her again. She was worth far more than any deal.

Perhaps it truly had taken losing her for him to realize how much he valued her, because he wasn't sure if he would have had those same thoughts before. If she had come to him, if she had told him she over-heard, he would have expected her to understand why he'd done it. Now he understood it didn't matter why, he should have never spoken like that to begin with. It didn't matter what her father thought, or how he did business, Alex should hold true to his own standards. Standards which didn't include running down his wife, just because the man in front of him didn't value her the way Alex did.

Thankfully, it seemed she had grown up as well, because she'd finally forgiven him. At least, he assumed that was why there were fingertips stroking sensually down his chest.

When he opened his eyes, she looked up at him. Although her eyes were still pink around the edges, and slightly swollen, she looked beautiful. Her face was no longer flushed, and she looked... lighter somehow. As if there had been a measure of sadness in her eyes which was now gone.

"Hello," he murmured, sliding his hand down to her bottom and rocking against her.

She winced and a little whimper escaped her lips, but she didn't stop stroking his chest, even though he'd just reawakened the fiery sting from her earlier spanking. Her reaction just sent even more blood surging to his already hard cock as she squirmed against it.

"Hello," she responded, almost shyly. Tipping her head back, she looked at him more fully, and he was overwhelmed by the trust he saw in her eyes. It was hesitant, wary, but it was there. "I'm sorry I threw a tantrum earlier... I should have just come to talk to you."

"Yes, you should have," Alex agreed, but his voice was also soft and mild. He kissed her, gently, tenderly. "I'm glad this time you came to me though, rather than running. I'd rather have you throwing things at me than leaving me again."

Grace giggled, blushing as she thought about her childish behav-ior. She almost wondered if her display had been another test for him. To see what he would tolerate from her. Wanting to know how he'd react. If it had been a test, he'd certainly passed.

"I won't run again," she said. Even though it was true, she could still hear the slight hint of uncertainty in her voice. This new rapport between them was still fragile, even if she was finally giving herself leave to hope. She wanted to think she would stay and try to work things out... but what if he did something awful again?

She squeaked as he rolled her onto her back, settling himself between her legs, pinning her to the bed. The position made her bottom throb a bit. Even though it had recovered somewhat during her nap, the surface was still quite sensitive. Still, she loved the feel of Alex's weight on top of her, solid and imposing. The head of his cock was brushing against her pussy lips, making her want to rock her hips and push him inside of her.

When she'd first woken, she'd started touching him, almost in wonderment he was there... but also because she'd been aroused.

"If you run again, I won't make the same mistake I did last time," Alex said quietly, his eyes boring into hers. His words had the feel of a vow. "I will chase you down and I will blister your bottom. First, for leaving me again, and secondly, so you tell me *why*. I'll admit, I'm not sure I would have handled it the way I should have, if you had come to me the last time. What I said to your father was wrong, and it did take our separation for me to realize how wrong. If you had come to me, I would have expected you to understand, but it's me who should have had a better understanding of how to be a husband. I thought I was happy with the marriage we had, but now I know I want more. I want what Edwin and Eleanor have, what Hugh and Irene have, and what I'm fairly certain Wesley and Cynthia are going to have. I'm sorry it took me so long to get my head out of my ass."

Grace reached up, cupping his face in her hands, feeling the wiry scrape of his facial hair against her palms. The tender, fierce look in his eyes was everything she could have ever wanted.

"I want that too," she whispered, unable to speak any louder when her throat felt so choked with his beautiful promise. Even the promise to spank her if she ran was beautiful, because it showed how much he cared. "I love you."

"I love you," he murmured back, his gaze flickering over her face, until he met her eyes again. The warmth and caring she saw in them slid through the last of her defenses, melting every sliver of ice still in her heart, and crumbling the remains of her walls to dust. She had no trouble believing he meant every word he said.

It would be so easy for both of them to resent the other. They'd both made mistakes, at the beginning of their marriage and throughout their separation, but neither of them wanted to dwell in the past. Alex had been focused on their future from the very moment he'd decided to reconcile, and Grace had joined him in that outlook after she realized he was serious and there might be hope for the kind of marriage she'd always wanted.

She drew him down for a kiss, rocking her hips against his, wanting—needing—him inside of her. Alex pulled his knees up to take his weight, allowing him to slide his hands down her sides, caressing and teasing the sides of her breasts, before cupping them more fully. Moaning against his lips, she canted her hips upwards, seeking him, as he thrummed her nipples with his thumbs.

Hot pleasure flashed through her, making her need simmer. She craved the intimacy of love-making, a physical enactment of their declarations to each other. Whimpering as Alex pinched her nipples, her fingers tangled in his hair as she kissed him harder, more desperately.

Groaning, he rocked, and the length of his cock slid through her pussy lips, coating the underside of his rod in her honey. Grace moaned as the head bumped against and then passed over her clit, making the little bud swell. One hand came down to rake nails over his shoulder, clutching at him. The slight pain in her bottom from her previous spanking was already fading, melding into the pleasure growing in her core.

She made an impatient noise, wriggling as Alex squeezed her breasts, pinching and rolling her nipples between his fingers. It felt so incredibly good, and at the same time it wasn't nearly enough. The sensations went straight to her pussy, which only made her aware of how empty and needy she was. He was rubbing the outside of her pussy with his cock, rocking back and forth, teasing the sensitive lips, but leaving her so empty and aching inside.

"Alex, please," she begged, moaning, as she pulled his head up and away from her lips.

His dark eyes glittered at her, filled with dominance and heat, searing her with his gaze. It utterly took her breath away and she gasped as he pinched her nipples so hard that her back arched to try and relieve the pressure on the sensitive buds. The pain made her ache even more to be filled. She clung to his shoulders, digging her nails in, as her pussy clenched around nothing.

"What do you need, sweetheart? Tell me."

Like he didn't know. He just wanted to hear her say it. She'd felt his cock jerking against her thigh as she'd pleaded with him.

"Please... Alex, I need you inside me... pleeaaa-oh!" Her entire body felt like it was throbbing as he pushed in, hard and deep, filling her completely with one almost brutal thrust.

Her inner muscles clenched and protested against the suddenness of the invasion, even as they sang with ecstasy. Alex wrapped his arms around her thighs, sliding her knees into the crooks of his elbows, spreading her legs wide as he leaned over her. She was completely open and vulnerable to him, her hands pressed against his chest, her pink pussy lips wrapped securely around his cock. They could both look down the length of their bodies and see her impaled on him, see him filling her. Grace shuddered and moaned, clenching again at the sight.

Doing his best to control his own demanding need, Alex began to thrust, slow and sensually, in and out of Grace. Because of the way he had her bent in half, she couldn't wrap her arms around him. She ran her fingers through the hair on his chest, before letting them fall down beside her head, writhing in pleasure as he took his time with hard, slow thrusts. Her pussy massaged his cock, shuddering and spasming as he buried himself in her, over and over again.

He hungrily gorged on the sight of her writhing before him, her breasts bouncing with every thrust, hands reaching up to grab at the pillow as she cried out when he ground himself against her swollen pussy lips and clit. He had absolute possession and control of her body, and she trusted him with it. Reveled in it. Screamed his name as she lost herself in it.

As she writhed in orgasm, he slid his hand between her legs, pinching her clit and rubbing it between two of his fingers. Grace screamed again, tears beginning to leak down her cheeks from the overwhelming shock of ecstasy. She grabbed at his wrist as the pleasure became almost unbearable, but she couldn't stop the twisting, rubbing friction against her clit, as he pushed her over the edge into torturous rapture.

"Alex!" She sobbed his name, her legs straining against his arms, trying to close, trying to stop the erotic assault on her senses.

When he finally released her clit, she only knew a moment's reprieve before he was pounding into her, harder than before, intent on his own pleasure. He rasped against her sensitive tissues, holding her open as he groaned her name, his balls tightening in anticipation. Grace's writhing and shuddering beneath him, her sobbing cries, had him losing all control.

The hot clasp of her pussy sucked at his cock as it swelled and began to throb, pulsing inside of her as jet after jet of his seed filled her womb. His weight rested fully on her, pushing him so deep he felt like they were melded together, the heat of her cunt binding them together. Rocking against her, he could feel the shuddering after-shocks of her orgasm, wracking her body.

Replete, he let her legs slide down and he held her close, dropping kisses along her brow and kissing away the tears that had fallen from the intensity of her pleasure. Grace whimpered, sweetly feminine, and all his. Their limbs were tangled together as he rolled onto his side, taking her with him, unwilling to relinquish his hold on her.

He knew this wasn't the end of their troubles. They would have to continue building their trust in each other, work on their communication with each other, and make the effort to show and share their love, but it would be worth it if he could hold Grace like this for the rest of his life.

EPILOGUE

The Honorable Lord Marcus Simon Villiers blinked solemnly at the faces peering over him. His rather wispy hair was a sunny golden blonde, his rosy cheeks utterly at odds with his dark serious eyes, and he pursed his lips as feminine cooing surrounded him from all sides.

"Oh isn't he just adorable?" Cynthia said, reaching down and tickling at his stomach. She frowned. "He's not ticklish?"

"No," Eleanor said, almost sadly, as she looked down at her progeny. "He's my serious little chap. A little bit too much like his father, sometimes."

As if sensing his mother's disapproval, young Marcus gurgled and smiled, making all of the women gasp and coo again. Just like his father, he already had a devastatingly charming smile. Eleanor laughed and shook her head as Irene, Grace, and Cynthia fell over themselves to tell him what a good, handsome, charming baby boy he was. She was sure Marcus was already all too aware of his effect on the opposite sex.

He was such a good baby though, almost as if to make up for the positive horror he'd been during the pregnancy. Once he'd started to move, he'd never stopped, which had been particularly trying at night.

She'd become so tired and over-stressed that Edwin had been going a bit mad trying to care for her. The labor had been difficult as well, and since then he'd treated her like breakable glass. The spankings and discipline she'd been promised at the beginning of her pregnancy, when she'd still had the energy to cause trouble, hadn't been mentioned by him once.

It was making her rather antsy. Not because she thought he would spring a spanking on her unaware, but because she had a feeling he didn't mean to spank her at all. In fact, for all they slept together in the same bed every night, he'd been remarkably reticent about being seduced, insisting she was still recovering.

Marcus was three months old and she was quite recovered, thank you very much.

"I hope my baby is as sweet as you are," Grace cooed at baby Marcus, garnering the attention of the other three women. She looked up at them and winked.

"You're expecting?" Irene asked, looking thrilled for her.

"Yes," Grace said, looking serenely happy as she placed her hand over her stomach. Eleanor had been relieved to see the immense change in Grace and Alex's relationship by the time they'd arrived at the Manse. They were so very obviously in love; he absolutely doted on her and Grace had found her happiness again. She was nothing but smiles most of the time—although she was occasionally the recipient of a look from her husband that Eleanor recognized very well.

Apparently Alex was still disciplining his wife when he felt she needed it. Eleanor wondered what she would have to do to make Edwin realize she still needed it as well.

"So everything turned out well between you and Alex?" Cynthia asked, watching with interest as Eleanor picked up the baby, who had started to fuss. He quieted, now that he was able to look around the room, winding a lock of his mother's hair around his chubby little hand. "You look much happier."

"I'm so much happier," Grace said, the smile on her face completely genuine. In fact, it didn't look like she could stop smiling even if she wanted to. "He says he didn't mean what he said to my father, he was just trying to be like my father in order to secure the deal... and he's apologized for that. We've both apologized, for the mistakes we've made, but we're focused on the future, not the past."

"Your past lovers don't come up?" Cynthia asked.

"No," Grace said. Then she smirked. "Although, Conyngham and I are still friends, which Alex tolerates. They actually get along quite well, as long as he doesn't think about how Conyngham and I began our acquaintance."

Cynthia made a face. "I can't imagine being friends with any of Wesley's mistresses. Some of them still write him the most appalling letters."

"How do you know?" asked Irene, her eyes widening in shock.

"We read them together," Cynthia said, with a shrug of her shoulder. She snickered, glancing around the room as if to make sure the men weren't within hearing distance, even though they had gone down to the stables almost an hour ago. The other women leaned in, knowing whatever was making Cynthia wary to share was probably going to be deliciously shocking. "Some of them make the most salacious suggestions about what they'd like to do with him. So then I do it with him instead. It's quite fun."

Eleanor and Grace both laughed, but Irene frowned, looking a bit indignant. "What do you do with the letters afterwards? He doesn't answer them, does he?"

"Oh no," Cynthia said, waving her hand carelessly. "We burn them. Although, being ignored doesn't seem to bother them. I actually met one of them, recently, and thanked her for all the wonderful ideas. She hasn't written him since, but she's the only one."

"It's a wonder Wesley hasn't spanked your bottom raw," Eleanor said, amused.

"He thought it was funny," Cynthia admitted. "I thought for certain I was done for when he overheard me, but he just laughed. Later, I cursed when I tripped getting into the carriage and he spanked me the whole way home! I never know what's going to set him off." The way she spoke, the women all knew she wasn't upset about that, more amused than anything else.

255

"Edwin hasn't spanked me since I told him I was pregnant," Eleanor blurted out. Irene looked a bit envious, Grace surprised, and Cynthia a bit horrified. "And he hasn't... we haven't..." It was surprisingly hard to say out loud, despite the frank speech she often enjoyed with her friends. Tears sparked in her eyes, of frustration and a little bit of shame her husband hadn't touched her intimately in so long. She didn't doubt his love for her, but right now that very love was making her feel unhappy because of the way he was expressing it. She clutched at Marcus a little bit tighter, and he started to fuss again, as if her upset was spreading to him.

"Oh dear..."

Grace and Cynthia leaned in on either side of her, comfortingly, as Irene reached out and plucked baby Marcus from Eleanor's arms. She let go of him willingly, not wanting to distress him just because she was upset. He settled again in Irene's arms, and she brightened at holding him, so much so that Eleanor felt a little brighter herself just from looking at them.

"I keep telling him I've recovered, but he doesn't seem to believe me," Eleanor said, sighing. She looked at Irene. "Do you remember, in Bath, he told me he was going to keep track of my infractions, tally them and hold me accountable later?" Irene nodded. "Well, he hasn't. When I mentioned it, he brushed me off, implying all was forgiven. I'd rather he spank me than not touch me at all!"

"Did you tell him that?" Grace asked, sympathetically. "He may need you to come right out and say it."

"I haven't, but I practically threw myself at him the other night, before you all arrived," Eleanor replied, wringing her hands a bit as she remembered her embarrassment when he'd told her she wasn't recovered yet, and tucked her into bed like she was a child, rather than treating her as his wife. "You know how he is, he thinks he knows better than me about everything. Even though he wanted me, he acted like I was being irresponsible by tempting him."

The rejection had smarted, and it was a damned good thing he made her feel loved in other ways, or she would have started to seriously doubt his love for her. It did help that he stayed by her side at the Manse the whole time, so she didn't fall prey to her old insecurities about his faithfulness.

It was cathartic to finally talk about all of this. Even with her own mother in residence, she hadn't been able to talk to her or Edwin's mother about this. It was just too embarrassing. Now that her friends were here, she was finally able to unburden herself.

Cynthia's head turned towards the window. "Where are they now? Are they still at the stables?"

Standing, Grace moved quickly over to the window, peering out. "No, they're at the kennels, looking at the Earl's dogs."

Edwin's father's favorite bitch had a new litter, which he was almost as proud of as he was of his grandson. Eleanor's lips twitched. She wasn't at all surprised he'd insisted on showing them off.

"Good," said Cynthia, sitting up straighter. The devilish look in her eye made Irene look at her warily, even as Eleanor straightened in anticipation. "I know exactly how we can show Edwin you're fully recovered... although it may mean sore bottoms for all of us."

"Of course it will," Irene muttered, but she listened just as intently as the others to Cynthia's plan, and she didn't even attempt to talk them out of it.

THE CAVORTING PUPS didn't hold Edwin's attention as much as his friends, because he'd seen them quite a few times before. His father was in his element though, happily showing off the litter and expounding on their bloodlines. Wesley wasn't nearly as interested as Hugh or Alex, but he'd always been more interested in horses than dogs.

"How was the honeymoon?" he asked, leaning back against the wall of the kennel, watching as one of the pups nipped at Alex's outstretched fingers.

"Edifying," Wesley said, flashing a quick grin.

"It must have been, considering you extended it," Edwin teased.

Gossipy letters had flown fast and furious when Wesley had sent word to his friends and family that he and Cynthia were visiting France and Spain, along with Italy. No one had expected him to be gone from business so long. Privately, Eleanor had told Edwin she'd heard there were many disappointed ladies in the *ton*.

"The pile of mail I returned to wasn't nearly as pleasant," Wesley said, shaking his head. "My partners did their best while I was away... but nothing beats the personal touch."

"You and your penchant for controlling even the smallest details," Edwin said, laughing. "I'm amazed Cynthia convinced you to stay away for so long."

"Well, she does have her ways." The smugly masculine smile on Wesley's face, made Edwin ache a bit. He'd been holding himself back from Eleanor for months now. The doctor had insisted she rest in bed the last two months of her pregnancy, and had warned him against claiming his marital rights—not that Edwin would have anyway, when she was so pale and weak.

The birth of his son had been joyous, but the time before that had been the worst hours of his life. Only the women and the midwife had been allowed in the room, while he'd been left to pace the library with his father and Hugh for company. Because it was such a hard birth, after the first few hours, the mothers had sent Irene out of the room as well, not wanting to alarm her. He'd felt so helpless. So useless. Even though he accused Wesley of being overly concerned with control, the truth was, Edwin was as well, and in those long hours he'd had absolutely none.

Eleanor could have died. The amount of blood on the sheets had been horrifying, and he could only be grateful she hadn't succumbed to any of the illnesses that often plagued women after giving birth.

While his father reassured him it was all a part of life, Edwin found himself reluctant to put her through such an event again. Especially so soon. She'd indicated her own willingness to return to love-making with him, but he worried she was pushing herself too fast. After all, they'd talked over some of her insecurities, especially when she'd been confined to the bed, and he knew she'd been watching him to see if abstinence would make him unfaithful. Of course it hadn't, but now that she was trying to seduce him, he worried she was doing so before she was completely recovered. Possibly out of guilt or insecurity. He wasn't having any of that, but it did make life difficult for him.

Especially when he was faced with three other happy couples, all of whom were able to make love to their wives whenever they wanted.

Over by the dogs, Hugh suddenly straightened from where he'd been leaning over, cocking his head to the side as if listening for something. Chuckling under his breath, Wesley elbowed Edwin and nodded at their friend's stance. He looked remarkably like a hunting dog, scenting the air, a comparison which made Edwin chuckle as well.

"Do you hear that?" Hugh asked, his brow wrinkling. "Who's going out riding?"

The sound of horses trotting out of the stables was nothing new, but as Hugh asked the question, Edwin realized how out of place it was at this time. All four of them and his father were in the kennel. His mother was out visiting friends. And their four wives were supposed to be safely tucked away inside the house, having tea.

Supposed to be.

All four men scrambled to the entrance of the kennels, just as feminine whoops of laughter rang out, leaving the Earl of Clarendon staring at their backs with bemusement.

GLANCING OVER HER SHOULDER, Irene could see the four husbands gathered at the kennel door, staring after the women with fierce purpose in their eyes. She turned her head back, trying to suppress the small shiver going down her spine, and concentrated on controlling her horse. Well, they'd certainly gotten the men's attention with the horse race Cynthia had suggested.

Apparently it wasn't enough to get Eleanor up on a horse, no, they all needed to be involved and the best way to do that was a race. Innocent enough... except Eleanor knew Edwin would be upset, Grace was pregnant, and Cynthia was purposefully trying to create trouble. Irene still wasn't sure how she'd ended up being talked into it, she just hadn't wanted to be left out.

Going by the expression on the men's faces, none of them were going to believe any protestations of innocence. Didn't mean Irene couldn't try though.

In the meantime, it felt wonderful to be on horseback. She loved Eleanor, but being cooped up in the Manse ever since the baby had been born had been hard on both of them. By default, she'd become Eleanor's main companion during the day, and that meant she'd been restricted to the same activities as Eleanor. Certainly she hadn't been on any wild rides...

Now it felt like she was flying, easily leading the pack of women toward the far end of the field, although Eleanor wasn't too far behind her. When she reached the line of trees, she expertly turned the horse about, ready to race back and win... but the men hadn't been content to wait by the stables for their ladies to return. Hugh and Edwin were in the lead, both riding bareback and already halfway across the field, with Wesley and Alex just leaving the stables.

She couldn't say why she did it, it just seemed instinctual, seeing the men advancing upon them like a hunting party.

"Run!" She screamed at the other women. Eleanor twisted around and, grinning, took off like a shot across the field, veering away from the men. It only took a moment for Cynthia to follow her example, although she headed into the forest, and Grace did her best although she wasn't nearly the horsewoman the others were. Irene could see the men cursing as they scattered, following their women.

She started to run as well, her heart pounding. Hearing Hugh calling her name brought her back to her senses. Just a bit. Reining in her horse, she turned again, watching him advance. The others were all out of sight, except for Grace, who had been easily apprehended by her husband and was already being led back to the Manse.

Hell and damnation. She shouldn't have bolted. But they'd just looked so intimidating as a group. Like the four horsemen of the bible, bearing down on them with a vengeance. By himself, even scowling, Hugh wasn't quite as terrifying—even though she knew her bottom was likely about to get a serious workout that had nothing to do with riding a horse.

Reaching her, still scowling, he jerked his head at the stables and started to ride back. Nodding meekly, Irene followed behind him, wishing she hadn't run in the first place.

Hugh didn't speak a word to his wife until they got up into their bedchambers. He was more than just a little annoyed with her. Not for getting on a horse, of course she could do that, but because they still apparently had a problem with her loyalties.

Sitting down on the edge of their bed, he silently gazed at her, knowing it was unnerving to her. She squirmed under his steady gaze, twisting her hands in front of her, looking utterly adorable in her guilt. Red tendrils of hair wafted around her face, having come loose during her wild ride. Seeing her ride like that always aroused him, but they had something else to tend to first.

"Get your hairbrush."

Irene paled, biting her lower lip, and his cock twitched at the pleading look she gave him before obeying. She hated being spanked with her own hairbrush, finding something humiliating in being disciplined with an implement she owned. One she had never considered as a spanking tool. It was a nice, sturdy brush, flat backed and wide, and Hugh sometimes thought it must have been made with the intention that it be dual purpose.

She handed the hairbrush to him, doing her best not to look at it. Sometimes she even blushed when she used it on her hair, if she saw him watching her brush it, and he knew she was thinking about its other use. Honestly, that was part of the appeal to him. He liked how every time she brushed her hair, she thought about why she needed to be good. He barely had to spank Irene more than once a month, and that was just how he liked it.

"Strip."

This she was able to do on her own, fortunately. He was able to sit and enjoy watching her peel off her clothes, seeing the pink in her cheeks intensify and travel down her neck. The shade matched her pert, pink nipples, which were already standing at attention. Once she was fully naked, Hugh patted his lap and Irene willingly put herself over it, which made his cock throb even harder.

"Do you know why you're being punished, Irene?" he asked, one hand resting on her back, the other rubbing the hairbrush over her bottom. He could feel the shiver that went down her spine as he made a circular, massaging motion with the hard wood.

"Because of the horse race," she said, sighing in resignation.

"No."

SMACK! Irene jumped and yelped.

"I don't care if you want to race your horse, you're an excellent rider."

SMACK! She shrieked again, unable to ask the question 'why?' as the hairbrush smacked into the other side of her bottom.

"Grace is not, however, *and* she's pregnant." Alex had told them while they were in the stables. From Irene's lack of surprise, Hugh knew she was aware as well. "Eleanor is still recovering from childbirth."

SMACK!

Irene yelped again, but some of her own temper came to the forefront. "Eleanor is perfectly fine! That's what she was trying to demonstrate!"

SMACK! Another yelp. Hugh rubbed the hairbrush over her already burning cheeks, making them sting.

"I suppose that was Cynthia's idea. Well, Eleanor knows perfectly well she isn't supposed to be pushing herself, and you knew it too. Which is why you're being punished."

SMACK! SMACK! SMACK! SMACK!

The flurry of firm blows against her bottom had Irene howling and squirming. Hugh was showing her absolutely no mercy, he hadn't even given her a warm-up spanking with his palm like he normally did, and she was having trouble adjusting to the fierce sting of the hairbrush on her cool, pale cheeks.

"I expect you to be a good influence on your friends, not be corrupted by them."

SMACK! SMACK!

"You should have come and told me as soon as you knew Eleanor was going to do something she shouldn't."

SMACK! SMACK!

"I am your husband and your first loyalty should be to me."

SMACK! SMACK!

He actually sounded a little hurt as he said that, and Irene felt the faintest flicker of remorse through her resentment as her bottom flared and sparked with pain. She hadn't meant to hurt his feelings... it was just...

"But they're my friends!"

SMACK! SMACK! SMACK! SMACK!

"And as your friends, they shouldn't be so hell-bent on getting you in trouble," Hugh said firmly. Then, to her horror, he turned the brush over and rubbed the stiff bristles against her flaming skin. Irene shrieked. The normally soft bristles felt like sandpaper, rasping over her sensitive cheeks, making her writhe and try to reach back to stop him.

A futile exercise. Hugh easily grabbed her hands and held them in place in the small of her back, leaving her to kick and cry as her stinging bottom was assaulted in an entirely new way.

"You're a people pleaser, sweetheart, and I understand, but the very first person you need to please is *me*. You need to choose me over your friends, especially when they're doing something which could be harmful to them, even if it's not particularly harmful to you. Don't just say 'yes' to everything they suggest, use your own judgment."

That was certainly something no one had ever said to Irene before. All her life she'd always had to say yes to whatever her parents wanted—mostly what her mother wanted. Now she mostly said yes to whatever Hugh wanted. But then, there were times when she told him no or asked him for something different. Most of the time, he didn't mind and it had made her braver.

Why hadn't she been able to do that with her friends? Was she worried they would no longer like her afterwards?

Why did she trust Hugh would still love her, but worried they wouldn't?

SMACK! SMACK! SMACK! SMACK!

Her introspective thoughts flew out of her head as Hugh flipped the brush back over her brought it down on her bottom with firm, crisp swats that had her howling again. The rubbing bristles had made her skin feel even more sensitive than before, and she was soon kicking her legs and begging him to stop. His point had been made. She needed to stop letting herself be drawn into the wild schemes of her friends—she wasn't going to be a snitch, but she could certainly try to convince them not to do things. And not allow herself to be drawn into their schemes even if she couldn't persuade them otherwise.

From the way her bottom was burning, this wasn't a lesson she would soon forget.

Although, when Hugh was finished blistering her bottom, and he tossed the hairbrush aside, she forgot everything but the burning meld of pain and pleasure as he climbed between her legs and pounded her into the bed, heedless of her throbbing bottom as it bounced against the surface beneath her. Clawing at his back, Irene screamed his name as she came, pulsing around his cock before he emptied what felt like a gallon of seed into her waiting womb.

Nine months later, he was willing to swear that was the day their daughter had been conceived, which would account for her stubborn, wild ways.

SEETHING, Alex had led Grace's horse back to the stable, reins firmly in his hand, while she haughtily maintained icy composure. She hadn't been very hard to catch. His Gracie was a passing horse-woman, but in comparison to Irene or Eleanor, or himself, she wasn't able to hold her own. Alex would have been hesitant to let her participate in a horse race even if she hadn't been pregnant.

Her hauteur only made his palm itch to turn her over his knee and break her ice princess shell. It was a facade that rarely came out any more, not since they'd spent months together, rebuilding their relationship on his estate. When it did, he had no hesitation about spanking it out of her.

It seemed she thought her condition would protect her, much as it had protected Eleanor during her own pregnancy. There was a definite air of triumph about her. Taking the wind out of her sails was going to be immensely satisfying.

He spotted Edwin leading Eleanor back to the stables, seated behind her on the horse she'd been using, with his barebacked filly following sedately behind. However, he didn't take any time to watch them, instead he dragged Grace into the house, making one quick stop in the kitchen. It was obvious from the confusion on her face that she had no idea what he might want with peeled ginger root.

"You can't mean to spank me!"

Grace looked both shocked and outraged when he ordered her to strip and turn herself over his knee. Raising his eyebrows, Alex held his position on the chair he was sitting on, and silently lifted his finger, indicating she'd better hurry. She glared at him.

"But I'm pregnant!"

"So?"

"Edwin loved Eleanor enough not to spank her when she was pregnant!"

"No, Edwin worried about Eleanor's health enough not to want to distress her. She had a difficult pregnancy from the beginning." He smiled smugly. "You, on the other hand, haven't had a single problem. If anything, you're healthier than ever. Besides, he still found ways to discipline her. But I'll be damned if I am going to punish myself by depriving myself of watching you climax for me. So you're getting a spanking."

And a figging, but he wasn't sure she understood what the finger of ginger was for, even though he was shaping it into a nice, tapered plug. Wesley had been a font for interesting ideas on creative ways to punish a wife, and for all Alex's talk, he wasn't going to be too harsh with Gracie even if she was the picture of glowing health. For putting herself and their unborn child in danger, she deserved a strapping at the very least. Instead, she was going to get a figging and a spanking.

Grace blushed at Alex's comment about watching her climax. It was true. She'd found that her husband loved nothing more than to bring her off with his hands or mouth, just so he could see her orgasm, before sinking into her and watching her cream herself on his cock. Watching her find pleasure aroused him like nothing else.

She knew she was arguing just for argument's sake though— although she had had a flash of insecurity for just a moment. Over the past months, she'd been spanked quite a bit, constantly feeling the need to push at him just to make sure his feelings were still true. Alex was consistent and firm, which was just what she needed to settle herself back down again. A spanking, some thorough love-making, and Grace's lingering doubts would be laid to rest all over again. Although she hadn't tried to run, ever. She hadn't needed to. Alex dealt with minor transgressions quickly and firmly enough that she felt constantly loved.

The only time he hadn't spanked her, when she thought he would, was when she mouthed off to her father. They'd gone to London for a week and Alex had invited her family over to dinner. It had been wonderful to see her mother and sisters, but her father had been stiffly cold and formal. That hadn't bothered her. But when he'd made a disparaging remark to her younger sister Adeline, because she didn't want to eat one of the jellies, Grace's temper had flared up. She'd been downright rude, but Alex had not only cut her father off from berating her, he hadn't even spanked her afterwards. If anything he'd been proud of her.

The funniest part had been that her father hadn't even been able to show his displeasure by cutting off his business with Alex. He needed her husband too much. At the end of the night, Alex had made it clear the Duchess and her daughters were welcome at their house any time, in fact, he insisted on it at least once a week when they were in London. Her father had looked like he was choking, but he'd agreed it was good to keep family ties in place.

Good for business was what he meant. Grace hadn't realized just how much her father needed the deal with Alex to keep his own finances above board. After they'd returned to the estate, she'd kept in touch with her sisters and mother through letters, the first time she'd been able to do so in years.

So no, she didn't really question Alex's love for her most of the time. Little doubts niggled on occasion, but he always laid them to rest. Of course he loved her just as much as Edwin loved Eleanor, and he'd never risk her health or safety. Unlike Eleanor, she hadn't had a single twinge of morning sickness, she wasn't even fatigued. She wasn't showing yet either, not really, although her stomach had become a bit rounded. It would be no hardship to lie over Alex's lap, and she trusted him enough not to spank her so hard that it would be any danger to the baby.

She stripped, watching him with the ginger, wondering what he was doing. Was he going to make her eat it? That seemed a possibility. Cynthia had mentioned Wesley soaping her mouth the last time he'd overheard her cursing. But Grace liked hot food, especially since she'd become pregnant, she'd started craving it. A bit of raw ginger wasn't going to be any real punishment.

Once Alex had her over his lap and it was pushing at her bottom hole, she changed her mind.

"Stop that!" She shrieked.

Alex just grinned at the outraged propriety in her voice. She was more upset about him putting something in her cute, crinkled rosebud at the moment, but in a minute she was going to understand why he was doing it. Holding her firmly in place, he swiftly inserted the thin finger of ginger. He'd notched it, the way Wesley had told him to, and her anus snapped around the notch, leaving just a bit outside.

Grabbing her wrists, he tutted at her. "You brought this upon yourself, Gracie. You should know better than to engage in horse races when you're *enceinte*. What if you'd been thrown? Or jostled?"

"The only danger to me was you," she snapped back, tightening her muscles and trying to buck. The sudden burn inside of her rear channel, as her muscles clenched, had her gasping. "Ow! Ow! That hurts, make it stop!"

The frantic sound of her voice and her writhing movements had Alex's cock rubbing against her side as she tried to dislodge the ginger root. He could see her bottom working to push it out, making her cry out as it burned even more.

"Just relax, it will burn less the more you relax," he said, making sure he had a firm hold on his wife and her wrists as he raised his hand. With that advice, he brought his hand down firmly on her backside, careful to catch her full on the cheek without jostling the ginger.

Grace cried out as he began peppering her bottom, going back and forth between the cheeks, making it impossible for her to relax. The ginger was going to work on her insides, her bottom feeling strange with something inside of it, especially something burning her sensitive innards. She howled, begged, and pleaded, twisting as Alex spanked her.

Surprisingly, the spanking seemed to help with the ginger, making her burn on the outside and distracting her from the growing furnace between her cheeks. Her legs kicked, churning, as she tried to escape the twin fires, but Alex had an iron grip on her, and his hand just kept coming down with firm, stinging swats. The juices of the ginger were leaking down to her pussy, making it swell and tingle, her natural juices flowing from the combination of the ginger and Alex's domination over her.

No matter how hard he spanked her, she was always aroused at the end of it... but this felt so much more intense. Maybe because her rear aperture was filled, but her pussy wasn't. That didn't stop it from hurting though. Alex spanked her until her bottom was throbbing, feeling just as swollen and hot as her pussy, but for an entirely different reason.

Tears were leaking down her face and onto the floor as she cried out, reduced to incoherent cries and sobs. It hurt, and she was already promising herself inside of her head that she wasn't going to do anything even remotely dangerous for the rest of her pregnancy. She'd almost prefer a strapping over the infernal ginger that burned even hotter every time she clenched around it.

Finishing the spanking with five swats to Grace's sit spots, Alex thought his cock was going to burst. Her bottom was a bright flaming red, and yet even when the spanking stopped she couldn't keep from writhing. The ginger was burning her from the inside out. The effects on her pussy were incredibly arousing, he could see the plump, dark pink lips between her slightly parted legs, ready and waiting for him.

It took him less than a minute to pull his cock from his breeches— he'd already undone them while Grace had disrobed—and pull her up so she was facing him, straddling his lap. Both of her hands were still behind her back, he held her wrists tightly, which thrust her breasts at him, tempting him with her cherry nipples.

"Wait!" Grace cried out, trying to pull away, her thighs already burning from the effort of not sinking down on top of him. Her knees were bent, but he wouldn't allowed her to straighten completely, and she refused to lower herself. "Take out the ginger."

"No."

The denial was swift and firm, and then he leaned forward to take her nipple between his teeth, using his leverage to push her down onto his cock. Grace's head fell back and she cried out as gravity forced her down onto him, his thick length sliding in easily thanks to her ample lubrication. His free hand squeezed her bottom, fingers seeking out the ginger.

The sharp stinging pain wrapped around her pleasure, enhancing it, as she was forced to ride him. Her nipples were tortured by his lips and teeth, her pussy filled and pleasured by his cock, the ginger in her ass pumped back and forth even as he squeezed her burning bottom cheeks. The strange feeling of two things sliding in and out of her, both of them burning in different ways, had her shuddering and sobbing with the overwhelming mix of sensations.

Even though she was on top, Alex controlled her every movement, taking her hard and deep, fucking her ass with the ginger, and sending her into a maelstrom of intense rapture. She screamed his name as she came, feeling him join her only moments later, filling her with his seed.

Hazy warmth enveloped her, soothing her aches, caressing her body, and she floated in a sea of comfort. The only sound that pierced the cottony enclosure of happiness was the soft, deep, beloved murmur, whispering the same thing over and over again.

"Sleep now, sweetheart... I love you, Gracie."

LOOKING over her shoulder one too many times proved to be her doom. Cynthia's horse balked at a fallen tree trunk across the path. She almost cursed too, but the sudden memory of soap flickered across her taste buds and she immediately bit her tongue. That was all Wesley needed to catch up to her though, he knew the Manse's woods much better than she did. It had only been a matter of time, but truthfully she'd been enjoying the chase and had hoped to keep it going a bit longer.

"Get off the horse."

Cynthia tossed her head, looking a bit like a fractious mare herself. "Or what?"

The white gleaming smile he flashed her, bright in the shade of the trees, was not encouraging. "Or instead of punishing you, I'll drag you back to the house, tie you to our bed, and leave you there for the rest of the afternoon."

She only hesitated for a moment. Then she got off the horse.

"Good girl," Wesley murmured, dismounting as well, now that his wife had both feet firmly planted on the ground. She scowled at him, but he could see through her. Cynthia needed the excitement, the pain and the pleasure, as much as he did. She craved it. But only if she felt like she really earned it. Bedroom games occupied them the rest of the time, but every few weeks she needed to misbehave in a way to earn herself a truly rigorous punishment.

Which Wesley was always happy to provide.

She got a regular spanking at least twice a week, but eventually she always needed more. Yet, when the time came, she fought against her punishment, tried to talk or seduce him out of giving it to her, and he knew if she ever succeeded she would be incredibly disappointed. The fight was part of the thrill for her, almost as if she craved being forced to his will. The idea that he might take her back to the Manse and leave her restrained, without any kind of gratification, was probably horrifying to her.

It was certainly a punishment he planned on using sometime, when she had truly earned it. The withholding of pleasure. Except he wouldn't just leave her there... no, he'd tease and torment her body until she was begging him for release. Today's silliness didn't amount to such a punishment though.

"Pick a switch."

"What?"

Wesley gestured to the tree beside him. "Pick a switch."

As he gathered the reins of both horses and began to lead them to a different nearby tree to tie them to, Cynthia gaped at him. "You want me to pick my own switch?"

"Better hurry or I'll do it for you."

Excitement and apprehension tingled through her at the dark look that went with his threat. She might never understand why she became so aroused at being punished by her husband, but did it really matter why? There was something wrong with her, she knew that, but it made both of them happy. The idea of being switched... it made her tingle even as it terrified her.

The tree he'd indicated had plenty of thin, whippy branches. Biting her lower lip, Cynthia found one that wasn't too thick, but wasn't too thin. She tried to break it off at the base, but the limb was strong. A second later, heat pressed against her backside as Wesley's arms came around her and he used a knife to cut the slender branch.

"Good girl," he murmured in her ear. "Now go bend over the tree and lift up your skirt."

Cynthia hurried to the fallen tree trunk, already anxious to get the bad part of being punished over with. Watching her, Wesley smiled darkly as he began to trim the branch, peeling off the bark, while her bare bottom began to squirm as she waited. He was careful to make sure the switch was smooth, so there would be no chance of splinters.

At least she'd learned her lesson about waiting. He did love to keep her anxious, never knowing how long he was going to take before he began the punishment. One time, he'd added five minutes to the wait every time she spoke. After that, she'd never tried to hurry him along again.

Bending the limber switch into a loop, holding both ends, he approached her from behind. For a long moment he just admired his target, smoothing his hand over her creamy bottom and tapping it lightly. She moaned a little, sounding both scared and excited. When he slid his fingers through her pussy lips, they came away wet. Wesley licked her cream from his fingers before stepping back.

"Hold still," he warned her.

SWISH! SNAP!

The shrill cry echoed around them as Cynthia's body jerked. The loop he'd made out of the switch had caught her simultaneously on the bottom and the top of her curved cheeks. She pressed herself hard against the tree, her body instinctively trying to get away from the painful, stinging implement.

SWISH! SNAP!

Fortunately there was a branch on the other side of the fallen tree she could grab onto, holding onto it for dear life to keep herself from reaching behind and trying to cover her bottom. If she risked her hands in such an endeavor, Wesley would be furious. He loved her cries of pain, but only when it pertained to torment he was purposefully inflicting.

SWISH! SNAP!

The thin red lines on Cynthia's bottom, combined with her mournful cries, were making Wesley's cock throb with need. Fuck she was gorgeous like this, bent over and vulnerable, taking the punishment they both knew she deserved, that she craved even as she cried out in pain. Every time a blow landed, her pussy clenched.

The thin welts burned, stinging at her skin like angry bees, drawing sobs and tears from her, despite the dark need welling inside of her. Wesley was careful not to overlap the lines too much, taking his time to ensure he didn't draw blood as he laid a delicate tracery of welts across her bottom. They almost looked like lace, as they crossed each other.

When he finally stopped, Cynthia's legs were trembling and almost her entire weight was being supported by the fallen tree. She was lost in a haze of sensual need and erotic pain, and she had no idea how much time had passed before he was suddenly pushing into her pussy. Moaning, she wanted to lift her hips to meet him, but her legs were too weak. It burned when his body pressed against her body, shoving her hard against the tree. Her skirts protected her tender skin from being scraped by the bark, but there was nothing to protect her welted bottom from the rasping of Wesley's body against it.

She cried out, shuddering in ecstasy as he pumped his hips, fucking her hard and fast. Since their wedding night, Wesley had taken her in all manner of different positions, but this was one of her favorite. Bent over and taken from behind, feeling his cock sliding inside of her, over the sweet spot, as his hands dug into her hips. Somehow she felt his domination even more like this than when she was tied face-up to the bed.

Pulling out, his cock covered in her juices, Wesley pressed his cock against the tight rosebud of her anus.

"Oh no, please!"

Cynthia's face heated as her rear channel opened for him. It hurt as her muscles stretched. He didn't take her back there often enough for her to truly become accustomed to it, enjoying the struggle every time he did. So she also never really quite got used to the shame of enjoying such a perverse act. Deep down, she knew she loved it, but that just made her blush more furiously, protest more adamantly. If Wesley ever stopped taking her in this manner, she would miss it, but she couldn't admit that, not even to herself.

"Ow, ow, ow," she muttered as he pushed deeper, not heeding her plea. It took her breath away every time he sank into her ass for the first stroke, making her feel so full, like there wasn't room in her body for air. "I wasn't that bad... it was just a race!"

"Which was whose idea?" Wesley asked, holding her hips tightly as he watched her crinkled anus stretching around his cock, all of the little wrinkles smoothing out to accommodate his girth. Her silence confirmed his supposition. "So not only did you get your friends into trouble, but then you ran from me." His voice lowered, growing gruffer as his cock was engulfed fully into her ass. Holding still for a moment, feeling the spasms of her tight sheathe around him, he leaned forward to whisper in her ear. "I think you deserve a little bad girl sex, don't you?"

She moaned, half in denial, half in pleasure, as he began to drag his cock back out of her body. Clinging to the branch on the other side of the trunk, she suddenly realized this might be why she liked this position so much. Because whenever he took her from behind, she wasn't just out of control, she was completely vulnerable to him. He could play with her anus all he wanted and there was nothing she could do to stop him.

Her pussy dripped as he began to fuck her ass, hard enough to make her squeal and yelp, the burning friction fighting with her rising pleasure. Every slap of his body against her bottom made her cheeks jiggle, the stinging welts feeling like they were flaming brands tracing her skin.

The overwhelming sensations were making her toes curl as a rising tide of ecstasy began to overtake the effects of her punishment. Her ass clenched and spasmed as his cock slid over her sweet spot from the other side, making her gasp and cry out, writhing before him as he impaled her over and over again. Cynthia's sobbing breaths were interspersed with Wesley's grunts as he ravished her aching bottom, skillfully pulling her from stinging pain to abject pleasure.

Their combined shouts of climax echoed through the woods around them. Cynthia clawed at the fallen tree as she came, her tight ass milking Wesley's cock, sucking his hot jets of cream deep into her body.

When they returned to the Manse, it was on foot, leading their horses by hand, in deference to Cynthia's painful rear. They walked between the horses, holding hands all the way.

~

"Out," Edwin ordered as he handed over the horses. "Take them for a long walk to cool down," he said to the young groom who took the reins. The rest of the stable staff had already scattered at his command.

Shifting back and forth on nervous feet, Eleanor tucked her hands into her skirt, anxiously fisting the fabric as she waited for his attention to come back to her. It returned after the door to the stables were closed, his dark, furious gaze making her tremble a bit. But this was what she wanted... his attention. His discipline. His recognition that she was able to act as his wife again. That she wanted to. Needed to.

"What were you thinking?" His question cut through the air, sharp and heavy with frustration.

Eleanor tilted her chin up, knowing her stubborn pose never failed to needle him. "I was thinking I deserved to have some fun."

"Fun? *Fun?* You think risking your health and safety is *fun?*" He advanced on her, his jaw clenched, eyes glittering with anger. It was rather sweet how protective he was of her, or it would be if it wasn't so damned frustrating as well. Hiding her smile, she rolled her eyes instead. Baiting the boar.

"My health is fine—as I've told you—and I was perfectly safe. I'm a very good rider and I know these lands like the back of my hand."

For a moment his jaw worked soundlessly, as if he was trying to get out an argument but was having trouble thinking of one. Stopping his advancement about a foot away from her, she could practically see the thoughts churning in his head. Holding her breath, she prayed he would come to the right conclusion. If he didn't, she wouldn't be liable for what she did next. Kicking him would be the least of it.

"Your health is fine." The flat statement didn't sound at all like a question, but she answered anyway.

"Yes."

"You think you're fully recovered."

"Yes." The defiance in her voice rang with challenge.

Edwin's cock was hard as a rock as he struggled to keep his emotions on an even keel. The flashing rebellion in his wife's bright blue eyes, her saucily tilted chin, her prodding, was all designed to make him lose control and he knew it.

"Then let's test that. Strip."

His voice was hard, demanding, but he couldn't fail to see the excitement flare on her face at the command. Clenching his fists, he thought swiftly through his options. Part of him still worried he was going to accidentally harm her, so he would need to be careful and not allow her to divest him of all his self-control. Another part of him recognized she must truly feel ready, since she was willing to take a punishment in order to receive his love-making as well.

As she stripped, he grabbed a horse blanket—a clean one—and tossed it over the hay, which had been stacked in the corner of the stable. The horse blanket would keep her from harming her tender skin, but it wouldn't be too comfortable either. Which was part of the punishment, of course. He wasn't going to let her take this too far.

To his surprise, she didn't even wait for his command. His gloriously nude wife swanned past him, without even the hint of a blush and bent over the hay bales, positioning herself in the center of the blanket. The creamy cheeks of her bottom beckoned to him, and between her legs he could see her glistening, pouting pink lips, framed by her damp curls. Edwin bit back a groan as his cock throbbed.

He hoped she truly was recovered, otherwise this was liable to kill him.

Tossing her blonde curls, Eleanor peeked over her shoulder at him, her seductive gaze tinged with an anxiousness that tempted him more than any mere seduction could. His palm itched.

SMACK! SMACK! SMACK! SMACK!

It wasn't the hardest spanking Eleanor had ever received, nor was it the most erotic. The blows were caught somewhere between punishment and pleasure, as if Edwin couldn't quite decide what he wanted to do with her. She wriggled and moaned, occasionally crying out when he caught a particularly sensitive spot. The slow burn was building with every sharp smack, making her wag her bottom up and down.

The horse blanket rubbed against her breasts, which were so much more sensitive since she'd given birth. Eleanor had decided she wanted to use her own milk for her son, despite social conventions, and Edwin and his parents had supported her, even though her mother had tried to talk her out of it. Right now, even though Marcus had fed recently and she had no more milk at the moment, her breasts felt tightly swollen and heavy as they rubbed against the blanket. Her sensitive nipples were like cherries about to burst, abraded by the rough material in the most delicious way.

When her bottom was a nice, hot pink, Edwin stopped and slid his fingers down between her legs. Her pussy was dripping wet, and Eleanor moaned as he pressed a finger inside of her, stretching her tight sheathe. He muttered a curse under his breath, his knees nearly buckling, as he felt her muscles clenching down around him. She was incredibly tight, probably because he hadn't done more than use his mouth on her in months. And that only before she'd given birth, and very rarely.

Eleanor whimpered, lifting her hips and her hot bottom, her body silently begging for more. As he undid the front of his pants with one hand, he slid a second finger inside of her, helping to stretch her inner muscles.

It felt phenomenal. She didn't care that they were in the stables, or that she'd just been spanked... she didn't even care if anyone overheard them. Edwin was finally touching her again, finally inside of her again, and feminine intuition told her that she was going to get everything she wanted. The hot, sensitive skin of her bottom protested as he turned her over, pressing her down on the bale of hay.

"I want to see your face," he murmured, pulling her legs up and pressing them against his shoulders.

His eyes flickered over her face, searching her expression for any sign of discomfort as he pressed his cock against her pussy and began to push in. Eleanor gasped, her back arching, as she bit her lip against a cry. It hurt, but she didn't want him to stop.

Seeing the discomfort on her face increasing, Edwin immediately stopped.

"Don't you dare!" Eleanor shrieked as he started to pull out. She reached up, grabbing him by his coat and holding him in place. "If you stop, I will take a crop to *your* backside! There's plenty of them in here! I'm fine... just... go slowly."

"If this becomes too much, you *will* tell me," he said, fiercely determined to get her agreement before he started again even as he wanted to laugh at her threat. His Nell would never be the type to lie back and let him have full control, and he would never want her to be. She nodded her head, looking relieved. He had to trust her to tell him if she was in too much pain, although he was watching her closely as well.

It wasn't entirely comfortable, her muscles had been sorely abused by childbirth a few months before, but she could adjust. She could take it.

Edwin rocked his hips, moving incrementally deeper, just a tiny bit at a time. It was slow and torturous for both of them, but he held onto his control with the skin of his teeth. As much as his body wanted to plunge into her, to bury himself in her slick warmth, he kept a careful watch on her face to ensure he wasn't going too quickly or too roughly for her.

By the time he'd worked his entire cock into her body, both of them were thinly sheened with sweat and he felt like he'd just run for miles. He closed his eyes, savoring the feel of her around him, of the intimate joining that they'd been missing for so long. The tight muscles rippled, massaging his cock, and she moaned again.

"Edwin... please... *more*..."

He started to move. Gently at first, and as he heard her gasps of slight pain turn to moans of pleasure, he thrust harder, faster. Despite the discomfort, Eleanor was so wound up, so needy, that it didn't take very long for her husband's steady thrusting to send her over the edge into screaming orgasm. She filled the stables with her cries of passion, with his name, as the pent-up dam broke and pummeled her body with waves of rapture. For just a moment, he felt regret over holding back for so long. As much as he'd wanted to make love to her, his need to see she was fully recovered had been far greater. Perhaps he had taken it too far, and next time he would trust her more fully. Having her beneath him, writhing and crying out with ecstasy, he didn't know how he'd managed to wait for so long.

Overcome by her climax, Edwin felt his cock throb and he shuddered as he pumped her full of his seed, unable to hold back any longer. He collapsed over her, leaving her legs hanging down, his hands caressing any part of her he could reach.

"I love you..." he murmured, nuzzling against her naked breast. Replete and satisfied for the first time in months. He didn't see Eleanor's slow, sleepy smile as he repeated himself. "I love you."

IF ANY OF the parents noticed the squirming, blushing discomfort of the four young women at the table during dinner that night, not one of them said anything. The men noticed, of course, and exchanged knowing looks. Irene blushed whenever any of her friends looked at her, despite Grace's sympathetic look and Cynthia's unapologetic wink. Eleanor was too lost in her own haze of happiness to really squirm too much, besides Edwin had gone rather lightly on her.

Happily sitting back in his seat, Edwin could only reflect on how unexpectedly this past year had gone. He'd married the woman of his dreams. In addition, he had a son already as well. Even better, not only was he blissfully happy, but his friends had all found the right women for themselves as well. He'd found a new friend in Alex, and the man's reconciliation with Grace made Eleanor even happier. If someone had told him this past year would bring so many changes to his life, he would have never believed them; but he wouldn't take a single thing back about this year. Not even the frustrations Eleanor had put him through at first.

He didn't think anyone else at the table would either. Surrounded by friends and family, sore bottoms or not, their warmth, love and laughter carried them into the night. Just like it would for the rest of their lives.

～

DID you enjoy the *Bridal Discipline Quartet*? Check out Philip's Rules, the first book of the Bridal Discipline Series; unlike the Quartet, each book is a standalone romance with a guaranteed HEA.

HUGH AND ELEANOR'S cousin Philip is hoping for the same sort of happy marriage he's seen his family and friends achieve for themselves, but there are a couple of obstacles in his way to marital bliss!

～

WOULD you like to receive a free story from me? Join the Angel Legion and sign up for my newsletter! You'll immediately receive a free story from my Stronghold series in a welcome message, and as part of the Angel Legion you'll also receive one newsletter a month with teasers, sneak peeks, and news about upcoming releases, as well as what I'm reading now!

ABOUT THE AUTHOR

About me? Right... I'm a writer, I should be able to do that, right?

I'm a happily married young woman and I like tater tots, small fuzzy animals, naming my plants, hiking, reading, writing, sexy time, naked time, shirtless o'clock, anything sparkly or shiny, and weirding people out with my OCD food habits.

I believe in Happy Endings. And fairies. And Santa Claus. Because without a little magic, what's the point of living?

I write because I must. I live in several different worlds at any given moment. And I wouldn't have it any other way.

I also write erotica, fetish romance, and dark offerings under the pen name Sinistre Ange.

Want to know more about my other books and stories? Sign up for my newsletter! Come visit my website! I also update my blog at least a couple times a month.

You can also come hang out with me on Facebook in my private Facebook group!

Thank you so much for reading, I hope you enjoyed the story... and don't forget, the best thing you can do in return for any author is to leave them feedback!

Stay sassy.

www.goldenangelromance.com

Breaking the Chain

Bound to the Past

Stripping the Sub

Tempting the Domme

Hardcore Vanilla

Steamy Stocking Stuffers

Entering Stronghold Box Set

Nights at Stronghold Box Set

Stronghold: Closing Time Box Set

Masters of Marquis

Bondage Buddies

Venus Rising Quartet

The Venus School

Venus Aspiring

Venus Desiring

Venus Transcendent

Venus Wedding

Venus Rising Box Set

Black Light

Defended

Black Light Roulette: War

Dirty Heroes

The Lady

Standalone Romances

Mated on Hades

Marriage Training

Masters of the Castle

Masters of the Castle: Witness Protection Program Box Set

Tsenturion Masters with Lee Savino

Alien Captive

Alien Tribute

Big Bad Bunnies Series

Chasing His Bunny

Chasing His Squirrel

Chasing His Puma

Chasing His Polar Bear

Chasing His Honey Badger

Chasing Her Lion

Night of the Wild Stags – A standalone Reverse Harem romance set in the Big Bad Bunnies World

Chasing Tail Box Set

Chasing Tail... Again Box Set

Poker Loser Trilogy

Forced Bet

Back in the Game

Winning Hand

Poker Loser Trilogy Bundle (3 books in 1!)

Made in the USA
Middletown, DE
05 January 2021